# TIME CAPSULE
## Mitch Berman

★_____★

"Terrifically interesting to read and to consider.... What a courageous, audacious gesture Mitch Berman has made.... What an absolutely perfect ear for dialogue he has. This is a brave and heartening book."

**Los Angeles Times**

"Animated and very real... Sweeps through all the emotions and expressions of humankind. Berman's style is wonderfully casual and real.... A vibrant piece of work. This is a book for one's personal time capsule."

**Associated Press**

"Like a Pied Piper laying down a hypnotic line of patter, he draws us along. We go willingly because he's fun and quick and sharp."

**San Diego Union**

★————————————————————————————★

"Berman has language and heart. . . . *Time Capsule*'s strength lies in the riskiness of its writing, in its evocation of raw, inexpressible feeling."

*Village Voice*

"Amusing and inventive . . . Recalls Richard Brautigan and Donald Barthelme."

*Publishers Weekly*

"Zany, brilliant, funny, and inventive. A science-fictional Huckleberry Finn . . . There's absolutely nothing like it."

Ishmael Reed

# TIME
# CAPSULE

## Mitch Berman

BALLANTINE BOOKS • NEW YORK

Library of Congress Catalog Card Number: 86-17071

ISBN 0-345-35165-7

This edition published by arrangement with G.P. Putnam's Sons, a
division of the Putnam Publishing Group, Inc.

Manufactured in the United States of America

First Ballantine Books Edition: April 1988

TO MY MOTHER AND FATHER

# I

# 1 ❊ Dream Solo

During the sixth take of the opening song firemen fell off ladders, skyscrapers gnarled and groaned, lovers were blown apart, welded together, cars spun wild, some still moving as they were torched alight, and my alto saxophone solo was interrupted. The fire-storms faded in New York, Washington, Philadelphia as they sprang up in Denver, in Salt Lake City, in San Francisco, Honolulu, Tokyo, Hong Kong. Civilization did not immolate itself in one instant: it took an entire afternoon. Finally the metal lumps or metal shells, cold to touch, their tires black puddles, lay strewn at random on the streets and highways.

In the total darkness of Redundant Records' Studio B, in the basement of a squat concrete building at the Hopatcong Cloverleaf on the fringes of the outskirts of the suburbs of the New York megalopolis, I slept through it all, half a ton of plaster on my leg.

Splip splip splip splip. Water was dripping right into my open mouth. A sneezing fit cleared my nose of plaster as I choked awake. I struggled for breath, wheezing

3

and gasp-gurgling and making muddy snorts. Air came into my lungs; I seemed to feel it spread through my arms to my fingertips: dusty close air, but air nonetheless. I lay exhausted from the war within my body.

It was absolutely still in Studio B, still of music and of breath. I got out my lighter: a wreck, a mess. Rubble everywhere, three stories brought to their knees. Howard D. lay close by me. I reached out to him. His cheeks were warm, but not warm enough; his raised hand cold. I turned his face to me, and blood spilled from his mouth. There was a box on his chest: AMERICAN LOCK COMPANY. A warehouse, I'd never known whose, was on the first floor. Boxes from above had broken open in the fall: a bright tumble of chromed padlocks nested in the dark splintered innards of Howard's bass. Billy Bo was buried under drums and walls and boxes. I was alive because only ceiling had landed on me. Albert? The soles of his winghis stomach beyond them: like the locks and the boxes and the drums, part of the still life.

Splip splip: the water had started again. I lay watching: water had soaked through the ceiling at the far end of the studio, run improbably toward me along the underside of the ceiling to the broken edge, and from there, still fifteen feet away, slanted impossibly down at the angle of rain in a high wind: lay watching and drinking, for I was dust thirsty. Behaving as no water should, it was aiming, and accurately, for my mouth.

When I had had enough, I turned aside. The water stopped. I jerked my head back; the water started on cue. I turned away; not a drop. I turned back quickly: splip splip. It always seemed to beat me, like the light in a refrigerator.

I tried to sit up. Flat back: right leg! Now that I'd moved, the leg, squeezed numb before, shot pain with every heartbeat up through my groin into my stomach. When I got up I would search Big Al's pockets; he always knew, and usually had, the right drug. When and if I got up: the pain was massaging my heart and lungs with a weighty hand, wearing me down like too much exercise. My thirst had been quenched, but the dripping continued, a nag, a medium-tempo goad. Get up, get up, get up, get up, get up, get up, get up!

This chunk of hell would have to come off my leg. I gave it a preliminary shove. No. I took a breath and shoved with all my might. No. It was as big as a grand piano. My hand fell around to the right and found a heavy metal disk, not lying flat but balanced on edge. I wheeled it toward me and heard a scraping: it was the base of a toppled music stand.

With both hands I raised and swung the heavy cast-iron base onto the solid hunk of ceiling, first holding it back, then letting the full weight come down. The crunching seemed a sound effect designed for the feelings in my leg, but soon the plaster gave along the steel struts, and I sat up and pushed the fragments off me.

What would I see? I remembered a war movie where a man's insides fall out loose when his shirt is torn off. But there are no guts in a leg. I would see blood, I'd see a smashed bag of bones with maybe . . . Shit: I'd see what was there. I snicked the lighter.

My leg was bandaged! A heavy blue denim was wound in thin strips around my thigh, a snug job tied off, with ludicrous loopy flourish, at the hip. And nestling in the bow was a heavy silver pillbox with the initials ASH.

Albert! I turned cautiously over onto my stomach, pulled myself by my forearms toward him. Albert! Stripped to his jockey shorts. His fat sweet face was smiling, a strange toothy grin that looked as if it had been worked onto his features according to some blunt-fingered mortician's idea of the average smile, as if Albert had had no time to put it on from the inside.

A dozen or more yellow Percodans stood out against the tarnished silver of the pillbox. I took three, then wished I hadn't; I put the flame out too. Everything, everything would have to last.

I knew what had happened. I had always known it would. I grew up in suburban Buena Park, half an hour from Los Angeles. In the late fifties passenger planes were not quite a novelty, but we stood off to the sides of the lawns that were still growing in, and pointed. The first sonic booms rattled the windows of my first bedroom. The kindergarten "duck and cover" drills came after the flag salute. I daydreamed maybe a year ahead, no more than a few. I was Max Debrick until a smartass buddy tagged me Debris, and once the other kids got to the dictionary, the surname stuck. I could not be anything in particular when I grew up because I would not necessarily grow up. There was no God; or if there was, he offered no guarantees. Ten, twelve, fifteen, eighteen, twenty-one, thirty—impossible ages, my faith in their impossibility unshaken by their achievement. I knew exactly what had happened. I had always known, even though the knowledge had been disguised, at various times, as a fear, a prayer and an expectation.

And I knew this: if I went out now, the fallout would turn me to broiled aspic. I had to stay buried as long as I could hold out against hunger, and the smell of rotting flesh.

A fear came over me—mixed up and muddled and pulled off its axis by the contradictory idea that it had all been a dream and I might still be dreaming—that if I allowed myself to sleep I would die. I needed to see my own hand. I flicked the lighter and my hand appeared, floating close, reddened and glowing in the firelight.

I reached for Howard's cold palm and clung to it. I could see his hands, brown and slim and fluid and not attached to anything, working the neck and bridge of the bass, but no sound came. There was nothing I could hold on to that wouldn't turn sour. The time. The time of day. I had to know.

I felt down Howard's wrist, but his digital watch had gone dead black. Slowly, I dragged myself to Billy Bo and dug out his pocket watch. A quarter to one, a quarter to one, the cool freeing orderly sight of a clock face. I pressed it to my ear.

It sounded like that trickle of water: splip splip splip splip. If I turned away, the water stopped. Why?

And the bandage. The bandage and the pillbox. The whole thing had Albert Sherman Honeywell written all over it. But how and when had he done it? Before he was injured? Made no sense. I stretched out; the Percodans were taking hold. So Albert had been felled by ceiling and boxes, had crawled over to me, dying, lifted the half-ton chunk of plaster, torn his pants to ribbons, uh-huh, bandaged me, inexplicably set the crushing weight back on top of me, and then, and only then, expired. Of course not.

Sleep swallowed me suddenly, sloppy sprawling pole-axed sleep. In my dream the song was "Oops" and the band Howard D., Bo Brummel, and Al. My solo began with ancient music, crunching percussive pre-music, went to crazy African tribal to woody Renaissance to tick-tock Bach through a capsule history of jazz. The sixth take ended the solo, and this time I finished. All the styles were compatible and everything fit. I held up my sax and fell straight back, fainting in slow-motion bliss; as I hit the floor in the dream I jerked awake. Exhilaration bore up under me; I felt I was floating, unwilling to give up my hold on the dream music, slowly down. There was a tap at my shoulder and quite distinctly Bo Brummel said to me: "Write it down, sucker." I flicked on the lighter; no one. I had still been half-asleep.

A good idea, wherever it came from. It was why I carried folded music paper. Every note was still sharp to me, except I got stuck during the Renaissance. "Yo, Billy Bo," I said in the imitation jive he always detested.

"What?"

Was I imagining again? I flicked the lighter and looked at my hand. It was just a hand.

"What?" the voice repeated.

"Billy Bo?"

Now came a long pause. "Riiight."

"But you . . ." I looked over at his body. "You're dead!"

"Riiight," said Billy's voice. Was he in pain? Was it hard for him to talk? What was it like? Was anyone else alive?

There was a very long pause. I was not inventing; Bo had been there. But I might never hear from him again.

"Skip."

Skip, huh? What the hell did that mean? But what did it matter? Billy Bo existed. There was a life after. There were dead spirits in the living world. Ghosts. It was too much to believe, but far too much to disbelieve: Albert's pillbox. The bandage. The trickle of water. The voice. Ghosts, and bent on my survival.

I lit up the music paper. So I was stuck. I'd simply do

what I usually did; leave a measure or two blank, pick up the thread, and go back later to fill in the spot I'd . . . Oh. Skipped.

The notes came quick and hot, too fast to write but lining up patiently until my hand could catch up. I was cooking now. "Damn you, Billy Bo!" I murmured.

"Too late," said the voice. And that was the last I heard of it.

I wanted to go to that place where Albert and Howard D. and Billy Bo were still joking and riding each other. Alive I would never hear Big Al's voice and horn again, or see Bo work himself up into one of his rages over an imagined offense; but I hadn't eaten in a day and a half or two days, depending on whether it was afternoon or night, and my stomach was waking up to the fact. Find something to eat or simply waste away: I lay passive and let my choice make itself. And my thoughts moved, as thoughts do, far and far and far away.

&#10086;

I'm the last to arrive at the studio. Howard D. thongs his bass for Billy "Bo" Brummel, who is tuning the tom-toms as carefully as if they were a melody instrument. My handwritten charts for "Oops," the appropriately light opener, face front at the music easels. Albert's tenor and soprano saxophones are on their vertical stands like strange gleaming plants. I'm expecting hearty greetings, good beer because tomorrow is my thirty-fourth birthday, and Big Al knows because he put it in the diary I gave him for Christmas. Bo Brummel, barely up to my shoulders even in his wide gray fedora, angular and greyhound-thin in his drapey double-breasted forties suit, his brown-pinstriped, cream-colored linen shirt; Billy Bo, a live exclamation point, comes up to me, and pulling a chain from his inside pocket, consults his pink gold pocket watch, its numberless onyx face adorned only with four tiny rubies, to announce: "As usual. Seven minutes late."

It's my third album on Redundant with the same musicians. From right to left: Billy Bo, back against the side wall, framed in two large and twelve tiny cymbals above, and high hat, snare, tom-toms and double bass drums

with black skins and silver letters BBB below, Billy Bo
peering out ready through a jungle of percussion; Big
Albert Honeywell, the man who plays sitting down and
has to pull two chairs together to do it, near the drums
because he likes them, approaching sixty wih all the reserve of a city bus coming on a yellow light, Big Al and
tenor; narrow Howard and his fat five-stringed double
bass of spruce, ebony and European sycamore, a strange
and expensive Austrian antique which he pays for, like a
house, on a thirty-year mortgage; and in that corner Max
Debris, né and still legally Debrick, so tall he makes his
alto look like a party favor, a left-handed alto, a saxophone sinister, a horn for that turned-around sound, Max
Debris, with too much nose and chin and strawish hair
and little claim to being the nominal leader of this band.
Hit it!

Well into the theme statement I realize that no one is
playing what I am; like Wile E. Coyote running off a
cliff, it takes me several seconds to get the idea that I
should be falling. The song they're playing, with con-
summate professionalism and smiles all around, is
"Happy Birthday." Billy Bo rolls out a pony keg of
Guinness Stout secreted in a bass drum, and Gerry Wichensky emerges from the engineering booth to drink
and urge us all to share a Hostess Ding Dong dinner with
him. That was the first take.

And now, looser and warmer for the beer, we start,
really start playing "Oops." Bo's a little heavy on the
toms, and Albert falls out of the ensemble. We stop rag-
gedly. "OK," someone says. "Three strikes and you're
out." That was take two.

Bo's hearing too much drum; he wants to carry the
rhythm on the cymbals during the theme, kinda splash
splash splash. Yeah, that way, we chorus. Albert studies
the chart, humming the tune in his cement-mixer bass.
One two three and yes: cymbals the right choice, Albert's tight with me. He takes a nice bluesy solo for two
polite choruses. My turn. I'm inspired, with ideas draining out of my horn, and off into a closing riff. A second-
chair-in-a-high-school-band yelpsplat lurches from my
horn, a horrendous screech that, amplified, is worse than
truck brakes, worse than a rake on concrete, than finger-

nails on a blackboard, a sound that could not possibly be a creation of the same God responsible for chocolate truffles, sex, the Alps, Greta Garbo, the Chrysler Building or the Etch A Sketch. "Oops" simpers to a close, like someone murmuring goodbye to a departing 747.

The monitor crackles into life. Although Studio B has a small fortune in sound equipment, including fine old McIntosh speakers, the engineer communicates with the musicians through a Radio Shack $9.95 special. Wichensky sounds like shortwave from Moscow. "I think you had a squeak in there..." What ears. That's take three.

Take four's playback: wwweeeerrRRRRR. "Sorry guys," grackles Wichensky. "Wrong speed. Here," and we boil out of the speakers mid-note, crisp, assured, snapping along, riding the ting! of the cymbals like surfers ting! muh-blunk muh-blunk the round earthy sound of Howard's bass. The drums lay out for the bridge, short questioning unison spurts on the saxophones, clipped notes skip-dancing over fast lava bass, and Albert stands to the mike. Vintage Al: warm shredded splay-legged blues, step-stamping along. I watched his shoes during his solo, and from in front now, I watch them during playback: short fat wing tips, wide shallow boats, the shadows underneath the toes opening like smiles and winking out. Albert's feet are a show unto themselves: the left taps smart on the beat on the beat On! while the right moves slyly from side to side like a man talking out of the corner of his mouth, moving in a different time, pulling stalling straggling behind the beat then all over it, spanking out a rhythm for a whole series of notes, some implied rather than played but the thing is you can hear them all anyway, listen you can hear them. Once I caught Albert's right foot doing 11/4 time while the left just kept 4/4-ing along, smiling wise and slow and regular amid the flurry of blue notes, silent notes, of crazy scales, of moaning and let-me-tell-you-a-story that came out of that horn.

I can hear myself up behind Big Al now with short boosting, heating big-band licks, then out as he turns raw and fast and mean and now very very blue again. Al runs chromatically to the highest range of the tenor and my alto picks up the baton, from its low brassy register to speechlike top and then into the shrieking falsetto. What a gimmick! I hate it already. But Albert's rich soothing smile is on me, and I listen to the rest of my solo in that grace and warmth. Take four.

Albert gets up to high-five me when it's over; Guinness jolts from the Styrofoam cup in his other hand. Wichensky's grainy voice comes too loud from the monitor: "Sounds like a wrap!"

"No," I say.

"No?" Billy Bo comes bouncing out from behind the drums, wielding sticks. "*No?*"

"My solo was just a lot of notes." There is a moment of silence, as if everyone is either contemplating killing me or commemorating my passing.

"Oh man," says quiet Howard D. "You gonna play till the morning light."

"Gonna play," adds Billy Bo, regarding me cynically from underneath that hat. "Gonna play till he's a black man."

"Do you maybe have another solo in you something on the order of the last one?" I ask Albert.

"*Run the tape!*" he rumbles.

". . . what?" crackles Wichensky.

"*Run it!*" says Albert. Bo goes back to the drums, giving the toms a whack meant for me.

"*Ten*-four, good buddy!" says Wichensky.

"You," says Albert, settling onto his chairs, "are a pain in the ass. And when you got an ass as big as mine, that's a lot of pain. Now, gentlemen: for posteriority!"

We count down, hit the tune together clean and crisp. Seconds later Wichensky's voice cuts off take five. "Hold it!" We peter out.

"That's 'Oops' again. You're doing 'So Low' next."

"Gerry, have they put you on salary or do you still get paid by the hour?" I yell.

He knows what that means. "'Oops,' take six?"

"Take six and last!"

"*Ten*-four, over, under and out."

It's the best one; I hear that right off. Bo's doing his light airy thing, and Howard D. swings in; Al clings through the twisty bridge, and at the launch of his solo slips me a large wink. And the stomping take-four solo comes out of him, note for note. I watch the slow grin appear under the 4/4 foot and the other fast-smiling maniac: 7/4, 3/4, 11/4. There it is—11/4! The same exact solo—no, he's refined it, trimming the fat here and giving the silence a chance to speak, jamming in a spiraling Roland Kirk downscale there. Motion and he's waving to me with his free hand; I hop to and feed him those licks. He soars over, growls under, and ends it singing sweetly. I come to the mike shaking my head. I've got my own ideas now! I'm sorting them all out into the air, and it's going well, it is going very very well. Albert is already smiling on me.

My legs are dancing on their own: it's the ground! the ground shaking breaking up! The mike falls away and plaster dust sinks on a line from the ceiling. Earthquake! No—no—not. Movement all around me, yelling, big things falling. I dive for a corner. Something squeezes my head.

※

And in the black shambles of the recording studio, lying on a floor that only seemed cold, I came out of memory and into my own body. I still had not decided to go on living, or didn't realize I had. But my lungs didn't stop pumping air, slow and regular as long as I paid no attention to them, and my heart squished along, slow and regular whether I noticed it or not. My stomach hurt for lack of food, hurt until I ground my teeth, hurt until I pressed down on top of it with both hands, hurt until I could think about nothing else, and then I knew that my stomach, with its simple chemicals and nerve endings, my stomach, with its simple ideas, had won the argument.

Hungry and nauseous at once, I began pulling rubble aside, overturning boxes and finding locks, locks, locks, finally grabbing a chart of "Oops" and tearing off a piece with my teeth. In a second my mouth was full of saliva and a bitterness beyond the range of tastes of food; the charts had been photocopied. I chewed and chewed until the paper would reduce no further, and I swallowed. Only then did I remember Wichensky's Ding Dongs.

I hauled myself to the engineer's booth and found the flattened white box. Peeling the foil from each squashed disk, I inhaled one after another until the package was empty. I washed it all down with a luxurious gulp from Wichensky's warm flat Coca-Cola. For the first time in a while, a thought caught up with me and I stoppered the upside-down liter bottle with my tongue. I would have nothing to live on but the Coke and the Guinness.

Now was the time to do something about the bodies of my friends. I decided to drag them here into the engineer's booth because it was enclosed, and to start with Albert while I had strength from food. Lying on my back to the left of his body, I brought my left knee up and pushed hard down and away. Big Al moved only inches each time. That was how I thought about him: Big Al, not some dead object to move. Albert was still Albert: playing jokes, helping. Bo's monosyllabic thump: a drummer through the very end. Howard D. was the last member of the Max Debris Quartet to get in touch with me. As I was dragging his wiry body to the booth, his voice, like the little cake in *Alice in Wonderland*, said "Eat Me."

Although I knew that a human being can live for more than two weeks without food, knowledge is not always enough. Nor is Guinness Stout, though it goes further. I never bothered with a cup: I would just put my mouth to the spigot like a baby. The alcohol shot into my starving head as if injected, and I went crawling through Studio B, blunted, slowed, creaturely, running the same unaccountable scenes in my head: my elementary school playground, the cramped bandstand at the Village Vanguard, my first apartment; an unidentifiable beach scene, gray-green waves hitting rocks, hitting and jumping up pale blue, jumping back, recoiling, retreating. As if in response to my thoughts, the building sighed from time to time, and a trickle of dust would whisper down somewhere in the long silence.

The beer ran out way before I thought it would, on the fourth or fifth day, and without it, my stomach clamped down tight to the size and texture of a baseball. A sleepy feeling, a dull mild throb, spread throughout my body, into my joints, so that they all felt like they needed cracking. My head pulsed with sharp pain when I did not hold it absolutely still.

In my better moments I collected Albert's reeds and cleaning gear. Wichensky, a chain-smoker, had another butane lighter in his pocket. I wrote down everything I'd ever known about radiation; numbering the items, idiotically, made me feel better. Don't eat fatty tissue. Do scrape off topsoil before lying down. Don't sing in the rain. I rationed out Wichensky's Coke and filled the plastic bottle with the dregs of the Guinness, letting a full bottle of foam-scum stand until it subsided into liquid, filling it and waiting. I stayed submerged for eleven days, and actually did a little bit of practicing in Studio B; once or twice I thought I heard applause. I got my dream solo down cold.

Up out of the cave, finally, limped a stone-sober white man with a growth of beard, an alto saxophone dangling from his neck, a pair of outsized Levi's tied in strips around his leg, a Swiss Army knife, an antiquated gentleman's timepiece and two disposable butane lighters in his pockets, and a music stand for a crutch.

It was dark for daylight. The visible fallout had cleared; after the studio, the air smelled sweet, and it seemed I could see for miles: nothing was taller than my head. In a high-hanging smog the sun was a bright patch of brown: I could stare at it. The insect sound of the pocket watch could be clearly heard. It was dark for noon.

# 2 ❋ The Abacus Bridge

"No mammal," in the words of my high school biology teacher, "wants to die." And so the holocaust let loose a storm of displaced spirits: wild angry jealous spirits, suddenly spirit spirits, spirits with all to mourn and nothingness, no thing to anticipate. Dead souls that outnumbered the living by a fantastic ratio. It was a riot of ghosts.

No: ghosts are white fluffy harmless things, low-flying clouds, little airborne lambs. Casper was a ghost; these things, like the Japanese yūrei, were ranging, raging spirits transformed by their hungers, dead souls condemned to wander yet unable themselves to do so. Jerked from life so instantly that they could not surrender to or even comprehend the fact of their own deaths, the yūrei commandeered any lump of sentient protoplasm that came within range. *To find out. To see.* Where they had come from. Where and what they were. That was all they wanted. And they needed live moving feet, needed to take readings available only through live eyes and ears; I became their unwitting guide to what they had left behind and to where they were now, and they pushed me toward the places of their pasts. I was the first living flesh the yūrei had seen since the holocaust, and they converged on me like vultures on carrion.

I had my own idea where I was going. I'd planned to walk Highway 181 south about five miles, take a left on Interstate 80 and follow it east for about thirty-five miles more, across cities, counties, and one state line as fast as I could throw my body down the road. With gargantuan naïveté, like an old man telephoning a high school girl-friend from his deathbed, I was heading home.

I was going *there*; the yūrei wanted me *here*. My will crossed with theirs like a pair of swords, each pointing in a different direction. Though the way was straight and paved—I-80, except near cities, was undamaged—it was no simple matter to get from point A to point B: I found myself veering to R and L and T, detouring to Q and Y, spelling out a message like the pointer on a Ouija board. Though the yūrei could manipulate very small objects, their influence in the physical world was weak. They did their main work directly in the mind, hiding beneath the conscious level, tampering with the senses, goading or squelching an emotion, skewing judgment, fanning the spark of an impulse until it burst into flame. They could lay a welcoming carpet of absolute stillness or make everything look strange, ill, wrongly composed on that other route I was considering. Once, as I decided not to take an exit off I-80, the pavement seemed to open right along the center, like a zipper. I took the exit. A day later, when I returned to the highway, it was smooth and unbroken, and, I realized, always had been.

I would find myself in a place where everything had been leveled except for charred telephone poles, prepos-terously upright, in a place that had been Totowa or Teaneck or Lodi, kicking at a pile of rubble no different from any other. Once in a while a voice came through: "Apartment" or "Born here." A yūrei's voice had a char-acteristic static crackle, like a far-off radio station. It was surprising how many wanted me to drop in at the office. That lead-colored gleam was someone's typewriter, a graffitied toilet stall, the Xerox machine, maybe a pic-ture frame from a desk.

The yūrei needed the vehicle of my flesh, and they needed it in usable condition; I was steered not only toward what they wanted me to see but away from what they wanted me to miss. I could be allowed to see nothing that would disrupt my mind, nothing that would impair my efficiency as a bearer of sense organs. I wasn't permitted to come across any dying men, not even many corpses. And though cans of food were burst or melted, I was fed: every so often a crazed bird would plummet from the sky and crawl broken-winged circles at my feet. I never got my own bearings; I was too busy getting them for others. My senses were usurped, my needs and desires diluted, and what was left of the dead filtered partially, sloppily, into me. I knew pieces of all of them, for only pieces remained, and those became part of me. I had become an anthology. Numbed, stump-stumbling forward in a kind of mindless continuous falling, the weighted music stand swinging me around like an unwieldy doll, I worked and fought unevenly on.

The George Washington Bridge put an end to my plodding as the blast had put an end to it: the great pylons had crumbled at water level, and a broken shoelace of cable moved gently with the current. I could make out dim outlines in the silt, the two levels of the bridge, cars. For the first time in days I laughed. The laughter started off hollow-sounding; it hung in the air, as if it came from outside me, then grew until I was out of breath and all the smile muscles in my face were exhausted. It was impossible to cross! The whole idea was ridiculous! A rubble hill in smoky water, a truncated mound, a massive amputation, just an island. Nothing could be living in Manhattan. I was free now to go west, to food and maybe some human beings organized around it.

But I didn't. I struggled back north on a path of seagulls and brown bushes, with a few junipers stubbornly hoarding the local supply of the color green. Under one I found a half-dead tabby; before I could think I had crushed his skull with the music stand. He convulsed once, front and rear legs scissoring together, and I turned away quickly, gulping down vomit.

I got out my Swiss Army knife, the silver inlay neat

and calming in its red casing. My keys jangled. The building key, the smaller brass dead-bolt key, the key to Studio B that never worked, each with VILLAGE LOCK 165 7TH AVE. SO. stamped on it. I set to the nasty business of stripping the cat's fur and fat from muscle. Butane-singed, it tasted like rabbit and gasoline.

Upstream from Manhattan, a sloped clearing in the Palisades seemed to suggest itself as a place where I might cautiously approach the Hudson. The water tumbled by as I advanced toward it; my desire to back out grew as the bank steepened before me. I put one foot in front of another to keep from falling; the surface was slippery, forcing me on. At last I staggered and splashed at the water's edge, unwilling and unable to make the journey to that magnet of an island, but this was not enough: the bank kept shuttle-sliding me forward. Cool water filled my boots. The music stand slipped from me and I grabbed uselessly for it in the water. I was in up to my waist before I realized where I was being driven. Swim with a broken leg?

"Help me!" I screamed. And as I swayed and waded and flopped in the water, always falling, but like those inflatable punch-clowns with weighted bottoms, always upright, a log floated by, then a plank, and another log, butting against each other, drifting parallel, coming together but remaining out of my reach.

I was chest-deep when I slipped, got a mouthful of water and a faceful of log. It was a raft! I hauled myself up and sat dripping. Floating face-down in the Hudson I would have been worthless to the yūrei, so they had knitted six feet of logs and planking together for me with fine sprung cable wire.

A sturdy pole maybe fifteen feet long lay diagonally across; as the current carried me straight south I jammed the pole into the water, into the river bottom: east, east, east! And south by southeast I bobbled, the water rushing thinly across the motley surface of the raft. I lost touch with the bottom and drifted downstream, parallel to the banks. But where the water ran swiftest I felt bottom again, and prodded my way toward land. I dragged myself and the raft ashore, and lay panting on Manhattan's soggy bank.

As it had in life, this island held a great fascination for the dead. Some had tried to make me swim, some had fashioned me a raft; some had pushed, some had pulled, but all had joined to call me here. And here they batted me around like a Ping-Pong ball, like a particle in an atomic accelerator, like a pencil point filling in a dot-to-dot drawing, like a half-dead, wholly disoriented saxophone player with a walking stick twice his own length. For three days I explored—or rather *they* explored—the great leveled city through my senses. I visited unknown and untold homes, offices, schools, stores, restaurants, bars, tanning salons, parking structures, spas, nightclubs, kennels, barber shops, hospitals. Great funnels of asphalt, earth and ash marked subways and sewers.

I could tell where streets had been, but not which streets. Central Park, a denuded plain, was clearly distinguishable. The modest boulders that had seemed quaint in the full-blown manmade hurly-burly were now the largest intact structures in Manhattan. From the southwest corner of the park on Fifty-ninth Street, I learned to find my way around by counting my steps: a hundred per numbered street.

Tethered to the park: east four hundred steps and south two fifty, dust, dust, red brick dust, this should be Carnegie Hall, Carnegie's white expectant stillness, the hiss of fiber on fiber as I lever myself into seat E-104, hiss of whisper, hiss of program, the band's brazen burst of sound, the burst of white light on brass trumpet, and later, from the stage, the weight of whiteness, weight of white hush, the weight of the audience and the notes of years past waiting in the white wood: this should be Carnegie, but all I find in the red dust is twenty-six cents, loose change, loosed from use and user, loosed from everything I might have thought before if I found a penny and a quarter on the street; the park, six hundred south and twice as many east, Citicorp I'm guessing, coffee and cashews with Might I have this seat? an old gentleman who produces a magnetic chess set and plays a good sharp game—as I study his seersucker suit, spotty and frayed at the cuffs, and over the visorlike hands shielding his eyes from everything not a magnetic chess set, his beetling still-black eyebrows—until he leaves his queen *en prise* and refusing to take back his mistake resigns with a Thank you kindly, young man a few moves later: the glass tower of Citibank turned back to sand and collapsed into its foundations, terrain so jagged and uncertain I can't poke through for pawns or pennies but must return to the park; the park, nine hundred steps down what had to be Sixth Avenue: Radio City? the skating rink? Time-Life? voices mix and merge and I find nothing, a broken bit of marble, a fire hydrant melted from the top down like a candle, nothing; the elastic tether of the known brings me back, finally, to the park, where I resolve to cut my tether and count south as far as I can.

South, south: I lived south. South twenty-five hundred paces and the Empire State Building or what I assumed to be the Empire State Building was a small lump on the edge of the blast crater punched square in the center of the land. Just as the curvature of the Earth reveals itself only at a distance, the crater appeared straight and endless from my perspective at its edge. Manhattan had been split in two.

The spongy powder at the rim lay striated by the fingernails of the wind. I approached the edge amid ripples of two feet, ridges of twenty, and valleys of inches, tapping the pole before me like a blind man; it had become an extension of my feet, poking where they couldn't, finding the subways and sunken basements, the breakage that lay ahead, probing for a hard shallow place to walk, feeling the light-packed fineness of the ash, of the dust really, beneath a flaky surface of dried mud from recent rain; and where the dunes and drifts abruptly ceased I sent my stick out onto the surface that dropped gradually away, brushing lightly over the clean empty interior of the crater while I stood back at its edge, brushed away ash to reveal the surface of glass. There was already a black glint of water at the bottom; at the first heavy rain it would turn into a lake, and not a small one. Primitive plants, mosses and algae, would grow there. In time animal life might begin again.

Now even the gulls had deserted Manhattan. There were only a few rats, which I couldn't catch, and the exponentially multiplied cockroaches, which I did.

Roaches roamed and swarmed like ants. Some stubborn reserve of squeamishness made me flick off their heads with a thumbnail. I would save the tiny bodies in my pockets until I had a couple hundred and make a small meal of them. They contained minute amounts of water, or what passed through me like water. I drank my urine, with the idea that my organs had absorbed all the radiation the first time through. Besides, it tasted better than cockroaches.

The hot filthy Hudson River seemed the only way that remained to me. If I headed uptown toward the raft along the Hudson's bank I would have New Jersey to look at; I could at least gaze west. But this is what I found when I reached the western edge of the island: a border of solid land perhaps a block wide. I could pass to my neighborhood, try to pick out Sheridan Square, the Vanguard, my own building. Manhattan had not been cut in half.

Nothing was distinguishable along the way, and I lost count of my steps. I wanted to believe the blast had fallen short—Twenty-third to Fourteenth Streets might be a dead loss, but not Greenwich Avenue, not MacDougal, not my own Charles Street. Like the yūrei, I would not believe my apartment building was not intact until I had seen it myself. The crater's edge rolled in; the narrow border of land grew wider and I followed it east. Block by block the dust congealed into ash, ash into chunks, the chunks into brick, cement, metal. Rubble grew up around the avenue, Seventh Avenue I was sure, and in the absence of anything big enough, whole enough to tell me otherwise, I invented a topology for my neighborhood. It was like trying to read a newspaper from its ashes.

Metal, a big clump of black or blackened metal, must have belonged to Village Lock, where the girl who made my keys threw her hips to 98-KISS; a silvery sheen, I decided, was part of the odd inventory of the twenty-four-hour Korean grocery at Seventh and Charles, a can, maybe, of Danish mussels or what the store's annual calendar advertised as "So Da." I had known a girl who worked there.

She was about seventeen when I had come in on a

muggy summer night to buy Roach Motels. She looked up from a big black book on the counter to say no to every word I tried: cockroaches, Roach Motels, bugs, traps, sticky; then she watched from behind the counter, distrustful of her own English, as I squatted, miming a box with one hand, and then a cockroach, index and middle fingers trotting across the floor, entering the box, getting stuck in it, the girl glancing back and forth from my face to my hands, her round face full of amused perplexity as if watching some indigenous American performance art.

"See?" I said, hoping she had at least heard the slogan on TV. "They check in, *but they don't check out*."

Finally I decided to settle for peanut M&M's, but while paying I saw that her black book was an English-Korean dictionary. I looked up "cockroach" and pointed to the Korean.

"Ah!" she said, breaking into a big smile. "To keel!"

That had been what? almost three years ago. I tried to come in at least twice a month on her shift, Tuesdays after midnight. I lent her my jazz albums (she liked "hard rock"), introduced her to my friends, enjoyed her steady progress in English, played with the store's gray cat, got credit when I needed it, counseled her sternly to stay in school. We always smiled and talked through the line of customers who came and bought, came and bought, but we had never learned each other's names.

If that was her family's grocery store, this, a block up, close to the edge of the crater, must have been my apartment building. Six floors of carefully tended and partitioned environments had been ignominiously mingled: my ancient rocking chair, cherrywood and inlay, the seat varnish worn through in the shape of buttocks; its opposite number in Mrs. Blair's apartment; old Mrs. Blair herself, who asked me to screw in a light bulb in March and blessed me, deaf-loudly, through December; the Schwartzes' tiny white dog named Rhino; the building's wrought-iron fire escape PAT. JAN. 8, 1891 where I had stood on warm nights, playing the horn tunes-only straightforwardly for the people who chattered and staggered past my street; and, finally, as I tried to push aside a big piece of concrete with my stick but found it required the strength of a leg, entryway tile.

The tile. Ours was blue and white in a bottle-cap pattern. My shoe cleared off a chunk, brown and white. More, and a message, cracked but entire, was spelled out in mosaic.

> PROPERTY OF THE
> HESS ESTATE
> WHICH HAS NEVER
> BEEN DEDICATED
> FOR PUBLIC
> PURPOSES
> XXXXXX
> XXXX
> XX

I was at the entrance of Village Cigars in Sheridan Square, two blocks below Charles. My apartment building, the locksmith, the restaurants, sex shops and the Korean grocery were back in the empty crater so in the air, in the stratosphere, circling the Earth, drifting, sifting down over strange places, in the Hudson and maybe the Nile, in every rain.

My legs gave out suddenly and I was sitting hard in the ashes, picking up two hands of ashes, letting ashes sift through and blacken my fingers. Little black slugs of wet rolling ash appeared in my hands, and I looked to the sky for rain. Rain! With no shelter in sight. It wasn't rain, I was crying, and I couldn't feel it and didn't see how—tears seemed tiny, lost in the expanse of my lostness. I covered my face in the ashes, brought two hands full of ash to my eyes, rubbed them on my cheeks, in my ears and hair as if they were water that would wash me.

❉

I am crossing an abacus bridge. I am walking on metal rods with dangerously wide gaps between them, and on the rods colored beads that move and slip under my feet as I go forward, always forward as time goes forward, leaping from rod to rod, the beads spinning out from under me, shuttling to the side, counting as I cross. One slip on the abacus bridge and the geometry of what is real, the delicate algebra of time and memory, the basic arithmetic of life and death will be altered beyond recognition.

I lose my balance and everything is interrupted; everything has spilled. I can steer my falling body toward either a rushing black river, a gorged, flooding river so thick and heavy it moves without sound, a vast sucking river of oil, or the short springy lawn of the house I was born in. I know that behind the house's bland and cheerful facade nothing stirs and that the street too is empty; if I land here I will wander alone among the small homes that once seemed so large, calling out the names of people who have moved away, too big for my memories, alive but as if I was never born.

✻

The next day, one month after my thirty-fourth birthday, feeling strength return to my leg, I took the keys off the ring, one by one, thinking of the doors they had opened, left them in a pile on the memorial to the Hess Estate, walked back up Manhattan, got on my raft and pushed off into the Hudson River.

I wondered how many people shared my birthday. I wondered what they were doing. Did anyone have anyone to share a birthday with? I watched the gulls flap and careen. I wondered how many people were alive, and where on God's green earth they were. I wondered if floating on your back down the river made you wonder, and I wondered whether I would ever get to read *Huck Finn* again. I was aiming for the southern tip of Jersey in the Upper Bay, and very nearly didn't make it.

# 3 ❋ Time Capsule

And so I'm writing this as if I expected you to sink into the sofa and prop up your feet, get a glass of apple juice, cup of tea, brandy snifter. What's your pleasure? As if everywhere lovers were loving flesh, firemen were fighting fires, Grandma was in her kitchen making salmon patties, drivers were driving and all was right, so to speak, with the world. As if you were part of what was or very far into what may be.

I'm putting together a time capsule for me and you, and what the hell, "for posteriority," as Albert said before they turned on the tape. Think of my time capsule as a book, or as a human being if you prefer, as me, and I as it. In this time capsule go Al's favorite album, *Suitely*, a picture of his smile, and his pillbox, when I'm done with it. And:

A real crutch of hardwood, with pads for my armpits. A history of negotiations to limit nuclear arms. Another good comedy, maybe *The Gold Rush*, in which Chaplin was right, trust me, about eating shoes. Think of my time capsule as a huge expanding recipe. I reserve the right to add ingredients at any time, though I won't take any out; enough has been removed already.

I'll add a secretary's typewriter, reconstructed from the rubble, the picture of her children, the lucky penny from her desk. Come to think of it, we'll need a four-leaf clover; let's not tear it apart. A dozen salmon patties in case you or I get hungry, six for one, a half-dozen for the other.

Look: I'm bundling it all up in Saran Wrap until it's rounded as a mummy, I'm putting it into a wide-mouthed Thermos and then into a no-frost Frigidaire, I'm wheeling it down the street to a safety deposit vault at your local FDIC-insured banking institution. Copies in Latin, Hebrew, Chinese, Cyrillic and Esperanto are enclosed. It is my gift to you, my message in a bottle, my time capsule. As people of my mother's generation used to yell when they didn't know if anybody was home, Yoo-hoo!

# 4 ❋ Play That Song

The seagulls followed my still, floating form down the opaque waterway. They gathered, swooped goonily, sniffing out the prospective bonanza. I sat up suddenly, hacking the air wildly with the sax. I didn't hit a gull; they did not even scatter, but merely, genteelly, receded. They had already forgotten me.

I looked at the saxophone: it was no weapon. I put it into my face and played for the first time since Studio B, played a single long note, listening for an echo from the distant cliffs. Breathing circularly, I pruned the sharp edges off my sound, rounding and fattening it. I was my own echo: I repeated the note, bent it, split it, and set off into a slow vamp, something I'd call "Carrion Blues," though it wasn't a blues at all. I quoted "Taps." I quoted Chopin's Funeral March. I even cut off a piece of "Goodbye Porkpie Hat." And I watched the northeast corner of Staten Island slip by. I had overshot! In the distance was the point in Jersey I'd been aiming for, in the far distance Liberty Island. I would soon be attempting the first solo raft crossing of the Atlantic Ocean.

I grabbed up the pole and jammed it down, down to my elbows in water. Too deep. Probably much too deep. I flopped belly-first and yanked water hard up toward me, long scooping motions splashing my face. In an astonishingly short time I was out of breath; soon my heart started flumping around like a bat in a bottle; then I started to wheeze, to cough, to hiccup, to practically retch with fatigue. And all that happened was that the front end of the raft wheeled lazily around to give me a view of the land that drifted so serenely, so imperceptibly, so implacably away from me.

The current was actually nosing me toward the Staten Island edge of the Verrazano Narrows, but so slowly that, flapping and milling, busy with panic, I couldn't see it happening. When it came clear that land was getting closer, not farther, and that my efforts had nothing to do with it, I lay on my back and panted with deep luxury. I examined my saxophone: the pads were drenched but intact. Bo's watch was still ticking. Five dry pills lay in Albert's pillbox. I still had my knife and lighter. Finally the wavelets lapped me close to shore, and I poled in.

I wouldn't be able to drag the raft across fat Staten Island. I kept the pole but bent one knee to the shore and launched the little raft. As I watched, the cables loosened and fell away: the water bore them gently apart from under, and two logs and five planks fanned slowly out in the tide.

⁂

Let's move back and watch my progress from a distance; don't worry, we can do this, it's not necessary to limp every step, eat every cockroach with me. I'll tell you when anything really interesting happens. Keep up that reverse zoom, please: I do better sometimes when I'm not watched too closely.

Imagine me now on a map. From Studio B on a curlicue path south, my course describes a big S, like the one in Staten Island, which I'm leaving now. What? On foot; the land has closed off. Well, yes, a little wading. I'm a small s as we pull back, like the s in speck; a series of coordinates, which coordinates are 40° latitude and 75°

longitude and don't figure to change much in the near future; a mere squiggle, an abstraction, a here-to-there.

❊

"Initial S as in Sam, McCullogh, M-C-C-U-L-L-O-G-H, sir?"

"Right." S as in Shannon. My girlfriend for three college years at Berkeley.

"Checking." After we broke up, I called Information at irregular intervals, not always drunk, to find out where she was living. Through adolescence I had suffered the idea that all my kindergarten playmates must be dead, since I didn't know what had happened to them.

"That's in Oakland?"

"I guess." I hadn't guessed. Shannon had moved.

"654-5034."

"Do you have an address?"

"3409 Telegraph."

I didn't write it down. I never wrote it down in the seven years since I'd seen her, not her phone and address, nor Julian's (twenty-one years), nor Judy's (twelve years). I didn't intend to make any use of the information other than to have it.

❊

Now my S is more of an essss. It winds and knots through upper New Jersey, New York City, and now back out west-south-west through Newark and Plainfield and plain west, plain west. Tufts of my hair are strewn along the way. I've been nauseous too, but able to hold back vomit so far. You're right: radiation poisoning, which, like most illnesses, ends either in recovery or death. The leg? Healed without complication, except that I too am shaped slightly like an S, or at least the leg is. But there's no pain, and it works. I'm hoping it won't be permanent. Finding no one to shout at me. I shout at myself: "Straighten up! Watch your posture!" You can imagine tiny dirt clouds, puffs really, kicking up from the map where I shout. From the middle of such an empty sprawl it's a yammering voice, a very little voice.

❈

"Nothing in Oakland or Berkeley, sir."

"Could you check San Francisco?"

"Checking." Maybe I had finally lost her.

"I have an S. McCullogh at 824-0128 with no address."

"But it is in San Francisco?"

"Yes sir. 824 is a San Francisco prefix."                    ·

❈

S for safari, for sojourn, for so long. S for Sol. For scorch and soot and scrub and scratch and scrounge. S for starveling. For slough slouch sag. S for scarecrow. Scabrous, sallow, scorbutic. S for sepulchral, for sciomancy. S for SOS. S for setback. S for Sell the farm, Sally. I haven't found a single human being, and I'm passing through Allentown. S for shitfuck.

❈

Shannon was no longer listed in Berkeley, Oakland, San Francisco or Marin County. But I remembered how she used to talk about Seattle; they did have an S. McCullogh with an unpublished number. She was slipping from me. Judy and Julian could no longer be found at all. I was losing track of people. They really were dying. I was getting old.

❈

S for the stubble that grows on the top of my head. S for the silly dance I do. Bless S, for it is the first letter of survive.

❈

There are so many knots and turnarounds on that map—geometric figures, other letters of the alphabet—it's impossible to call my path an S any longer. As we pull back we can see more surface: Pennsylvania, the Virginias, Ohio, Kentucky: more places that speck, that squiggle can lead. Even now, if the end of the strand winding out toward Harrisburg, Pennsylvania, could speak to its opposite number in Studio B, it might scold: Don't go south. Skip Manhattan. It might say, "Can't you start me in another direction? This one didn't work. It turned out lonely."

"Keep going," says Studio B, with the easy resolve of the ignorant. "Keep going."

"Where is everyone?"

"How should I know? You're the traveler. I guess most are dead."

Staten Island cuts in: "Have you been practicing?"

"Have I been what?"

"Playing the horn."

"No, good idea."

That crosstalk on the line may be a snarled wire, or something else, but I'm doing the best I can: stringing a line of communication between all the places I've been and all the times of my past to replace the fallen lines that used to knit them together, the telephone lines. All telephones everywhere go into the time capsule so all people everywhen can talk to each other.

༄

It was a ritual: my sister and I would agree to hang up after talking for an hour (New York to Olympia, Washington). Ellen would get off, and I would stay on, listening to dead air. She'd pick up the phone and we'd both start giggling. "Get off, you asshole!" She'd hang up again and I'd stay on, sometimes for a full minute. Ellen always knew I'd be there when she picked up, and laughed when I was. We could only really hang up after counting "one, two, three, bye" together. Then we would hang up; or at least I did. Maybe she's still on the line.

༄

You may be wondering what those little black things are, coming up out of the map. More bugs? No: musical notes, audible flags of the spirit. You can see them, rising up on a wavy five-lined staff. It's like Harrisburg is wearing a scarf. Get closer: it's music, good music. It's me.

An unnaturally warm early summer night with a warm brown moon. There I am, my pupils and my horn bright flickering points of firelight. A fire, not because I'm cold, but because without it I think I see eyes in the darkness, plenty of them.

So there's music in Harrisburg. It's started with "Cherokee," medlied into "Parker's Mood," a strong gusty "Summertime." And I burn, I yowl, I moan squeak and howl with the voice of ten thousand ghosts of jazz. I got rhythm and I got Lester, I got Pepper, and I got Rollins and Hodges and Miles. Lockjaw! There's Bird, I think, and the coda's Coltrane.

The front half of me is dripping fat beads of sweat, my back in cool darkness. You saw how I lost a whole state on the Hudson? Now I've lost the eyes beyond the circle of light. Or I've converted them to smiling, audience eyes, and—why not?—I'm taking a bow. Thanks... thank you very much.

Back in the real, in the dry rocks and bushes, two meat hands are actually hitting each other: plaplaplaplap. Plap plap. A voice sings out, a full voice that comes from a live voice box:

"Hey, man, do you know 'Strangers in the Night'?"

Fixed, only my jaw moves. "Y-y-y-you ... ?"

"Yeah I mean it." Twigs rustle impatiently. "Why say what you don't mean anymore? Play 'Strangers in the Night.'"

I am thinking of my journey. But thinking is too organized a word: my journey is rushing through me: water, crows, infections. I've crossed one entire state on my own two feet, two states on one foot. And here, standing right in front of me or about to be standing right in front of me, is my first, my very first human being since the sky fell in. I am thinking about him. Believe me, I'm thinking about him. And what he wants is that I play him the worst song in the entire world.

# 5 ❋ Trying to See in the Dark

Can we leave me standing there for a few moments? Moments of Who's out there? What does he want? Does he have a gun? I'll still be there, breathing shallowly and trying to see in the dark, when we get back; I'm not about to walk away. My wandering has ended in wondering. Leave me there, caught in the thickness of the moment like a fly in amber.

Because now I will tell you about the original Time Capsule.

It doesn't seem as if there could have ever been a first Time Capsule: every letter sent, every leftover, every bank account, every tomb of every king, every bone buried by every dog, every genetic code in every human being is a kind of time capsule. But nothing called a time capsule had ever existed until the Westinghouse Electric & Manufacturing Company buried a torpedo-shaped vessel made of a copper, chromium and silver alloy called a Cupaloy on September 23, 1938.

The Westinghouse Time Capsule was a little taller than a man, seven and a half feet, and considerably narrower, eight inches in diameter. Each of the hundreds of carefully chosen items—even the lady's hat and the baseball—were meticulously prepared for their "journey of five thousand years": wrapped with rag paper, linen twine and glass wool within a Pyrex inner envelope the length of the Time Capsule, which was then reinforced with glass tape and set in a water-repellent wax base; air was sucked out through a tube, the contents washed with inert gas and bathed in a preservative humid nitrogen. Finally, the inch-thick joints were chilled to below-zero, screwed together, and allowed to swell tight at normal temperatures. The citizens of the year 6939 (whom Westinghouse termed "futurians") would have to cut open the Time Capsule with a saw; a dotted line was tattooed on the shell to show them where.

"When the time comes to dig for the Time Capsule," G. Edward Pendray, the Westinghouse publicity man behind the whole idea, wrote to the futurians, "look for it in the area known as the Flushing Meadow, Borough of Queens, New York City, on the site of the New York World's Fair 1939." For there, "at high noon at the precise moment of the autumnal equinox," and as reporters, workmen and officials from the Fair, Westinghouse, the City and the Museum of Natural History doffed their hats, the Time Capsule was lowered through the fifty-foot, steel-lined Well of the Future, as a gong borrowed from a Chinatown shop "tolled solemnly." The Time Capsule hit the marshy Flushing Meadows subsoil with what one observer called a "slupping sound, like that made by a large dog eating canned kennel rations mixed with raw eggs."

# 6 ✳ Wolf, the Night Prowler

"Who are you?"

These are the words I wrap my mouth around, but shock has sent the blood rushing shouting through my head. I'm frozen in the glow of the fire like a rabbit caught in headlights. Playing the saxophone is just one of a thousand things I couldn't do to save my life.

A black man about fifty, skinny and straight both above and below the waist but hinged forward at it, steps now into my clearing, thrusting out a long face with a long long jaw, a yellow-brown face catching so much firelight it seems to give some off, dangling like a lantern on a pole. He is unarmed. He is not tall.

He's talking, but the solid drumming pulse in my ears blankets his words. Threatening me? Telling me his name? I force a hopeful smile, but there's a randomness to my grin, an uncertainty that flickers across the tense air to his features.

My ears pop and suddenly I hear him:

"...man, I'm hungry. You got some food for me?"

*Wolf*. The name is in my head. He's Wolf, I don't

35

know why. The outrageousness of telling me *he's* hungry makes me smile, really smile. His hands open as if explanations, like white doves from a magician's, will issue from them.

"I haven't eaten," he begins. "In . . ." His eyes close and his fingers scratch the air, figuring, calculating, computing; pluses, minuses, sines, tangents, differential equations; clawing out an invisible history of mathematics from first grade to Ph.D., from Euclid to Einstein, adding millennia to eternities and multiplying eons by centuries until he exhales triumphantly and his eyeballs snap djing! back into view like the total into the window of a cash register.

"I haven't eaten," he declares. "In one and a half days."

Now I can't hold it in. He doesn't move his head, regarding me only with his eyes as my adrenaline straitjacket opens and I come spilling out of it, drowning in my own laughter, speechless, limited to gesture. I lay a greeting hand on his shoulder that soon is clutching for support because I'm falling, laughed limp.

"I asked if you got any food." He sniffs the air above my crumpled form, still peeping at me out of the bottoms of his eyes, and steps back to scan me critically. "Didn't your mama teach you to answer a direct question?"

"There are no mamas anymore, Wolf."

"There are *always* mamas," he says. "That's the trick of them."

When I raise myself to my haunches and reach into my pockets his eyebrows lift with me, expectantly, inspectingly, but as I pull out, and hold out to him, two handfuls of cockroaches, Wolf reels, his head shaking in contradiction and nausea. He repeats the key word—"Food"—once for emphasis—"*Food*"—twice for deafness—"*FOOD!*"—three times for completion and disbelief and exasperation and because cockroaches are, goddamn it, not something to put in your mouth.

"Don't you . . . ?" My fingers are withering in his horror, dry black insects slipping through. "Eat them?"

"Man." The pause is designed to remind me what species I belong to. So far I've stood there deaf and then dumb, called him a name that isn't his, laughed like a loon, collapsed, given him cockroaches to eat, asked a foolish question and got a foolish answer. "You better come with me," says Wolf. And he's leading me out of the clearing.

I'm stepping on sharp stones, turning my ankle in holes, crunching gravel. We pick across brush and pavement, slowly because it's become smoggy dark, moonless; Wolf is stumbling all over the place but never quite falling. "Eat roaches, hnh?" he says, forcing a calm voice through several glances full of hysteria. "You ain't crazy?"

"No, I don't think so."

"No." He is slow to agree. "But close, damn close. Cockroaches. Well."

We walk in silence for several minutes. Wolf's hair, compact on top, bushes out on the sides as if he's been wearing a cap: the outline of his head resembles a mushroom cloud. It's hair as it grows in from scratch. I run my fingers through my own; the same, short on top, long around it, and none comes out in my hand.

The central city we are approaching is in reasonable condition; a Bob's Big Boy restaurant even has some partial windows. The missile must have sailed far wide of its target. I dredge my memory for Harrisburg: Oh.

"Wolf?"

"Mm."

"What happened to Three Mile Island?"

It's his turn to laugh. He sweeps a hand wide, as if making me a present of the worthless land. "Take a guess."

"I remember reading... if a reactor is bombed there's more fallout... a lot more, all over the place."

Slowly, nonchalantly, without looking up, he replies. "That so?"

I fight back an impulse to tweak his nose, slap his face: "Hey! Listen!" But he won't. And we pass a shopping center; on the narrow walkway, near a store called Jimmy the Hot Dog King, is a little red-orange clump of plastic: a Big Wheel, those low flat things that kids used nowadays instead of tricycles. I remember, at five, trading in my tricycle for my first bike, and my mother trying to teach and getting upset with me and then my father, a nervous man who had an old-fashioned pencil mustache and was so thin and folded he seemed to have been printed on paper, coming out to yell at her for yelling at me.

Out of nowhere Wolf shouts: "Yeah, I know. I *will*, I *will*! Of course I will!" He stamps his foot like a petulant child. "Jesus."

"Ghosts?" I ask gently.

He stares down and ahead, his nagged expression an answer. Suddenly he bellows: "Will you *shut up*!"

I jump. But then he sighs, "Yes. OK, I'm sorry, alright? I'm sorry. I should've said 'be quiet.'" Now he's nodding and shaking his head, twitching in mute conversation, like a dog with more than one flea bothering him. It's hard to watch.

I clear my throat shrilly, and my voice lurches out. "What did you do?" I have to repeat the question before his dreamy voice answers.

"Do?"

"For a living."

He frowns into the sheer distance of the subject. "An engineer, civil engineer."

"Streets and sidewalks, that kind of thing?"

"Sewers and unemployed for the last nine years, *that* kind of thing."

Later, much later, as we approach the first of his empty traps, he asks: "How come you call me Wolf?"

"You just..." Reasons, resemblances boil up and simmer down, a stew in which I can no longer make out individual ingredients. "I'm not sure. Do you mind?"

"Wolf," he says. "Wolf," weighing it. "No, I like it. It's right. Wolf, the Night Prowler!" He frames an imaginary marquee, his hands T squares.

Wolf's rat traps are cages made entirely of coarse wire mesh: bent into boxes, broken into squares for the cage doors, separated into single gauge for door hinges. Wired down in each is a flick of some tissue, a rat eye or brain or something equally unsuited to Wolf's palate. The doors hang down from the cage ceilings, permitting entry, but not exit, unless the rats figure out that they must pull the door, instead of pushing as they did to enter. We come across six, seven empty cages, only two of them still baited.

"The ones who get away," he says, "are too little to eat. No meat and too many G rays."

Sour grapes. But I think of my own diet, and feel suddenly useless beside this display of purpose.

We climb down an open manhole to what Wolf calls the Main Line, "cause this is where the fat rats live." Sightless, I misjudge the bottom rung and crash to the floor; it isn't wet. "Sorry," says his voice, and there is cigarette-lighter light. I am nose to nose with a rat the size of my face, whiskers twitching as it decides if I am good enough to eat, the cage's wire outlines congealing around it as my eyes focus. I sit up, and Wolf is grinning down, blue butane lighter in hand. Past him are eight empty cages and two more crammed length and breadth with live rat meat.

"It's Thanksgiving on the Main Line!" He strings up the wiggling cages on a length of wire, wrapping the excess several times around his hand. As we pass an Orange Julius, a Peoples Drug, a Hardee's restaurant, grizzled Wolf, face speckled with a graying beard, prey dangling from a fist, looks like a fur trapper heading home.

Home is a hollowed-out 7-Eleven. Two and a half walls are intact and a piece of ceiling is poised for the instant when it can create the most possible damage by falling. I move my good left leg out of range.

"Naah," and Wolf waves a palm upward. "Don't worry. I did a structural analysis. It's safe. I don't know about you," he says, occupied with twigs and matches. "But I've survived as long as I have by outsmarting inanimate objects."

In the quiet night there is a low whistling sound. It is coming from the rats, frantic, crowding away from the licking fire. One starts chattering his teeth, a mechanical noise quickly taken up by the others, frightening despite their helplessness, or because of it.

"I can't stand when they start in with the teeth," Wolf says, too loudly. I've already got the mouthpiece on the sax. "Yeah, why don't you make yourself useful and get some noise up?"

I do the only food song I can remember: "All You Little Rookies." Wolf dangles the wire cages over the flame, forcing a torrent of squeals out of the rats that I cover with some of my own. When it is quiet again there is mainly the smell of burning hair. Wolf opens cages and jams a stick mouth-to-bowel through the rats. As he rotates the carcasses over the flame another smell rises up: meat cooking. It is a good smell, even mixed with hair, and I have to stop playing and open the spit valve on my horn. My instrument and I stand drooling on the smoke-marked linoleum.

Wolf slides a broiled rat off the stick; grease drips. I get out my knife, and Wolf halts at the sight.

"A Swiss Army knife?" He plucks a pair of black half-frame glasses from a crate and, putting them on and turning my little red and silver pocketknife in his hands, suddenly appears twenty years older. "See, a good knife is one of the few modern conveniences you don't find in a 7-Eleven." And he pulls out from behind him a bottle of Lea & Perrins Worcestershire sauce, one of Heinz ketchup, and another of Louisiana Red Tabasco. "This is *civilized*," says Wolf, taking up my knife and skinning the rat in half a minute. "This *is* civilized."

# 7 ❈ Got To

I am watching a skull come to life. Muscle grows on bone, and as worm-forms surface from within, eating and excreting flesh as earthworms do soil, skin on muscle.

When the skull has become face the worms make a return trip, etching away the skin, and I can see that the veins inside their bodies are not blood, but a silvery fluid, and the tiny striations not body segments but a numbered scale. Slip-slithering around the earlobes, into and out of the nostrils, skirting the lips and entering that darkness, crawling through hair and leaving scalp behind, they are animate thermometers, mercury creeping. They burrow beneath the face, leaving trails of bubbling, popping, then cooling, scarring flesh, an intricate mask, a flaming batik, glowing red, glowing with expression, with slow realization, embers exhaling dim, breathing bright, fading, then glowing.

❈

I wake on fire. I touch my face: all there, all full of feeling. I kick the newspapers and flattened cereal boxes off

41

me. No chill comes; no fever.

Wolf is asleep—Don't wake him, I think reflexively
—and snoring like a chainsaw. Now he's whining
smooth and high through hardwood, now blatting
through a low flatulent vein of balsa wood, loose
chunks flying. Spectacularly, ostentatiously asleep like
this, Wolf is a lump of pliable flesh waiting for my
inexorable idea. A Kellogg's Corn Flakes box with a
moisture-deformed picture of Tony Dorsett heaves
gently on his chest.

"Wolf," I say. "Hey you! *Wolf*!" I kneel to poke him.

"Wussamugga . . . ?" he says, and turns over. The saw
starts easily, hitting a vein of granite, ratcheting down-
gear to pine and settling there in a satisfied, self-con-
tained purr.

"This area is hot, Wolf, do you understand, very hot.
Three Mile Island means—I don't know—a *lot* more
fallout." I'm mulling over the idea of patting his cheeks,
bouncing his face easily from one hand to the other, until
he grogs awake, continuing the pendulum motion on his
own for a moment. But what if he's one of those people
who wake up swinging?

"Hey! up, get up! You know what's going to happen
to us? We're going to lose our hair again, except this
time we're going to get bloody diarrhea, start vomiting
and then we're going to *die*, you dumb fuck."

He hawks up a ball of phlegm, calculates by my voice
that I'm somewhere in front of him, and turns his head to
spit it out.

"I had a dream that scared the shit out of me. We're
going to fry here."

His head stays turned away. The only argument he
wants to have is with the idea of consciousness.

"We're leaving, Wolf."

Wolf's eyes are a quarter open now, examining his
long dirty fingernails. "Could I see your knife for a minute?" he asks politely.

"You'll never see that knife again unless you get up
off your ass. We've got to leave."

"'Got to,'" Wolf repeats, lit by gentle amusement.
"'Got to.'" He opens his eyes a little more, gauging my

seriousness, brewing a rebuttal. "The way I've always felt," he begins, "either you're gonna die or you're not."

This is the fuse, I'm sure, of a long string of cliché firecrackers: when it's his time, he'll be taken; he'd already be dead if it was meant to be; everybody's gotta die, etc., etc.

"Naah, that's not it," says Wolf, waving his palm from side to side in an "erase" gesture. "What it is is I can't leave Dad and Mama."

"What?"

"Yeah, they're here. Stuck here, as a matter of fact. They can't go anywhere any more than they could when they were alive." He scratches his temple sleepily. "You serious about this leaving shit?"

"You've got . . . you can talk to your parents?"

But he sits up suddenly, cradling his chin in a hand and his elbow in a palm. "Show him? Yeah, I *know* I said." He turns back to me, shrugging. "They want to meet you."

"Now?" I've got a chill.

"Yeah." Pause. "But I think they'd appreciate if you, you know. . ." He looks at me, blinking tactfully.

"If I what? If I what?"

"If you, you know. . ." A hand makes limp vague circles in the air. "Made yourself *presentable*. Shaved." He sits cross-legged, smiling placidly.

"*Shaved*?" I'm up and stamping. "This is ridiculous! How *can* I shave? I *can't* shave! Of all the goddamn, all the idiotic, all the motherfucking—ow! Ow!" Someone's yanked my hair, pulled me straight up almost off my feet, and let go. I fall in a heap, rubbing my head.

"I would say," chuckles Wolf, rising with a great cracking of joints, moving slowly to the ice-cream case, and tossing me a can of Barbasol and a Gillette Good News razor still in its original package, "you used a word that Mama doesn't like."

# 8 ✸ $29,157,601,226, 911,936,193,863, 914,956,813,455, 379,220,042.90

A whole book could be written about the Westinghouse Time Capsule, and one was. The *Book of Record of the Time Capsule of Cupaloy*, designed by Frederic W. Goudy, was published "as a contribution to the people of a future age," printed on specially manufactured one-hundred-pound rag paper, hand-sewn with linen thread, bound in buckram and stamped with gold. For it Dr. John Harrington of the Smithsonian Institution created "A Key to the English Language," consisting of a phonetic spelling system called High Frequency English and a Mouth Map showing exactly where the palate produces the thirty-three sounds of this language. "The Fable of the North Wind and the Sun" is translated into High Frequency English ("Dhj Fecbjl jv dhj Northwind aend dhj Sjn") and twenty other languages, the Lord's Prayer into three hundred. The *Book of Record* also gives instructions on how to find the Time Capsule from the locations of the planets, in case the coordinates of 40°44′34″.089 north and 73°50′43″.842 west and the idea of a New York City, with its Borough of Queens, have become moot to the futurians. Over the caption "An 800-Pound Parcel to be Delivered in the Year 6939," a sepia-toned photograph shows the Time Capsule suspended by a cable above the heads of thirteen middle-aged, mainly smiling men, squinting up at the small missile as if it gives off light.

The *Book of Record* was sent to hundreds of libraries around the world, dozens of monasteries and three Tibetan lamaseries (it was returned from Calcutta marked "insufficient address") with a plea that the book be reprinted and retranslated as it and the language deteriorate. Other than the *Book of Record*, the only volume to make the Time Capsule was the Bible.

Special texts were written for the Time Capsule by Thomas Mann, Karl Compton, Robert Millikan, and Albert Einstein (who observed shrewdly that "people living in different countries kill each other at irregular time intervals . . .") and printed on Permanent Paper in Nonfading Ink.

What else went into the Time Capsule? Thirty-six Articles of Common Use, each selected by Westinghouse "for what it might reveal about us in the archeological sense" (a woman's hat, a pack of cigarettes, an alarm clock, a baseball, and something no home would have been complete without, a Westinghouse bactericidal Sterilamp); forty-five sample Materials of Our Day (artificial leather, asbestos, aluminum, stainless steel, silicon, and some peculiar alloys manufactured by Westinghouse: Beetleware, Hipernik, Hipersil, and oddest of all, since the entire Time Capsule was made of the stuff, Cupaloy); and thirteen Miscellaneous Items (twelve types of seeds, the two books, a dollar bill, silver dollar, half dollar, quarter, dime, nickel and penny. The Monroe Calculating Company, doing its part for posterity, announced that if this $2.91 were deposited in a bank giving two percent annual interest, it would, in 6939, be worth $29,157,601,226,911,936,193,863,914,956,813,455,379, 220,042.90).

The greatest educational value per cubic inch was provided by ten million words and a thousand pictures on microfilm, most comprehensive on the subject of Our Industries, including photographs and descriptions of

America's major businesses, the *Encyclopedia Britannica*'s entry on "Motorcar," excerpts from Westinghouse's 1939 catalogue, timetables from seven different railroad companies and a full-length biography called *A Life of George Westinghouse*.

# 9 ❋ All the Same, All the Same

As one afflicted with the tandem curses of tough beard and tender skin, I never enjoyed shaving, but using an ordinary razor blade on three months of unfettered facial growth is like giving yourself a haircut with a butter knife. "OK?" I keep asking, pulling inch-long whiskers from the implement of torture. "OK?"

Wolf looks at me each time I ask, shakes his head slowly. I scrape on.

"How come you don't have to do this?" I say, finally getting down to skin on my right cheek. Damn! Through skin.

Wolf grins smugly. "I'm *family*, man."

"Well this is really fucking stupid," I say stupidly. "Can't they see me already, I mean what *is* this?"

"Can't see you at all. They don't got any eyes. They can't exactly smell or hear either. All that's left is up here." He taps his temple. "Whatever you want to call that."

"So what am I doing this for?" The blue razor looks up at me, hairy and quizzical.

47

"All they can do is get an idea of what *you* think you look like." I start making noises of pain and objection, but he holds up a palm. "Don't get the idea you're gonna be able to fake em out. They'll think right through you."

I go back to shake, spray and shave. Quantities of Barbasol pool on my shoes. "How come you know so much about yūrei . . . about ghosts?"

"Ghosts? When a white man dies, maybe *he* leaves a ghost behind; black man leaves a shade. Anyway, I don't know anything about ghosts *or* shades. All I know is dybbukim."

"What did you say?"

"Dybbukim." He eyes me, hands on hips. "You're not Jewish?"

"My mother was. I'm half."

"Half-Jewish, hnh." He turns partially away, smiling, then back. "I got a riddle for you: what do you call a kid whose father is three-quarters Irish and one-quarter Chinese—now listen carefully—and whose mother is half black and half Cherokee?" He gives me a second. "Black. That makes *you* Jewish."

"So what is a dybbukim?"

"Don't you know *anything*, faygilah? The -im makes it plural. One dybbuk, many dybbukim."

"I'll remember that." I go to work on the mustache.

"A dybbuk is someone in your family who died. Hm, hard to explain beyond that. Let's see . . . You had the regular kinda shades—sorry, ghosts."

"I had a different word for them too." I blow air out of my nose; shaving cream's gotten up there.

"Yeah, 'ghost' comes up a little lame. But you had em too, right, the voices? always want you to do something, go somewhere for em."

If I talk I'll eat Barbasol; I nod vehemently. I'm not crazy or he is too; it's good to know either way.

"A dybbuk . . . Well, a dybbuk's like that only more so. They never stop harpin. Not *ever*. A dybbuk gets next to you, stays in your head. First thing they did when they found me was chase off all the run-of-the-mill dead souls, and good thing, they were drivin me crazy."

"I had the others, but no dybbukim."

"Yeah?" Wolf lowers his eyes to me. "Poor sucker.

When I was half-starved a week after the blast they led me to this 7-Eleven. Then later—this is after I ran out of the food lyin around here—I was standing at the door wondering just what the hell was out there to eat, and I saw something moving way off in the distance. I figured a dog. It was a big bundle of wire mesh rolling at me all by itself. I made rat cages. See, they're always worrying about parent things—like am I taking my vitamins? Mama was heavy into vitamins. She made me quit smoking, just shredded all the cigarettes I could lay my hands on. In winter they'll probably wheel up a rack of coats. Nasty scratch you got there."

I wipe my cheek, and my hand comes away pink.

"Your problem," he tells me, "is that you keep going against the grain when you should be going with the grain."

"My problem is that I've been asking a razor blade to mow a lawn."

"Hold on." He rummages around in the ice-cream case. The place is organized, even tidy; there's very little on the floor except for a few rat cages and the remains of last night's fire. But the ice-cream case is full to the horizontal sliding door.

"If you have another can of Barbasol in there . . . ?"

Bent over, he turns his head to squint at me. "You used up a whole *can*? Incredible." He dips his head back into the freezer and consumer items begin to spill willy-nilly out of the cornucopia, Bic pens, a box of Maalox, take-out foil packets of mustard and catsup, a cardboard rack of nail clippers, and several small yellow tins of Bayer aspirin. "A whole *can* of shaving cream," he mutters, coming out with three new razors in one hand and a can of Gillette Foamy in the other. "Some people are just naturally wasteful. Now take my advice: *with* the grain, then *against* the grain."

My skin is shriveling under the shaving cream.

Wolf comes closer, squats low to the floor, extends his hands, palms down, out in front of him, rests his eyes on them. "I'll tell you what worries me: if I leave, what happens to Mom and Dad?" He stares steadily up at me. "Be like killin em."

"Yeah but Wolf, staying here *is* killing you."

"All the same, all the same," says Wolf, as if that means anything.

When I'm finally done he has me stand up. "Turn around." I do. "Tuck your shirt in." And: "Not bad." He comes up and fastens the second button on my shirt; I didn't know I still had it.

"Now," he says. "Just get yourself in a comfortable position, cause if you don't your ass is gonna be sore. Found that out the first time. Whole damn thing fell right asleep." He lies flat on his back; I follow suit, propping my head up on a low display shelf. "Now," he says.

I close my eyes and tell myself determinedly to relax. Soon I start to itch; just psychological, I tell myself, keeping my eyes clamped and scratching an arm and a shoulder and a knee. A chain-reaction itch. Ignore it and it'll go away.

Nothing dramatic happens; I'm just comfortable. I imagine I'm sending roots into the floor; they come from my toes and fingers, then my ankles, knees, waist, wrists, feel along the floor for cracks, find them, and burrow straight down slow into the cool earth beneath. I am very comfortable.

"You feel it. That's what we feel." I know what Wolf means: stationary, solid, still, irrevocably *here*. "Why aren't your parents able to leave? Can't they go anywhere?"

There is a feeling of chuckling. A woman, maybe Wolf's mother. "Haven't you ever known any *people*? Well *they* all stuck in one place?"

"I guess . . . No." I've got to admit.

"*Now* there."

"You mean because everyone alive is different, dyb-bukim—you people—"

"Call a spade a spade. Specially when it's a spade shade." That's Wolf's contribution.

And a new, stern, distinctly masculine presence comes out of the background: "Charles, I am going to have to ask you to hush your mouth."

*Shame* from Wolf. Hung-head Wolf. *Sorry.* And I am realizing my ears aren't hearing a voice from anyone; the only one actually speaking is me.

I concentrate tremendously on each word: *Can you hear me?*

They're laughing, and as the laughter subsides someone says, "Don't have to shout!" I'm asked, "What do you do?" or not really "do," more "What moves you?" or "What are you about?"

"I'm a musician."

"Show em." That's Wolf.

I send up a plume of question marks.

"Gotta think it to play it, right?" he asks. "So think it."

So think it! A musician's dream. First I realize I'm not stuck within the limits of my technique because I'm not using my fingers and mouth and lungs to play. I'm not restricted to an alto saxophone, to the whole saxophone gaggle at once, to a big band, or even to sounds the human ear can hear. Imagine shaping all the notes in a chorus of crickets, a playing card clothes-pinned to a bicycle frame, the pained cry of train brakes coming through fog, the *thrumm* of tires on a metal bridge—and if you can imagine it you can play it! Ideas, directly, can sing.

And I do have a story-song for Wolf's parents. The first part is about Three Mile Island: footsteps in plutonium vaults, locks locking in lockstep, a great waiting of poison. The nuclear attack itself is an ellipse, a bow to those who were there.

Now: the silent feather of fallout stretching blurring in the winds of weeks. Spreading, permeating dirge music: the hot dust in the air, in the rivers and reservoirs; the tempo picks up as that air, those rivers rush burning through the human body, my body, through Wolf's. This is the crescendo I want them to hear, not just the bomb's big bang.

Now? To short questioning phrases, technically inexpert, on unaccompanied alto saxophone, I project onto a bright blank screen the shadows of Debris and Wolf, slowly shrinking as they approach it, arms around each other's shoulders. The Debris-shadow slips on his bad leg, but Wolf-shadow keeps him from falling. Strange, colorful beasts intrude on the edges of the screen, and the Debris-image, pied-pipering with his shadow saxophone, entices them to dance harmlessly around, then off. The two approach a shadow city, its tall ramparts beginning to topple. Wolf-shadow waves a hand and blueprints fill the screen, propping and firming the city.

I've made my argument, my solo's over. A silence, a thousand one a thousand two, then a kind of nod, a "we heard you" fills the breach. They need time to let the ideas sink in and settle down: losing their hold on the living world, losing their son, and he must think about losing them. I make it a question, and their silence is my answer.

First I am aware of those tendrils from my toes and fingers detaching themselves from me, staying back in the soil, staying behind; then I am cut loose from what is around me, touching but no longer a part of it, which is to say I am a human spirit in a live warm body, a body lying on a floor and blinking awake and looking up through a broken roof at a brown summer sky.

The transition was sudden. Everything was violently bare and simple around me. There were no edgings of light on anything, no little symphonies waiting inside of objects, inside of tales and ideas; no story-songs, just stories and songs.

Wolf was laid out like some Egyptian king in his sarcophagus, flat on his back, his fingers locked on his chest, twitching and spasming. I envied that other life he had, was having now, had had all along. But from the stark outlines of life in the present, Wolf was no fun to look at. I was alone now.

Still dazed, I went outside. I leaned against a wall, slid down until I was on the ground. In back of me were the ruins of Harrisburg; but west was nothing but the dirt, bushes, and highway, nothing but surface.

※

I was twenty-one again, in my parents' home, in the plants and cats and neat dishevelment, absentmindedly working out chord inversions at the piano, waiting for the phone to ring with a friend with a car and something to do.

The phone rang. Doctor-something from the hospital: my parents, an automobile accident, the freeway, rather serious. Parents? Yes, both. I called a cab. "Nothing in your area." But I begged and told them why and it would be eight minutes.

I wrote a note to my sister, Ellen, at school, a sweet dreamy actress, a sophomore with her first boyfriend. I told her I was at the hospital, and it was Mom and Dad, and I'd call as soon as I—

I crumpled the note and wrote another, telling her only that it was important she stay at home. I threw the first note out in the garbage pail under the sink. Bundled in the cabinet door were folded shopping bags from Ralph's.

Jerked into a strange state in which time moved very slowly, I flew through the house. In my parents' bedroom I picked up the wedding picture from the dresser: they were young, so young. I remembered my mother when she was my age, their fight when each of them had tried to give the biggest T-bone steak to the other, shoving the plate back and forth across the Formica table like a hockey puck as the broiler's heat filled the room: the fight, and how I had broken it up by crying, "Are you gonna get a divorce?" And in their closet, her left side and his right, I embraced the worn, paling clothes, squeezed them together and tried to send strength to them through their bathrobes and cardigans. I went out and waited for the taxi in the empty driveway.

When I came home Ellen was at the kitchen table, the note I left for her beside the crumpled one I'd thrown away. The door below the sink was open and a few pieces of garbage from the pail were on the floor with her books and Pee-Chee folder. Brenda, our little mama cat, was in her lap, and Ellen was stroking her. She had taken a glass of milk from a full gallon.

❊

I felt like rushing back into the battered 7-Eleven, telling Wolf's parents not to listen to anything I'd said, not to let him leave with me even if he wanted to, because whatever we find out there it won't be family.

Garbage was piled up about four feet high behind the corner of the two solid walls. Hard to believe all this was the doing of one person. The layers of detritus told the history of Wolf's first few months the way rock strata tell a lake's.

On the bottom were muddy cartons, the names half-legible, recognizable by pattern and color: Tide, All. Rusted dish scrapers. Desiccated balloons and Golden Books from the toy rack. Everything Wolf had figured he didn't need. Apparently one of his first acts had been to clean house.

Next were the perishables: frozen turkey à la king, sliced American cheese, Häagen-Dazs. Chocolate—chocolate chip, the son of a bitch.

Finally there were the boxes, wrappers and most of all cans. Without thinking, like a hungry dog, I was nosing through for shreds of food. Everything was unnaturally clean. I picked up a Campbell's Old Fashioned Tomato Rice can, imagining overturning it sluup! into my Paul Revere saucepan, smashing the corrugated red cylinder of soup against the side of the pan, breaking up stray lumps of tomato with a fork, pinkening with the milk, fire at maximum, and turning it off as the first good-sized bubbles formed around the edges, then eating the soup, burning my tongue but eating it in quick shallow half-spoons anyway, feeling a rush of tang and salt and hot at the back of my throat, and pressing the soggy rice grains between tongue and roof of mouth. And that was just the beginning—there was much more to dream of: Fritos and Mystic Mints and Milky Ways.

What about Wolf? Still in conference. Bodily electricity flickered randomly across his features, his fingers. I could tell nothing from him.

There must be something in that huge junk pile I could salvage. The food was gone; the tools had been kept, and used. I got down and started pushing cans aside, noticing for the first time how bad it all smelled. Pain gave dull notice under the heel of my hand: a half-buried child's jack. And in plastic bags I found two sets of marbles, one of clear colors, the other of cat's-eyes, price-tagged $1.29 each.

A thin layer of ash over the dirt as I kneel; I'm trying to remember something. If I don't chase too hard, it'll come back to me. I draw a circle in the dirt; don't you shoot to knock the other guy's marbles out of the ring? Something like that.

Now I remember: the cat's-eyes in the ash conjured up an image from a dream, and borne on that single image the rest of the dream trails into my mind. It's like the corner of a piece of paper sticking out under a door: pull, and the whole thing comes through.

It was a dream, and it was about my cat. I was chasing Brenda through my apartment; I'd reach for her and she would slink away, eluding me without apparent speed, without effort, without seeming to notice me. Finally she was up on a windowsill and didn't move away as I reached out; didn't move at all. She turned color like a leaf to gray and gray-white, and when I touched her chunks of ash came away in my hand.

Brenda used to lie in a patch of sunlight on my floor, warm and happy beyond purring, exorbitantly comfortable, an animate pelt spread out on the warm hardwood. She would get up occasionally, reluctantly, when the rotation of the Earth left her in the dark. Her short coat, thick and warm as a chinchilla's, glowed with all the earth tones, and the sunlight seemed always to heat them warmer, emphasizing the reds: rust to brick to redhead red. Brown: every brown, every brown. And yellowings of red and brown, including patches of orange that presaged one pumpkin-colored male kitten in each of her three litters.

She was born in our house when my parents were still alive. Although, at nineteen, she was completely blind, had had strokes that left her with a loud high child's voice and a tendency to walk in circles, she had never lost the plucky delicacy I loved. In earlier days, when she was healthy, I took her on road trips; she was a great traveler, standing like a dog at the car windows, forepaws on the armrests. When she had a stroke three years ago I told my sister I'd swear off touring until Brenda either got better or died. Ellen said I was being ridiculous, and she used my decision as an excuse to move to New York.

And when I went on road trips Ellen would come to stay with Brenda, who was too fragile to be moved even across town. So the night I went to the birthday session at Redundant Records my entire immediate family was in my apartment.

Cats first, then people. It's simple to weep fat pure tears for an animal; animals are easy. But with Ellen I remembered more than the best of my own behavior: my sharp elbows in the back seat when we all drove to Chicago, to Yellowstone, to Sequoia, tip-of-the-iceberg evidence of which had been preserved for all time in our innumerable home movies. Laughing at her when she used to appear in the early-morning hours as my mother and I sat talking in the two armchairs: Ellen would come out of the dark sleeping part of the house and stand there, eyes closed, in her pink nightgown and fine long drifting dream-hair, a wanderer from another world, a living yūrei, just stand there behind the piano in the corner of the living room for the longest time. She thought she had already said hello. Mom would ask her if she was sleeping well and she would say yes. Once she announced abruptly in a sleep-roughened voice: "We're not Eric."

"We're not?" I said.

"And Derek."

"No?"

"We're not . . . Eric and Derek!"

And she went back into the darkness. Presently a toilet flushed, and her door creaked closed. Mom and I giggled.

But with Brenda I only remembered making her purr, pushing her rabbit hind legs as she lay on her side, arching back across the smooth floor, front paws moving as if swimming. I fed her, I cleaned out the cat box, I took her to the vet.

Where had I been when I had that dream of Brenda? I knew only that I'd chugged with sobs, awakened and kept crying; she had changed color, she was dead. For months after the crash, Ellen had heard Mom's airy soft soprano, singing "Toot Toot Tootsie, Good-bye." She had used it as a lullaby.

I was in the dirt, my hands working automatically, arranging the marbles for a game of solitaire: the solids over here; the cat's-eyes there. I was about to shoot when a dim shadow came over me.

"So who's this Tootsie and is she coming with us?" said Wolf.

# 10 ❋ Where's the Bathroom?

"Yeah? Yeah?" I stand up smiling; my eyes feel wild, like they did the first time I tried marijuana.

"Yeah yeah yeah." He won't look at me.

"Don't you want to come?" I'm slapping dirt off my ass.

His hand waves back and forth in front of his face, windshield-wiping the whole idea away. "Not a question of *want to or don't want to*," he says. "You don't do everything because you want to. Like I didn't want to take off in the car, leave my parents behind. I did it cause I *had* to."

I don't know what to say, so I don't.

"The thing is," says Wolf, "I miss em already."

He's walking; meandering, I think, following anyway. "Gotta clean out my traps. Close up shop." All the way to town he stays a little ahead of me, his gait constantly changing its mind: one step he's got a bad right leg, the next a bad back, and on the third, his back and right leg are fine but he's got a weak left knee that won't quit; fast, slow, eager, reluctant, he does a kind of slump-straggle-stutter-step. Khaki has torn below his knee, flapping against the calf. He's about 5'8', I'd guess, with the kind of body that never weighed more than 125. We reach the sewers, as dark as before, and climb down the rungs. We've got two rats.

"Better hold on to these." Wolf hands our catch over to me, and begins carefully flattening the empty cages at the seams. "I'm gonna see my parents one more time. Haven't said goodbye yet. Oh—they said something about looking. It had something to do with you. Looking for you."

I give him a questioning glance, but he's avoiding my eyes. "Not looking for *you*, lookin *for* you." He shrugs. "I don't always get what they mean . . ." he says. "Don't always know."

"I understand," I say, and I don't.

We return to the 7-Eleven, set everything in a pile. "OK. Like before," Wolf says curtly. We lie down, and the familiar feeling of deep rest, of rootedness comes over me more quickly than before. But it's a long time before his parents arrive.

"You." They're here. "We got someone for you."

"Me?"

"Max?" A new presence; who? "He's not there. He was never there." It's a girl; she's crying.

"I'm here. I'm here."

"He's not here." The presence is turned away, re-treating.

"Ellen! Ellen it's me!"

"Let her know your name," Wolf prompts.

"Ellen, it's Max, Max."

"Your name *in the family.*"

"It's Fatso, Ellen." She hung that on me when I was seventeen, as tall and even skinnier than now. Ellen's ransacking our minds, my words, searching frantically, spottily for something she can recognize. "Fatso" doesn't ring a bell; it's too recent. She's gone back a long way, like a hermit crab hiding inside the smallest central spirals of its shell.

"Ellen, I'm Googy!" The very first thing she ever called me, when she had no teeth and "Max" was too much for her infant mouth. The nickname hung on until I was about ten. "It's Googy. Are you OK?"

And she's all around me like a rain. "I don't know where I am. I'm scared." She's crying wildly, and I seem to feel it too, the hard shudders. "Where's the bathroom?"

"Keep up contact," Wolf's parents seem to tell me together.

"I'm sobbing like I did in my Brenda dream, and try to think my arms around Ellen, wherever my arms are, wherever she is.

"No! Don't! I'm scared!" She's panicking.

"What's wrong?"

"*You* scare me. You're ugly and hungry."

"Do you know where you are?"

"Yeah, uh-huh. We're in some place that's . . . We're at home, right? Where we were?" If the idea of tears means anything, there'd just be a few; if she had a real voice it would only be cracking. "I hate when you quiz me."

"I know, sorry. I'm sorry, dig me, Pygmy?" At 5'10" she was the shortest member of the family.

"You're in a different place, it's you, right?"

"You kind of know, don't you?"

A long pause. "I'm dead?"

"Yes, you are." I imagine putting my arms around her shoulders.

She wrenches away: "Ow! You're hurting me!"

"Jesus, I'm sorry, Ellen! I won't do it again."

"It burns . . . it burns to touch you. You're made of different stuff now. Where are you?"

I don't know how to answer her. "I'm in Harrisburg, Pennsylvania. I found one guy, we're going on a long trip."

"You gotta walk?"

"Yeah."

"Long walk." A pause. "Who are all these people?"

"Old people. And the guy I'm with, he's their son."

"Can I come with?" It's the same question, in the same odd phrase, she always asked, whether I was driving to Thrifty for nose drops or flying to New York for the Newport Jazz Festival.

My answer was usually the same as now: "Yeah, can you?"

"Can I come with?" she repeats.

"Yes." I send out my response as clearly and deliberately as I can. "Can you come?"

Nothing from Ellen for a long time. Finally I begin to hear the faint tune of "Toot Toot Tootsie, Good-bye."

"Ellen!" I try to summon Wolf's parents. "What's happening to her? Ellen! I'm still here!"

"She's just a little tired now, that's what it is," someone tells me. Wolf's mother. "She's got to go, we don't have too much strength, fading now. Hard to keep up contact this long."

"Does it hurt to be touched?" I can still feel Ellen's pain at my touch, from the moment when you see yourself getting burned but don't yet feel anything except the knowledge of impending hurt, to the slow way it fades, long after the thing that burned you has been removed from your inflamed skin.

"Everyone's different. Told you. We're fading now."

*"Mama! Dad!"* It's Wolf, and it's his voice. A voice is such a loud thing. "Mama! Goodbye!"

"Honey. You was loved."

No one's there any longer, and smoothly, without any noticeable point of transition, our bodies materialize in their surroundings, which is another way of saying that an empty Slurpee machine, an overflowing ice-cream chest, an electronic cash register with dead eyes and two and a half walls in a broken 7-Eleven seem to grow into existence around us.

Wolf is up on his feet, unsteady then straight. "We gotta go, man."

"OK." I'm sitting with my arms around my knees, collecting myself.

"Sooner the better." He gives me a hand, and we're standing.

"Wolf, you think she'll follow us?"

"Best she can." He's got a big canvas sack, is picking up things, flattened cages, extra wire mesh, a good dozen multicolored butane lighters, string, making selections. He takes the Tabasco. Leaning so deep into the big freezer he practically falls in, he produces a can of

Borden Sweetened Condensed Milk and holds it up wordlessly for my admiration. He fixes a black cord onto the earpieces of his glasses and hangs them from his neck.

"N'lookit this," says Wolf, waving a dog-eared brown hard-cover: *America: The Sherman & Sherman Guide.* He opens the flyleaf, reads aloud a name, "'Ezekiel Sheridan Dunster,'" and closes the volume with soft respect. "Remind me to tell you about this book sometime." *America*, too, goes into the bag, "so we can find our way," and we leave the 7-Eleven, the mound of garbage, the rocks and twigs for smoother ground.

I check Billy Bo's watch. This has become my ritual at auspicious moments; I may not have any idea what I'm going to eat next, what I'm going to do when the holes in my shoes get bigger, whether or not there's a God or a California, but I do know the exact time. It's 7:04 p.m. Now, with his reading glasses swinging in his stride, Wolf seems less a corrugated survivor than a wayward librarian. He is already doubled over under the weight of the canvas sack.

"I'll take that," I say politely.

"Would you?" He thrusts it on me; not so heavy. Yet. "Bad back," he says to seal my fate.

Wolf's legs are on automatic pilot, simply moving him forward across an empty lot, a broken street, and his eyes are staring down and ahead; though he is the one who knows where we're going, I can't escape the feeling that I am guiding him.

"Wolf?" I say finally. His eyes don't change their focus, but the brows raise slightly. "How come your parents were stuck here?"

"I don't know, some people just . . . They were old people, y'know. Yeah, very old people. I was their youngest. They just wouldn't leave, and they had some warning."

"Warning? We didn't get any warning!" I stop cold.

"Feet," says Wolf. "Feet," he says, meaning mine. When we are mobile again Wolf continues: "It wasn't from the TV or like that, just a kind of intuition my mother got. Oh, she was always predicting things." He smiles, his eyes on a far point. "Yeah, she'd get this look—no matter what she was doing she'd always have to go lie down—*the look*, and then we'd all come round the bed primed for the last words, and she'd say, very weak, her hand kinda up and kinda shaky, say like, 'Something bad is going to happen...' And the thing is, nothing ever did!"

"What?" I'm fully awake.

He shakes his head. "Not to any of us. And next morning Mama'd be at the breakfast table with the newspaper. 'There!' she'd say. 'MAD-DOG MURDERER MAULS MORE, now here, look at that, that's certainly a terrible thing now!'" He chuckles. "Good game she was running. Like betting on every horse in the field for the price of one. See, whether a train went off the rails in Saskatchewan or the milkman's kid got the mumps, Mama had it covered. Automatically." He snorts. "The fab-u-lous gift of prophecy. When she had a headache, Dad used to say, 'Not tonight dear, I have an intuition.'

"Right before *this* shit came down"—Wolf's arm swings an arc—"Mama had one of her famous intuitions, a full package deal with the look, the bed, the prophecy. Well we all had too much respect to laugh outright, but I looked to Dad to see if maybe he was sneakin a little smile on the sly. But he grabs my arm and says, 'I feel it too, son.' You understand now, this *never* happened." Wolf's eyes flash up at me.

"See when he called me 'son' it was serious. And then he reached into his pocket and gave me the car keys, and I *knew* he was serious. Ever since I cracked up his Buick when I was fourteen, he never so much as let me *wash* his cars. Old man held a grudge for thirty-eight years. And here he's standin in front of me: 'Now get outta here right away, son. Somethin *is* gonna happen.'

"And I was backing out the room, I was talking. Asking them to come and they weren't answering, just in their own world waiting for It. They didn't see me anymore, or their bedroom, or the house they lived in for thirty years; it was like it was all already gone. The sight of them sitting together on the bed gave me chills, I went running. That was it, man. That was it."

It is getting dark. I lead dazed Wolf down a bank, onto the shoulder and Interstate 81. It makes me think of the old West Side Highway when it was still standing but off-limits to cars. It was a park really, a desolate strip. You'd look down four lanes and see nobody for a mile; but off to the side not fifty feet away was the Wall Street rush-hour smashup. I think of Wolf's parents. "Jesus. They knew."

"I want to tell you—not only them. I was out there on 83, it was weird enough being behind the wheel of Dad's Olds. The seat didn't quite fit me and the mirrors were off and I was on the highway at night driving out, out like a maniac. Maybe eighty-five, ninety. I was weaving through other cars like they were standing still.

"And you know what I saw? Out of every five or six cars going normal speed there was always one guy like me, skidding around turns, hunched down low over the wheel. I passed a guy in an old VW Bug with one headlight—he was only goin maybe seventy but he felt it. And the farther I got the more of them there were, until at the end it was maybe half the cars were just fifty-fiving along and the other half were madmen, feet clamped to the floorboards, steering only, not slowing down, *running*, like the world was a video game and their quarter was about to run out."

# 11 ❋ Man of the Year

The final component of the Westinghouse Time Capsule was a fifteen-minute newsreel prepared by RKO-Pathé Pictures. This special film of *World Events* would show the year 6939 how the year 1938 moved along.

The big noise in the 1930s, and especially the late 1930s, was Adolf Hitler. When, for example, in March 1938, the Nazis took Austria, tens of thousands of Jews were arrested; thousands more had their property confiscated or were put to work scrubbing public latrines and sidewalks in front of jeering crowds. In Germany and even Italy, where anti-Semitism had never been particularly popular, there were decrees, arrests, beatings, all flagged and illuminated by the large white letters now required on Jewish shops.

But lo, when the Time Capsule's film of world events came back from the developer, Europe—not just the Nazis, not just the Jews, but the continent itself—failed to show up. According to the newsreel, the highlights of early 1938 were a military parade at Fort Benning, Georgia, "showing tanks and other war machines," and a fashion show in Miami. The futurians were to be treated to such scenes as these:

> a. General view of a luxurious scene in which the audience is seated around a swimming pool, watching models displaying advance summer fashions.
>
> b. Two girls in long beach coats.
>
> c. Two girls in long beach coats opened to reveal bathing suits, wearing enormous straw hats.

By August 1938, a month before the Time Capsule was buried, Adolf Hitler, paying little heed to anybody else's war machines—let alone to their long beach coats and enormous straw hats—had marshaled 1.5 million men under arms and openly announced his intention of taking over the Sudetenland region of Czechoslovakia. The fifth annual Nuremberg rally took place during the week of the Time Capsule's interment. Hitler had gained a reputation among foreign reporters for his habit of hurling himself to the floor after a nerve-racking day of politicking and chewing on the edge of the carpet. *Time* magazine named him Man of the Year.

For the second half of 1938, the Time Capsule's newsreel included a speech by FDR at Gettysburg, with "veterans of both sides, attending their final reunion, present"; a lengthy sequence on Howard Hughes, "celebrated aviator, who made an around-the-world flight as 'Air Ambassador' for New York World's Fair 1939"; and some footage depicting a "typical episode in the undeclared war between China and Japan."

In 1939, 1940, 1941, 1942, 1943 and 1944, while Russia rocked, the Pacific boiled, the lines of attack and retreat, attack, strafe and retreat etched across Europe, Asia and Africa, the Time Capsule, resting peacefully in the swampy quag beneath Flushing, Queens, slept the sleep of the ignorant.

When the atomic bomb was dropped on Hiroshima and Nagasaki in August 1945, interoffice memoranda flurried through the corridors of Westinghouse. Even then, it was decided that exhuming the Time Capsule to include a description of the event would, according to G. Edward Pendray, "spoil the whole venture."

It was Pendray, the goateed publicity man who wrote on science in the popular press when not engaged by Westinghouse, who invented the phrase "Time Capsule." Although one of his subordinates pointed out that "capsule" meant either "a dry dehiscent seed vessel made up of more than one carpel" or "a small gelatinous case for containing a dose of a nauseous drug," Pendray stuck with his choice because he liked the way it sounded. He had originally called it the Time Bomb.

# 12 ❋ Open the Doors and See All the People

Wolf is a nicknamer: in the last weeks he's called me Debrick, Deprick, da brick, da beak, Debris, de Camembert, Debird, Max, Facts, Maxillary, Maximus, Gluteus and My Man.

"Here," he says or I say. And side by side but facing opposite directions, like two men about to duel, we begin pacing away from each other, each dragging one plowlike foot behind him, turning the radioactive topsoil with a curving motion of the instep, sweeping small arcs of dirt behind and to the side. Finally we have scraped out, scalloped out, staked out a rectangular plot about ten feet on the long side, soft to lie in and look at. Wolf calls it Homesteading.

"Gluteus Max, you are one selfish motherfuck," he tells me, his face dangling near and yellow, long and jaundice-yellow. We're facing each other, lying on our bellies and propped up on our elbows. The dirt was moist and light grayish-brown when we started out in Harrisburg, with a wet-forest fragrance, mushrooms and mashed rainy leaves. Soon afterward it changed to a coarse crumbly brown, with a slight dry smell of sage and eucalyptus. In this soil we've scratched two concentric circles between us, like a target, as if to direct any spare missiles that might still be up there to the spot. And, here's-the-church-here's-the-steeple fashion, I've interlaced my fingers, am corralling all the marbles, cat's-eyes and solids, each and every one. I've won them, they're mine. "One monumentally selfish motherfuck," Wolf concludes roundly. "You're like the man who whips his slaves to death, then yells cause he's got nobody to pick his fields."

"You're an asshole. 'Slaves.' Fuck you." Master of the witty riposte.

Wolf shrugs, and flicks his thumb a few times, shooting phantom marbles. "Nah, doesn't work." He dons his glasses and grimaces with phony concentration. "I keep *trying*. Still doesn't work." Then he rolls over on his back, eyes closed, hands folded on his chest, feigning deep relaxation.

Nothing is left but surrender. I shoot marbles one by one gently into the dark acquisitive mass of his hair. By color, texture, and static electricity, Wolf's hair seems to collect bits of everything he comes in contact with; it is our trip historian, keeping leaves, dust, soil, keeping records and now a third of my marbles. I have retained all the cat's-eyes, the solid blues and most of the big "boulders" that can knock two or three little marbles out of the winner's circle.

"More," murmurs Wolf, his eyes closed behind his half-framed glasses. "Parity."

Round Two is the first weeks of play turned upside down. Before, Wolf spoiled his game by an excess of caution, like a pool player who lines up every angle with the stick, measuring the exact point where the cue ball must hit the six, then ripping the felt as he misses everything. Now Wolf is gambling recklessly, fecklessly, and collecting ruthlessly. I have become a limp balloon, drained of my competitive turgor.

"This is great," Wolf enthuses, knocking my favorite boulder just outside the outer circle. "Just like having an unlimited supply of quarters in a video arcade."

"No, no, no." I am a grim teacher, down low to the

dirt, sighting his red cat's-eye. "That takes the whole point away from it." I fire hard and miss everything, overshooting.

Wolf smiles into the middle distance. "Missile Command, man, that was my favorite. Missile Command." This is our two-rails-to-nowhere Conversation Special. "I used to come alive on the gray screen. *Then* you'd get the smart bombs, bloo! bloo! those smart bombs. I'm tellinya, I was great on the smart bombs."

"C'mon, Wolf."

"Oh yeah." Sitting cross-legged, he notices the marbles as if for the first time, bends forward and carelessly fires a boulder. It clacks into my lone well-placed marble, a yellow cat's-eye that sat complacently in the very center of the inner circle, and now goes skittering far out of bounds.

"Wolf, the idea is to have a reason to keep playing. So you don't lose your quarter. An incentive. It doesn't make *sense* unless you play for keeps."

He gives his all-encompassing sweep of the arm: "*They* were playing for keeps. We're playing for *fun*."

I have no answer to this. But Wolf has to push his advantage. "Shiiiiiit," he groans as he rises to his feet, lanky, prowling. "Things have *changed*, Bambi. You just may need to learn one or two new things, Peter Pan, about what does and what doesn't make sense. It ain't the same world it used to be, Heidi. In case you haven't noticed." He bends down avidly, speaking to my face. "We don't got to play by the rules for the rest of our natural lives."

"That's why I want to. I mean, there's no one around, there aren't even any books to read, we eat rats, we don't bathe; it's all unacceptable. So now we've got marbles and I think we should play with them the right way."

"Shiiiiiit." I've learned that two of these in a row mean he's going to drive some sense into this dumb motherfucker if it takes till next Friday. "What I wonder," he says deliberately, "is what a sweet babyface jackass like you's gonna do when we hit the first city."

"What I have to."

Wolf removes his glasses thoughtfully and folds them with a snap. "You kill if you have to?"

"Why would I have to?"

"You could have to." Hands in pockets, the Strolling Inquisitor, a profile marred only by the fingertips protruding beneath frayed khaki. *"Would you kill if you had to?"*

"It depends . . ."

"No shit," he says with slow sarcasm.

"Yeah, I would."

Wolf subsides, settling back on his haunches as slowly as the sun goes down. The smog produces reds at sunset, but there's not enough light coming through to make the colors pretty; dull magenta fades to smoky purple to smoke.

"Think there's going to be any cities?" says Wolf.

"Cities I don't know. I bet at least organized settlements, more like villages. Shit, who knows? maybe cities in the midwest."

"The Midwest." He says it with a capital M, like the one in Mecca. "How we gonna get to the Midwest? I don't think we're makin ten miles a day."

We've gone through this one before: he tells me how unrealistic it is; I explain how many days it'll take to get to for example Ohio; he says if we live that long; I say yeah yeah yeah you made it this far didn't you? But Wolf lays back with his hands behind his head and surprises me. "The world's biggest museum."

"What?"

"I'm thinkin anywhere they dropped a neutron bomb. A museum's just one big building, right? Well, how many buildings in a city . . . thousands? Any city'd be the biggest museum in the world. Chicago, St. Louis, Cleveland. Shit, Wichita."

"The world's biggest museum," I say.

"Yeah, and the world's best cause it wouldn't be *arranged* by anyone to show off. Like no one went to Chicago and organized it to be looked at."

I chuckle. *"That's* for damned sure." And relax, propping my head on my jacket. "Any of that pigeon left?" We caught our first the previous night; it just wandered into a rat trap, a fat turbulent bundle of feathers and wire waiting to be plucked and roasted.

Wolf is quiet for a long time. "Know when I was a kid I used to daydream about it."

"About what?"

"About What if everyone in town was frozen except me."

"Me too. Except I used to think about just my high school, not the whole town. Algebra class only, in fact. All I wanted was for Algebra II to be frozen."

"Algebra, huh?"

"Yeah." I smile dreamily as if I've answered the question.

"Why Algebra?"

"Because one seat up there was a girl named Judy and I wanted to be able to take all her clothes off."

"What she look like?" He rolls over, props up on his elbows, frames his face in hands.

"I could imagine her whole body looking at just her shoulders where they came out of her shirt—those sleeveless T-shirts? I used to wait for when she leaned forward to pick up her books at the end of class, cause then I'd get to see a few inches of skin between her shirt and pants."

"Mmm-mmm-mmm." A noise of approving lechery.

"She was this little blond girl with a huge smile and these fat cheeks. Pink and rounded everywhere, like you could take a bite out of her and it would be OK, it wouldn't hurt. She was like some fruit. My glands were going nuts; I grew like eight inches senior year, and at least half of it must've been Judy's fault. Old Brownell would be up at the blackboard droning on about whatever Algebra II is supposed to be, and I'd sit there looking at Judy and sucking on my spit. When class was out I'd go practice my sax and chew clear through the reed."

Wolf chuckles sympathetically.

"She was my girlfriend in third grade. I used to go to her house and watch *Felix the Cat*."

"Girlfriend." There is a little derision here.

"She *was*. We called each other boyfriend and girlfriend. I gave her rings. There was a stack of wood in back of her house, and we used to go out there and I'd try to get her to kiss me."

"Cockteaser," Wolf growls.

"This was *third grade*! My mother kept asking where I got so many splinters."

"Back to Judy." He doesn't want to talk about mothers.

"Judy didn't turn out to be a cockteaser, just the opposite. She had the best body in the high school, and everyone knew it."

"In the uh, biblical sense."

"God, the stories. *This* was the little girl who wouldn't kiss! I never told anybody that; I would've been a laughingstock. She was fucking *everyone*."

"But not you."

"But not me. She was real real friendly, like she'd come up and stand close to me with a knee curling around my leg, and kind of skim my chest lightly with her hand. She made it with each of these guys exactly once—that's what they said—and never again. My mother used to tell me Judy wouldn't sleep with me because she *respected* me."

Wolf likes this a lot; he's laughing. He likes it too much.

"I think there was some truth in it." My voice hits D above middle C, making it an inadvertent question. "She called me up once in a while crying or something, and she treated me like I was special even at school." I pause. "Judy Leighton," I say weightily, looking to Wolf for a response. There isn't any.

Finally he renders judgment: "Little manipulative cockteaser."

"Not entirely. She went crazy. She attempted suicide when she was nineteen."

Wolf shrugs. "*Crazy* little manipulative cockteaser, then."

"You don't know what you're talking about." I am amazed to hear myself sulking this way. Amazed, but helpless to do anything about it.

"Hey, sorry," he says with no conviction.

"Forget it," I say with less. "I'm going to play a little." I rise to my haunches.

"One second, Babe." He holds up a finger. "Before you stomp off you tell me *why*."

"Why? Look, I'm willing to think you just had a bad day."

"But I haven't." He puts his hands behind his head, like someone in a hammock in Tahiti. "Just had a nice meal, just went through some nice memories concerning how pretty and nice things used to be. About to hear some good music. The fact is I'm a man utterly at peace with his world." Wolf puts his hands behind his head and looks miserable.

"I tell you all about this girl and you just sit there calling her a cockteaser. You don't care if she was so fucked up she tried to kill herself, you don't hear any of that, she's a cockteaser anyway. She's in third grade? Fine. Cockteaser. Every single time I start to enjoy thinking about her you go 'cockteaser.'"

He spanks the flat of his fist on the ground. "It ever occur to you that *I* was enjoying it too? You ever stop and think that maybe all those nice little memories you feed and water every day aren't so nice, that maybe what they really do is fuck you up?"

"What the hell," I ask him evenly, deliberately, "do you think you mean?"

He sits up to educate me, his hand and hook-crooked finger poking like a slow metronome: "From now on I got no use for anything that doesn't help me go on living. Cause if I can say I don't need no mother and father and I don't need no home—and I did say that, I said all that back in Harrisburg—I definitely do not need any god-damn little cockteasing Judy Shango that I never knew anyway."

"Christ, she was just a girl. She doesn't have to *represent* something."

"You don't decide whether she represents something. She means something to *me*. Something I can't have."

"Shit, Wolf. Everything that used to be is something you can't have."

He lets his back fall softly to the ground. "You remember you're the one who said that."

Abruptly, I grab the sax and get up, feeling stiffness in my feet and upper legs. I take off the mouthpiece cover. I just want to get away. And I do want to play, so much that I almost rush it. But if I don't get some feel—sometimes a specific line, usually just a rough idea—of what I'm going to do, the whole session flounders. It takes forever to play my way back.

I know what I want. I want *sound*, not notes; size and sound. What comes out of me are long phrases exactly the duration of one natural breath, sometimes a spray of multiphonics, sometimes just a single drawn-out note. Rhythmically it's nothing, very square cut; the harmonies are from preclassical music, a set of intervals I've learned to use when I want to think about other things or not to think at all. It's the tone, a kind of rusty-battleship mix of Sonny Rollins and Coleman Hawkins, that blows me along, on and on without interruption in the same style.

I return to the dying campfire rejuvenated and composed. As I approach, Wolf removes the book *America* from his chest and doffs his half-frames. Cross-legged, I lay the horn on my lap, take off my shirt, and unroll the sleeves. Wolf turns onto his side, facing me, resting a cheek on his fist. I will not, I have previously decided, talk to this person. I may consider reconsidering in the morning. I spit copiously into the cleanish inside of a shirt sleeve.

"You play pretty well, y'know."

"Thank you." Sucker for a compliment.

"Yep . . ." he muses, "play pretty well."

I'm not going to bite twice. Wolf lies there watching as, methodically, nonchalantly, I polish the bell. Unlike Big Al, I never used to like a shiny horn; but now that my saxophone is the only thing in sight that isn't a variation on gray and grime, I buff until it's like a mirror. I don't know if a slow grin is seeping over Wolf's face. Probably.

"Know what you look like fussin over that piece of metal?" I slip him a withering glance. "You look like something out of a corny western, the sheriff with his six-gun. John Wayne. Wyatt Earp. Yeah, old Debris. Blowin for the lost world."

A smile comes inadvertently to my face, but I wipe it away, pinching lint off the pads in what I hope is the equivalent of casually filing my nails.

"I mean," Wolf rolls on, "why couldn't you play some

more humble instrument...the ocarina, the ukulele? No, it has to be the *saxophone*. See now, playin the *saxophone*, and playin it so well...The way I look at it, like they say on TV, you are a man with a *mission*."

It's easy for me to look sleepy. I let my face sag, one eyelid droop slightly lower than the other; when the entire expression is in place, I turn it to him.

"And that mission," he declaims, "should you choose to accept it, is to make people happy!"

"To make people happy," I repeat dumbly.

"Beginning with me." Wolf sits up and crosses his arms decisively. "Play 'Strangers in the Night.'"

❋

I remember cities, I remember every city. And every city is the same through a windshield: the traffic lights at each intersection a wide flat triangle of greengreengreen, and within that another, the next, and within that another, a series of arches, a receding canopy, not quite infinite, like the images in facing mirrors, the yellow up ahead advancing down, marching down on the car, green passed to yellow and then yellow to red and you wait redredred you wait right there.

❋

It is a most mysterious thing. "Wait a minute," Wolf will say, and will not be budged from a freeway exit or a WELCOME TO WALNUT BOTTOM sign until he has fished his guidebook *America: The Sherman & Sherman Guide* from our sack. "There might be a 7-Eleven in this burg."

"The book tells you *that*?"

Wolf, scholarly and patriarchal in his half-frames, is poring over the index. "Uh-huh," he says distractedly. "Tells me everything."

"Let me see it." I grab for *America*. He twists away without taking his eyes off the page, protecting the book with his body.

"No," he might finally say. "No 7-Eleven." In this case we bypass the town.

But he might say: "Hnh. Meenymeenymeeny," burbling along with whatever he is reading, an index finger moving swiftly across the page. And then, for purposes unknown to me, we plow ahead into Greason or Scotland or Chambersburg, uninviting turf.

Wolf, for what it's worth, is never wrong: if he chooses to stop in a town, we do invariably, uncannily find a 7-Eleven store there. Inside, Wolf goes immediately to the back of the counter, and whether everything is in place and well preserved, a Levittown dream of the future, or a shambles of jagged glass and Formica, he works through the ruins as closely and gingerly as a detective afraid of smearing fingerprints: the time-release safe that, as he once explained to me, opens an hour after you tell it to; the closed-circuit video monitor; the cash register; the microwave oven, the massive stainless steel Slurpee dispenser, all of it mute and unrevealing. Finally, swearing exactly as I remember my father doing when he disassembled the garbage disposal and found he couldn't put it back together ("Son of a *bitch*! You *god* damn son of a *bitch*!"), Wolf destroys the rest of the store with quick savagery, kicking fallen display racks, upturning shelves. I ask him what he's doing and the answer is always, "Salvage. Wouldn't you like another can of condensed milk?" Once, chest heaving, destructive futility in his eyes, he simply said, "Clues."

Salvage: at first I bought it. But after we failed to find so much as one can of Puppy-Chow in a whole skein of picked-clean 7-Elevens, it came clear to me that Wolf was acting under some compulsion, might even be trying to find someone who is keeping one step ahead of us.

I got that idea when we found the grave. It was a dusky cool dusk in a small town named Fort Loudon, and I stayed outside as Wolf stepped through a door frame empty of glass to begin his archeological expedition in yet another 7-Eleven. The sky hung humidly, uniformly brown, looking warmer than it was, and a pair of big birds, buzzards maybe, circled far overhead. A light breeze kicked up, and I heard a faint flapping sound.

Around the corner of the store a wooden land surveyor's stake jutted out of the ground, a strip of orange plastic tied to the top and fluttering noisily against it. The large birds dipped and flew off and two or three fat drops of rain, the kind that still make me look up for air conditioners, hit my head. I turned my ankle in a hole and sprawled forward. Not six inches from my face a human hand protruded from the dirt. In the distance, a crash and Wolf's voice: "Son of a *bitch*." The hand had very little flesh on it, just fingernails and bone and cuticles, and it was faced down in a relaxed position, as if it liked the feel of the soil.

It seemed for a moment that the corpse's smell had reached my nostrils, and I let out a scream; as I hop-hobbled back toward the 7-Eleven, desperately pogoing, I realized it was not the scent of dead flesh but the taste of live panic.

Wolf had emerged from the doorway and was leaning against the building with one hand on a hip in an attitude of infinite exasperation. The rain had come in earnest. "Well well," he said. "If it isn't the boy who cried Wolf."

"Out back . . . out there . . . where the stake . . ."

"Yeah? yeah? yeah?" Wolf kept interrupting, and soon was rushing by me, into the downpour, past me, and to the stake.

He had yanked it from the ground when I caught up with him, and was on his knees sifting handfuls of dirt through his fingers, his face slick and his hair matted from sweat and rain. A laminated card appeared in his shaking hand.

"Read it! Read it!" he shrieked, shoving it at me.

"7-ELEVEN STORES CORPORATION," I recited dumbly. "Employee I.D. Joel Shuman. D.O.B.—"

"Max," he said, my plain name, pulling from the dirt a Baggie with a scrap of paper in it. And as I took the paper out Wolf put his glasses on and the two of us sat squinting at blue ink that had already bled so faintly into the fiber of the paper that the water running in rivulets down off our noses, guttering in the ground, and stripping a dead man's knee of its thin cover of dirt could do it no further damage.

Wolf stood, face upturned, and hurled the slip of paper to his feet.

"Go ahead!" he screamed, his glasses asteam and opaque. "We can't read it anyway! Go ahead! Rain on it!"

# 13 ❄ Ladies, Generals, Poets, Statesmen and Babies

Brigadier General John J. McNulta, then of Bloomington, Illinois, fought in the Civil War for the 94th Illinois Volunteers. After the war, he moved to Chicago, made a large fortune as the receiver for several railroad companies and ran for Congress against the first Adlai Stevenson. He died in 1900, at the dawn of the new age; but then everyone dies at the dawn of a new age. He is the only general who left a time capsule behind him.

It was an etched glass bottle containing several tiny bundles wrapped in linen and wound dozens of times with thread. A note was placed in the bottom: "*11-79. To Be Kept Unopened For 100 Years.*"

On a sunny day as good as any other in November 1979, the McLean County Historical Society declared that the century was officially up. Kathryn McNulta, ninety-four, the general's daughter-in-law, was there in pointy glasses with her three grown grandsons. Also present was Mrs. Emma Hoffman, the oldest participant in the ceremony by two years, whose father had served under General McNulta; so were the mayor, the police chief and even some reporters from national magazines. There was a band. Civil War songs were sung, uniforms were displayed, and the broken stopper and the slim parcels were removed from the bottle with forceps.

In General McNulta's time capsule were two photographs of the general and one of his wife Laura. A ceremonial ribbon. The menu, program and seating plan for an 1879 reunion dinner of the Tennessee Army Veterans. The program described no less than fifteen toasts, until finally someone raised a glass to "the babies, as they comfort us in our sorrows, let us not forget them in our festivities." To which a literary guest named Samuel Langhorne Clemens responded: "We haven't all had the good fortune to be ladies; we haven't all been generals, or poets, or statesmen; but when the toast works down to the babies, we stand on common ground." With that, draining his highball as fast as gravity would take it, he put an end to the toasting.

The guest of honor was former president Ulysses Grant. It was General Grant who provided McNulta with the inspiration for his time capsule, as revealed by a note in curlicue script wrapped around a glass tube sealed with red wax: "*Cigar given to John McNulta by General U.S. Grant, November 14, 1879, must not be opened for 100 years and then smoked by some one of his descendants who has rendered good service to his country.*"

A century later the cigar was finally smoked by General McNulta's three great-grandsons. Unlike cigars given out on other occasions by Ulysses Grant, this one did not explode.

# 14 ✳ Fire

It's like Wolf gives a jump without leaving his feet, that's
how quick he straightens up. Suddenly he's got about
four inches of height I never knew about. Not for long:
he's looking straight ahead, looking, bending, looking
like an invisible fishing line attaches him to some point
on the horizon and if he stares hard enough he can reel it
in.

I follow his eyes: terrain, land to cross, nothing. But
Wolf is running, if that's what his clumsy involuntary
progress can be called; he's a collection of discombobu-
lated parts jerking forward as if the thing he's watching,
the thing he's attached to, is stronger than he is.

He comes to a stop maybe fifty yards out, watches for
a moment. Then, in rapid succession, he:

- punches the air, jabs it about five times before
  throwing a right so hard it yanks him forward,
  slow-motion, to the ground
- slugs the dirt, not beating it with the flat of his

81

fists like a child in a tantrum, but with the knuckles, pauses, glances up at the horizon and slugs the ground one-two again

· gives a wide open-throated yell, something like "ooOOOOOOOwOOOOOOaaaaaghhhHHHHHHHHHH!" and just when I think he's done, "makamakapureaaaaaaaaahh!"

· takes off his left shoe, of all things, and throws it as far as he can

· tries to do a front flip and collapses flat on his back.

When I arrive, this quivering, ululating advertisement for psychiatric medication, this one-man convention of epileptics, is heaving like a quarterhorse and making a noise like a whistling teapot just come to a boil.

"OK Wolf, what is it?" I lean over him. He's purpling. "Are you alright? Hey Wolf! you alright?"

He's laughing, coughing, laugh-coughing, doubled up, knifing along the ground, barely able to nod his head. I'm only a tiny part of his overall amusement.

"You saw something."

Wolf says nothing, but slowly, like a charades player, taps his nose.

"What is it? C'mon, what is it?"

He lets his inner noises die out; but as I help him to his feet, his arm rises straight out from his side, pointing.

"What?" I say, squinting. "Way out there?"

"Wayyy out there . . ." he whispers.

"What? Another town?"

"No." He's got me by the elbow. "Fire."

I strain to see it too, but can't. "How far do you think it is?"

"Half a day, maybe less. I don't know."

"Half a night," I correct. Blue-black grades to gray to reddened gray on Wolf's horizon. "You sure it's not just the sunset?"

"It's fire."

"Jesus," I say, still squinting.

"Feet," he says.

We walk steadily, Wolf a half-step ahead, trying to speed us faster. In another half hour I think I see it, in an hour I do. And now both of us are hurrying along in silence.

Constantly I am checking Billy Bo's fine watch. It was exactly seven o'clock when Wolf discovered civilization; it is now 8:17 p.m. A diffuse patch of gray rises, the moon wrapped in steel wool. At nine we stop so I can fix up the horn and run some scales. On second thought we spray our faces with Barbasol and try to scrape off some beard, using each other as mirrors. We go on in double time. The moon crawls; we are beating it.

Suddenly Wolf erupts with: "Hello. I am Charles E. Dewey, Junior. I am a civil engineer by training and experience and can assist you in designing a drainage and sewage disposal system that will undoubtedly be of great benefit to your community. Now this is . . ." He extends an open hand toward me. "This here is my friend who." A peremptory throat-clearing. "This is Mr. Maximilian Debrick who will function as an assistant to me and provide musical entertainment in the nights ahead. We are confident that we will be of immeasurable—"

"Wolf."

"Will be of immeasurable . . . What?" He turns to me, his jaw working, snappish.

"Let me do the talking, will you?"

"Let *you*? What you gonna say?"

"I don't know. That's why I'll be better."

We go on. Wolf is sullen, and when he talks it's in a grumble, as if he's boycotting not just me but the very process of articulate speech itself. Unwillingly, as we approach the fire, his spirits lift, he steps a little higher. Finally the book *America: The Sherman & Sherman Guide*, previously owned by E. S. Dunster, appears in his hands. "Pennsylvania . . ." he says, flipping the pages. "Luzerne . . . Lycoming . . . Will you hold on a minute?" We stop in the road and he reads, holding the book up in front of his face. "Town covering da-da-da square miles . . . fine family-style restaurant . . . historic home of yeah yeah yeah," he mutters impatiently. "Ah."

He turns the book sideways. "Yep," he says, smiling, nodding. "Yep yep yep."

"Whup?" I ask.

"This," he says, closing the book with a snap, "could be the place. Feet," he orders, briskly striding on.

I'm caught flat-footed, have to trot after him. "What place? Wolf? What place?" But he just raises a hand over his shoulder, waggles it dismissively. There is nothing to do but try to keep up with him. In a few minutes, slightly winded, I hand him our satchel to slow him down; he accepts it without a word, and soon is swinging it eagerly, like a boy on his way to school and in love with his teacher.

"Shit," says Wolf, glancing at me, staring at the fire with wide white wild eyes. "People!"

The town is coming clearer. It's a puzzling site for a settlement; judging by the rubble, a small village that suffered a direct hit. It's leveled. I see no standing structure that would give shelter.

"Maybe," says Wolf, finally slowing down a little. "Maybe they're hiding."

"You think they're scared of us?"

"Well no . . . maybe they're . . . what I'm trying to say is."

"Is?" But before he can answer I hear it.

Listen." I hear the fire, whipping and snapping in the wind like a mainsail on some hellish ship.

It's not broad but maybe forty feet high. As we get close enough to feel heat Wolf lowers his voice in the din. "Why they need a fire that size? Unless they're roasting dinosaurs." He sniggers a little, but the sniggers scrape to a halt. "Or some other big animal."

We look at each other. "Why don't we stick together here?" I say.

"Yeah, you get out your little knife. Just in case."

And side by side, sometimes back to back, we edge around the enormous fire. Wolf gets my attention by periodically tossing his head up, pointing with his nose at some patch of darkness in the shadow of a wall, some hollow that, now that you look at it, does seem to be throbbing with life. A wiped-out train station down the block looks suspicious to me. All the shadows are moving, cast by the fire; more than once I'm fooled by our own.

"Listen!" he says, and I feel a tingling in my scalp. "I'm not sure—no, there it is again. Don't you hear it? They're laughing at us. Weird noise."

"No. What's it sound like?" I can usually hear anything.

"Like men laughing, or growling, very deep. Listen."

I stand and listen. Sweat runs off my nose. "No, I don't hear it. Listen Wolf, let's get away from the fire."

He doesn't budge.

"Come on. If they're going to kill us they could have done it already."

Wolf shakes his head but follows me slowly, carefully to the train station. I know I saw something move in there. No, I think I saw something move.

I shout foolishly into the black doorway: "Hello!"

"Fuller Brush man!" calls Wolf, his voice quavering with false bravado. We've got our lighters out, but they don't do much besides cast doubt on what is just beyond their glow. We go in. I shout again, and this time we hear a scuffle.

"Sounds like rats," says Wolf.

Gigantic sticks of charcoal, the pewlike benches for waiting passengers, crouch in the darkness. Behind them? Neither of us is willing to poke around.

We hike out of the town at twice the speed at which we entered it, conjecturing in hushed voices. Where are they? What if they come out after us while we're sleeping? They could. Are we far enough away yet? No. Why would they hide like that? Maybe there aren't any people. That doesn't make sense. Are we far enough? It's a full mile before we start speaking at full volume again, and two before we bed down. I'm up until dawn, grinding my teeth, hot, afraid to let my eyes shut all the way. Wolf tosses and churns, asleep in name only, all night long.

I dream of fire and open my eyes on a startling bright sun. I sit up, squinting at the town. The flame looks different in the day, a clear pale blue at the ground, transparent a few feet higher and above that a shifting, inconsistently opaque yellow. Everywhere it's the wavy lines of heat, and everything behind, the train station, a hotel, looks like a rained-on watercolor, lines dripping.

"What do you—" I start to say, but there is no one to say it to. Wolf is gone.

I jump up without bothering to put on my shirt. Kidnapped? Run away with them? All ideas are dumb. I walk fast toward the town; I dash toward the town. My mouth tastes of ash.

Wolf is squatting by the great fire, a figuring, logical look on his face, empty of feeling. "Hi," he says, without so much as an upward glance. "I haven't seen anybody you'd know."

There doesn't seem any point to searching, but I do anyway, poking through rubble, peeking into the sewers, checking the burned-out cars for signs of life. There's a Volvo 444 like the one that used to park outside my building, upholstery charred, the metal tubing of a kiddie seat in back. In the hotel I find three letters from a red neon sign: VAC, and part of an A Vacancy. Behind the benches in the train station? Nothing. Nothing but broken glass and rat shit. I return, finally, to Wolf and the fire. He is still squatting there, catatonic, unhappiness in his eyes.

"Gas leak," he pronounces. "That's how it keeps going with nothing to burn and nobody to feed it. Burst gas main underground, and the firestorm touched it off. Stayed lit. That's what happened. There never was anybody here." I sink to his level, and he looks at me like he's never seen me before. "Where's your ... your ..." His hand waves limply, vaguely at me.

I drop my eyes, realize I forgot the saxophone. Wolf taps my bare sternum. "Don't leave home without it."

※

Some night Wolf and I will wander into a deserted city; in the morning we'll awaken to discover a city populated entirely by shadows. As in Hiroshima, the forms of the inhabitants will have been projected permanently on the broken walls, the sidewalks: shadows forever on their way to work, shadows at lunch, shadows right-angling down stairs, naked shadows stripped of props, stripped of purpose, stripped even of the solid shapes that cast their images on the blank page of a swept-out city. People in the purity of position and activity; guess their intent. Was that boy chasing a ball or running from something? Him with his hand held up: just a man greeting someone? A clairvoyant shielding himself from above? A lunatic who thought he could stop traffic?

Over on the playground, by the hopscotch squares and the tetherball poles that have shed their fruit, kids stood in the bright and brighter sun, making shadow-figures with their hands. Making the only joke anybody else could ever get. Look: this is a bunny, this is a dog with his tongue hanging out.

# 15 ⁕ Dirt

Wandering Wolf, wild Wolf, wary Wolf, chary Wolf, yesterday's big bad Wolf; firelit by night, steel-blued by dawn, browned by brown sun; Wolf of granite, Wolf of stone, Wolf is there but nobody's home; it's Wolf minus Wolf, wind-up Wolf, Wolf of steel, Wolf of gears, and when the gears turn blinking Wolf, the mere and only sign of life, a sign that Wolf sees out but there's nothing in to see, no keeper of the flame: Wolf squats by the fire, utterly symmetrical, elbows on knees, fingers locked under grinding and still clean-shaven jaws, dew-browed, in a fever of frustration, the jagged edge of the hotel looming over him like a hospital chart. A bead of sweat appears at the tip of his nose, growing until inside it quivers an inverted miniature landscape, and drops.

"Come on." I put my hands under his armpits and drag him backward hard enough to splay his legs straight out in front of him. He's soaking wet.

"Hey, let off! You let off me!" He's flapping his elbows like an enormous duck, flapping free. "I'm thinking."

"Think in the shade." Irritation has crossed his face and passed immediately; it's a little scary that he isn't even bothering to sulk. He merely looks in my direction as long as I continue to be a source of sound. "The human brain is not supposed to be stored at over a hundred and fifty Fahrenheit." I've got him out of the blaze but not into the cool. "Come here now," I order him, pointing at my feet, my voice booming, and he obeys.

We're sitting quiet, backs against the wall of the train station. Sometimes I picture us from a few feet away: two tired travelers come to rest in a strange town. Holes in the clothes and long hair; that makes it maybe 1968. Beers and a joint would complete the picture. Maybe a guitar and they'll sing "House of the Rising Sun." In that two-shot, in every two-shot, it's as if nothing dramatic has happened; you'd need words from us, a soundtrack, to figure it out. The soundtrack hasn't any words on it now anyway, just the background crackle of the flame and tape hiss. But pull the camera back—no need to do it gradually, just kerchunk back into long shot—and now you see what is behind the two of us.

No: I'd rather stay in close-up, watch Wolf's face, let it fill the frame: the one part of the landscape with features, the one part that's in motion, and it is constantly in motion, planes shifting as his chin works, rolling hills of lips becoming waves as he silently works over the words to come; and all the changes happen so fast, and all of them mean something. It is a marvelous thing to gaze at someone else's face.

"Now I'm going to tell you why I'm staying here," Wolf says at last.

"*Here*? Staying *here*?"

"Now you're cooking with gas." He gestures toward the flame. "This fire gets a lot of attention, see what I mean? Specially at night."

"What are you trying to say?"

Wolf points to the ground. "That right here is the only place we've been where anybody else is ever gonna come."

"How can you possibly know that?"

Wolf locks his arms crossed. "*You* askin me that?

'Know,' shit. How we *know* there's ever gonna be anybody out there anywhere? We don't know, that's the answer, we don't know shit. Except that this is our chance." But his face, his hands lend no support to this enthusiastic transcript, seem completely unaware of what it is saying; Wolf is hollowed-out, enervated, his emphasis automatic.

"Your brain's been parboiled. Say you're right; maybe some guy does come dragging along in six months. Then what've you got?"

"What do I got if the guy's a girl? I got a chance to start from scratch. Build something."

"You think we have to start back at Adam and Eve? And you can just sit on your ass and Eden's going to come to you? We've got to find *people*, Wolf, a bunch of people. Some kind of community that's already going. That's what we're looking for."

"Shiiiiiit." He gets to his feet, and walks around arms akimbo. "*You* look. *You* go draggin cross-country jamming your sax in windmills. *You* go discover the pot of gold somewhere over the rainbow." With each "you" he stabs the air in front of my face, so I spend most of his diatribe with an index finger one inch from my nose and an urge to bite it. "*You* go takin your raggedy-ass roach-fed hopes and dreams and dreams and hopes round and round this great empty Midwest of yours. And when you find your Shangri-La you just send your pal the Easter Bunny hoppin back out to Flametown and there I'll be."

"Are you finished?" I've bloated with anger; it's filled me with hot air, dragged me up to my feet, words and reason left behind like ballast heaved from a balloon, and I'm towering over him, putting an arm around his shoulder, a strong arm, and jerking him around. "Are you *finished*, you little piece of shit, are you *quite* finished?" I've got us staggering around like a couple of drunks, flop-wheeling careening, and turning nasty tight turns for italics.

"Let me go, Debrick. Let me go!" Wolf is repeating through this, his feet flailing for balance, and when I do he's suddenly weak, thin, boy-sized, backing away and leaning against the wall, shoulders hunched and hands in pockets.

"Is that how it breaks down?" he says in a small voice. "The last two men on earth and because you're bigger, you're right?"

"I'm sorry." How could I? "I really am. Did I hurt you?"

"You hurt my pride, man. Hurt my feelings." His eyes glisten but there's fight in his face, like a kid who's been yelled at by his parents and still thinks he's right.

"Listen to me now, Wolf. I'm as serious as you are. I believe what I believe. I'm sorry about pushing you around, I am. I think we're going to find something out there."

"I think I'm gonna find something right here. You believe in the Easter Bunny. Each of us can go think what he wants to think. How do you *know?* that's the point. I'm in pain, you hear me? My legs hurt all the time, my back doesn't give me any peace. I'm at the point I wanna *know.* I want proof."

"Wolf, remember me? How am I supposed to give you proof? How am I supposed to do that?"

"I don't know..." His back slides down the wall and he links his fingers behind his head, bending his elbows forward like wings. "I don't know...you don't know ...nobody knows."

I squat in front of blank Wolf, and there we are looking dumbly at each other, two infinitely questioning, infinitely puzzled men, men who might scratch their heads if they were able to perform complex motor tasks, men whose tapes are on Pause, men at sea, a pair of bookends, a Derek and an Eric.

I'm the one who breaks the spell. I retrieve the canvas rucksack from where Wolf has dropped it, and slowly, methodically spread out its contents in a semicircle around Wolf. The rat cages go in one pile, the shaving stuff in another. The butane lighters like big cheap gems in the dirt; the nail file; the can opener. I fan out attractively our frayed and mildewed Rand McNally road map of the United States.

Wolf watches this process with dull curiosity. Finally, when I produce our treasure, the tin of sweetened condensed milk, he is moved to say flatly, "Why are you doing this."

"I just thought you might want to have one last look at all this stuff," I tell him airily. "Before I take it with me."

"Huh huh," says Wolf, watching me closely as I put the items back into the rucksack. "You say the funniest things."

"Well." I stand up, extend a handshaking hand. "It was nice to meet you."

And now I can feel it even with my back turned, even as I stride away from him, the old spirit surfacing in Wolf, rising slowly like a bubble in cold oil.

"Where," he begins, and the power in his voice tells me he's on his feet, "do you think you're going with all my earthly possessions?"

"*My* earthly possessions," I say, not turning, not stopping. He can't see the smile spread across my face.

And in a second Wolf is there beside me, short, wiry, feisty. "I'm not foolhardy," he says. "So I wouldn't try to take that back by force." He's trotting every third step to keep up with me.

"No," he adds a minute later. "What I'm going to do is wait until you're fast asleep one night and find a nice rock about the size of a grapefruit, preferably with sharp projections, and see once and for all if there are any brains inside your skull." I glance at him; his smile is beatific. "Not tonight," he croons. "Probably not tomorrow night. But some night."

I say nothing, feeling my calf muscles complain. We hop over a brambly embankment and get back on the freeway. I step up the pace.

"I often think about deterrence," Wolf's voice comes from the blue. "It's really one of the major issues in society. See now, take a man who is motivated to commit a crime; murder's probably the best example. A man can want to kill a particular person so badly that nothing else seems nearly as important. It can come to seem that killing this, uh, special individual is the right, proper, just and necessary thing to do. Now will the idea of penalties stop him? You have to admit it's an interesting question." He raises his eyebrows at me sidelong, his hands clasped behind his back. "I say, you *have* to admit it's an interesting question."

"It is," I say, wondering what planet I am on. "It is."

"I think we'll be able to agree on this much," says Wolf, grave, scholarly, brandishing an index finger: "If the man with murder on his mind looks to his left and looks to his right, and sees no one except his victim, absolutely no one to witness the crime, no one to arrest him or even ask him if he won't please go to jail, he will not hesitate. He will kill. And can you blame him? Not me, I couldn't. No," says Wolf. "*I* certainly couldn't."

Asphalt passes under our feet. The city of flame is behind us now, far enough behind us that I have relaxed our pace.

"You'll be pleased to know," Wolf announces suddenly, "that I've decided to bury you *with* your saxophone." Pause. "If we're on a patch of soft soil. You'll understand I won't be able to provide burial services if we're on clay. Can't afford to throw out my back."

We reach an overpass. Down below, a red Corvette has smashed into the pylon at freeway speed. Rust grows in the body's cracks.

Half an hour later, Wolf is ready to speak again. "In any case, there'll be a proper funeral, though I can't guarantee good attendance. Yes," he muses, "I'm going to enjoy being the executor—of your estate, of course. That's something I like to take care of, all the arrangements." He looks at me shyly. "I've even gone ahead and composed an epitaph, if..." He clears his throat. "Here Lies a Man," he declaims, "Who Spared No Moment of His Life the Full Weight of His Inanity."

I chuckle. "That's very good."

"Thank you," he says. "It'll have to do."

"... who spared no moment of his life ..." I repeat admiringly, trying to edge in on his vanity. "I like that."

"Fine," he says crisply. "Thank you. Please go ahead and have as much fun as you can in the time remaining to you."

❀

Days pass. From horizon to horizon Wolf and Debris step stamp limp and lump along. Along before and beside a hill, a clump of trees, a town of cold ash, along beside and on top of a whole intact and upended tanker, back wheels in the air over the road, front end in a ditch beside it, evidence of a fire, oil spill a mole in the light skin of the Earth, alongside and on top, climbing like kids on a toy train in a park, except that these kids are grown, and this toy train is a dark blue oil tanker, and in this unmarked oil tanker are two skeleton drivers and on that steering wheel two hands still hold fast, one bones, one flesh, and then only the hills hear, only the towns watch, alongside and past, and the side of the Earth with Wolf and Debris on it, stick-men, slow ants, spins into the dark.

Periodically, for example as we come to some railroad tracks, the big wooden arm of the crossing sign sheared off by some runaway vehicle, Wolf will read a dated entry made by Ezekiel Sheridan Dunster in the margins of our guidebook *America*: "10/30/83. Halloween in Wolfsburg. Jack-o'-lantern sibling came a-haunting, all lit up from inside by brotherly love. Sold him a pair of wax lips." Or west of Wolfsburg: "7/9/83. Manns Choice, Pennsylvania. Miserable. Who was Mann and what was wrong with him?" Or west: "12/22/82. Christmastime in towns called Brotherton and Husband. Need Sisterville and Girlfriendtown, but not on map."

Except to search for and through 7-Elevens, where Wolf has resumed his strange quest with renewed vigor, we leave the stripe of road only at night; the dirt's a softer bed, and in it we can scratch our ritual battle-ground of marbles.

Yesterday we crossed into a new kind of soil entirely, sandy stuff over a moist, almost odorless red clay. "Like a pig in shit," grinned Wolf as he moved his forearm across the surface, defining a circle with his thumb and within it another. He regards the new dirt as a good omen, a kind of fortune cookie served up by the planet itself. And somewhere, maybe in some 7-Eleven along the way, he not only lost the desire to kill me but became the force behind this mission.

"Play," urges Wolf. "Play it, Sam." I shoot a boulder listlessly, knock one of my own cat's-eyes out of the circle. "OK." He sets down a fist of marbles. "What's on your mind, my boy? If you can't tell me who *can* you tell?"

I roll over onto my back. Shooting stars? Fireflies.

"What do you think 'Garibaldi' means?" I woke up a week ago from a dream I was sure was of Ellen, but all I remembered upon waking was one word—"Garibaldi"— and one idea, that I had to seek out someone with that name.

"Garibaldi, huh? You want to know what I think?" He sets his cheek on his palm, eyes bright with cheer and platitude. "I think it means nothing. Haven't you ever woke up from a dream with a great idea, scribbled it down, and looked at it in the morning? Might say 'The door to all roads is Maheunyheuny.' Might say 'Garibaldi.' Means nothing. Static electricity on the brain."

I find this bogus scientism vaguely comforting. But still. "What about the ghosts?"

"What about em? I just figure they went to wherever they were supposed to go." He pats my leg comfortingly. "Probably happier there."

"None of this shit is good enough for me, Wolf."

"Why?" He folds his arms. "It's good enough for me."

The fireflies zip and dance. "I'm beginning to wonder if we'll ever reach a city."

"We will indeed." He explained matter-of-factly one night that the odds were overwhelmingly against our being the last two men on earth, solidly in favor of the other survivors having organized into something like cities and marginally in favor of our finding them. The thought, bound up and twisted and conflated with the prospect of still more clues and corpses and 7-Elevens, has been driving him up with the sun and on when I want to rest, on when I don't on and past the hills and trees and tankers and hills and trees. "We will indeed."

"But where? I wish I knew."

"Me too, Cheez Whiz." This is the latest in a direct line of succession from Debris, deCamembert, and da Cheese. He calls me twenty different names to make up for the fact that there are only two of us. "But what's it matter? We *know* a town's up ahead somewhere. We *know* we're gonna hit it."

"What's 'up ahead'? Ohio? Nebraska? California?"

This is intended to sober and chasten; instead Wolf whistles "California Here I Come" through his teeth.

"And what're we going to find there, Wolf? It might be awful."

"Nahhh . . . ain't gonna." Over the hill and through the dale, brick by yellow road brick, Wolf has been compiling the inventory of the imaginary city, which always as now includes: "Beef for dinner. Women. Beds with sheets. Women."

I shake my head. "Women for dinner, beds with women in them. You must be some idiot with women, Wolf."

"Do alright," he mutters, fading, disgruntled.

※

And all the 7-Elevens have graveyards. And in each grave are Baggies, eulogies Wolf calls them. And all the eulogies are in the same water-soluble blue ink, impossible to read.

One morning Wolf neatly folds the slip of paper with a shrug of his shoulders. "No better than the others," he says. He is sitting down. He no longer swears or breaks cash registers. "But it's a nice day. We're getting warmer."

I blink in the rare sun, close my eyes. The light filters red through my eyelids. "Getting warmer?"

He fishes around in our sack for a small nail clipper. In Wolf's unvarying routine, he works on one nail at a time, first cutting, then cleaning with the tip of the file and finally filing each nail until the tip is smooth as polished stone, first the left hand from pinky to thumb, then the right. I timed him once; the entire procedure takes more than twenty minutes and, once begun, can rarely be interrupted. "Still can't tell if it's him," Wolf murmurs. "Might be. *Might* be."

I take a seat, remove Billy Bo's watch from my pocket and wind it. "Who, Wolf?"

He looks past me for a long time, finally raising his eyebrows and nodding twice firmly. "I knew Ezekiel Sheridan Dunster." He digs *America* out of our sack and hands it over. "People called him Zeke," says Wolf, craning his neck to look.

I flip through the book. There is as much written as printed on the pages, in a tiny, unbelievably tiny hand, precise squared-off letters about half the size of the small print in the dictionary. The point of Wolf's nail file comes into view. "That's done with a mechanical pencil."

"Oh."

Wolf takes a deep breath and lets his words out on a sigh. "Z was an odd bird."

"Guess so."

"Don't have to guess. I'm *tellin* you," flares Wolf. "Z was a friend, a close friend, so watch your mouth." I squint at Wolf, trying to figure him out. He settles down quickly, resumes work-in-progress on his ring finger and finally announces, "Z worked at that very 7-Eleven where you found me."

"Oh," I say, wondering what is required of me. "Yeah?"

"Not just that one, though . . ." Wolf shakes his downcast head. "Dozens."

"What?"

"Anywhere from one night to eight months each. Depended on whenever somebody shot at him. Somebody always did."

"*Shot at him?*"

Wolf inspects his middle finger, finds it lacking, goes back to filing. "Or at least pulled a gun. Then he figured his time in that particular town had expired and he moved on. Z started his 7-Eleven gig out as far west as he could imagine. In Salt Lake. He hopped back east from one 7-Eleven to the next, until he wound up where he'd started out, which was Harrisburg. He was the best draftsman in P.S. 22, that's why his writing is so neat. Mr. Thurmond used to tell us, If anyone from this class goes on to make it—really makes it big . . ." He tails off.

". . . it'll be Zeke," I supply.

Wolf's voice shifts up into a tone of instruction, and his eyebrows go with it. "See, 7-Elevens are very vulnerable to robbery. They sit all alone on a strip of road, or maybe next to a couple of other stores that close at normal hours like everything on Earth except 7-Elevens. So for a guy who needs some cash in a hurry and is willing to wave a gun to get it, there's always a 7-Eleven, twenty-four hours a day, just sitting there waiting, and one duck sittin in it."

"Ezekiel Sheridan Dumpster."

"Dunster," Wolf enunciates carefully, as if trying to teach me lip-reading. "*Dunster*. He didn't mind givin em the money—he wasn't loyal, he was in it for other reasons—he just didn't like being shot at."

"Reasonable."

"The man had stories! The guy who waved a little toy gun at him sayin, 'I'm Astro Boy. Gimme all the money or I'll vaporize you!' Z gave the guy a ten and he went away happy. Once when a guy had a real gun, Z not only handed him the cash but got the guy to believe there was film inside the closed-circuit video monitor, just cause Z had always wanted to see someone shoot a TV. He used to . . . he used to . . ." Wolf is looking off, laughing.

"What?"

"Try to talk to practically every person who walked through the door, specially women. Thousands of women . . ." He leaves off, shaking his head. "Shoulda had a contest, 'You are the One Millionth Woman Zeke Dunster has tried to pick up,' given away a Mrs. Smith's frozen pie or something.

"He'd spend all his time developing these opening lines, just isolated in his little lit-up cubbyhole, lost in his thoughts. He'd've started out on the main road, gone down it a little past the point where the average person runs out of gas, to where it took a detour, drivin till he was pretty far from civilization and his idea of the kinda remark that would sum up the crux of the modern world and do it in just exactly the way that would take somebody he'd never met before and was just waiting for their frozen hot dog to pop out of the microwave, and turn em into an instant friend-for-life, would be something like, 'Whatever happened to those wax lips kids used to wear on Halloween?'"

Wolf clips his thumbnail with a loud thk! "And if the person stared at him Zeke figured it was cause they just didn't remember the wax lips so he'd say, 'There were those wax teeth too, like vampire teeth. When you were done using them you could just chew them up—they had liquid inside em, they had flavor.' The customer would be grabbin his hot dog and running out the door not even fuckin with the mustard, and there'd be Z, leaning out over the counter and yellin after him, 'Those wax teeth . . . they had flavor . . .'"

"How many 7-Elevens did Zeke work at?" I ask.

"Thirty-one," says Wolf without hesitation. "Salt Lake City, Gusher, Dinosaur, Goodland, Black Wolf, Boonville, Mount Comfort . . ." He chuckles, and goes back to trimming his nails. "Black Wolf. Ended up back in Harrisburg where he came from in the first place. He swore after ten years he'd come home. And that's what he did."

Wolf lets the silence stretch out, so I step in. "It must've been strange for you"—he looks up at me sharply, making me stutter—"you know, after, to be living in the 7-Eleven with his ghost."

"He didn't leave a ghost," Wolf says curtly.

"What—you mean . . . ?"

Wolf looks at his hands, brushes off the nail dust on his shirt, stands up and begins walking again. "I mean he left a *shade*. He was a black man."

I rise, and jog a few steps until I'm caught up with him. "Well with his shade, then. But all alone in that 7-Eleven."

"Look," says Wolf irritably. "Let's just let a dead man lie." And picking up momentum both verbal and kinetic: "Can't you let *anything* lie? No, shit no, nothing's settled till the full Maxillary investigation runs its official course, his big nose gets itself jammed into every little cranny, make sure all forms are filled out in triplicate, calls put through so every source has an opportunity to confirm or deny, receipts handed on to the accountants for tax deduc—"

"OK, OK, OK, OK, OK," I break in soothingly.

❈

I've told of trees and towns and tankers. Another way of relating distance would be to catalogue our diseases. And every runny nose, every wart and every pimple fuels our endless paranoia of radiation poisoning. If Wolf runs a hand through his hair and too much shows up between his fingers, or my leg begins acting up, if any real or imagined ill besets either of us, the other must immediately examine him, pulling back his eyelids, looking inexpertly down his mouth, poking in his ears.

To start small, one of us always has a cold, and just when he seems about to be rid of it, lends it for safekeeping to the other, in whose care or specifically sinuses, nose and chest it resides until it can be returned, undamaged and undiminished, to the original owner; one of our continuing discussions concerns who was first to blame for it, this marathon, vituperative, ever-mutating affliction for which "cold" is a poor short squirt of a word.

Wolf, paying double now for a fortunate childhood, woke me one morning, and turning to me a face as wide and elliptical as a football, said "I thing somein's wrong w'my cheeks." He had the mumps, and soon after, chicken pox. These illnesses were not funny before modern medicine, and they are not funny after it. The mumps hung us up for a week.

We are living on rats and roaches and the odd bird, on flesh alone, and our digestive tracts have turned to vinegar from mouth to bowel. Everything, meat and spit and air and water, tastes sour.

Our feet are constantly producing an array of welts, blisters, corns and abrasions, and I've learned what bunions are. The Swiss Army knife plays podiatrist nightly; we have to keep our feet in walking order. Athlete's foot crawled up my legs and all over my balls. To give them some air I've taken to carrying my pants rather than wearing them.

What else? Well, the human mouth, particularly mine, is susceptible to canker sores after a nuclear war, and the teeth seem looser, rattling in your stride. We are collecting antiquated diseases and passing them to each other, and now I think we have scurvy. On top of everything else. On top of that infernal, eternal cold.

But when Wolf stops stock-still, intent on something far in front of us and slightly toward the left, does it matter whether or not he is the current repository of a mere cold, whether his words, literally transcribed, are "A town! A fuckin city" or "A towd! A fuckid city"? No, no, a thousand times doe.

What matters is this: Does Wolf lean his head forward, giving an impression similar to the one he gave as we approached the city of flame, namely of physical connection between himself and something on the horizon? Does he amaze and astound with a vocal and calisthenic performance the brother of and encore to that at the bleached ramparts of the aforementioned Flametown? He does indeed. Does he, specifically, remove his left shoe and heave it toward heaven? No, it is our entire canvas rucksack of molding goodies he throws this time. Does he screech and caw and scratch and punch the air? Yea, and more. And what is it, finally, that he says when he collapses supine, chest heaving, finger pointing past his feet which themselves point toward the horizon?

"A town! A fuckin city."

# II

# 1 ※ Home Sweet Homestead

Off in the distance there's a brown ball—even I can see it—a brown moving ball that keeps extending its front end until it's like a caterpillar made of dust.

"A car," says Wolf. "I don't believe it. Gotta be a car."

"What do you see? Tell me." Wolf's the one with the eyes.

"OK, it's a jeep...two people...*People*, Christ! Two men, got blue clothes. Think maybe it's some kinda uniform...Uh, put on your pants. The driver's a kid... other guy's bald, got glasses, sunglasses, the mirrored kind...Put on your fucking pants."

The jeep rolls toward us, each of its details coming clear a few seconds after Wolf relates it to me. The first thing I notice is the clothing of the two men: instead of a mass of pennants, flaps, sunburned skin, dislocated cuffs and dissociated collars, they wear shirts. They come from a place where there are needles and thread. The jeep slows and, a hundred feet off, stops.

The men, the exoskeleton of their car: a single organism, hard heavy body, two mobile peering fleshy heads. On their faces is neither the flickering alertness nor the horizon-scanning calm that alternate on Wolf's as he watches them; instead, they retain the cocked-eyebrow-of-measured-assessment, prefabricated phrase-faces, expressions learned in childhood, set and polished in the surface of the television screen. The two men are from another, older world and haven't had to reinvent their own faces from the inside. To Wolf and me they are a new species. What must we look like to them?

The older man puts a bullhorn to his lips, like some strange bug all eyes and round loud mouth: "*Do you have any identification?*"

Wolf and I stare at each other. I am struck by the softness of Wolf's face, its flux, the way experience has carved lines of flexibility, change, preparedness and a kind of ambiguity into it. I see him at this moment as the others must. Two men from civilization ask us who we are.

"Max Debrick and Charles Dewey!" I yell back.

"Junior. Charles Dewey, Junior," adds Wolf in a murmur.

"We're American citizens!" I shout foolishly.

The jeep has been advancing again in tentative spurts, and now slows to a halt. The man with the glasses gets out and advances slowly around the edge of the car, eyes on us, feeling along the hood like a blind man. He raises the bullhorn, and now that we're so close, his blurred muffled amplified voice rattles our teeth: "*I repeat: do you have any identification?*"

Wolf jerks his hands up. "Got a full set of fingerprints," he says, wiggling all ten aloft.

"*Keep both hands above your heads and do not move!*" The man scrambles back into the car and gives a short order to the driver who stands up in the car holding a submachine gun, not pointed at us, but sideways across his body, for demonstration purposes, an odd cheerful expression on his face.

"No, I'm afraid we don't," I say quickly. I'd like to bring my elbow down on top of Wolf's head.

"*How do we*"—the bullhorn crackles, goes dead; the man hollers muddily into it for a second; the kid sneaks a sidelong smile; the man takes down the device and yells unamplified—"How do we know you're who you say you are?" He has a blaring, oratorical voice, like he's using a bullhorn even without it.

"I guess," I shout back, "you'll just have to trust us."

"Come *on*," says the kid with a commonsensical shrug. "You gotta prove it to us *some*how." He looks like every kid in every World War II movie, the kind Richard Widmark calls "Dogface."

One of Wolf's eyebrows is about two inches higher than the other, and counting. "Prove it," he says slowly, softly. "What do you want us to *do*?" he screams. "Piss and shit for you? In that case you better give us food and water. You want two arms and two legs? You want the whole set of internal organs from gallstone to cerebellum? You want a whole set of American memories, discount-priced? Bugs Bunny! Joe McCarthy! Cheryl Tiegs! Sirhan Sirhan!" And Wolf's walking slowly toward them, as if proximity will drive home his argument.

"Wolf!" Get back.

"Mister, you better not come any farther," says the boss man. Wolf keeps advancing. "Fire some warning shots."

The young Dogface fumbles with the side of the gun, feeling for the safety, as Wolf walks forward. The kid is looking all over the gun. Wolf is not fifty feet away.

There's a rickitikitiki of popsnap fire. A row of tiny dust storms springs up from the dry dirt where the bullets hit far to Wolf's left. Little bullets; they don't seem much to be afraid of. The bullets are spraying left twenty feet ahead of Wolf, just a polite barrier that he ought, really ought, not to cross; now coming right, toward Wolf, right, right.

BABOOM!

The ground explodes. Wolf's hurled about one foot up and five feet back and scrambles gibbering the rest of the way into my arms, jelly, witless. "Ogodpeople gonna go and trya kill me!"

But they're just as scared, watching gap-jawed as the dust settles into the crater between us. A land mine. If Wolf had been allowed to walk a few feet more he'd be not-Wolf. He is still writhing against me, fish-wriggling gripping me, incoherent, a collection of syllables and most of them obscene.

"Shit," exhales the Dogface, paling into translucence. "Shit." The other man's lips are going buh-buh-buh-buh but making no sound.

I pry Wolf off me and give him a look. Nothing's missing, and there's no blood, but he doesn't seem to recognize me. I slap his face twice, bringing nothing into it except color.

"Look at him," says the Dogface, releasing his death grip on the steering wheel to point at Wolf. The two heads bow together and whisper unintelligibly.

"Come on over," calls the kid. "You're safe. Get in the jeep and we'll go back exactly the way we came."

I have to half-drag Wolf along and into the jeep. The Dogface sits in front of me; Sunglasses is in front of Wolf with the rifle in his lap. He keeps sending sharp looks back at us as we bounce along. With his reflective glasses and stone-set seriousness, he looks like a Secret Service agent. The jeep picks up speed.

"I'm Kenny," says the kid, sending his voice back to us but watching the ground, where Budweiser cans mark a wide lane back to the city; next to me wild Wolf, his long hair loosening, flying behind him, keeps shooting me incredulous Can you *believe* here we are in this car heading for a real city? grin-grimaces.

"Max Debrick," I shout, then wait for the other two to give their names. "He's Charles Dewey," I say at last. "Junior."

"How far did you come?" Kenny says.

"From New York."

"On *foot*?"

"Yeah."

Kenny shakes his head. "Lucky you didn't walk here yourselves. Last five hundred yards is a killer."

"Yeah, this is great!" calls Wolf. Then to my dismay he makes a five-year-old's "driving" noise: "neee-oowwwwww!"

Kenny's Dogface features spill down sharply to the right, like a cinder-block bookshelf with a cinder-block removed. He has never met anyone like Wolf. Neither had I. And now we approach the strange settlement in silence.

The city has a wall, like a medieval city, a wall first of dirt and then of wood, some planks painted, some not, rough-cut lumber, split telephone poles, a few charred interior doors from buildings, a tumble-down or about-to-tumble-down wooden miscellany, and above that a tangle of barbed wire and the third-world gleam of broken glass.

"Welcome to Homestead," says Kenny.

"Homestead?" I tap him on the shoulder, getting a disapproving glint from Sunglasses. "You call this place *Homestead*?"

"It's *called* Homestead," yells the kid, shrugging behind the wheel. "It's *always* been called Homestead."

Set at ground level is a wide gate of Cyclone fencing, locked with heavy chains, the forms of men moving behind it. The jeep halts in front of the gate and the chains come snaking loose. I envision our triumphal procession through the streets: no skyscrapers or ticker tape, of course, but maybe some curious kids and definitely some women, the banging of pots and pans; faces, at any rate, lining the streets, welcoming, forthcoming with food, eager for stories and music, and bearing, from their humble stock, gifts which we graciously decline.

But no: one man dollies out a little metal tank while three others, armed with tommy guns, look on from behind the Cyclone fence. The tank, maybe some kind of industrial vacuum cleaner, is plump with a long hose; the man is gaunt, grave-faced: together they look like master and dog.

"Got to strip for the germicide," says Kenny, dropping his pants and revealing a small blaze of red pubic hair. Wolf and I follow as the tank-man looks on.

"Hey Kenny," says Wolf. "You got any restaurants here? I could really go for some Thai food." It's a relief just to hear him on speaking terms with real words.

A goopy green liquid, like Prell Concentrate, sputters for a second from the nozzle, then pelts at us. I shade my eyes to look at Wolf, whose face is first spattered, then covered with tiny green freckles, then solidly green, as he clenches and gasps and spits against the ooze-bubbly mixture. The man with the hose gestures for me to take my hands down, has us turn around and completes the procedure. He moves on to the jeep. Kenny wipes down from his forehead with his hands, and turns his freckled face to me, a startlingly pink oval cut into a field of emerald. "It's a bitch, isn't it?"

"At least now we get the water," says Wolf. "Man, our first shower since the apocalypse! Good thing too, cause my eyes are starting to burn."

"Mine too," now that he mentions it. Water! It's going to feel so good. And my eyes are vanishing in stinging soap.

There is no water. The bullhorn man, his reflective sunglasses the only not-green part of his face, just says, "We can go in now."

"Go in? Looking like *this*?" Wolf stands with his arms folded, noble and immobile, a monument in green gel.

"C'mon, hurry up." Kenny is rubbing his eyes. "We got showers inside."

"... can't deal with this shit..." Wolf's muttering. "*Got* the stuff to wash us down but *don't* have water..."

But that is how we enter Homestead: blind, naked, green goblins, eyes sealed so tight by will and pain they won't open again until the soap is washed out. Somebody has us by the elbows. "Two steps," he calls. And a little later: "Watch it. Rough ground." We go over some dirt, some bricks or cobblestones, jolt down a couple of stairs, cross plenty of asphalt, and are finally told to stop; we stand around until, without warning, cold water hits us, hits us hard, like a shower of sand. Still, the viscous soap takes a lot of rubbing; my skin squeaks.

"AaaaaaAAHHHH." Wolf's noises of stoic satisfaction are the kind best made alone. He's singing in a key that's a new addition to the world of music. "WOOOoooOOOoooOOO!"

The water's off and six men stand on bare concrete. It's a large outdoor area with brick walls and about a dozen shower heads, piping suspended from the low ceiling by rusty wire. One of the heads has slipped loose where the wire is rusted through and dangles at eye level. The shower gives the impression of a temporary creation that has already outlived its prime. *Six* men?

"Magamagamaga . . ." says Wolf, shivering and stamping his feet.

"Wolf. Wolf."

He shakes his head, sending another minishower in my direction.

"Wolf, we've got company."

"No, *we've* got company," says the man who's joined us, dressed, wildly, in a conservative business suit and tie. He steps into the wet. "Welcome, gentlemen," transferring a stack of clothes into his left hand to extend his right. "Don't worry about your wet hands. Harry Sawyer."

"Max Debrick."

"Good to have you here, Max." He's plump and comfortable in his pinstripes, exchanging names and handshakes with Wolf. Kenny and Sunglasses step off to a deferential angle. "I'm here to show you around. After you dry off and slip into these, of course." He hands me a pile of dark purple clothes topped by a towel. There is underwear. There are socks. I stare dumbly at it all for a second; then my fingers take over and begin their unconscious work of tugging, smoothing, buttoning.

"I get green," says Wolf, stepping into a fat man's overalls. "Cause I'm Irish."

As we dry and dress Sawyer takes a breath and winds up for a long sentence: "Homestead is a small community by the old standard—"

"Women?" Wolf cuts in hoarsely.

"Pardon me?"

"But you got women?" Wolf leans his neck forward in midbutton.

Sawyer smiles. "Yes, there are women in Homestead, Mr. Dewey."

Wolf clears his throat. "Just checking." He fixes his collar with exaggerated nonchalance.

"We have two hundred thirty women in a total population of nine hundred fifty, more or less. That makes Homestead, incidentally, the third-largest city in the United States."

"There are others?" I ask.

"Four. Each city has a special role to play in the reorganizing economy. Homestead is the fuel-production center. Washington—it's actually up in Vermont, but we still say Washington—is the coordinating center. The largest city is Denison, Iowa. Agriculture has become labor-intensive again, as you might imagine. Denison is growing rice and soybeans and sunflowers. We're living primarily on dried milk, live poultry and stored foods until their harvest comes in. Industrial Reclamation is up near Cleveland. Exploration is out in Arizona, or maybe Utah by now; we've lost contact. Their sole job is, or was, to find stragglers."

"Like us," says Wolf.

"Exactly. And to organize them into small settlements. Arizona is set up to give them a few resources and plenty of advice. It's kind of the experimental center; they have only about seventy. Others wanted to join them, but we couldn't let them go. They had skills we needed here or in Cleveland."

"What kind of skills *do* you need?" Wolf is keen.

"There's a continuing demand in Production. It's, ah, blue-collar work."

"What about professionals?" says Wolf, quickly donning his glasses.

Sawyer turns to me as if I've asked the question. "You've put your finger on it. Our main problem. We have almost no middle-level professionals; instead of plumbers or dentists or mechanics, we have bureau chiefs and politicians and generals. Administrators... managers... Men whose abilities are useless, and whose temperaments worse than useless, when it comes to the nuts and bolts of setting up a community."

"The shitwork," says Wolf.

Sawyer smiles generously. "If you will, Mr. Dewey."

"Chuck." Wolf grins back. Chuck? *Chuck*? "Shitwork is what I do. I'm a civil engineer by training and experience; I design sewers."

"Sewers?" He likes Wolf better already. "You might be very useful."

"How about musicians?" I pipe up.

"Musicians?" He looks at my shiny horn. "Jazz, I suppose?" I nod. "Well, maybe, maybe. Listen..." he says to Sunglasses. "Get Mark Chester to come down here. Tell him we brought in a civil engineer." Sunglasses

nods, and Sawyer catches him as he leaves: "And someone from Production as well." He turns back to Wolf.
"I'm getting a hold of some people in Planning, Chuck; I
think you'll have a lot to say to each other."

"Great." Wolf's rubbing his hands together. "Great."

I examine myself: the purple pantlegs come to un-
timely conclusions somewhere in the middle of my shins,
and lower, much lower, white socks, elastic exhausted,
flap around my ankles. Wolf's overalls are big enough for
another Wolf to get in with him.

"Ready, gentlemen?" says Sawyer.

And Chuck and Debris and several men they don't
know march out of the shower into their new Homestead.

# 2 ❄ Shovels and Sewers

We are in a large open area, paved in ancient cobblestones, bordered on one side by a string of long pinkish structures of unmistakable industrial origin, old but intact, one tall story, dirt piled high on top (that's for fallout; I remember some government planner telling our high school civics class we could, "with enough shovels," survive a nuclear war).

"Nice color, isn't it?" Sawyer smiled at Wolf. "Coral. They got it by mixing brick dust with cement."

On the other side are scattered several smaller buildings, not made the same way or during the same era as the others but probably at the same time and as haphazardly as the city walls, of wood.

"This is the Yard. Over there you see some of our, uh, original architecture," says Sawyer. "That's the sewage treatment plant, Mr. Dewey, such as it is. The munitions dump. The chicken coop. And the far building is the garage."

"Log cabins," says Wolf in amazement.

Sawyer's smile comes just short of grimace. "That's the basic method of construction."

Wolf's eyebrows hoist themselves to a diplomatic height. "It was good enough for Abe Lincoln."

Sawyer emits that kind of stylized business-world chortle that comes too soon and lasts too long, a sort of I-assure-you-that-your-witticism-has-found-an-appreciative-audience vocalization. Wolf, in his turn, causes his eyes to form little freeze-dried crinkless of shared mirth. I have never seen him manage to make such an appalling expression.

Now another of these men appears in the same strange costume: suit and tie. Not, upon closer inspection, the nine-to-five suit-and-tie, but a variant dependent on repair rather than recent manufacture for its respectability, one elbow and both knees mended by inexpert hands. The man is short and compact, full of caffeinated energy, bounding toward me across the wet concrete with a broad fixed smile; he doesn't *seem* like someone who would get so hopped up by the appearance of a wayward jazzman, but what the hell, I give him my hand and he practically removes my arm from my socket so happy is he. I feel a sudden unwary warmth for this enthusiastic little man—like a kid at Christmas and me his gift—with his bursting effusive glee and glinting glasses, one lens of which is badly chipped.

"Max Debrick," I say, a goony smile spreading over my face.

"You're not . . ." begins the man, dropping my hand as quickly as you might a leper's. "Charles Dewey, the engineer?" The thousand Christmas lights of his soul wink out one by one, and all I can do is point across my body to Wolf.

"*Mister* Dewey!" says the man, grinning winningly at Wolf in renewed incandescence. "Mark Chester!"

Pumping each other's arms, they seem to form a single organism, maybe a mechanism, like a hyperactive oil derrick.

"You know something about sewers?" asks Mark Chester.

Wolf removes his glasses slowly with both hands, half-closes his eyes and delivers a sphinx smile that says he does indeed know something about sewers, that he, in fact, wrote, bound, edited and illustrated the book on sewers and has only to squint a little, the way he is doing now, to summon it up verbatim (cf. *Sewage Systems and You*, 17th ed., by C. E. Dewey, Jr.: "§43.2. The Activated Sludge Process"), that some of his best friends are sewers, that he designed the Paris sewer system in 1860 and has since advanced to self-cleaning sewers, trompe l'oeil sewers that look like shopping malls, surrealistic sewers (soft sewers, The Persistence of Sewers), medical sewers that exchange feces for diagnoses, minted after-dinner sewers, sewers for socialites, and the great Singing Sewers of Siberia, where the mournful winds play songs across the holes in manhole covers and the streets are named according to the chords thus formed, Boulevard C Sharp, Avenue Em⁷. A world of sewers, in short, a shitpot of sewers.

"Good," says Chester. "Great, because we had a cholera outbreak from seepage. We lost almost two hundred people."

"Cholera?" croaks Wolf, losing all his composure and a good deal of his balance.

"Yes, because we ran out of chlorine. In fact we have no chemicals whatsoever for detoxifying sewage. And when a corpse got into the water supply it was even more costly," says Chester. "We hadn't thought to take a vaccine for typhoid, and we were helpless against it."

"Typhoid fever?" says Wolf, temporarily a white man.

"So you can see we've had some very serious problems."

"Oh yes," says Wolf. "I can see that. I can certainly see that."

"Hopefully it's all behind us." Sawyer clears his throat. "We have a man coming from Production to talk to you," he says to me in a different tone.

"Production? I don't know anything about production. Producing what?"

On cue, a man about fifty, wide, more fat than burly, in blackened khaki overalls, with a blackened face and a mining helmet in his hand, appears in the doorway. "Coal," he says pleasantly. "Coal is what Homestead is all about." 15:30 has been feltpenned on a yellow plastic rectangle dangling from his neck. Every part of the man has been dusted in coal except for the yellow rectangle and the palms of his hands, one of which catches mine in a firm grip. His bald pate has been wiped streakily clean. His liquid, humorous brown eyes drop from my face to the floor. "We're sitting on top of a hundred million tons of known and accessible coal reserves."

"Coal?" My voice has slipped into whine. "I don't know from coal. I'm a musician." I say it extra-slow, one hand draining green germicide that yo-yos viscously in the air from the saxophone's spit valve, the other hand tapping the instrument, in case everyone has somehow missed it.

The big man dips at the knees to look at it. "A left-handed alto? That's amazing." He looks up at me. "I used to have a left-handed tenor, swear to God. I thought I was the only one. A Selmer. Nice horn. Do you mind if I . . . ?" His hands are parallel to his chest, fingers wiggling in the timeless, universal mime for Can I Play It? This coal miner intends to slobber into my saxophone; my practice has always been to refuse.

"Here," I say, ducking out of the strap. He slips the reed into his mouth, takes a breath and looks up at me with the apologetic basset eyes of a man who knows he is about to do something slightly ridiculous. And he plays an unridiculously fast lick, cleanly articulated, that leads into a faster one; it's Bird's classic break on "Night in Tunisia" with only two squeaks.

"Well," I say when he's stopped. "Wow. You play."

"Strictly amateur, strictly living-room," he says, giving the sax a last longing look before handing it back. We are alone; Wolf and Sawyer and Chester have slipped away. Wolf! I'm suddenly helpless without him, as if a doctor just told me I'll never be able to use my legs again. But I am using them; dazedly, I am following this fat, saxophone-playing coal miner out into the brown sunlight.

"I don't get it," I say. "Is there some huge mistake? Music is what I do. It's pretty much *all* I do."

"Lucky bastard." He turns to smile wryly, shrugs and continues walking. "But then I always thought *I* was an aerospace engineer. Even went to the trouble of earning three degrees that said so. In Homestead they tell me I'm a coal miner."

"You've got a Ph.D.?"

"Sure. Half of us do—no, that's an exaggeration. I worked for Boeing, then for the U.S. government. In the seventies I taught at MIT."

"I don't understand." Or don't want to.

"Oh—Gary Tascheira."

"Max Debrick."

We stop to shake hands. "Sorry about the dirt." He shoves his hands into the bib of his overalls. We are at the end of a passageway between the short sides of the low pink buildings. A man in a suit crosses the far end of the passage with a purposeful stride, and disappears.

"Why do I dig coal?" my companion asks the air, palms up. "Why are you going to dig coal? An excellent question. An unanswerable question."

He continues walking, me in tow. We are crossing a paved four-lane bridge; I stop to look down at the still, muddy river. "The mighty Monongahela," Tascheira murmurs. He sees me looking back across the bridge at the long string of pink buildings we've just left.

"Kiss em goodbye," he says gently, near my ear. "And welcome to the other Homestead."

At the end of the bridge six men with tommy guns, in the uniforms of the U.S. Army, sit on wooden blocks. Not full uniforms; one man has the pants and jacket but wears a loud floral shirt. Another is Army from the waist up, civilian from the waist down. The uniform is like some skin disease, a greenish rash affecting different parts of each man's body. Still, the overall effect of them together is overwhelmingly, terrifyingly that of men in uniform. And all have guns.

"Hi, Buck," says Gary Tascheira, too loudly.

"Yeah," says one of the men.

"Who are these guys?" I ask when we get a little past them.

He chuckles. "We're getting to that."

We pass through another, smaller row of old mills, and begin ascending a broad slope on a dirt path. "Wait a minute," I say. "How did this place survive intact?"

He sighs. "I'll tell you if you'll just walk—we've got

to be at the mine checkpoint by three-thirty. Now see these hills? The Bomb plays hell with buildings and human beings, but it doesn't do a whole lot to sheer earthly geography. The hills protected Homestead from most of the direct effects of the Pittsburgh blast, and the hundred feet or so it knocked off the top just made it easier to get at the coal inside."

"How did you know in advance?"

"Where we were in Washington—underground— there was a printout with a hundred or so possible places for settlement indexed by probable blast damage, proximity to usable natural resources and so on. Homestead was one of them. They had one T-6, an experimental Army reconnaissance craft, and they sent it out . . ."

"And *Homestead* was the place?"

He holds up a finger. "Don't forget the four other thriving settlements sponsored by your government and mine. Anyway, the T-6 only got as far as Nebraska before half the instrument panel went down and they had to land. We got the reports by radio on the ground they'd covered. See, they *have* guns and they *have* tanks, but the difference is when one throws a bolt now, it's forever. If some sand gets in your gun, you might as well toss it away."

We have reached the crest of the ridge. I turn back to look over low Homestead, across the mills, the bridge and the Yard. Behind the munitions dump and the sewage plant, near the gate where we must have entered, is a wide pick-up-sticks pile of uncut lumber. Wood seems to be the only available building material.

I stare out for a long time, until Tascheira's voice drifts back to me. "Pittsburgh."

He is facing the other direction. I turn and the impression of height gives me vertigo. Homes and factories, homes and factories, a rooftop profile tapering down now instead of up to the city center, the hypocenter, the down town. Only the streets are a constant: implacable, imperturbable, they can be made out trundling to the edge of the hypocenter, roads to nowhere. Rain has turned the crater to lake. Cities, it occurs to me, have become part of nature now, subject to change only through natural processes: the erosive wind, the rain, the pull of gravity, the thrust of vegetation.

Tascheira tugs my arm and we walk along the ridge.

There are eight guards around a wide-mouthed tunnel in the ground. Tascheira executes an exaggerated salute. "Shalom, Superbuck," he says, unclipping the pass from around his neck and tossing it at their feet.

"Who *are* those guys?" I hiss.

"In the mines," says Tascheira, "there's about one guard for every twelve of us. The guard gets to live with the bucks and eat buck food, so he knows which side his bread is oleomargarined on. He's a lieutenant or a captain in the army. He has a tommy gun and knows how to use it." Tascheira sighs. "Sooooo. You want to see what the mines look like?"

"I don't ever want to see a coal mine as long as I live."

He breaks into a smile. "That's the spirit; neither do I. Come on."

Down into each side of the tunnel slopes a pair of cable-car rails on a mild grade that join in a U where we stand at the tunnel's mouth. At the turnaround is a coal-blackened wooden car, about fifteen feet in length and five in width, with four huge posts, sections of a telephone pole, running widthwise across the floor, serving as benches. We sit on the rear bench, Tascheira holding a long lever from the floor in his hand. A brake.

"This is a slope mine," says Tascheira. "The coal seam's only about a hundred twenty feet deep, so we can use a gradual incline to get at it. Makes haulage easier than a shaft. There's one ventilation shaft at the far end of the mine. A big fan sits at the top sucking out the bad air and bringing in the good through this tunnel. Theoretically, at least. Actually..." And he raises both hands to his throat. The car, having started slowly, seizes this opportunity to pick up speed. "Hold on," he says, braking jerkily.

"Not all the machinery is homemade, by the way. The cutting machine is an Eickhoff-170, state-of-the-art, if coal mining *is* an art. We call it the Shovel cause all it gives you is shit. Looks kinda like a long bulldozer with a big chain saw up front to slice the coal. You'll see it.

You'll see too much of it. We salvaged three Eickhoffs from the Greenwich Collieries out in Barnesboro and cannibalize one for parts."

"What are *you* doing down here?" I ask him.

"With a Ph.D., you mean? Look at it from Buck's point of view. Have you been seeing a whole lot of B-1s buzzing overhead?"

"No."

"Then what is Gary Tascheira good for? Do you think they bother to save any *real* miners? Even any real janitors?"

On the left track comes another slow wooden car piled high with irregular sheets and chunks of coal. "Frankie baby!" bellows Tascheira to this pile of black rocks.

Something dark stirs amid the camouflage of coal. A man. He doffs his hardhat and sings into the knob of the brake: "I did it myyyy wayyyyy..."

"Frank was an archeologist," says Tascheira. "Specializing in Pompeii. Everyone they collected in the Washington shelters was overqualified for this Mickey Mouse community...academics...architects...analysts. The mines are full of them, though you'll never see any military men above the rank of sergeant. Half the aboveground bucks went to college and became army officers." We've come to the bottom, and a second turnaround in the tracks.

He brakes the car. "End of the line." Several helmeted men and a couple of women are loading oversized wheelbarrows with coal chunks, and a man, dressed in khaki overalls and blackened like the others, follows with a wheelbarrow full of large chunks. Tascheira dons his hard hat, letting the chin strap dangle. "So those of us classified as useless chip coal off the walls. You're a musician. You have my condolences; I'd like to hear you play. This is Shaft A, familiarly called Asshole. They run up to H. Come on. Meet the folks."

# 3 ❀ The Works

Time throws a yellow shadow over the printed page. Leave a newspaper in the open for a month, or a book on a shelf for fifty years, and it will spot and darken like human skin. It is as if the light of the present in the room you are in does not fall directly on the paper. Open that book, open that time capsule, and remember.

In 1892 the largest steel manufacturer in the country, and in fact the largest company of any kind, was Carnegie Steel, the forerunner of U.S. Steel. Carnegie's flagship plant, the biggest and most modern steel mill in the world, was located in Homestead, Pennsylvania.

At that time the nation's union movement was spearheaded by the fledgling American Federation of Labor; its strongest constituent union was the Amalgamated Association of Iron and Steel Workers, with 24,000 skilled dues-paying members. The Amalgamated excluded semi-skilled workers, Slavs, Hungarians and blacks as a matter of course. The union had only about four hundred, or one-tenth, of Homestead's employees, but they were among the highest paid.

Andrew Carnegie, in Europe throwing vast quantities of money at noble causes, sent a delicately worded cable to his right-hand man, Henry Clay Frick, to the effect that there might be one too many unions at his beloved Homestead Works.

You may imagine an illustration, an engraving in the realistic manner of period political cartoons, showing Henry Clay Frick, his angular, squarish face enveloped in an angular, squarish beard, a large man in an old-fashioned black suit behind a larger black desk. This man sits at this desk holding in both hands a missive he has just received from his master, scowling with a face made to scowl. A huge question mark, with one or two more curlicues than the ones we make nowadays, hovers over his head.

Frick made the Amalgamated a preposterous offer entailing massive pay cuts, refused first to accept several compromises and finally to negotiate at all, announcing that if the union failed to accede to his demands by June 24, 1892, he would hire nonunion employees.

The Amalgamated rejected Frick's terms, surprising him by holding a mass meeting of all employees and somehow convincing the nonunion employees to join in a general strike.

Frick closed the Homestead Works. Having stockpiled enough steel armor plates (the Works' prime product) to last for months, he intended to begin importing outside workers. Anticipating trouble with the Amalgamated Association, Frick wrote to Robert Pinkerton:

> We will want 300 guards for service at
> our Homestead mills as a measure of
> precaution against interference with
> our plan to start operations of the
> works July 6, 1892. . . .

He expected

> some demonstration of violence . . . most
> likely by an element which usually is

attracted to such scenes for the
purpose of stirring up trouble.

Trouble was stirred. Wait and see, wait and see.

# 4 ⚬ Model City

I spend what seems like a very long afternoon looking for distinguishing features in an endless succession of coal-smeared faces, shaking hands and carrying sheets of coal until my fingers are weak, trailing the Shovel, soiling my purple clothes, working up a tremendous hunger and slamming my too-small hard hat into low-hanging ceilings and light bulbs. Gary Tascheira only chuckles. He's the foreman of my crew.

In the evening there's an across-a-desk interview with an utterly focused, businesslike little man: I beg for a job as an entertainer; he asks me my shoe and hat sizes. I ask to room with Charles Dewey, Jr.; that's impossible, out of the question. I *made records*, I say; he gets on the phone and orders a hard hat and mining boots. He calls someone else, has trouble with the telephone, swears to show me he's a regular guy, seems puzzled by what he hears, writes my housing assignment on a scrap of paper and sets to signing documents of great importance.

I stumble out, my ears hot, the key and room number in my hand. 59 PLANNING. Fucking Wolf, abandoning me to these animals! Hardly anyone is on the streets as I head out toward the bridge; they must work long hours. A guard turns me back. "Production," he says, jerking a bayonet over his shoulder toward the mines, and then pointing at the mills, "Planning."

Planning? Tascheira told me the miners lived in the barracks on the other side of the river, but here it is in one of the pink buildings, 59, an index card tacked to the door, and all I've seen so far is two men in suits and no armed guards.

The door is unlocked. I avoid stumbling over the pile of khaki overalls, boots and hard hat placed just inside the entrance. I turn on the light. DEBRICK, reads a note in precise, regular capital letters on top of the heap. PLEASE DISCARD PURPLE UNIFORM IMMEDIATELY. They either want me to walk around naked or wear these.

I'm glad to get out of the dirty clothes. There's no sink, so I wipe my face and hands on the inside of the shirt before handling the new clothes. On the inside of the door is taped an unrolled piece of silvery acetate, reflecting, like a funhouse mirror, a variously squashed and elongated me. Nothing fits except the boots: the sleeves are half a foot too short, the shirt won't tuck in and the overalls grab me in the crotch. The cuffs are even shorter than the sleeves. The hard hat fits, but I take it off.

I explore the empty room. Fluorescent lights. Two beds, plywood on cinder blocks, with two sets of linen. Two sets of linen but no sign of another person. Whoever I am living with doesn't have a whole lot of personal belongings; none, in fact. Fucking Wolf. Leaving me to share a room with some colorless, odorless sanitized-for-your-protection little bureaucrat. Some disgusting, antiseptic—

The door opens.

And closes. "Eyaah!" whinnies Wolf, holding both hands up and Zorba-dancing. He's dressed in purple clothes like the ones I've just shed. "What a day! This is great, just great! What a place!" He collapses dizzily onto the bed, hugging himself, kicking air. "Homestead sweet homestead!"

"So you're my new roommate," I venture.

He sits up, appraising me with sudden grave concern. "You're a mess, Maxillary."

"I asked to room with you but they told me absolutely not."

"Rules is rules," Wolf pronounces. "But..." He smiles slyly and deals me a wink. "When you got the right friends, rules is bent."

"Friends? The fuckers sent me down to the coal mines."

"I couldn't do anything about that, buddy."

"*You?*"

"Sorry. I tried. They wouldn't buy you as my assistant; said they'd find me an architect or something. But I did get us this room. They have two types, converted metal shops and offices. I asked Sawyer which kind *he* had and since he said 'office,' *I* said office."

"What makes you a big shot around here?" I sit down on the bed; now that I do, I can never get up as long as I live.

One hand bent genteelly at collarbone level, his head at an angle aristocratically raised, Wolf is astrut. "Not 'a' big shot. *The* big shot. Do you realize that outta six hundred miners, only one is allowed to live on this side of the river? You. That's power, bub. Swing. Sway. The purple duds are just temporary. Tomorrow I shall be wearing a suit and tie. Vestments of the first quality." He puts one foot on the chair and leans forward, folding both hands over a knee. "See Maximus, I'm the only honest-to-god civil engineer in the house. They got plenty of generals and plenty of planners and plenty of urban this-n-thats but only one civil engineer. They put me in charge of a whole unit. They got no choice but to." He stands chest-out straight and flares imaginary lapels. "The big cheese himself, and you're lookin at him!"

"That's great, Wolf." And I'm struggling to stay awake.

"It is great, isn't it?" Sober Wolf sits down on the edge of his bed. "All my life I had trouble getting work as a civil engineer. I dressed too this. I talked too that. *This* and *that* when what they meant was *black.*" He leans his elbow on the corner of the desk, cheek on fist. "Yeah, or crazy; I got that too. I *was* crazy, man, I was crazed with being useless for so long. It was like all I could do was read, eat Mama's food, wash her dishes and make a joke out of everything. I used to sit up nights at my old drafting table designing model cities in one-to-one-thousand scale. I put in every driveway, hydrant, storm drain—shit, everything, I had plenty of time." He runs his fingers lightly over the desk's surface. "There was a place right around...*here* where I carved my initials back in high school and I had to watch out or the pencil would go through the paper." His stare is almost glare: "Nine years out of work, Max, nine *years*. Naturally I didn't tell *these* bozos that. Gaps in the résumé, tch tch." The mischief chases quickly into his eyes. "Shit, look at this room! We got beds"—he prods his—"real beds with soft mattresses."

"And Wolf, these sheets are all cotton. Not fifty-fifty, all cotton."

"Izzat so?" He's at the light switch. "Look here now. All I have to do to plunge us into darkness is *that*"—and true to his word, he does—"and all I gotta do say I decide I want light is *that*!" Click. "Let there be darkness," he intones. Click. "Let there be light!"

"You're getting carried away." Jesus, he's driving me crazy.

"I'm *be*in carried away, there's a difference," he says inattentively. "Now look at this! Each got our own dresser. Each got our own half a desk. Look in here—genuine goddamn fine-point pens." He holds one up dramatically in front of his face, clipping his syllables like a TV announcer: "We subjected this Bic pen to a nuclear war *so strong* that it virtually wiped out an entire planet. And...*It still writes*!" To demonstrate he makes curlicues on the desktop.

"Wolf." Calm down, lower your voice, peace be with you.

"Oh yeah, I guess I shouldn't mess the..." He's up and pacing. "Wolf and Debris return to civilization!" And twirling an index finger aloft as I watch through half-closed eyes: "Wolf and Debris find their Shangry-La. Accept no imitations—youuuuu-topia and none other. The land of milk and honey, with a cherry on top!"

I check Bo's pocket watch. "Speaking of food."

"Is it dinnertime already? Lord I've never *been* so hungry!" He's out the door, poking his head back in to ask· "You comin?" but not waiting for an answer, and I sink flat back to the mattress, drinking in the sudden silence, more hungry than sleepy, staring at the ceiling.

It's that white porous schoolroom stuff with the thousands of holes in it. In fifth grade we used to try to count those holes; but you'd lose your place, there were so many of them. Years later I saw a chart like that, thousands of black dots on a field of white. One dot in the center was circled. It stood for the total explosive power used in World War II, and the entire field represented Russia and America's nuclear arsenals.

I was dreading the cafeteria with its eyes and elbows; I was the new kid in school, and I was stalling. My belly wouldn't let me do it for long.

The hallway, with its soiled blue marble-patterned linoleum, its row of closed doors, its dull echo of massed sounds, seemed as empty as any stretch of landscape Wolf and I ever crossed. I felt ridiculous, *was* ridiculous in my shin-length khaki overalls, forearm cuffs. I pushed up my sleeves to make it look intentional and followed the murmur of voices.

A long narrow room occupied by a long counter and an aisle came first, and mercifully, none of the voices just beyond the wall, beyond the swinging door could see me as I wandered wet-mouthed, boggle-eyed past macaroni and cheese, tabouli, pot cheese, peaches like glowing suns in the stainless steel, and finally took a tray for the return trip. My first meal.

I began with three of the main dishes: macaroni, chicken meatballs that smelled good, rice with beefish gravy; four smaller plates of condiments and salad balanced on their edges; a half-dozen tumblers adorned the foodpark like the tiny trees and plastic people on an architect's model; and diagonally folded brown napkins garnished the four corners of the tray.

Finally my great work was at its end; with luck, with care and balance I could manage without spilling to bring this edible edifice to a place at table. Still following voices, I backed through a door.

And into another human being. As that din of voice

opened up to me my ankle hit another, I stepped sideways on a foot, and Disaster! I was falling down amid
several elbows knees and ankles, pot cheese and
peaches, orange juice and spinach and hair and meatballs
and long black hair, napkins and milk and rolls and coffee, a woman's blue eyes startled and startling—all of
which seemed to hang suspended around me in that infinitely split second when Disaster opens his raincoat
and exposes himself to you—like a multicolored mobile
before falling, along with half a ton of glassware.

Hundreds of faces were on me. And only one of all
those faces was black. It was easy to spot him: alone
among the people in that room, he was standing at his
seat; alone among them he was applauding.

"Sorry, are you OK?" I slurred to the woman.

She was already on her feet, a tall kinetic pillar of
glare towering over my crumpled form, her fists clench-
ing and unclenching, her plain straight dress paved with
food from hem to collar, her black hair already settled in
an oddly stylish shoulder-length blunt cut with bangs, so
fine and glossy it seemed to be of one piece, her generally well-organized features unifying themselves in an
expression of instant, severe and irrevocable dislike. In
my hot state of embarrassment she was so magnificent
that I wished I had a hat to take off. "Fucking Christ!"
she said, and disappeared.

I knelt before my feast and began sweeping it into the
tray with the edge of a halved dish. The macaroni, idiotically, had bounced right-side-up intact. Hairy-shinned,
impossibly tall and awkward, I headed blindly for that
one black face, a vortex of food and wreckage sprawled
out in front of me, topped by the unruffled cube of macaroni. My long hair slapped against my face; there was
tabouli in it. The one black face said:

"*That's* my buddy Max."

# 5 ✳ Arks

An old book exhales, like a speaking mouth, when it is opened. The smell is that of microorganisms, which are what make air more than a combination of a few different elements, eating paper. The smell of an old book is the bad breath of History.

And so we read that three hundred and sixteen men —mainly kids and drifters drawn by the modest promise of a day's pay and a solid meal, ignorant of their mission and almost everything else, their sole qualification for the job simply that of being men—assembled at Pinkerton headquarters in Chicago, where they were dubbed "detectives," put in the command of Captain Frederick H. Heinde and railed in a darkened train to Bellevue, Pennsylvania, arriving across the Ohio River from the Davis Island Dam at ten-thirty in the evening of July 5, 1892. The water was calm, the sky cloudy and peaceful; an engraving puts a fat moon in it. The temperature was about sixty-five degrees. The barges looked like little Noah's Arks. Most of the men had never fired a gun at anything larger than a raccoon.

131

Waiting at Bellevue in the lapping waters of the Ohio were two roofed freight barges owned by Carnegie Steel: the *Iron Mountain* had been converted into a dormitory, with sleeping berths lining its 125-foot sides, and the *Monongahela* into a floating dining room, replete with twenty waiters and a steward. Dozens of coffin-sized cases, then 316 men, were put on board, and two small tugboats, the *Little Bill* and the *Tide*, pulled the barges off down the river. The sun was sliding through the heavens at several thousand miles per hour, the moon was in one or another of its phases, the planets were just so. Anything could have been predicted.

# 6 ❈ River Crossing

Fzzzzzz! The Eickhoff-170 shears smoothly through a vein of pure coal. Or, coal and rock, not smoothly: zzzt!zt!zzzt! It's the sound as it comes through or around the wax plugs in your ears. You can't follow behind the Shovel while it cuts, because it spews coal chunks and pebbles like a superpowered lawn mower. When the Shovel's roar dies down, and it rests idling at the end of the longwall, another sound seems to well up, but really it has been there, smothered, all along: a tape of Julio Iglesias played at rattling full volume on a hand-held cassette recorder. It's the only tape we have.

Now one man walks ahead with a tool that looks like an ax with a long cutting edge, and breaks down the sheet into chunks.

That's Tascheira's job. He let me try it once: you bring down the ax (which is called, like the person who wields it, the Chopper) again and again every few feet; by the time you're done with one long sheet of coal you're ready to surrender ownership of your arms and shoulders. Tascheira is the only man on our crew with

133

the right build for it: he's a bowling ball, with his bald head, bull neck, sloping shoulders, big chest, bigger belly, and short spindly legs. He works with inhuman speed and concentration, usually finishing the entire hundred-foot longwall before we've picked up half the coal. Then he sits at a card table in the corner doodling on a small pad of paper he seems to carry everywhere, or just lost in thought, or both at the same time.

Early mornings are best because I'm not working yet. I walk out alone, am watched like a curiosity all the way through the Planning Quarters, go by the guards, pause on the bridge over the Monongahela, wish I had a penny to make a wish, go by more guards, climb the hill, look out to see if Pittsburgh's changed, and leave my pass with the last set of guards, all without exchanging a word with anyone. I'm an anomaly in Homestead; I do not fully belong on either side of the river.

Once in the mine, I get a lukewarm greeting from everyone but Tascheira, who seems to have adopted me, and the three guards on duty down under, who impartially ignore everyone. And the Shovel starts up, and there is a lot of noise, and then we start carrying coal, and the coal dust gets everywhere, in your hair, up your nose—where its smell is different from house dust, not musty, but pure mineral, like unscented talcum powder —in your eyebrows and sometimes your eyes. Sooner or later you will have to open your mouth to breathe, upon which you will inhale a teeth-squeaking fine grist that turns your spit black. And the human arm has an unbelievable number of tendons and muscles, and your biceps seem no longer good enough to hold up your arms, but Fzzzzzzz! the Shovel is operating at top efficiency today and as soon as you stop knocking into people with your sneezing fit there's another hundred feet of coal sheeting to carry to the cars. Now that the Shovel is silent, you can hear the worn cassette blatting through the tiny speaker: "Ah-morrr, Ah-morrr . . ."

By mid-morning we have a car full of coal and take turns driving it up the shaft. This, everyone agrees, is the best part of the job; as you drive the car up to the little square of bright sky, tranquillity sweeps over you like cool water. Once a fight broke out between an art historian and an investment banker over whose turn it was to drive the car.

In the past week two explosions have collapsed Shafts D and G. No one was hurt, and the whisperings on the Planning side of the river are of sabotage. The quota of bucks assigned to our crew has doubled in quantity and suspiciousness, and I've been working under a constant fear that either they or the roof will come down on us at any moment.

My days pass slowly in an acrid pressure of dust, sweat, and a vast expanding fantasy life involving the woman in the cafeteria, either a kiss and a bold nocturnal escape from Homestead to our own small shack with salvaged furniture and a vegetable garden, or, as my body slams and strains in the hot overalls, every sexual position I've ever known, all from the tiny aperture of an image of a woman with food on her dress, the same way a spider's web has its starting point in a tiny hole in the spider's abdomen, the way a teenage boy might spin from a single glimpse of an actress stepping into a taxi-cab a whole imagined existence that, when his bedroom lights go out and his day comes to rest, collapses in upon itself until it is once again only an outline of a memory that seems no longer to have even been his own, that recedes from him the more he tries to grasp it, the way the thin fabric of the woman's dress defined her hips and shoulder blades as she moved away from me.

❋

"You want a day pass out of this shithole?" Tascheira asks me one day across pannikins of oily stew. "I'm going across the river to fix a couple jeeps. I need a grease monkey, and I get to pick my own. It's one of the innumerable perks."

"You fix jeeps?"

"Anything with wings or wheels. I worked my way through J.C. in a garage," he says, picking up his tin and licking it clean. "The old man who owned the shop finally handed me five thousand dollars, in cash, in 1961, and said, 'You're a bright boy, Gerald. Go to college.' I was supposed to pay him back when I got the chance."

"Did you?"

"Naah, he died. No family." He wipes his face with a coarse brown napkin and rises. "So I'll meet you at nine? Your place."

In the morning Tascheira shows up at my door with a yellow pass around his neck and an armed guard at his elbow. "Well," he says, strolling in past me. "Sheets and a desk. So this is human life." He hands me a yellow pass; like his, it reads 17:00. "Buck here's along in case we might decide to take a spin. Max, Buck, Buck, Max. Let's go."

The garage is dark. Tascheira points to oversized key rings hanging from a row of nails. "Sixteen cars," he says. "Guess how I figure out which keys work in which car?"

"How?"

"I don't. I have to try each one. All this massed alleged brain-power, and not a soul thinks of putting numbers on the wall above the keys. Hey Bucky," he says to the guard. "Wanna make colonel? Take your tongue out of your superior's ear and whisper it to him."

"Eat shit," says the man, making a move toward Tascheira.

"Listen," says Tascheira, stepping up to his belly, "you're either going to shoot Homestead's only mechanic or restrict yourself to the use of your wits." He turns his back, unhooking all the key rings. "In other words you're completely helpless. Now which car?"

The guard stalks to the front of the garage and thumps a hood. Tascheira goes around the other side of the car and tries the first set of keys. The motor kicks over. "Lucky," says Tascheira. "I've always been lucky. But you have to pay for luck one way or another, don't you believe that, Buck? Hmm, sounds like it's missing. Show Max the tools. I need plugs."

The man nudges a large tool chest with his foot. "It's a six," calls Tascheira. I get out six sparkplugs.

Inside of five minutes Tascheira sits behind the wheel, gunning the engine. "Tough," he says. "Yessir. Requires an expert. Number two, Buckaroo?"

The man moves to the car near the entrance. This time Tascheira has to try several keys, and though the motor starts smoothly, the jeep takes off with a jerk and hits the car in front of it. Tascheira, after yanking the gearshift, hops down. "Clutch." He squats, gathering an armful of tools and laying them out next to the car. "You've seen these before? You know what they're called?"

"I think I can figure it out."

"Splendid." Tascheira fixes his bulk on the flat low wooden dolly and slides under the car. "How come no one says 'splendid' anymore? Maybe nobody ever really did. I need the trouble light. Can you believe they don't even have a light in this room? Dumb buncha fucks, don't you think?" I put the light in the outstretched hand that appears from under the car. Soon he's giving curt instructions like a supine surgeon. "Pliers. Small crescent. Five-eighths open-end wrench."

The guard, feeling safe for the moment, stands leaning in the entrance, smoking a cigarette. It seems you have to be a military man to get one.

I stick my face into the space between car and ground. "How come you're so hard on that guy?"

"Let me tell you something." Tascheira dollies out from under the car and blinks up at me, gravity spreading his face even wider than usual. "There are natural enemies in this world. Cobras and mongeese. Black ants and red ants. Fire and ice. Me and that guy with the gun. You and the guy with the gun, if you're smart." He cocks his head. "What's the matter? He's only doing his job?" He pronounces the cliché mincingly, acid nasality in his voice.

"Something like that," I say sheepishly.

"His job," says Tascheira. "Is to shoot you if you refuse to be miserable. So that takes care of that." He wipes his mouth with the back of his forearm. "If it's me you're worried about, forget it. I'm their fair-haired boy." My eyes slip inadvertently up to his smooth scalp. "Fair-headed boy, then. I can come over to this side of the river anytime. They need me as a mechanic."

"You mean you're in the mines of your own free will?"

"I'll tell you what I always tell them," he says, disappearing under the next car. "I'd rather be a karma mechanic than a car mechanic. Like I say, you have to pay for luck. Do you have any idea what five grand would be worth nowadays?"

I think about it. "Nothing."

He laughs. "Socket set, please."

When he's done he tosses the key rings at the guard. "Sonny," Tascheira tells the man as he grabs around on the floor for all the keys. "I want you back by midnight."

※

And then I have an entire afternoon off in which to explore Homestead. In the middle of a workday, Planning is a ghost town, as I discover wandering around the lumber pile, or veering away from the alarming smells of the chicken coop, or watching some miners putting up the frame for Wolf's new sewage plant, or getting myself kicked out of the vicinity of the munitions dump: the guards are lounging around, smoking an occasional cigarette, gossiping in slow voices about the people they work for.

In the corridors doors open and people burst into the silence carrying architectural drawings; doors shut. Neatly lettered cards bear the names of occupants. Harry Sawyer's office is flanked by two armed guards.

"Do you know where I can find Charles Dewey?" I ask one of them.

"Dewey . . . you know a fella named Dewey, Rob?"

"Don't think so," says the second guard.

"Black fella," I say.

"Oh yeah," says the first. "The engineer. He's in 19, 20, 21, one of those."

Here the offices have room numbers but no names and no guards. I try 21; the door's open, and, setting in my mind a picture of Wolf, wearing his glasses and bent over a drafting table, a cup of ersatz coffee gone cold at his elbow, I push in. What meets me instead is the blue ice stare of the woman I bowled over in the cafeteria.

I'm standing there. "I, uh . . . have the wrong room," I croak, and rush from the room.

※

Sometime during the following week, as the mining crew rode the last car up to twilight, Tascheira asked me:

"Why don't you bring your little Selmer to work tomorrow?"

I looked at him and sighed. "I don't think so, Gary. The work itself is all I can manage."

"So you only play for Buck?" he said loud enough for the others to hear.

"Cut the shit. I haven't picked up the horn since I got here." I lowered my voice. "Gary, they're saying the miners caused the accidents."

"You must miss the saxophone, then," he said as loud as before. "Maybe you could play for us." I shook my head with great vehemence as the evening sky hove joltingly in view. Gary Tascheira was smiling and beating my upper leg with a thick-steak palm. "Excellent," he said. "I never have had a chance to hear you play."

# 7 ❈ The Thing You Need Most

When the lights go out in our room they go *out*, and nothing, absolutely nothing, can be seen; it's a strange sensation after months of sleeping outdoors, where, as vision grows more acute, forms grow in definition, in depth, and the shades of shadow grow into purples and browns. Inside silence has a different sound, too, close around you as the ringing in your ears. Half-asleep—and that half is my mind, conjuring and connecting in free-wheeling heedless defiance of the plugged-in body it is housed in—I see the days as laps around a track, and as I run I see myself on other days, other laps, knee raised, fists pumping toward a finish line I cannot see, an un-painted line, a nonexistent line, and all there is is me, first wind, second wind, flagging, tiring, feigning energy —how do you pace yourself for a race that never ends? —more days, more and more of me, passing and being passed by images of myself in a kind of enforced, inter-minable déjà vu. All I can do is count imagined holes in the ceiling—but here my body gives a heave-twitch, that neurologic border sign marking the entry to the sleep-world—but I've forgotten the first count . . . and the pillow is soft . . . but I drift while trying to start the count again, the pillow soft as a woman's lap.

Time lapse, blessed lapse, running in a circle, running, slowing, lapse of laps, lapse of light and lapse of synapse.

Snap. Flood light! Lights, camera, Wolf: "Aye mytee, it's me, Cap'n mizzen-the-hatches-button-the-britches Charles E. Dewey, Junior, here to stay and make em pay! Avast and awyke, me hearties! Up and at em, Adam! Rise and shine or into the foamy brine!"

"Wolf." I open my eyes for a second: Wolf is leaning over me, thumbs in his belt loops, pleased with himself and content in the world. It's a better thing to close my eyes. "Shut the fuck up. I was sleeping."

"Oh . . ." He's tiptoe-staggering backward with exaggerated solicitude. "I thought you might be mildly interested in hearing how Homeboy here has been busy Krazy-Gluing this city together while you rolled and lolled and messed your sheets dreaming of the beauteous Juliet. Please won't you pardon *my* ass for interrupting?"

He has a right to his irritation, after listening to my nightly disquisitions on the woman I bowled over in the cafeteria. But Wolf's tales of life and work, littered with phrases like "disposal of solids" and "anaerobic treatment tank," have been, for me, late at night, bone-tired, soul-tired, dog-tired, an irresistible invitation to sleep. I've been wearing out his patience, the careless way you wear the same shirt to clean the kitchen, do your laundry, paint the house, and are surprised when one day it's in tatters. "OK," I force out. "Talk."

"Such a warm invitation," says Wolf, pulling up the desk chair. "How can I resist?"

"Resist if you want to. Just do me a favor and turn out the lights."

"Uh-unh," says Wolf. "You'll just fall asleep. Well—if you promise."

"Sure."

"So we've figured out that the first thing we got to do," he begins, getting up and turning off the light, "is build separate treatment plants for each side of the river, with three tanks apiece. In the holding tank we rake off and burn the large solids, then in the anaerobic tank the bacteria inside the sewage breaks it down. Oh," says Wolf. "Anaerobic—that means without air."

"Ah." A simple syllable that leaves the mind free to wander.

"Yeah, and then the sludge goes into an aerobic tank and air is pumped in. New breeds of bacteria keep breaking down the sewage; we take samples every so often to check how it's doing. When it's pretty much harmless we drain it out into the Monongahela downstream of Homestead, keeping some behind and using it as a culture for the next batch, like a sourdough starter. I told you this stuff last week."

"Mm," I say. He might have.

"Don't worry; there's no quiz. Now today I put it all down into a memo and this guy who's what passes for a secretary took two hours typing one page on a little manual job with the f missing. And you had to be there to see the way they circulated that page." He chuckles. "Someone has to bring it around to each guy, stand there while he reads it, then take it around to the next guy, stand there while *he* reads it . . . Had to be there, had to be there." Wolf laughs softly, cracklingly. "The way I look at it, they're tryin to organize a society without the one thing you need most. See, they thought enough to pack all this weird dental machinery and the complete works of Shakespeare and Erle Stanley Gardner on microfilm —but they forgot to take a Xerox machine. No spare parts, all the wrong kinds of expertise—I don't know how long they expect to keep this whole fat lollapalooza running on Scotch tape and rubber bands. Anyway, the main thing holding up my sewage plant was resources." You can hear that a man is lying on his back, hands behind his head, by the slightly distant, slightly guttural sound of his voice. Wolf is in full soliloquy. "Resources. We have two materials here: wood and coal. If we built the tanks of wood, how we gonna stop the sewage from leakin right through em? So one day at lunch General Itkin mentioned he'd majored in chemistry, and said he might be able to remember how to distill tar from coal. See, we'd make the tanks watertight by coating em with tar!" He pauses for response, then rushes jubilantly on:

"Two resources and only two, and still we can set up a half-decent sewage plant. Someday we might even be able to use the methane gas as a power source, and dry out the sludge for fertilizer. It's so perfect, so goddamn economical, so—"

I can restrain myself no longer, and burst out: "What *you* need, Max, is someone to *listen* to you, a shoulder to cry on. C'mon now, who could be a more natural choice than me, Wolf, your oldest and only buddy? Go ahead now, go right ahead."

Wolf springs up. He's turned the light on, is kneeling by my bed and batting his eyelashes: "However *was* your day, Maxy sweetums? Does our little Maxiwax maybe want his strained spinach now? Is oo feeling bad? Tell Daddy ebwyting."

"Wolf, have you ever even *seen* a coal mine first-hand?" He gets up and slops himself backward on his bed, staring wide-eyed disgusted at the ceiling, silent except for a drawn-out, exaggerated sigh, the very picture of passive resistance, still as a felled tree. I supply both sides of the conversation myself:

"Pretty grimy down there, huh Max? Yeah Wolf, pretty fucking disgustingly grimy, but that's not the worst part. Oh no? What *is* the worst part, Max? The work, Wolf. The work itself."

He chuckles, not moving his eyes from the ceiling. "Do you good."

"Up yours." I get up to turn out the light, return, and try three positions in half a minute, none of them comfortable.

I can hear that he's turned his back to me, is speaking to his own wall. "Y'see I was dumb enough to think you might, just once, want to hear what *I*—"

I have a small explosive tantrum consisting of arms, legs, sheet and blanket. "The fucking condition I'm in, Wolf, I want to hear only two things: somebody telling me I don't have to work in the mines anymore, and Julia saying anything, anything at all as long as it's to me."

Wolf orates into the darkness: "For never was a story of more woe than this of Juliet and her Romeo." He snaps the light on and, bending a knee there near the door, still faced away, stutters like Porky Pig, "W-w-wwherefore art thou, Juliet?" Ever since he found out for me that the woman in the cafeteria is named Julia, he's been studying Shakespeare on microfilm with the express purpose of insulting me. It's almost, but not, touching.

I push all the bed stuff to the floor. "Will you do me one favor, Wolf? And lay off the Juliet shit?"

Wolf pivots to regard me, arms crossed, and utters one curt syllable. "No."

I sit up in bed. "What?"

"I said no I won't lay off that shit." He's in motion now, approaching, pausing to stab a finger at me, pacing past. "I come back here every day after putting in twelve hours, my mind buzzing with politics and personalities and technical shit, words you wouldn't even understand, my head chattering so I can't even think of sleep, and when I come back here what do I find? The world's biggest five-year-old cryin cause he's got to do the first day's work in his life. Or if it's not that, it's the girl. But always, always"—with each word his open hand slashes the air back and forth—"moaning, wheezing, whining, wailing, wheedling, and whimpering." He stops in front of me, hands on hips as if bracing to give his lungs more power. Instead he speaks with grit-teeth softness: "I wanna tell you: I don't need a six-and-a-half-foot albatross hanging round my neck. Don't need the business." He snorts. "Dizzy fruit climbin the walls over some willing little number he can't even get it up to talk to."

I'm on my feet, in his face, tapping his chest. "Don't fucking talk about her like that! You don't know her."

"For all *you* do I might be right." He sits facing me across the back of the chair. "OK, I do you this favor and stop talkin shit about this girl—"

I open my mouth but he makes an "erase" gesture. "I'm not finished. By no means. I do you that and you do me this: stop calling me Wolf."

"What? What's one got to do with the other?"

"You scratch my back, et cetera, that's what it's got to do with it. Wolf's not my *name*." He rises, inflated with dignity. "I'm Chuck, but you can call me Charles E. Dewey, Junior. Think you can remember that?"

I get up shouting. "Don't pull that trash on me, Wolf; I

know who the fuck you *are*. You can scrape the shit off your shoes but I know where you've been. I've seen you suck the eyeballs from a fucking rat!"

"Here," says Wolf, pointing down, "here I'm a human being with a human name." His anger is the deadly kind that quiets as you yell at him. "It's called bein adaptable opposite of coming home and holding your head every day, say 'please sweet Jesus deliver me painlessly into a better world where there are no coal mines and the women come fallin at your feet.' When I had to eat rats, I ate rats; now that I don't, I don't. Simple logic. Things change, I'm a whole other man than the one I had to be before."

"Well, I liked that man better than the prissy shithead with the rented suit standing in front of me."

This sends Wolf off down the room, gesticulating, spitting as he speaks, an overwound toy. "That just shows what a jealous motherfuck you are, got to drag everyone down to your level. *He* has to go down and scratch in the dirt so *I* got to be called some wild animal." He whirls to face me. "And rented, shit. I *earned* this suit."

"How long you think they'll let you keep it, Wolf? How long before you finish your sewage plant and they send you down to the mines? How long before this whole fat machine comes down around all your ears? The miners hate you bastards, you know that? And they're right!"

"You identify so much with them, why don't you go live there?" He bows slightly, extends a sweeping arm. "Feel free. Go join your buddies blowing up the mines."

"*What*? The miners are the ones who stand to get killed in those accidents."

"Then how come none of them *have* been killed?" He waits half a second, and pounces. "Anytime you want to, just up and take your ratty carcass across the river where it belongs. You just remember who got you a room here in the first place."

"In the first place, go fuck yourself with a broken Coke bottle."

"Well," says Wolf, standing at the chair. "I see we got a real intelligent conversation going here." He strides toward the door and stands silhouetted in a vertical crack of bright light. "I'm going to count to ten real slow. It'll take me about four hours." He flings a hand to his breast. "A thousand times good night!" The door closes with a click, and he's gone.

Click, and he's back. "A thousand times the worse, to want your light!"

And he's gone.

❋

I don't know when or how I've come to be aware, hours later, that Wolf is in the room again, but there he is, slipping off his clothes very slowly, quietly in the darkness. My dreams have been of gunplay, adventure, painless murder. I'm awake and refreshed, but each of Wolf's small movements irritates, seems *designed* to irritate me, until I am twitching, itching with annoyance.

Wolf's voice, surprisingly immediate, surprisingly gentle, breaks the hot silence:

"You ever do anything besides music, Max?"

Trap! "What are you getting at?"

"I'll get at what I'm gettin at when I get at it. Come down off your hind legs and answer the question."

"OK." I collect my thoughts. Not much to collect. "I picked filberts, for one thing. That's physical work."

"You picked filberts," he repeats slowly. "When?"

"I was thirteen—no, fifteen, at least fifteen."

"Uh-huh. For how long?"

"Two or three weeks."

"Hnh," he snorts. "That your whole résumé?"

"Look, Wolf, you can't make me ashamed that I've been able to make a living doing something I loved."

"Hey, I'm over here. Nobody's sayin you got anything to be ashamed of. You got very good at one thing that brought a lot of people something they needed, pleasure I guess."

"Thank you," I say automatically.

"Now you're in a different world, and people in a different world need different things. Wake up to it, shake hands with it, exchange business cards with it," says Wolf, yawning exorbitantly.

"Wolf: I'm not getting used to it. I don't want to get used to it. I refuse to get used to it."

"That's just it: you refuse," says Wolf. "But like it or not, refuse to or not, you'll *have* to. I just want to leave you with that idea, cause I'm in no mood to poke my nose in all the available wrinkles of this argument at two in the a.m. *These* people need sewers and they need coal. You think after ten years of having nothing but fun you got a right to object?"

"Fourteen years."

"Fourteen years, then. A-rooooo!" This last is another yawn. "Now g'night."

I kick off the sheet. "This is exactly the weak nonsense I thought you were trying to pull. I don't buy the theory that says if Wednesday is fun you've got to lick toilets all day Thursday. If there's a God or some kind of floating principle of justice, how come *this* happened?" *This*, in the Max-Wolf argot, means the bombing, and there is no answer because the line of reasoning is unanswerable. Good. "Go ahead, Wolf, tell me again about your long and productive history of service to society. Your sole contribution is building a couple of wooden boxes that may someday make it possible to burn a few turds. Impressive stuff, Mister Charles E. Dewey, Junior, Sir. So don't throw the work ethic at me, you marginal asshole. How long were *you* out of work? Nine years?"

Nothing back from Wolf. That was dirty, dirtier than the insults screamed earlier, low and dirty and getting lower and dirtier each moment that goes by without a word. The quiet grows stifling, the thick air we share; in it I can hear, almost feel him breathing slowly and deliberately, struggling for control. Speak, Wolf, say something.

I flick on my lighter. Wolf is asleep, has been asleep I don't know how long, and I'm left with that peculiar seeping embarrassment, that feeling of having revealed myself, even though there was no one to reveal myself to except me.

# 8 ❈ The Tide Turns

When you turn the page its corner crumbles in your hand. Someone long ago may have dog-eared the pages, leaving you wondering what fell off the ends of those brittle sentences. The page is broken, the words, the knowledge lost.

But in 1890, in another century, two years before the Homestead uprising, Henry Clay Frick had hired the Pinkertons to squash a strike against his own coke refinery; both his firmness in dealing with labor and his monopoly on coke needed for steel manufacture had induced Andrew Carnegie, the wealthiest man in America, to offer him a high post and a substantial interest in Carnegie Steel. Within two years Frick had become chairman and general manager, and in fact he died a richer man than Carnegie.

Knowing Frick's record, the men of Homestead were ready for anything, Pinkertons or a posse of deputies, and had set up a watch along the Monongahela River. As the *Iron Mountain* and *Monongahela* passed the Smithfield Street bridge in South Pittsburgh, a scout wired

Homestead: "Watch the river. Steamer with barges left here." The Amalgamated Association's strike committee sent men and rumors running along the riverbank. The boats were slow.

One of the tugboats, the *Tide*, developed a motor problem and dropped back, leaving the sturdy *Little Bill* to pull the two barges by itself. Through the night the barges bumped together, giving the Pinkertons in the upper tiers some nasty spills and generally preventing sleep. At three in the morning the barges reached the B & O railroad bridge at Glenwood, less than two hours from Homestead. A heavy fog had descended over the water; through it the edgy Pinkertons could hear scout call out to scout along the banks of the river.

The union strike committee, with a certain sense of drama, sent a horseman dashing through the streets of Homestead giving the alarm. Long before the barges arrived at the landing outside Carnegie's Homestead Works, as many as ten thousand people had gathered on the banks. Three or four thousand of them were armed, organized, bellicose, full-grown males.

# 9 ❋ Happy Hour

A woman is running her fingers through my hair. Spread
out on the pillow in the nest of her black hair are my
thick unruly tufts, plants without roots. I reach up to feel
my head, but know before I do that I am egg-bald, cue-
ball-bald, and suddenly I am explaining, inflating a
comic-strip word balloon, telling her It's OK, I'm normal. My words degenerate into clinical syllabification
(something about "unimpaired vital functions"), scientific symbols, undecipherable abstractions and then (the
air going out of the puckering word balloon), into silence. I reach to my mouth but know before I do that it is
only a lipless dent in my face. I reach down to touch my
penis but know before I do.

It's a dream. And perversely, because it is a dream, I
wake with an erection.

❋

Once a week two drinks per person are handed out, and
all the planners, planners plus me, gather for an evening
in several small rooms centering around the cafeteria,

which is still impossible for me to enter without a twinge of remembered humiliation. I go anyway, hoping the slight flush of alcoholic warmth will embolden me to speak to Julia.

Two drinks per person—homemade beer and some equally nasty vodka—are poured at the beginning, and everyone seems to quaff the first drink as fast as possible and nurse the second, unconsciously obeying old habits of talking with one drink in hand. Not me: I drain them both at the beginning, get a quick fix on Julia, and proceed to hesitate at the fringes of whatever group she's in, lurch and hesitate, rethink and hesitate, hesitate and hesitate, without, however, finally inserting myself into the conversational knot. Still, I am always hoping, and she never seems particularly interested in the men who surround her.

Tonight I have showered for the second and last time this week (water ration), combed my hair, prayed to Ellen for help. I appraise myself in the distorting mirror: a presentable male person. It is possible to like the way I look. The overalls fit, more or less, now that I've taken the hems out and added a couple inches of fabric to the suspenders, and they are freshly laundered.

I am now shaving, shaving and despairing, as always when I get this close to a mirror, of my nose. Roiling up from the peaks and whorls of foam like the prow of a Viking ship, the nose occupies a space best described by a word like "prepossessing," which seems too long for its own good. My nose, like a bad reputation, precedes me into a room.

I think of my nose as quietly and independently alive, contemplative of disposition, serene, placid in the knowledge that unlike my dwindling supply of brain cells, it will continue to grow throughout life, will continue imperceptibly to swell and puff and inflate itself, sprout carbuncles, annex territories, and finally lay claim to the front portion of my head in its entirety. It is meditating on my face, its great bulb the belly of a great fat man, a kneeling Buddha, and the narrow flares of the nostrils the Buddha's skinny legs.

Courage. I force myself out into the hall and toward the hubbub of conversation. Courage! Avoid mirrors! Tonight, as I tell myself, out loud because it's even more ridiculous, will be the night.

And tonight, in the cafeteria, in the middle of four men, Julia catches my eyes, and I—it's ridiculous; what am I, sixteen?—actually have to go into an adjacent room, designated as the library, and sit down to catch my breath. The library has about five books, a much-thumbed copy of *Penthouse*, and a microfilm machine. And Julia, leading two stubborn men into the room!

Her hips and shoulders are slender in a blue linen dress; her face and fingers long, sharp-cut. It is her fingers I watch, playing restlessly, almost twitching in the air. The men are talking about movies, by default mostly to each other. One is decent-looking, the other not. It's a hopeless topic: what new movies could they recently have seen? What old movies? Julia looks once straight at me, a look of understanding, almost conspiratorial, then says abruptly to the men, "Excuse me. I have to go to the bathroom."

She begins quickly to leave, but pauses with the door open. I can see her from my chair, her face turned to me, measuring, deciding, but the men's view is blocked by the door.

The vast grating assemblage of liver and lever, tongue and groove, diaphragm and diode clack-clambers to its feet and there I am, the man who knocks over women he doesn't know, the one-man food fight, the macaronic man, in mid-step, in half-step, in stutter-step, in stumble-step, between the proverbial Scylla and the proverbial Charybdis, between proverb and adverb and ad lib and pronoun, and there she is, hand on the doorknob and about to leave the room.

Magic! Something whips against my ankle. The braided lace is snaking loose from one high boot, lifting up now into the air and out on a beeline for her. My bootlace wraps itself crisscross, in the nature of bootlaces, along the length of her upper arm, twisting thwip-thwip-thwip indecently around her until there's only enough left for the bow, which is tied with supernatural speed. Positively supernatural. Ellen has answered my prayer.

Julia turns back to look at me standing there, from my

feet up my long hesitating body to my face, and her surprise turns to smile turns to

"Why not?" She's smiling insouciantly, holding the door open. I am with her in the hallway. She pulls at the bow around her elbow and the lace comes loose, just a string, inanimate purpose served, for we are walking down the hall side by side. "Here." She hands the boot-lace back to me. "I'm not ready to be tied down just yet."

Nothing in Homestead is very far from anything else, and it turns out that the women's quarter is much like the men's. Her room is narrower and far longer than mine and Wolf's, housing an enormous and antiquated punch press, along with a desk, three architecture books, a small sink and two beds. She waves me onto one and sits opposite on the other, smiling at my boot, its long tongue lapping openly forward. "That's easily the strangest way anyone's ever propositioned me."

"I think my sister helped me out. Ellen," I blurt.

"So you're still in contact with her." I nod; it's safe to nod. "My last ghost left me a while ago. At the beginning I hated them—they were everywhere."

"Yeah." For a while now every word I say is going to be dumb; might as well keep them as few and short as possible.

"But now that they're gone, I don't know...I miss them." She catches my eyes, tries to hold them when I look down. For the first time I notice her shoes, narrow, oddly fashionable high heels of a darker blue than her dress.

The door opens and a woman, compact, sandy, comes into the room. She covers her surprise at my presence in rushing monologue. "I *was* going to tell you all about the big day in Security. You know what they want to do now? They want to bug the Production quarters. They're pretty sure the miners caused the accidents, and they think they're planning something bigger."

"He's a miner," says Julia, nodding toward me.

"Max," I say.

"Do you need the room tonight?" the sandy woman asks her. Julia looks at me, and this time I do not drop my eyes.

"Yes," she says.

"OK." And immediately the sandy woman is in the desk, taking a towel, soap, a toothbrush, deodorant, and talking. "They plan to use wireless receivers, isn't that idiotic? Just because we have the equipment doesn't mean it's going to work. They'll find a way to foul it up, and once they do it'll stay fouled up. Nice to meet you," she says at the door.

"Thanks, Rosalie," says Julia.

"Night." And we're alone in the room.

"Max," she says. "Meet Julia."

Her eyes, the humor and anticipation in them, and beyond that simply their color, the light tones of her skin and black of her hair, the angularity of her face and arms, the fact of her closeness to my senses, is cooling and quenching.

She takes off her shoes with her feet and I watch her calves for a second as she moves to the desk. "Listen," she says, "I'd better show you something very unromantic right now." She pulls open the large bottom drawer. In it is a collection of condoms, contraceptive suppositories and sponges, spermicidal gels and foams, all bearing the manufacturers' imprints, and a good dozen diaphragms.

"Choose your weapon," she says. "They packed enough of everything for each of us to stock a Planned Parenthood clinic." She takes a can of foam and an applicator, sets them out on the desk with the pens and pencils and regards them suspiciously. Suddenly her features relax. "I shouldn't worry so much, you were . . . out there, anyway."

She tails off. "Oh shit," and she puts a hand to her mouth. She comes over and touches my shoulder. "I'm really sorry I said that."

"I probably am sterile, you're right."

"I don't want kids anyway," she says hastily, not meeting my eyes. "Do you? I don't." I have nothing to say. "People used to talk about how they didn't want to bring children into this cruel world, remember?" I nod mechanically. "Well, now . . ." There is a nervous silence again as she moves to the wall and props a pillow behind her back, a silence that prolongs itself until even the rustle of clothing is an embarrassment.

Julia begins to speak rapidly: "We had this science teacher in fifth grade who kept talking about the Nuclear Age. Math and science, Mr. McCabe. I don't know why I'm talking about this. Anyway, Mr. McCabe heard somewhere about plant seeds that had been exposed to radiation, and there were all sorts of mutations. It turned out you could buy irradiated seeds, so that became our science project. One day he called us in alphabetical order and we came up and he gave each of us a small clay pot, a lunch bag of potting soil and a lima bean."

"Like a priest handing out wafers." Then again, maybe better not to say anything.

"Yeah, exactly." She smiles, simply glad I've spoken. "'Each of you is going to have your own plant,' Mr. McCabe told us. "Each of the plants is going to be different from any plant ever grown before.'"

She leans her head forward, cuts a new part in the side of her blunt-cut hair with a fingernail. "There was a long sill that got the morning sun, and we put all our little pots up there. They had labels, a row of pots that just said Ben, Darryl, Lori, Julia."

"Remember that plant in *Mad* magazine named Arthur?"

She laughs, taking her hands down off her hair. "I remember Arthur."

The sudden red in her mouth has a quick adrenal effect on me: everything warms up, the outlines of her face and body seem to redden and soften, and my visual perception of beauty heats into its base elements: the need to touch and taste. Her calves, her small ass in her dress, her black black hair. I move back near her on the bed. "So what happened to the plants?" I know to ask.

"Only about four sprouted, and they were spindly, twisting around like those things . . ." She sends an index finger swimming through the air.

"Corkscrews?" I've had that happen to me recently; when you haven't seen things for a while you forget what they are called.

"Corkscrews. Thank you. And Don—he was a boy I liked—Don's lasted the longest. It was white and never stood straight, it just twisted around and around along the soil until it reached the edge of the pot and then it died. Mine never came up at all."

Julia's eyes are wet. I press her head against me. She turns her face away. "What a silly thing to cry over," she says. Her cheek is warm against my chest. "Remember how kids used to say 'human beans'?" I feel her sob once and go rigid, struggling for control.

"Cry," I say, turning her face to front.

"I always *wanted* to have kids!"

"You can't be more than thirty," I tell her. "It'll be all right." I feel her tears through my shirt.

She shakes her head against me. "Not with me. I haven't had my period since . . ."

I squat in front of her. "That doesn't mean it's permanent. Sometimes it goes on for a couple of years or even more, but it starts up again."

"And sometimes it *is* permanent." She dries her eyes with a sleeve.

"Yeah. With me it might be. I was out early. But you were down there a long time—"

"Seventy-one days."

"I doubt you got enough of a dose when you finally came up. Listen, I honestly doubt it."

"That's what they always tell us." I like that rebellious *they*. "I always just assumed they were lying, to keep up morale."

"Maybe not." I kiss her forehead and stand up. "Maybe not."

"You're very sweet, after what I said to you. Thank you. I'm OK now."

"I lost most of my hair when it started, but it grew back."

She reaches out tentatively and touches my head. "You need a haircut." She tugs my hair as if to see if it's real, and a groan of this-could-be-pleasure comes out of me.

"Do you want me to give you a haircut tomorrow?" she says.

I sit on the edge of the bed, my back against her. "Would you keep doing that? It feels so good."

"This is nice," she says. "You cheer me up. I *like* you." She sounds surprised.

I pull her hand around to my mouth and suck the side of her index finger and up to the tip, licking hard where skin meets nail. She gives a small moan and we are kissing.

Every pore in my body is grateful for hers, for skin on my skin, for the warm sleepy flexibility that lets us fit together as if boneless, grateful even for a few strands of her hair that get caught in my mouth, for the skein of sweat through my clothes where our bodies make contact.

Then we had sex. Made love. Fucked, screwed, balled. Had sexual intercourse. Fornicated. Engaged in sexual congress. Excuse me, but who devised the terms used to beggar and bugger this selfish, selfless, annihilating, rejuvenating, perfectly mad, perfectly sane, perfectly imperfect act? Please send down some new ones. Quickly, so we'll have words for fucking that we can use in our wordy little mouths and minds without betrayal when the fucking is over. For we will use words; they are ratchets, and once you turn the mind forward on these little clicks and clacks there is no turning it back to the point it was at before. Words are pins in mounted butterflies; after a while you forget they are there, but they hold the display together with an invisible and brutal precision.

# 10 ❋ Don't Shoot That Boy

Publishers in the nineteenth century were well aware of the uses of illustration in books intended for adults. They stuffed their books full of ink drawings, photographs, engravings. No matter that the illustrator's version often seemed so far from the text's that it appeared he had not read the book at all; the reader was given something to look at when he got tired of words.

So: 316 men in two boats pulling into a landing, ten thousand waiting for them. Above the landing a steep hill had been steepened by industrial slag from the Homestead Works far up the slope. In the week past, Frick had prepared for the Pinkertons by lining the route from the river to the Works with a twelve-foot wooden fence topped with barbed wire. The end of the fence dipped into the water, and that is where the *Little Bill* drew up with the *Monongahela* and the *Iron Mountain*.

A great shout went up, and the Homesteaders reduced the heavy fence to firewood before the Pinkertons could so much as extend a gangplank. No photograph exists, but a man who wasn't there made an engraving of the scene: men, boats and river are spread out in a fine panorama that gives no hint of the kinetic, no clue of the turmoil to come.

Captain F. H. Heinde had two hundred and fifty magazine-fed Winchester repeating rifles and three hundred pistols distributed to the Pinkertons. Now they were ready to make their landing, and the gangplank was set out.

"Go back," shouted the workers from the shore, and this is the caption of the engraving, spelled out in lovely cursive letters. "Go back, or we'll not answer for your lives!"

What did Captain Heinde do when he saw ten thousand individuals who looked like they meant business and told him loudly and expressly that they did in fact mean business? The captain courageous ordered his men forward.

According to the later testimony of Homestead's Captain O. C. Coon,

> When the plank was thrown out my attention was called to a man on the barge; he had a gun in his hand; there was a boy on the shore; he was tantalizing the man; the latter raised his gun to shoot the boy; I said to him: "For God's sake don't shoot that boy, for he is only a boy."

A shot was heard—no one knows who fired it. Captain Cooper, on the *Iron Mountain*, turned immediately to the barges and bellowed, "Fire!" Scores of Winchesters were discharged into the dense crowd on the bank, and more than thirty workers fell.

The workers fired back, and in that first volley mortally wounded two Pinkertons, injuring a dozen others. Captain Heinde was shot through the leg.

Another engraving shows men, standing, with rifles, prettily arrayed along the tops of the barges, and several polite dozens of riflemen displaying themselves on the river bank, as if this was the Revolutionary War and both sides were the British. You can be sure that in the real barges, on the actual tugboat, on the banks, there was wetness, there was mud, and men were crawling, men were swearing. In the background, in life as in the engraving, are the steel mills and hundreds of smoke-stacks.

Now both sides retreated for an extended battle, the workmen constructing sturdy barricades of scrap steel and pig iron on the upper reaches of the hill, and the Pinkertons cutting loopholes into the sides of the *Iron Mountain* and the *Monongahela*.

The wounded Pinkertons were loaded into the *Little Bill*. The tug's skipper, Captain Rodgers, promised to come back as soon as possible, and chugged off. The sun had risen. It would be a hot day. Immobile, outnumbered in the barges, sitting, squatting, hiding in the barges, rats in barrels in the barges, the Pinkertons smelled one another's sweat and waited.

# 11 ❊ Ichi, Ni, San, Shi

Such strange reactions to music. When I first played for just the thirty or so men and women I work with, about half, the usual ratio for music of any kind, seemed to thoroughly enjoy it. Even those who looked confused remained polite, paying attention and applauding at the ends of songs. It was a good but hardly an exceptional audience.

For the second performance, on a Friday, Gary Tascheira decided to take my act to a much larger group, the miners' main cafeteria, and everyone (except for the Secret Service-serious guards, out in force, who just stood scanning the crowd) was wildly enthusiastic, whistling and stomping and remarking excitedly to each other. At the nucleus of all this noisy activity was Tascheira, beating his hamlike hands furiously together, moving swiftly along the benches, his bald pate glinting palely in the fluorescent light as he bent to say a cuple of words to each party, smiling broadly and pointing at me all the while as if to knot everyone in the room together into one ecstatic organism.

"That was great, just great!" said Taschiera afterward as the crowd was dispersing. "Listen, we'd like you to do this every Friday, if you would. It would be very important for us." He had my arm in an uncomfortably firm grip.

"Thanks, thanks very much," I babbled reflexively. Strange way to put it—*important*. "But I don't know about every Friday. It was hard to put this thing together." I had recorded four primitive saxophone rhythm tracks over Julio Iglesias; "Rock Around the Clock" had been a lot of fun.

"No," Taschiera said urgently, "it's got to be every Friday." The concentration on his face broke up, relaxed, and he let go of my arm. "What I mean is—we really don't get any entertainment at all, and you know..."

"Yeah, I know. But—you play, you know what I'm talking about—this is *work*."

"Uh-huh, uh-huh, uh-huh." He waved impatiently. "You'd rather carry shit full-time, I suppose?"

"No, of course not, but that isn't the question."

"That is the question. I'm the foreman; I could say, oh, maybe, Max always rides the shit car, something like that. You could take it real slow, you know, to work on your stuff." I gave him an incredulous look. "Look, as long as the work gets out, Buck won't get hopped up."

Taschiera kept his promise. It was a lovely week, full of music. I played at lunch, I played on the slope as I drove the shit car. The acoustics were excellent, with a crisp sound because of the hardness of the surface and a spectacularly long decay. I would start toward daylight with just a phrase and a vague idea of working on it; I would have a melody by the time I reached the mouth of the tunnel, and on the way back down I'd write the bridge. Sometimes I just hit the brake to give myself more time.

The other crewmen didn't seem to resent my new privileges. Taschiera was becoming obsessive with his diaries, huddling over them constantly, having to be told when the Shovel had completed a run. When everyone else was carrying coal and Gary was sitting at his card table, I came up quietly behind him. He gave the barest start, just a twitch toward covering up his writing.

"See?" he said, waving his hands wide. On the pad were orderly little rows of facial caricatures: boys, girls, men and women executed in competent but unexceptional strokes, packed tightly lengthwise in five rows across the three-by-five paper, perhaps fifty faces to a page.

"Can I see it?" I asked.

Every page was like that, five rows of tiny cartoon faces, all of them different: some had freckles, glasses, cigarettes, earrings, dark hair, smiles, hats, mustaches.

Tascheira grinned and shrugged his shoulders and said, "See? My little cartoons. My Thousand."

I stared at him; the Tascheira I knew wasn't crazy. He just smiled pleasantly up at me and reached for his peculiar notepad. "Don't you have some practicing to do?"

❖

Why not? Two years ago a cable had arrived from the great Japanese flutist Akira Tanaka. An Italian record company called Black Saint would sponsor us, an American jazz band, fronted by a white man, to play in Japan. "Why not?" said the response coauthored by me and Howard D. and Billy Bo Brummel. Big Al couldn't come.

The night before our train ride from Kyoto to Hiroshima, Billy Bo had gone to his room, homesick, to call his wife, and Akira, Howard and I stayed up drinking sake. Sometime during the night the sake got cold, ran out, and we became morose, discussing what we all regarded as the inevitability of nuclear destruction in our lifetimes. Finally the three of us fell silent, a run-down music box, a slow ritard: Howard, whose pouchy face made him look twenty years older and forty years sadder than he felt when he didn't feel sad, who never spoke much even when spoken to; Akira, staring down and away, slowly shaking his head; and me, scratching the itches I'd developed from living in my clothes: the three of us silent but unwilling to be alone in sleep, until the sun cast bars of light and dark on our faces through the venetian blinds. Then we roused Billy Bo in the hopes that he would cheer us up, which he accomplished by chasing us out of his room and down the hall in his boxer shorts.

The next day Akira took us to the place where, between the forks of the placid Ota River, Peace Park nestled in its shelter of tall evergreens. On the far side of the river, in a residential neighborhood, we stopped at a small statue of a turtle that supported a narrow black tablet, about fifteen feet tall, with a few characters in gold. "This is the monument to the many Koreans who died in the bomb," said Akira. "They are bitter that it is not allowed in the park. That in death they remain—is this the phrase?—second-class citizens."

"The phrase," said Billy Bo, "is niggers."

We crossed a small stone footbridge, and the Atom Dome came into sight, hovering ghostly to the north, the curved and rusted metal bones of its frame visible no matter where we stood within the park. In a moat at the end of a walkway leading from the mouth of the museum stood a sculpture of a rainbow ten or fifteen feet deep, a tunnel really. The placard, in Japanese, German, French and English, explained that it represented peace.

"So many symbols," shrugged Akira. "We will catch a taxi now, OK? I want to show you something."

After a short ride we got out at the foot of an enormous apartment complex, dozens of twenty-story buildings that, despite their concrete modernity, were old beyond their years. Many of the closely packed windows were curtained by newspapers.

Howard nodded and said, "Projects."

"The Moto Machi Apartments," said Akira. "Not part of the usual tour."

We entered a square courtyard ringed with wooden benches. Sitting singly on the ends of the benches were perhaps a hundred old people. A few flowers grew in small rectangles of dirt. A man walked near us in the short slow steps of the aged, began coughing from some place deep inside him, dropped his cane, and started bending very slowly. I handed him the cane, and he took it without acknowledgement. A newspaper slipped from the fingers of a woman on a bench and fell outspread in her lap. She continued to stare ahead as if still reading.

"Howard," said Billy Bo, handing him the monogrammed handkerchief from his breast pocket and putting an arm around the taller man's shoulders. "I'm afraid you're just a regular wet rag today."

"And history," said Howard, blowing his nose, his luminous eyes showing above the handkerchief, "history just gave me a squeeze."

Afterward Howard and Akira went off together and did not return until we were halfway through the sound check in BunkaKaikan Hall. It was unlike Howard to be a minute late for anything—a gig, a rehearsal, lunch. When they finally arrived, out of breath, Akira raised a hand to deflect questions. "I was giving him a Japanese lesson."

Our concert opener, "A.M." (After Mingus), elicited a great washing ovation from a generous audience, and Howard D., the same Howard D. who was so quiet Bo called him Marcel Marceau or M & M, lay his bass on the stage and stepped to the mike.

"We visited Peace Park today," he said, and repeating himself carefully in Japanese, "*Watashi tachi wa kyō Heiwa Koen e ikimashita.*" His deep voice rang out in the hushed concert hall, and for the first time I realized what power it held. "In this time, we are all Japanese." He took a deep breath and closed his eyes as if about to dive into water. "*Ima, kono . . .*"

"*Konotoki,*" prompted Akira.

"*Ima, konotoki, wareware wa mina Nipponjin da.*" Howard bowed, hands at his sides, and turned back to us.

"*Ichi, ni, san, shi,*" Howard counted, and we were off into his lovely tribute "Dolphy Dauphin." I pointed to Howard for a solo, but he held up eight fingers to Billy Bo, who responded melodically with mallets and brushes, trading eight measures for eight of Howard's as Akira and I took turns comping softly behind them. I played breathy slow-tolling notes for Billy Bo and Akira slipped back and forth between pure flute tones and half-vocalizations as Howard bowed the highest warm-cello reaches of the bass, holstering the bow to punctuate the long lines of his thoughts with ringing octave harmonics.

Together flute and bass made a single unearthly instrument.

After the concert Howard was mobbed. There he stood, a lone black face floating above fifty roiling heads talking Japanese with great emotion and rapidity. All he could do was turn his stone-serious face from one to another, nodding as if he understood, and sign things thrust at him.

An old woman hung patiently back until the gathering around Howard loosened. Despite her Western wear, there was something old-world ceremonial about the way she approached to a distance of five feet, and stopped there.

"I . . . am," she said slowly. "Shoko Connery."

Howard bowed. "Howard Derrick."

"Yes," she said, slipping a bulky electronic Seiko watch from the thin bones of her wrist. She held it out at arm's length to Howard, who stood rooted, pleading with his eyes.

"It is a good enough watch," she said roughly, stepping forward to seize his arm and stretch the band over his knuckles. Howard smiled at it and bent to kiss the woman's forehead.

She sniffed, wrinkling up her cat-face in distaste. "Your breezes are poison with hunger. You will come to eat."

There was no refusing the old lady, at least not for Howard. He glanced around at the rest of us to ask if we were included in her invitation. She looked me up and down, blinking as if I was some sort of pachyderm that presented special feeding requirements, then began to walk away, certain that we were following.

In the dark safe streets we made a strange group, a tall young Japanese man, two blacks and a gangling white, spearheaded by an aged woman, tiny but erect, who walked at a pace that kept all of us busy. At an open-air stand, similar to the Korean grocery stores in New York with half of the goods outside and half inside, she filled lunch-sized paper bags with white onions, scallions, snow peas, celery, bok choy, garlic and several vegetables I'd never seen before, her fingers picking with a quick sureness through the bins.

I went to the tiny flower booth next door. Communicating in mime, the girl made suggestions and arranged the bouquet. The old woman was emerging from the vegetable stand with Howard and Tanaka, who carried the bags. She took my arm and bent the flowers toward her to smell them. "I think those are very pretty."

Shoko Connery lived in a squat modern wooden house. The door was unlocked, and she pushed inside, snapping on a light. She moved to a household shrine set back into the wall, pulled open the black lacquered door frame and switched on two light bulbs behind gold screens. Three golden steps receded to the rear: a small standing Buddha, gaunt and robed, seemed about to descend to the step below, where three thin black tablets, tiny versions of the one in the Korean memorial, stood on pedestals; flanking a pair of small vases on the bottom stair were sticks of incense and two candles, and Shoko Connery struck a match and lit them. She turned to take the flowers from me, putting a few in the vases. She handed the flowers back and rang a small brass bell in the center of the bottom step. She knelt on a square cushion, closed her eyes and bent her head toward the prayer-steeple of her hands. On the wall above the shrine a large sepia-toned photograph of a rather homely white man, with wavy light hair and large ears, looked down on the room.

The living room was a mixture of old and new Japan: a row of Kabuki masks variously leered and cowered and challenged from a high shelf, amid framed watercolors depicting flowers, an assortment of brown leather books and porcelain vases. On a Sony Trinitron TV sat a triptych of color photos of three Eurasian adults in early middle age, and nine smaller pictures of children trailing off to one side like ducklings swimming after their mother.

Leaving the shrine door open, Shoko Connery arose. She went into the large kitchen and came out with a Sabatier chef's knife. "That where I pray is called a *butsudan*," she said. "It is a home for the dead within the home of the living." She shook the flowers free of water, wrapped them in brown paper towels, gently squeezing, set them on a cutting board and brought the knife down, severing all but a few inches of their stems. An involuntary syllable came out of me. She removed an oversized volume bound in flaking leather from a shelf, laid it open on the table, dipped a calligraphy brush in an ink pot and wrote three characters on a blank page. "Now we have only to wait until the ink is dries," she said, arranging the flowers on the page and shutting the heavy volume with a soft thud. "It is easy," she said, "to preserve flowers."

She went to the kitchen sink and began rinsing the cutting board and vegetables. "You honored us today with your music." She turned to Tanaka. "Did I say that right? I have trouble with their tenses." He nodded. "But it is what you say in between the ... musics that is ..." Her hands groped through the air.

"Important?" said Tanaka. "*Kichō dawa?*"

"*Kichō dawa*, yes." She brought the vegetables, a dozen stacked bowls and the cutting board to the table, sat down and began cutting the celery on a bias, the knife chock-chock-chocking uptempo. Howard sat down across from her. "As you say today," she told him, "It could happen again." She picked up the celery in cupped hands, dropped it into a bowl and pulled the bok choy toward her. "And if it happen now," she said, trimming the edges, "it happen to all the whole world." Howard nodded. "I am a lucky woman. I have live to be so old that I must sit down to prepare your meal. That was my husband," she said, pointing to the picture on the wall. "He was never lucky. He came here from Scotland to study our old art and he met a young Japanese girl. Got into trouble, is that how you say it?"

Billy Bo sat down grinning. "That's *exactly* how."

"He made me pregnant so we get marry," she said bluntly. "Oh, it was a big trouble in my family." She picked up a double handful of carrot disks and put them into another bowl. "But we were happy two. He teach me English I speak like my mouth so full of rice, and we have five years together. August nineteen hundred and forty-five years, the kids and me, we go off to my mother's house. In Osaka. My husband usually come with us for these visit, but this time he stay behind to write article about landscape painting. He was a good man, but never lucky. You see? I am almost done cutting."

"Your husband . . . ?" asked Tanaka.

"As he say today, in the great fire. And after it happen, the city more full of yūrei than human being. So many I could not choose which one was my husband. So many yūrei," she said as Tanaka nodded. But she waved her hand impatiently toward the rest of us, staring at him. "*Imi o oshiete agensai*," she said.

"Yūrei means a ghost," Tanaka told us. "But our language recognizes more than one kind of ghost. A yūrei . . . is a ghost who flies or walks. He wanders. He is a ghost who has no home. If a man dies suddenly or is wrongly killed he becomes a yūrei. At certain bridges and old city gates there are said to be yūrei from ancient times. I have heard about the yūrei of Hiroshima and Nagasaki."

"Thousand-year yūrei," said the woman, waving a dismissive hand. "I am an old wife but I would not tell such thing. But the yūrei in Hiroshima"—she stopped cutting and looked at each of us in succession—"I have heard them myself. They were full of questions. Then they go away, and so I say there are no thousand-year yūrei. They go away, and that is why many who live go batty. They miss the yūrei."

"Batty?" said Tanaka.

She smiled. "Did I say that to you? Yes, *kichigai to iu imi desu*, my husband say that to me. He call me his batty bride. The he kiss on my nose. He give me very much funny kind of love. I would not have trade him for a serious kind." And we watched her in silence as, blinking, she reduced a knob of ginger to matchsticks.

"My kids still alive. Three. You see them on the TV. The boy is forty-two year. He go to Washington State and win award in school. He work on airplane for your government and send me too many dollar. The middle girl is only one year smaller than her brother. And my baby, she give me grandchildren, each year another grandchildren." She smiled. "In America you have Catholic? She"—waving a thumb over her shoulder like a truck driver—"is like a Catholic."

She took two of the bowls to the counter next to the

modern gas stove, and Billy Bo and Howard carried the rest. She brought two woks to the stove, where she mounted a broad wooden footstool and poured a few tablespoons of oil into each wok from a large can.

Standing on the stool, she turned the heat to maximum and overturned the chopped vegetables bowl by bowl into the woks. "For this one"—she stuck out her spatula at me—"the *stove* need to be put on a chair."

Soon the guests were seated around the table before steaming plates. At my place was a huge oval serving platter with at least five pounds of stir-fried vegetables on it. "This how much I make for my six healthy grandchild. I think enough for you?" She came to the table with her own plate and chopsticks for everyone. "Now we say grace, OK? like my husband teach me. Maybe I do not believe his God, but it make sense to do anyway. You speak so well," she said to Horward, "you say in Japanese and then in English."

The rest of us turned, unable to suppress grins as Howard's face darkened in embarrassment. "I don't speak Japanese," he said. "Only the few words you heard me say today."

"Oh." The old woman smiled. "I am sorry to you. You say in only English then."

Howard D. put his napkin in his lap and closed his eyes. He didn't seem to know if he was supposed to fold his hands flat or set them in a praying position, so he compromised by resting an open hand on a loosely clenched fist. "I want You to be listening to me now. I'm saying grace for Mrs. Shoko Connery and my friends, so *my* past behavior is out of the question." He cleared his throat. "We are very grateful to be here with each other and we thank You for the food we are about to eat. I bet Your mouth is watering. May You keep us all healthy and look down one day and see this lady making a meal such as this for her great-grandchildren. May You make it happen."

✧

I was ready to play my second and, as it turned out, my final Homestead concert. I had soggily conceived of it as some kind of suite for the working man. There was a plaintive first movement, a growing-resolve middle movement and an explosive finale in which I got each long cafeteria table singing apparently unrelated three-note rounds while I played a unifying theme. The idea was that the audience would have a sense of participating in the creation of the melodic solution to a problem posed by the rounds.

Through it all Tascheira played Kibbitzer King once again, grinning and gabbing and skittering through the room and gesticulating at me and distributing leaves from his little pad everywhere he stopped in the crowd. The guards homed in as soon as they saw paper, but Gary just smiled and showed them the cartoons he was handing out. They looked and rolled their eyes at each other and left him alone, a big happy kid giving everyone his dumb drawings. Afterward, he handed me the last sheet from his pad. On the back, in rococo-loopy lettering, it said: "*Friday Lunch Concerts Brought to You by Gary Tascheira*."

I stood flipping the scrap of paper around in my hands. "Oh yeah, I wrote that on all of them," he said. "A real collector's item someday, I bet. My little cartoons."

Outside, across the river, fumes began to rise from Wolf's unfinished sewage plant: sulphur, rotten eggs; shit, not coal, shit. Raked off by miners, hauled off by miners from the holding tank, burned by miners, the smell got up your nostrils and clung there, nested in your hair, permeated your clothes, sheets and blankets, inflected the tastes of foods, and did not go away during those last few days, not when you slept, not when you awoke, nor for a moment. It was as if Homestead had already started to stink, in anticipation of being dead.

# 12 ☀ ••• — — — •••

After my first night with Julia, there was a next, and a
next, until her roommate finally stopped asking and
found another place to sleep. Soon I'd moved in almost
everything of mine but, for some reason, the saxophone.
It is time, past time, to visit Wolf.

Reflexively I try Julia's key, discover my mistake and
use the right one. Wolf has overturned his mattress and
is in the act of stuffing *America: The Sherman & Sherman Guide* into a neat slit along the underside seam.
Evidence of guilt is everywhere: my Swiss Army knife
open to the fat blade; cotton batting speckling Wolf's
hair, strewn over the floor, floating lightly down in the
air. But unpanicked Wolf knows me by sound and, as he
would have me believe, by my smell. For, head slightly
raised, he is sniffing the air.

"The fair and blood-engorged Romeomeo!" he declaims. "O flesh, how art thou fishified!"

It's been weeks since I've been in the same small
room with Wolf, but the constant screen of irritation

through which I view his every tic and gesture turns on instantly like a TV with a picture of nothing but static.

"You're hiding that book," I state. Only dry facts will do. "Why are you hiding that book?"

"Hark," says Wolf, sniff-snorting again, "and snark, 'tis he! He speaks, and how he reeks." And he is placidly combing the floor for bits of cotton fluff.

One of his worst qualities, it is suddenly apparent to me, is his way of avoiding a question. We've spoken a dozen words to each other and already my cheeks are flushed and I'm in a state where I am subject to alternating desires to burst into tears and break things, particularly parts of Wolf.

"So," I say. "What's with the book?"

"Lock the door," he says, nodding at it.

I turn the lock. "The book, Wolf. What are you doing with it?"

"The book?" he echoes. "Simple. I have stuffed it into this mattress."

"Why?" I ask, my lips grimacing over clenched teeth.

"My back," says Wolf. "The mattress was too soft."

I roll heavily onto my own bare bed and watch him. Only my father, I've often reflected, had this power to upset me so easily. "Talk to me, Wolf."

"Well," he begins, "pi equals 3.14159265, and the rain in Spain falls mainly—"

"Wolf. About the book."

His jaw snaps shut. "No dice, Romeosky."

Only my father. My father and Wolf. And Wolf, who sits cross-legged on the floor beside me, meticulously working through his hair and adding the white bits to a pile in front of him. And Wolf, who is at once as frustrating as a father and as infuriating as a child.

I close my eyes. I will begin again with him. Like my father and I used to do if we had an argument: "Good morning," we'd say, even if it was neither good nor morning. "Look," I begin. "You explained the whole thing about the guy who owned that book . . . Dunster. But you never told me why he's so important to you. And remember—you told me to ask you about the book someday."

"Wrong day," says Wolf.

I get up and open the door, slamming it with all my strength. I step back into the room. "How do *you* like it?"

"Oh, a lot," says Wolf with phony voluble geniality. "It's great, really neat, uh-*huh*, enjoy it, jeez, wow, thanks and hey—thanks again for asking." Wolf has been talking to me like this for a while now, at least since I moved in with Julia; I'll see him in the halls, say hello and get this forty-five-rpm chipmunkery out of him. "Gee. Great. Wow," he'll say.

"Lock the door," he breaks in on himself in a coarse voice an octave lower. Donning his glasses, and with them that familiar aspect of geriatric superiority, he watches me closely, as if focusing on something with much finer detail than a human face. "Sit down."

I do.

"You may have noticed," he begins, picking through his words—and an image flashes into my mind of the rough-delicate way he took the uneven terrain in the darkness outside Harrisburg—"that it's been getting a little hot around here."

He's watching me so carefully, with such an air of cynicism, that I am impaled on a sudden fear of betraying false innocence. Never a good actor, and always worst when not acting at all, I say, "I don't know what you're talking about."

Wolf stands up immediately and paces the room, hands in pockets, slowing to a halt in front of me. "One of us is an idiot."

"I'm at a great disadvantage," I tell him. "I'm so innocent I don't even know what it is I'm supposed to be innocent of."

"Look," says Wolf, putting a foot on my bed and leaning down toward me onto his knee. "There *is* something going on in Production. That much we know."

"Yeah. A bunch of intelligent humans are being forced to do disgusting and unhealthy work."

Wolf whacks his knee sharply. "That's my Max, the pathological whiner." Good to see I annoy him as much as he does me. "But what's going down across the river is more than that. We're pretty sure there's some kinda plot bein hatched."

"A plot."

His near hand wiggles vaguely in front of my face. "To seize control, pull a coup or just escape . . . We're not sure what."

I stare at him as he goes to the desk, rummages around in the wide drawer, selects a pair of scissors, a pack of needles, a spool of white thread, and sits down again by his mattress. "Why are you telling me this?"

After a couple of passes, Wolf successfully threads the needle. "Like I said, one of us is an idiot, and I'm beginning to think it's me." He knots the thread and begins sewing the seam. "They've been telling me, Keep an eye on him—that's you, Debris—He knows something, and I've been telling them all along, No, no, no, he's too dumb."

"Thanks."

"God's truth," says Wolf, holding up two Boy Scout-oath fingers. "Who do you think planted the land mine that about danced my legs out from under me? A couple of miners who escaped months ago. So," and he goes back to his stitchwork, "Planning is worried. Whenever two people pass more than a couple of words, a guard is there. Wherever three people are together, quiet or not, a guard is there. Wherever three people are together, quiet or not, a guard is there. They even tried bugging the mines and barracks but some mechanical genius gummed up the system. They don't let anybody write anything down."

"I didn't know that."

He smacks his leg. "Faygilah, you are a miracle of nature. You're not just a little slow. You're so dumb you could make an onion cry. Tell me: what else don't you know."

"What the hell they think *I* have to do with all this."

"Think about it a minute," he says, smiling and shaking his head slowly, "if that doesn't lay waste to your attention span. Who is the only person who's addressed just about every single miner?"

"I don't address *anybody* down there. *They* think I'm a spy or something."

"Nonverbal communications," says Wolf.

"What, body language? Guilty eyebrows?"

Wolf cuts the thread from the needle, ties it off, and lets the finished mattress whap back to the bed. "Guilty music."

"*Music?*"

"Dot-dot-dot dash-dash-dash dot-dot-dot. Just a bunch of tapping, right? But it spells SOS. Music's got a leg up on Morse code—rhythms *and* notes."

"Me?" I'm slow on the uptake. "They think I'm sending out coded messages with my saxophone?"

Wolf says nothing, rocking back on his heels, shrugging, smiling benevolently, spreading his hands.

"It's not me or you, Wolf. They're crazy."

He shoves his hands into his pockets. "It's a possibility, got to admit it. That's why I hid the book. Cause I figure what's in it is my business exclusively. Should things get"—he clears his throat—"uneasy around here." He shakes his downcast head. "Such a shame if anything happens before my plant is finished." Wolf turns away sharply and his voice takes on a removed sound. "That doesn't mean I buy your story or I'm on your side. I'm on *my* side."

"Your side being infinitely preferable to everyone else's."

His back shrugs. "My side being too small to share."

"Generous bastard. When you're done with your sandwich, be sure to share your Saran Wrap with me."

"I'm exactly as generous as I can afford to be."

"He said as he took a quarter from the blind man's cup."

"You're the blind man!" Wolf turns on me, pointing so hard it practically hurts. "I try to tell you but you just don't want to see what's happening. I used to call you an albatross but what you really are is an ostrich. A fucking *ostrich*." His eyes slip down to my crotch. "A *fucking* ostrich. 'Everything's OK long as I got my head buried.'"

"Shit Wolf, what's the story? Women are dangerous?"

"Not 'women,'" he says.

"What's that supposed to mean?"

His hand rises to his chest, index finger right-angling at me. "That while you are jazzing fair Juliet for joy," he says, coming closer until the tip of his finger rests against my nose, "she's pumping *you* for information."

✻

That was the weekend of the Happy Hour Raid. Some fifty or sixty men and women in mining overalls stormed the town from the rear. They had the element of surprise, two tommy guns and chutzpah. When they were done they had more: they raided the ammunition dump.

Julia and I, on her bed with Homestead's only Scrabble board, heard some distant voices, and then a dim popping from the Yard on the far side of the building. We began dressing to see what was going on. If Julia was a spy, I'd decided, I could stand the way she spied. I had one shoe on when a planner whom I recognized as some kind of mucky-muck burst into the room, without knocking but with a gun.

"I'm convinced he doesn't know anything," Julia reported with an air of instant judiciousness, as if she'd been grilling me relentlessly.

I was held in her room for about four hours, in the shadow of the giant defunct punch press. They asked me repeatedly what I had heard in Production. Nothing, I answered honestly, unable to keep my eyes from shifting periodically to the Scrabble board. I could make Y-A-R-A-K, for thirty-two points, with the Y on Double Letter and the R on Double Word. More men filed in and repeated the same questions; I tried to ruffle the smooth surface of my practiced answers with throat clearings and apparent thought.

Soon they shifted focus to whether I had ever seen "written matter" distributed by Gary Tascheira. Harry Sawyer and the bullhorn man (who sat down too near the Scrabble game and upset all the tiles) spoke to me now for the first time since my arrival. It seemed my ex-foreman was prominent among those whose whereabouts were now unknown. They were certain he had passed notes of some kind, but no copies existed in Production. Could I supply a copy? No, I said, but they searched me and my belongings anyway.

Only now did Sawyer fill me in. It had begun when a few miners staged a brawl in a bathroom on the second floor of one of the barracks. The bucks rushed in to break it up and upon emerging again were ambushed by all sixty miners who lived on the second floor. Aided by staged disturbances throughout the barracks, the sixty miners snuck out the back of the compound and, instead of approaching over the heavily guarded Monongahela bridge, had gone all the way around to the Cyclone fence at the main entrance. They sank Choppers into the guards' skulls; ten men with the two captured tommy guns went prowling along the top of the city wall, where they covered the rest, who charged the ammunition dump. That was when Julia and I had heard the shooting: the men with the tommy guns were killed but replaced. The ammunition dump was taken, and all manner of explosives were hurled and fired from the doors and windows—grenades, sticks of dynamite, bazooka shells. It was a standoff: the miners couldn't come out, and the bucks couldn't get in.

Finally a single M-1 tank rolled majestically through the wooden wall of the dump, bringing down the roof and, after careening and firing erratically in the Yard, got control of itself and headed for the main entrance at its top speed of forty-two miles per hour, snapping the heavy wire of the Cyclone fence like vermicelli, the gun turret facing rearward and lobbing shells back into the Yard. The bucks rushed into the ammunition dump and searched the wreckage. To their surprise, they found nobody. All in all thirty bucks and fifty miners were dead. Gary Tascheira, eight or ten other survivors, some serious explosives and an unknown number of machine guns were all squashed together in that tank, which rolled out the entrance pursued by nobody and off into the night.

As Sawyer slowly, methodically told the story, sorting it out for himself as he spoke, sitting on the edge of Julia's bed and smoking one after another of the cigarettes that were so rare in Homestead, the door kept opening and uniformed men streamed through to the bullhorn man, who was furiously receiving information (bits of paper were found in the feces of all the miners who had died in the battle) and giving orders, one of which that I be put under "house arrest," which entailed stationing one soldier outside the door and another—

Kenny, the dogface, as it turned out—under the window. It would not be so bad, Sawyer reassured me; I would have privacy within the room and I could move about the compound under armed escort.

I returned to my old room that night. When the guards left me at the door I dug Wolf's annotated volume *America* from the innards of his mattress and pulled out the small page of penciled cartoons I had hidden at page 123. I stared fruitlessly at fifty-five tiny caricatures of boys, girls, men and women. Why did some of them have eyelashes? Why were some shown in profile? What did cigarettes mean? Never much good at this kind of game, I could not break the code. Tascheira and his little cartoons. He had called them his "Thousand." I pictured him smashed in at the controls of the tank, bumped and crowded and jostled by eight or nine other men in a space designed for two—it had to have been him, no one else could have got the complicated machine under control so quickly. Bald Gary Tascheira. I wished I had recognized my Garibaldi when I saw him.

# 13 ☀ Don't Let It Touch the Ground

Since the Happy Hour Raid it has become general knowledge that something big, something *transforming* will happen soon to Homestead, and everyone has reacted in one of two ways: either to do too much and laugh too often, to become larger and louder and faster than life, as if each action is something you can put away and the more you deposit the more you get back when accounts come due; or the opposite, to do less and less in the fatalistic conviction that nothing will make a difference, that trying to affect events is like waving a paper fan at a tornado.

One reaction or the other: there are no in-betweens. In the halls some people talk to themselves and others talk to no one at all. In the cafeteria, half of the crowd excitedly yaps about unexciting topics, the decline in coal output or plans to rebuild the ammunition dump, while the other half says nothing, inertly staring, bringing forks to mouths, forks to mouths. You get the feeling they'll keep doing it even after their plates are empty. On the bridge a buck went bananas, shot three hundred bullets straight up into the air, while his partner stood slack-jawed, not even watching. Half of Homestead has become A and the other half Z, and none of us remember the rest of the alphabet.

So watch us now, the tall skinny man with his pedal to the floorboard and the tall pretty woman with her brakes on and her battery down to zero. He's up on his feet gabbing, and gesturing when he feels it appropriate, which is far too often, walking around and around in a small room with two beds, a desk and a punch press, going fast and getting nowhere; and she's on her back on the edge of her bed, one knee up, an arm hanging down, the fingers curling indolently up from the floor.

"I still don't see how we did it," I am telling Julia. "It was like God threw the Book of Regulations at our family: you can have exactly two children, one boy, one girl, a mid-sized car and a mid-sized dog. The dad has to work at a job he doesn't like and the mom has to be a housewife. You get one black-and-white TV, one monaural record player and one ticky-tacky house in a smog-ridden suburb. Now go out and be happy."

"Were you?" Her face is turned slightly toward me.

"We were dumb enough to be happy. No, not dumb but simple, simply pleased. We used to play this game, what we did was throw a balloon into the air and all of us try to tap it back up before it hit the ground. That was the whole game. You know what we called it?"

"What," asks Julia flatly.

"Don't Let It Touch the Ground."

"And what happened if you did let it touch the ground?"

The question surprises me. "I don't remember. We lost, I guess."

"*Who* lost?" I can't decide whether she sounds just bored or bored and slightly annoyed.

"We did; all of us."

"Then what did you do?" Just bored.

"Jesus, I don't know. We probably just started over."

Julia nods slowly. "Dumb *was* the right word."

I laugh. "We were idiots! We loved that game—it kept us going for an hour at a time. You know, there's no reason . . ."

"What?" Julia gives a little jolt, awakened by the sudden intention in my tone.

"We could play it here. We could." I begin looking around the room.

"It won't work," says Julia, sitting up. "We're not six years old and it's not 1959. Besides, we don't have any balloons."

"Oh yes we do," I say, moving toward the desk, all boyish enthusiasm, maybe enough for two. "We have some great balloons."

"*Max*," she says with a kind of passive urgency.

"Shit." I'm rummaging through the famous contraceptives drawer. "Where are all those rubbers?"

"Sit down, Max." Julia's voice, hard-edged, ungiving, is a shock. I sit down on the other bed. She is cooler and more angular than ever, sharpness without respite, and her level, composed eyes spell out a slow, giant joke, not necessarily funny, that takes me a full minute (There's this man. His wife's on a trip and he takes another woman home. No contraceptives. They decide to use the wife's diaphragm. It's gone. "How about that?" the man chuckles. "She must not trust me") to get.

"Oh shit, Julia."

We stare at each other. She gets up and sits next to me. "What do you want me to say? I still like you very much. I never stopped."

"I believe that," I mouth, my voice squeaking along. Her earnest face is down and toward me as if I'm a puzzle to her. I start crying out of sheer bottled-upedness. She's stroking my head, misinterpreting, and it's insufferable, claustrophobic.

I'm on my feet suddenly, taking short steps and giving sharp small kicks to low objects in the room. Another man and I never thought to think of it. Maybe more than one other man. (My heavy boot against the base of the defunct punch press: a warm dull pain.) Of course more than one. Dumb *is* the right word.

"Max, come here, will you?" Her voice is small and distant.

I need to lie down. I do, on the edge of her bed, and she wedges her legs under my head.

"You mad, is that it?" she says, spreading her fingers through my hair.

"Mad." The word turns awkwardly in my mouth. My mind blanks and a long time goes by before she speaks.

"I'll tell who he is if you want." Nothing will come out of my mouth, so she says, "I don't really care about him."

"Them," I say.

Finally, in a voice muffled by caution, she gives up the syllable. "Them."

There is a long silence. "Julia, tell me why."

"You've seen why. We came here from Washington in flat-bed trailers. Everything was destroyed—everything. None of us had parents anymore, none of us had friends. We just came up out of the shelter and everything was gone." She's been squeezing my head in a tighter and tighter grip until her hands are cupped over my ears, muffling her voice. "I needed anything I could get, do you understand?"

I nod, prying her hands loose and moving them down to my cheeks.

"They were *there*. They held me and I held on to them because they were all I had."

"And now?" I ask.

"And now I'm supposed to tell them I've found my one and only and if they get lonely at night they can just go order an inflatable doll from central supply?"

Is that turkey-necked geezer who runs Construction —Sitwell or Shitwell? Is that who you're fucking? Do you audition during lunch hour? Or do you just go Eeny, meeny, miney, moe? What the fuck are you talking about? I thought I *knew* you."

"Don't say that," she says, her face bittering up. "You know me." Tears fall from her eyes to my cheek.

"Julia." Sitting up, smearing the wetness outward across her temples with my thumbs, I state the obvious in a slow obvious voice. "I'm not sure how well this is going to work out."

"Work out!" She wriggles her head out of my grasp, her face cruelly incredulous. "Work out into *what*? A little family in Buena Park playing Don't Let It Touch the Ground? We can't—there's no sperm, no egg and no

Buena Park." She puts both hands on my chest and looks straight at me. "Max, I'm giving you all I have left. I'm loving you the best I can."

My mouth purses into a nasty smile. "First among equals."

Crack! shock, then sting—she's slapped my face. And tries to do it again; I catch her wrist. Her other hand comes up, balled into a fist, but I have it too.

"*What do you want*?" she cries, her voice shaking with the struggle to get free.

I try to speak with dignity, as if it's no great effort to restrain her. "I'm not going to sound stupid."

And she's laughing, not an expansive laughter that reaches out to me, but a percolating one that bubbles up behind a closed mouth. I let her go.

"All right." My eyes are blurred up; she must've missed, hit my nose. "Anything to amuse. Love. Love or whatever we can manage with each other. A fuck of a lot more than what you think we can."

She straightens up suddenly, her features knitted tight with concern, as if she's just discovered I have a brain tumor. "Max. Your face."

There's blood everywhere, a smear on my chin, great blots on the sheet. It's from my nose.

"Here, lie down." She goes to the sink, returns with a wet paper towel, slips her leg under my head and presses the towel against my nose.

"Julia, you understand what I mean?" There's a pathetic nasality in my voice as I look up at her.

"Shh," she says, laughing lightly, wiping my nose, daubing at my chin. "Shh."

"I just want to know if—"

"Shhhh."

And that must be the way we fall asleep, for you do fall asleep after fighting as after fucking, except that at some point she slips out from under and into bed beside me. I wake up sometime in the middle of the night and there's a little bit of moon coming in the window. She's curled up in bed next to me, naked, trusting, her face the only part of her showing, her cheekbones softened by sleep, her cheeks smooth and rounded. It's how she must have looked when she was sixteen.

※

I dream of a ride in the old P.O.P. Amusement Park that I haven't thought of in twenty years. Everyone stood in a big round room that slowly began to rotate, picking up speed until the floor, made of interfitting leaves like a camera diaphragm, receded until nothing supported the people except centrifugal force.

Julia and I and a number of others are there on that machine, amazed, not touching one another, spinning, spinning and spinning. The bottom's dropped out but we're still standing.

# 14 ❋ Silas Wain and Little Bill

The efforts of the Homesteaders over the late morning and early afternoon of July 6, 1892, to wipe out the invaders were certainly not comical for the participants, least of all for the Pinkertons trapped in the *Monongahela* and the *Iron Mountain* (who early in the morning had begun sending out men with white flags, but since both flag and man were shot down each time, had discontinued the practice by noon). Described afterward, summarized and compressed, the Homestead struggle leaves in the mind a succession of extreme images, exaggerated poses struck in freeze-frame, an inevitably comic residue.

The main thing that occurred to the workers—and recurred, and recurred, with astonishing ingeniousness—was to set the barges on fire. First they piled lumber on a large wooden raft, soaked it with gasoline and set it aflame and adrift directly upstream of the landing. Water soaked in, however, and only a sputtering mass reached the Pinkertons. The workers then commandeered the town fire truck, filled the pump with oil and doused the barges. But the oil turned out not to be flammable.

In the local office of the Amalgamated Association cooler heads hovered over the telegraph receiver for word from the front, and planned ways to induce the men to accept a Pinkerton surrender. Good news at noon: the governor had refused the sheriff's urgent request for the state militia.

Back at the landing, the *Little Bill* had returned, festooned from bow to stern with tricolored bunting and dozens of American flags. Captain Rodgers had evidently figured that the men of Homestead would not dare fire upon Old Glory.

They dared. The *Little Bill*'s cabin was summarily and unpatriotically deglassed, and the man at the ship's wheel had gone from standing to supine. That man was good Captain Rodgers, wiser but still unable to steer a boat without seeing where it was supposed to be going. The *Little Bill* turned blind circles in the shallow water.

The strikers, doggedly returning to their schemes of immolation, opened up a natural-gas main at the landing, enveloping the *Iron Mountain*. Fourth of July rockets fired at the barge caused only a harmless explosion.

The inexhaustible Homesteaders hit upon one final way to burn the barges. A railroad freight shuttle ran from high up the slope behind the Homestead Works down to the water exactly where the *Iron Mountain* and the *Monongahela* lay at bay. The workers loaded the train car high with lumber and barrels of gasoline and sent it down the hill, flames leaping a hundred feet into the air. Thousands of women and children screamed soprano approval; the sharpshooters of Homestead, kneeling behind piles of I beams, put aside their rifles and watched the train of fire whirl down the incline; and the brawny Pinkertons uttered a low groan. But for all its momentum, the car stuck in the thick mud of the riverbank, and damaged only the *Little Bill*, still helplessly demonstrating its turning radius at water's edge.

The Pinkertons watched in dismay as the charred *Little Bill* left the scene, and though it is written in old books that several committed suicide by jumping ship, more likely they were trying a difficult escape. A captain stopped the exodus by threatening to blow out the brains of the next man who tried it.

About this time the residents of Homestead discovered that the town armory contained a small cannon; like many of their weapons, the twenty-pounder dated from the Civil War. From a difficult angle high up on the hill opposite the Works and after a good deal of inexperienced fussing, the workers finally managed to ignite the cannon, and to their astonishment the first shot took a wide swatch from the roof of the *Monongahela*. After a few uncontrollable misses, the final cannonball crossed the river and took the head clean off a young, unarmed steelworker, Silas Wain, who was merely watching from the mill yard.

# 15 ✴ X

The first blast knocks half the windows out.

Without thinking, on war-movie reflexes, I throw myself to the floor. It knocks the air out of me. "Get down!" I gasp.

Julia just stands in the middle of the room with her arms folded. We've been arguing, and this tableau is like an instant replay: me yelling, she equanimous, me whipping my arms around, she retreating into utter passivity.

*Rrrmm!* A second blast shakes my stomach as what's left of the window glass shimmies to the floor.

Julia moves to the frame and looks out. There's a quiet now, and in it I'm babbling about how dangerous it is to stand there, stand there exposed, but she only announces in a detached icy voice that sort of floats down to me, "The fall of Homestead." Her profile of mild concern in the twilit window could be that of a wife whose husband is a little late from work.

Her ungodly calm fills the room, borne on a light breeze from outside; but voices cut through, shouting in the distance, and they are answered by gunfire, and then more and more voices, hundreds of voices raised in a great cry, and my body is charged with an uncontrollable electricity.

"Christ! this is it." I'm up and taking her arm. "We're getting out *now*!"

She shakes her arm wildly but can't get free. "You're hurting me!"

I grunt, hauling her to the door, grabbing for the door-knob, throwing it open. But she snags a strong leg inside the doorjamb and yanks free in a sudden fury.

"I'll fight you," she pants, backing off, hunched low. "I'll kick you if I have to. You'll be fighting me every step of the way."

I point helplessly toward the noises. "Those are guns! Guns!"

"It's not that I don't understand," she says very clearly, as if speaking to a child. "I am refusing to go with you."

"Refusing . . . ?" I look around crazily, conjuring support from the walls. "What else can you *do*?"

She shakes her head slowly. "I can't live out there."

"We *can* survive, Julia. I did survive."

"Survive," she says, her voice receding as she fades back into the room. "I live *here*. I won't let them take everything away from me twice." She sits on the edge of a bed, just sits with her knees together and her arms hanging limply at her sides, and asks blankly, "Do you really have time for this argument?"

"They'll kill you." What I should do is knock her over the head and drag her away from this place; what I do is step in and stand awkwardly in the center of the room. "Probably all of you."

She murmurs something very quietly, and makes herself say it again. "I'm staying here."

I envision myself softly closing the door behind me, running out the back way, across the bridge, down into Pittsburgh, hiding in the sewers, working out through the suburbs, catching rats and sleeping in the dirt, and with all that a single frozen image, as if I'm not here now, not actually seeing her but must just remember, of Julia sitting alone on her bed, sealed in this room as in a crypt, very white and with a hand to her mouth. None of it has happened yet, and already it has become a memory.

I sink to the floor and crush her lower legs to my chest. "Please, Julia, please goddamn it! Please come with me."

Julia takes my hair and pulls my head gently back. She kisses my forehead. "Hurry, Max. You'll have to hurry."

I am slow getting up. "Come with me," I say.

"I can't." She smiles at me. "Goodbye, Max."

And now it's true: I'm closing the door softly behind me. My armed guards have fled. The hallway is momentarily silent, and I stand there for a second, lost between Julia's door and the faint noises of havoc, between my first day in Homestead—when I left the room I shared with Wolf, stared at the same blue linoleum—and this day. No! Her smile: too gentle. She doesn't comprehend what's going to happen. I try the door. Locked. I slam it with both fists: "You don't understand! You don't understand!" I pound and pound, but the mute dead door does not open. Something jerks free in me and I'm running crying through the bleary corridors.

The firing of guns comes muffled to me, dulled by the dreamlike quality of everything that's happened, dulled by distance: it is coming not from the back side where the miners poured over the bridge, but from the Yard around the front of the mill compound. In the Yard, in and around the ammunition dump, the showers, the chicken coop, the sewage plant, they are yelling, swarming, shooting large and small guns, and the rear seems deserted. That way!

But first a single irrational thought runs through my head: *Where will I find a saxophone out there*? And I detour to the old room. Wolf's mattress is cut up, overturned, wildly plundered. I snatch my silly instrument. Wolf? Where is Wolf? Now it's out.

Twice people come past me down the corridors, first a man in a suit and then a woman in her underwear, their legs milling, like dogs trying to change direction on a smooth surface. They have the same idea: the rear exit, out across the bridge, out across the mines, and out.

I fall behind them, I get lost in the corridors, in the

renewed screams and sounds of gunfire, in my own blind gulping fear, and finally I find the exit those two were running for, the big double door to the back of the compound, and as I run up there they are, half in the doorway, half out, shot to death and laid across each other in an X, the man in the suit and the woman who was, I remember now, whimpering, soft and high, words that made no sense.

I've never in my life seen a person who was shot. It sinks in: those guns I've been hearing. And sinks in: a massacre, a massacre. I shrink from the two corpses, scramble back through the corridors as far from that door as I can.

And finally I stand transfixed at a window in the women's barracks, staring out into the Yard. It's nothing like Tascheira's raid; these people are running pell-mell, helter-skelter, running wild through the Yard, consuming everything before them like a fire. What feeds their power, gives them strength and advantage is not their meager arsenal, nor even their multitude, but a willingness, more than a willingness, a need and passion to rip and destroy. Some still wave picks and hammers, many have guns, others have Molotov cocktails, and almost all have torches, thick stakes with a kerosene-soaked cloth wrapped around the end, the scraps of cloth burned and peeling, peeling and flying, flying and veering bright and sudden like moths aflame, torches that make them look fanatical and dangerous and numerous beyond their numbers, torches that glow in the twilight and through the billowing blackish clouds of smoke that well up everywhere in the Yard.

My body gives a sudden awful thrill: Julia! I saw her running, saw her dead. But no, that wasn't Julia, it was a woman I don't know.

Until their offensive sweeps completely across the Yard and leaves a breathing space behind it, there is nothing I can do but stand and watch the men and women who used to grunt and swear alongside me in the dark dusty tunnels, the black cathedral. Stand and watch them tear apart this city like a brittle sheet of coal.

# 16 ❋ The Hitchhiker

As I watch a man, running with a crazed jerky silent-movie athleticism, hurl a torch into the ammunition dump, pause and wait and when nothing happens, grab a torch out of another man's hands and charge into the dump, as I watch a big white-red explosion before he can get out and a scatter of smaller ones following, as I watch behind a window in the women's barracks, maybe the only intact windowpane in Homestead, standing and watching without fear as if the thin glass will protect me from the sources of the fire that lights my face, a violent satisfaction floods through me, a savage rooting interest in the men who destroy; and as the men who destroy begin to win out—for those who destroy are always stronger than those who preserve—as they set torches to the lumber pile, first one and then, frustrated by the slowness with which the great stack of wood takes to fire, hundreds of torches, hundreds of men, men living by the rule of fire that has consumed all of us, as I watch the men and women in victory and try to imagine them in peace, a queasiness weakens my legs, rising slowly and gathering momentum, jolting my heart as it goes by, sending out a shock of adrenaline to my neck, my fingers, my face. The word escape hisses in my ears.

Cars! The garage! They haven't reached it yet.

And I am running straight across the Yard as fast as I can, immediately winded, the saxophone banging against my chest as I try to draw breath. A woman in khaki appears from behind the flaming lumber pile, a nightmare figure with a tommy gun, engulfed in fire, face red and sweat-shiny.

"No, no!" I scream. "I'm a miner!" She waves me down and I press my face to the concrete. The saxophone and I are denting each other and my cheek burns. Even the ground is hot tonight. The tommy gun chatters.

"Urgh!" gurgles a voice behind me, a death more Hollywood than Hollywood. The firing stops; she was shooting at him: suit and tie. I scramble to my feet.

It's Wolf. He's fallen backward in a twisted heap, one hand clutching a shoulder and the other his stomach, a leg pinned under him at an impossible angle, his mouth a strange snarl, his eyes wide open. I scream his name into the wild air.

But a hurled torch cuts a high arc that glows hanging in the sky until it lands at my feet with a shower of sparks, and my legs are moving under me, backpedaling, turning from the sight of Wolf, jogging, running, sprinting away from him until the garage, wavering in heated air, is only a few hundred feet off. No one is around the garage, and the small side door is ajar; the guards must have left to run or fight.

It's dark inside and quieter, full of the sound of my breathing and heartbeat. I bump into a rearview mirror. The keys—I've seen them—hang in a row along the wall. I grope for them; no. I shove the side door farther open to let in light. There are all sixteen sets of keys.

The nearest jeep has a spare tire, and I grab another one leaning against a wall and toss it into the back seat. Good enough. I grab up all the key rings off the wall. Trial and error? Oh Christ, Christ, out of control. I force my shaking right hand to insert keys by locking onto it with my left. The long keys with the square head. Not *this* one. Every square-headed key on every ring fits in;

they just won't turn. Voices. Coming closer? Sounds like. I'm just dropping all the useless key rings to the floor-boards. They'll be here soon, burning, shouting, shooting. Not this one. Not this one. Damn, if I hadn't stopped for that spare tire! Not this one. There is a single key ring left in my hand. The motor turns over, god-damn, at the last second, the voices are very near, and I hear someone shout "Garage!" The motor turns over! And dies.

Bright light in the dark room—torchlight. And the motor kicks in. Voices precede the men into the garage, and now the men. No time to hike up the big door— God, make it thin enough to give! The men swarm to-ward the car as it starts, slowly, so slowly, to move.

In slow motion: the crawling car, the men, their torches, one landing in the passenger seat, the garage door giving, bending but not breaking, a hand on my left arm, slipping from my arm, wood everywhere, sunlight!

The door splinters and the jeep is rolling slowly into the Yard. Faster, goddamn it! There are men and women everywhere, falling out of the way. Please no guns. Veer-ing crazily, I toss the torch from the smoking seat beside me. There are no guns, just torches, hurled torches that fall short because the jeep is finally picking up speed as I approach the place where Wolf lies in the same grotesque position. Coming near his body, I slow down momentar-ily and pray in some way, but rifle fire starts up from somewhere and I'm forced to accelerate again.

As I pass Wolf's body one arm suddenly sticks straight up toward the sky. Some bizarre death twitch? It is a hand with one thumb protruding. Wolf is alive and Wolf wants a ride.

I screech to a halt and haul him up by the arm.

"Step on it!" he shrieks, his upper body across mine and his legs wriggling in the free air outside the car. "They're shooting at us!"

"I am!" I'm flooring it and we are going almost no-where. Clambering across me, putting a knee in my groin and able in his effort to speak only two words at a time, he says "Are you...planning to...get this...fucking thing...outta third gear?"

"Oh." And we are zipping along—no, zip-limping

along, they've hit a rear tire—but even so going much faster and soon on the road to Getthellout, the breeze drying the sweat from our faces.

"We're alive!" I shout into the wind. "They torched the garage—I saw them! And I have all the keys." I look over at him. "Wolf, how did you do that?"

He is feeling his ribs gingerly, prodding his stomach, "Ever hear of playing possum? Soon as I saw that gun I..." He's breathing with his mouth open, still winded. "Besides, I *was* hit by a bullet. Don't ever get hit by a bullet. Knocked the air right outta me."

"Knocked the *air* out of you?"

His mouth shuts with a snap. "Never mind that. What *took* you so long? I thought you'd never get a car."

"There were sixteen sets of keys, and—"

"Don't tell me. You had to try every single one."

I, a wrung dishrag, say nothing, so Wolf rolls on: "All the motherfuckin idiots in the world to choose from and I had to pick not only the dumbest but the one with the worst luck."

"No, the second-worst luck," I say. This sends him into a fury, bouncing up and down in his melted seat.

"The *worst* luck, the *worst* luck. Second-worst, shit. Did the car start on the *second* set of keys? No." It's plain at least he isn't hurt. "Oh no. For *you*, Third Gear, the car refuses to start until the very last key. You are *the* man with the single worst luck in the world."

"The second-worst luck," I insist. The hills of Homestead have become a blot in the rearview mirror on our wending course through the outskirts of Pittsburgh, where I finally stop the car behind enough of a factory wall to hide it from view. "The guy with the *worst* luck is now going to change our tire."

# III

# 1 ✸ The Mechanics

"One problem," says Wolf.

"Yeah?"

"I've never changed a tire. Always brought my car to Frank's Garage. *When* I had one, which wasn't often." He folds his arms and smiles complacently. "So I guess it's up to you."

"Wolf. *I* don't know how to change a fucking tire."

"What?"

"No. I've never owned a car. I lived in *New York*, Wolf. I've driven about twenty times in my life. I know where to put the gas in, that's about it. I don't even have a valid driver's license."

There is a long silence. "At least *that's* no problem," Wolf says.

"What?"

"The driver's license."

"I realize that. Wolf, we are in deep shit."

"Don't *say* that." He leaps from the car, goes around it rubbing his palms together, full of impotent industry.

"The first thing is to get these nuts off." He disappears beside the car. "Unhhh—! Unhhh—!"

"Wolf." Using his bare hands?

"Unhhh—! Nope, can't do it. Here, you try."

"Wolf. I am not going to try. We need a tool, a kind of four-pronged thing."

"Oh yeah, a tire iron, right?"

"Right. Besides, what do you think we're supposed to do when we get all the nuts off?"

"Don't you see, duncenik? We slide the bad tire off and put the good one on."

"With two thousand pounds sitting on top of it?"

"Oh . . . oh yeah. We need one of those things . . ."

"A jack, Wolf. We need a jack."

The trunk contains one tire iron, one copy of *Playboy* from which all the pornography has been cut out, and one empty milk carton.

"No jack, Jack," says Wolf.

"We're dead. We'll have to walk again."

"No!" It's amazing how quickly we got used to having a car. "I have an idea."

An hour later I am behind the wheel. Wolf waves me slowly forward, and I stop with the right rear tire suspended over the small ditch we've dug.

"Neat job," calls Wolf. "This'll work. I think so."

When I get out, the right rear of the car shifts its weight suddenly, slumps down into the ditch.

"Aiee!" screams Wolf. "My hands!"

Oh God. Now I've done it.

Wolf grins over the side of the car. "Just kidding. Still, I think you'd best get back in the driver's seat."

Another hour passes, full of my grumbling about the inappropriateness of practical jokes in certain situations, Wolf's cheery platitudes yelled over the back of the car concerning the necessity of keeping one's sense of humor; and then my grumbling about how long it's taking him to change a lousy tire, and his axioms, bromides, homilies and chestnuts concerning the importance of Doing The Job Right.

Finally we are both in the front seat, and the car is moving cautiously forward.

"We did a great job, a really great job, didn't we?"

says Wolf, greasy and jubilant. "That's teamwork for you. Hey now, more speed, Reed. Give it some juice, Bruce."

"Wolf, what if the battery goes dead? Or a spark plug blows out or whatever spark plugs do?"

He is crestfallen. "Or we plain run out of gas."

"Yeah. Maybe we have a hundred miles to think about it. And then we walk."

"Never," says Wolf. "I have an *investment* in this machine. "Shh! Shh!" And, joggling with the motion of the car, he assumes the posture of Rodin's *Thinker*. A ruined McDonald's passes behind him, fallen arches. After a long pause, Wolf makes his announcement. "OK. We got to cannibalize another jeep." He holds up his index finger, and one by one, each of the others. "Carry the parts around with us. Hope to fuck we can figure out what to do with them. Try to find a hose and suck gas out of other cars. Plus"—he adds his thumb—"I'm hungry."

In college, at Berkeley, I lived in the same place, walked the same streets for five years, the only time I ever held still for that long. In a variety of mental states and at all times of day and night I had seen Telegraph Avenue; I had watched health food and record stores come and go, had marked certain buildings as hangouts for wire-rimmed scholars, for sorority girls, for street people. But one day a friend gave me a lift in the back of his pickup truck and Telegraph was utterly new to me. In five years I had never seen that street by motor vehicle.

And now, from our jeep, the new but familiar landscape is transformed in the same way that, many years ago, Berkeley was. I feel an exhilaration, an impossible command, a power over terrain expressed as speed.

Like Berkeley, this is ground that I know from up close. I've lain in the dirt, sifted dirt through my fingers, run from rain, captured animals, nibbled on the bushes. I've counted my steps when my legs begrudged every inch. And now I sail over land, having transferred my brain to a superior body. If birds were made to fly, and fish to swim, then, too, man was made to drive.

We do find a hose, a full tank of gas, several blankets, a box of stale Lucky Stars cereal and the State of West

Virginia, but no jeep, and when we let the motor clunk to a halt near a little ashen town called Triadelphia, there is no other sound. Where, to paraphrase the song, have all the crickets gone?

"Well," says Wolf, rubbing his arms in the cold air. "Summer is officially over. We've eaten, such as it was. We made ourselves a fire, such as it is." He nudges the sputtering pile of chips with his black shoe and folds his arms with a certain air of finality. "What we need to ask ourselves at this point in our lives is this: What's next?"

"Sleep."

"In general."

"Oh." I shrug, take out Billy Bo's watch, due for a winding. "We go west, I guess. Maybe try to find that group Sawyer told us about—you remember?"

"Oh yes. The explorers sent out by the U.S. government to organize stragglers. The unit put together by the same folks who brought you the glories of Homestead."

The name gives me a sudden chill. "Pass me a blanket."

He does, and when I am comfortably wrapped removes his glasses from his jacket pocket. One lens is whole, the other shattered. Wolf picks the frame clean of jagged glass shards as he speaks. "So according to you, we go west, heading for the sunset on general principle. Hnh." He gives a grunt-laugh, extracting from the same pocket *America: The Sherman & Sherman Guide*. "Well, me and Mr. Ezekiel Sheridan Dunster, to whom I owe my life, incidentally, have got a few other ideas." He blows tiny glass splinters from the edges of the book, then holds it flat against his stomach: there is a neat small hole in the cover that widens into a large hole toward the back. He opens the book, and nesting there in the index is a flattened, splayed spent bullet.

I lean forward, squinting at Wolf's belly. "You're kidding. *The Sherman & Sherman Guide* to America saved your life?"

"The very same." His eyebrows hoist. "I don't take such things lightly."

"And so now a fucking tourist guide is going to tell us what sights to see? I can't believe this."

"Sit down, Max." He is speaking quietly, almost inaudibly, tracing a twig in the soil.

"I *am* sitting."

"A man can *look* like he's sitting and still be pacing up and down. Don't argue with me." He wraps himself in a blanket and sits there in it. We face each other like two rival Indian chiefs negotiating a truce. "You asked me once what was so important about Ezekiel Sheridan Dunster. So put away your toy, sit down and let me tell you."

I pocket the watch. "Fine. Talk."

"You remember I told you Zeke was a black man, so he left a shade behind him?"

"Right."

"I lied. He didn't leave a shade behind." He raises a peremptory palm. "Because Zeke didn't die, not as far as I can tell. And now *really* sit down." He puts aside his twig. "You set?"

"Yeah yeah. Go on."

Wolf raises his head, and firelight comes into his eyes. "Ezekiel Sheridan Dunster was a name my big brother Eddie thought up for himself fourteen years ago."

I am speechless, so Wolf continues. "He worked in 7-Elevens for an even decade. I used to go every year and find him wherever he was. Called up the Southland Corporation's main office, found which 7-Eleven he was at and drove out to him. Mama always packed me something to give him. So to keep Mama's gift fresh and because I never had any money for a hotel anyway I made it a straight shot every time." He takes a deep breath and shakes his head. "I'd arrive at some crazy hour and no matter when it was Eddie was always there—he worked a double or triple shift—and I'd fall out bone-tired in the parking lot and those buzzing 7-Eleven fluorescent lights would be enough to give my eyes a headache right on the spot.

"And I'd bring Eddie whatever Mama'd made me to bring. One year it was his favorite cupcakes, chocolate with mint frosting. She did em up nice, with a sprig of real mint on top of each one.

"So Eddie or Zeke or whoever he was would stand back behind the counter and kinda squint at what I'd brought him like it was no wonder he left such a crazy family, and then he said, 'I *got* cake,' waving behind him at all the products, Hostess cupcakes, Sara Lee, Pepperidge Farm, Drake's Cakes, always twenty-six different kindsa shit to choose from. 'I *got* cake,' he'd say, and he never ate Mama's cupcakes, or her cookies or her pies, he never touched any of it. Just left it out on the table in whatever hole he was inhabiting until I had to eat it on the last day of my visit just so it wouldn't go to waste." He takes up the twig again, begins picking at the bark. "And when my week was up and I'd be getting ready to leave, he'd say, 'Tell Mama I liked the cupcakes.' And every year I told her."

"Wolf?"

"Don't interrupt."

"What makes you think he's not dead?"

"A number of things. For one, Dad and Mama couldn't find him, and that's all they did—bug me and look for Eddie. If *they* couldn't find him he just wasn't there to be found. And in all this time he never rung me up on the heaven-to-Earth hot line."

"So you think he's out there somewhere?"

Wolf's shoulders give a twist of impatience; not with me, with the idea, as if he's gone over it too often before. He balances the twig on his finger. "Yeah, he's out there. Two weeks before the blast he took off in my car, I thought he was just running out for some beer but he never came back. Remember how I told you when my parents sent me off to the freeway in Dad's car?"

"Yeah, right before the blast."

"The reason I had Dad's car was cause Eddie had mine. Well I didn't go straight to the freeway. I had a hunch all of a sudden and I went skidding out to the 7-Eleven on Houcks Road. Eddie wasn't there, but 'Zeke' had been. He left this book." He pauses. "Of all the drivers zooming down the freeway that night I was the only one who had any idea where I was going. That's cause Eddie wrote—well, look here." Wolf opens the front cover of *America*. There big block letters say BERMUDIAN—SAFE HARBOR.

"That's where I went toward, Bermudian," says Wolf. "Little town of about three and a half people. I never quite made it; damned car ran out of gas in the middle of nowhere. Turned out it was the best place to be; the rest of the cars stayed on I-83 straight into the York blast." He closes the book and holds it flat to his chest with both hands. "That's twice this book has saved my life. I think by now it's earned my respect."

"So you figure on going around the country finding every stinking 7-Eleven, turning them all upside down and swearing like an idiot."

"Not *every* 7-Eleven, just the ones where 'Zeke' worked. I told you: he started in Salt Lake and worked back toward home. What he did was this." Tracing the twig in the soil, Wolf scrapes out a figure that is either supposed to be a cow or a map of the U.S. "He took a detour from Utah down to Colorado, then went due east on I-70 and I-81. This book tells us exactly where he stopped along the way." Wolf holds it up instructively, taps it. "Whether you knew it or not, we've been retracing his steps out west from Harrisburg the whole time." Wolf makes a dotted line ending in an X where the cow's heart would be. "And I believe Eddie did exactly the same thing after the blast."

"You do."

"I do." He crosses his arms. "But even if I'm wrong, all I'm saying is we continue on the same route we've been traveling all along. And when we do look in those 7-Elevens, I'm figuring on finding *clues*. Hard evidence."

"Great." Now I really am up and pacing. "Mankind has been bombed into oblivion and we, the standard-bearers of the human race, are going to go rummaging through twenty-four-hour convenience stores looking for Twinkies with telltale dents."

"You—you go and deedle your horn awhile. I've seen you like this before. Go head." He makes a vague, gentle shooing gesture. "I got some thinking to do."

"You"—I walk up to him pointing—"will do your dangerous thinking now, out loud, in front of me."

"Fine." Wolf snaps the twig in half, drops the pieces to either side of him. "First of all I'm wondering, say you leave me right now right here, which you are free to do by the way, how far you're gonna get, a man who can't catch his own food talkin to himself in a vehicle he doesn't understand. How far you're gonna get before you turn your rig around—*if* it's still in running order—and go hunting for me. And I'm wondering how you're gonna find me in this great big country if I decide I don't want to be found. Now sit down and hear the rest." He lowers two flattened hands as if he is a conductor and my body is the orchestra.

I glower for a while, then slowly, dumbly, humbly, I comply.

"*Eddie is alive*. Like I said, Dad and Mama told me."

"Did they tell you where he is?"

"It's not that easy. All they knew is where he isn't. He hadn't poked up his head anywhere they could find him. And they could find *anyone* who crispy crittered in the big bad boom. They found your sister for you."

"That's true."

"So Eddie is alive. Start with that. Now we don't *know* we're gonna find any clues. But what I wanna know is this." He pauses.

"What?"

Cross-legged, he holds up both palms with a patient smile. "Who cleared out every 7-Eleven store in the northeastern United States?"

"That's easy," I burst out. "Scavengers."

Sitting there in his striped acrylic blanket, he repeats the gesture, the guru bestowing the Seventeenth Beatitude on his flock. "Nothing, if you haven't noticed, is easy. Did you ever wonder who buried that 7-Eleven clerk in Fort London? And who . . ." He raises both eyebrows, sets his hands flat on the ground for the clincher. "Who forced that oil tanker off the road and killed the driver?"

"The one we saw months ago, before Homestead? Those men died in the blast."

He lets one eyebrow slowly settle. "They did, huh? You didn't happen to notice the bloodstain in the ground?"

"The oil spill? It was out in back of the tanker, fifty feet from the driver."

"A deep red oil spill much too small for a tanker that

size. And did you see the driver's hands? Still had skin on one of em."

"Are you saying your brother Eddie killed—?"

"Not just once. You know what Eddie's address was before he started working 7-Elevens? The federal maximum security prison in Tallahassee, for killing a man with a .22. Eddie was a sharpshooter in Korea, carried a .22 as a matter of pride; he used to say a good marksman didn't need to make a mess. There were tiny bullet holes in the driver's sternum, did you look?"

"No," I say heavily, the walls of this argument growing high and close around me. "I didn't look."

"Eddie forced the tanker off the road, the driver ran out around the back of the truck trying to get away. Eddie shot twice and dragged the driver's body back behind the wheel."

"Jesus."

"Why? That's a hard guess." Wolf lies back, resting his head on his hands, stretches out. "Eddie *was* a hard guess, always."

So Wolf has a crazy brother alive somewhere, with a gun, a great quantity of gasoline, the complete stock from a hundred 7-Elevens, and homicidal impulses. "Wolf, I agree with Eddie."

"How's that?"

"We *don't* want to find him."

"Naah..." Wolf smiles up at the sky. "He's a mean fuck sometimes, but he wouldn't hurt *me*. Once, in high school, Eddie was a big hotshot senior, I was a sophomore running with this guy Harold. I asked Eddie for five bucks. Eddie said no, and I called him a cheap bastard. He got so mad he beat *Harold* within an inch of his life. Never touched a hair on my head. I'm his little brother."

"How is that story supposed to make *me* feel, Wolf?" I get up, hands on hips, spinning a half-turn, a small oasis of activity in a quiet landscape. "I'll tell you: it makes me feel like your friend Harold. It makes me feel great." I lean into his face. "Great, Wolf, great, fine and excellent."

Wolf sits up and speaks quietly. "Now I'm going to

tell you something my mother used to tell me. 'Be quiet,' she used to say. 'Sit down and be quiet. God *sees* you.'" He dons his damaged glasses, peering at me with one normal and one enlarged eye. "Even if I can't."

# 2 ❋ The Lassen Cutoff

A man's best pillow, it has too frequently been said, is his peace of mind. Yes, but for some men, for most men at most times, the best peace of mind is another man's expertise. And as I trust myself to Wolf's guidance, so other overlanders, on other trips westward, have put themselves into the hands of trail guides assumed to be more experienced and knowledgeable than themselves, but who were often merely more determined. Man is that animal that looks behind him, and so let us look back once again at those who went before.

Peter Lassen, ex of Denmark, ex of Boston and St. Louis and Oregon City and San Jose and Santa Cruz, finally settled down in 1844 on a plot of land in a lush but unpopulated part of the Sacramento Valley. Lassen served a wide radius of territory with its only general store, but not a single customer made his residence within a much wider radius. So in 1847 Peter Lassen undertook a return to Missouri to lure pioneers back to his California ranch, which he had dubbed "Benton City" in honor of expansionist Senator Thomas Hart Benton, and to secure a charter to found a Masonic lodge there.

Quite oblivious to the discovery of gold at Sutter's Mill a few months before, Lassen returned to California in September 1848, Masonic charter in hand, with twelve covered wagons. How he got back to Benton City is not merely a story unto itself, it is the whole story. Within a year some tens of thousands of emigrants would follow him down the Lassen Cutoff, as his trail came to be known, and massive Saint Joseph's Mountain, near Mount Shasta, would be no more.

Peter Lassen led his pioneers on regular western trails until Goose Lake, near the headwaters of the Humboldt River. From there on he trusted to his knowledge of the terrain. It was not a thing to trust. Lassen took the wagons across the Pit River, and back across and back across, as many as thirty times. Subsequent explorers found tracks indicating that the Lassen party had marched west some fifteen miles at one point, turned around and trudged back. Lassen led the pioneers down House Creek, where surrounding cliffs were so steep that the wagons had to be lowered by rope. He used Mount Shasta as a landmark one day and Saint Joseph's Mountain the next, going toward each peak in its turn, with no idea in his head that there was any difference between them.

Finally, at Poison Lake, out of food, plainly lost, the men in the party threatened to hang Lassen, who swore that if he were allowed to scale Saint Joseph's Mountain he could point out the Sacramento Valley.

At gunpoint the men took their captive 10,457 feet up the mountain. Lucky Peter: it was an exceptionally clear day, and the promised land was barely visible. But even after the dramatic ascent of Saint Joseph, the men and women under Lassen's guidance would not have survived without the providential appearance of a large party of Oregon prospectors bound for Sutter's Mill, who supplied them with food and escort to Benton City.

When the miners showed up, nobody in Lassen's party had tasted bread in a month. All in all, Lassen's cartographic filigree had led them three hundred miles out of the way.

# 3 ✳ Open 24 Hours

We find a crate of motor oil, another of antifreeze and a magnificent set of tools in a Zanesville garage, and soon after we do find a Jeep CJ-7, an ordinary civilian four-wheel-drive vehicle, but never and nowhere an instruction manual that tells us what to do with it. For three days we are encamped between two impenetrably complex vehicles, like a pair of paleontologists trying to figure out, if the knee bone's connected to the shin bone, which ganglion of greasy metal might be the knee bone and which the shin. Finally we give up on the larger task of trying to understand what we are doing and set about the smaller one of simply removing everything we can carry: fan belts, wheels, spark plugs, a couple of pistons, fuel lines, compressor or what we think could turn out to be a compressor.

And in the little town of London, Ohio, we find a whole undemolished 7-Eleven picked clean, as if nothing more severe had happened than a telephone call to a rather thorough moving company.

"Eddie's work," announced Wolf from the center of

the bare floor, amid empty shelves and empty counter, empty news rack and empty icebox; hard surfaces, hard facts. Even the light bulbs have been removed from their sockets. The cash register sits with its dollarless drawer open, a jaw jutting in belligerence or surprise.

Wolf strides around the empty room, hands in jacket pockets, a finger poking out the bullet hole; he pivots neatly on his heel, Sherlock Wolf, Wolf Poirot, Wolf Spade, Wolf the sniffer-outer, and utters judgment. "Eddie's work. No doubt about it."

"No doubt? Have you already dusted this place for fingerprints, Lieutenant?"

"Don't have to." Wolf folds his arms. "Look at the safe." He jerks his head toward the counter. "It's wide open."

"Yeah?" I go behind the counter. A little armored cylinder is removed from its burial place in the floor; nothing's in it. "What does that prove?"

"Prove," he says. "*Proves* nothing." One hand scratches at his chin. "But it does lead to certain conclusions."

"Like whoever worked in this 7-Eleven heard about the blast and got the money out of the safe before he took off."

"That's one possibility," Wolf concedes. "A remote, wheezy little possibility. Picture this guy dashing out with about two seconds' notice; he's gonna stop to fuck with the safe? Besides, the clerks at 7-Elevens don't have access to the safes; that's the whole idea. Like I told you, they're rigged on a time delay. Naah. That safe was cracked by an expert."

I state the inevitable. "Eddie."

"Eddie. You know how long he was in prison?"

"Ten years." Pedantic son of a bitch.

"Right. And how long did it take to get a doctoral degree?"

"Five years or so, I guess, but what's that—?"

Wolf wags a reproving index finger. "The point is this: Eddie had enough time in the pen to get his doctorate two times over."

"His doctorate?"

"In crime, my boy."

This sinks in. "So the assumption is your brother learned safecracking in prison. But you don't know, do you?" He looks down. "You *don't* know." I stamp the floor. "Wolf, you call this a clue? This is thin air! This is shit!"

"When the Indians were on the trial of an animal," Wolf raises a finger and an eyebrow, "they used to *look* for shit."

"That's it." I grab his elbow and push us out the door. "Don't say another word."

Wolf goes silent, stays silent as we get into the car and pull out of the parking lot, makes one false twitch toward verbiage as we get back onto I-70, thinks better of it, stays silent as London, Ohio, falls behind us, falls into the past.

Even the days are cold now, prematurely bitingly cold; we drive with half a ton of jeep junk in the back seat and half a ton of blanket in the front. We look like sumo wrestlers, our little heads poking up out of vast motley mounds of wool and acrylic. Those are from a nice brick duplex, also in London. There we found a cup of coffee on the kitchen counter, frozen solid, the mug shattered around the brown block of ice and pieces of burst ceramic fallen to all sides. A saucer rested on top, placed there to keep the coffee hot. In the top dresser drawer were lined leather gloves; I had to cut off the fingertips so they would fit. We drive until we get to New Paris, until we've completed our European tour of Ohio, until our noses and ears and my fingers are numb.

"We're getting warmer," says Wolf suddenly.

"Warmer? *I* was about to suggest we stop and build a fire."

"A fire's fine," says Wolf easily.

"But you just . . ." I cut myself off: he says we'll build a fire; just build the fire. Safer than trying to figure him out.

There are dead bushes everywhere, crispy from the cold, which we grind into kindling with our feet, and chips and branches, which we put on top of them. Soon we have more fire than we've had since the burning of Homestead, more fire than we need, and we are sitting in front of it, stripped of blankets, faces red with blood and the reflected light of the flame.

Reading his shredded book behind his uni-glasses, Wolf is a pathetic sight, covering with a hand the eye behind the lensless frame and squinting the good one, mumbling as he tries to decipher words chopped short by the bullet.

Day fell today like a curtain: we awoke under a dim sky in which the sun could not be located, and the day simply continued until, as suddenly as it had begun, it stopped, and there was no light, no stars and no moon. Day fell, and cold fell, and night fell, like a curtain rung down between sun and Earth.

"It's damn cold for this time of year, Wolf. Much too cold."

"Mmm," he says, reading.

"I think this is it." I pause. "Nuclear winter."

"Mmm," he says, a syllable of amiable inattention.

"We'd better change our plans and go south," I tell him.

Wolf removes his glasses, rubs his eyes and looks up. Clearly, he is about to respond at long last. "We're getting warmer."

"Excuse me?"

"Wolf looks at me straight on. "We're getting warmer to Eddie."

"Eddie?"

"Yeah." He closes the book. "Cause as we work our way west we keep discovering little clues—the grave, the tanker, the open safe—each of em maybe not even good enough to be called a clue, but all together too much to ignore."

"You want something too much to ignore? Try nuclear winter. Try twenty degrees below zero."

Wolf shifts uncomfortably. "They didn't know *how* cold it would get."

"So what do you call *this*, autumn? No sun but no clouds, temperature falling maybe thirty degrees in a week. You think it'll be any better tomorrow?"

"No." Hunched up with his arms around his knees, Wolf looks around at the sky. "Tomorrow will be worse."

"That's why we've got to get our frozen asses south and wrap ourselves up in blankets and buildings."

"If we don't find something soon, yeah, we have to. But we will."

"How soon, Wolf?"

"I don't know. I'll tell you—I can't stand the cold. One winter I followed a girl out to Colorado. It got so cold there..." He shakes his head. "So cold your face froze and the only way to move your lips was with your hands. Give me... six more 7-Elevens. Then, if we don't find a good clue, we'll—"

"You've got three."

"Three? Fine." He cracks a smile. "S' what I wanted anyway."

But we do not find anything in Indianapolis, nor in Monrovia, nor in Marshall, just across the Illinois border. That's where Wolf, behind another stripped counter, stands with his hands clasped behind his back, looking down, toeing the open safe. "I guess you've got me," he shrugs. "I said three more 7-Elevens. I gave you my word of honor as a gentleman."

"Great."

"The only thing is, there aren't any more gentlemen left." He looks up at me. "And if there was, *I* wouldn't be one of em."

"Wolf! Are you—"

"I'm giving you my *new* word of honor as a gentleman: we go on only until the weather gets too grisly to continue."

"It *is* too grisly to continue."

"It's getting uncomfortable, that I'll admit, but not impossible. I have a deal for you: when it gets down like Colorado into the teens and the snot starts to freeze in my nose and my eyeballs squeak in my head, the second I have trouble speaking because my lips are numb, we turn left and head for Mexico."

The next day it is so cold I refuse to drive, and sit with blankets wrapped around my entire body, head included. I can't see, can barely stir, am in essence attempting to hibernate in a moving jeep. Wolf, at last glance, was wrapped as well as I except where the cloth was tucked in over his forehead to form a loose hood

above the eyes, like some kind of cold-weather bur-
noose.

"Wolf," I give a muffled shout. "Welcome to winter in
Colorado! Human life is not possible in these conditions!"

His voice comes slow, tripping over itself, a moo with
its batteries running down. "Mmbook say-said s-seven-
eleven uh-up a little way."

"Wolf!" I strip off my headdress to get a look at him.
"You wouldn't be having difficulty talking, would you?"

He grimaces, mobilizing his facial muscles for a supreme effort. "Ah *cannn* dawk."

"You can talk, huh? We're taking our left turn *now*."

He nods, grimacing in what might be a smile. Can he
have heard me correctly?

"You got that?" I shout. "The very next left."

As we pass a GREENUP—EXIT LEFT sign, I slide over
and put my hands on the wheel, forcing the car left. He
jams an elbow in my ribs and I let go for a second, getting my wind for what will be a final, successful attempt
to take the wheel. But Wolf, the onward-man himself,
turns onto the exit under his own power.

"Didn't theak I woo-ould, hah?" he says thickly, now
really, unmistakably, jack-o'-lanternly smiling.

And now, a hundred yards off, what Wolf was driving
at hoves into sight on the left, and the car moves, slowing, toward the left side of the road: another goddamn
7-Eleven.

"*No!*" I bellow, seizing the wheel with my right hand
and protecting my ribs with my left. He struggles, but I
am stronger, and the car edges back off the shoulder into
the road.

Wolf slams on the brakes and, unbalanced for the
fight, I roll off the seat onto the floor. He's out of the car,
slamming the door, and wrapped in his unraveling bur-
noose, the loose folds of the blankets hanging off his
arms, strides toward the entrance of the Greenup 7-
Eleven, noble and driven, Wolf of Arabia. As I climb out
of the car the glass door that says OPEN 24 HOURS is
slowly, softly, pneumatically closing itself behind him.

I lumber toward the store, my knees cold, my face

numbing. Suddenly a voice comes from inside: "*Yubba-dubba-doo!*"

I break into a stiff-legged run, and there, behind yet another cleaned-out counter in yet another cleaned-out 7-Eleven, is Wolf, grinning obscenely and pointing to something below the level of the counter.

Nestling in the safe's brushed-stainless container is a pair of half-frame reading glasses identical to Wolf's except that both lenses are intact. Wolf stands poised, glasses in hand, feisty and fiery. "Wanna bet the prescription's right?"

Days of cold string out in front of me: a vast line of white frozen asphalt, littered with chunks of rubber from brittled tires, and at the end two statues standing like warnings to the animate, two statues with eyes as hard as marbles and icicles dripping from their noses, one tall and light and the other small and frost-lightened, statues in poses characterizing and caricaturing disagreement, statues at loggerheads, each pointing in a different direction with the fixity of wooden signs on a country road, one pointing left and the other pointing onward ever onward. We have again, once again, reached a crucial point of decision in our journey: when the flames of Homestead snapped and snarled, in the quiet city of fire; when Harrisburg burned still more silently; and when, many nights ago in another world, one man standing in darkness yelled the name of his favorite song to a man standing in a circle of firelight. "No Wolf," I say. "I don't want to bet."

"Good," says Wolf, bespectacled. "Cause they do fit. They fit perfectly. They do fit and I for one arm ready for anything. Bring on the cold!" he shouts, brandishing a melodramatic fist-to-the-heavens. "The brothers Dewey are ready!"

# 4 ❊ A Rough and Ready Company

In 1849, Peter Lassen had made it back to Benton City by the bacteria on the skin of his teeth. There he and Missouri emigrant Saschel Woods had founded the Masons' Western Star Lodge No. 2. And in Missouri, in New York and England and Virginia and France, and everywhere you could shake a stick at, the forty-niners began their westward rush in earnest. It was one of those rare years, like 1776, that entered the language. By 1852, the population of California would triple.

Alert to the unprecedented commercial opportunities afforded by the emigration, Lassen flooded the eastern newspapers with press releases accounting his "discovery" of a "cutoff," or short-cut, to the land of gold, bolstered by endorsements of the Lassen Cutoff attributed to the same men who had forced him up Saint Joseph's Mountain at gunpoint. Their names were attached to statements which predicted that the Lassen Cutoff would shorten many a trail-weary sojourner's dreary overland trip to California, would make it a veritable piece of cake. Agents were dispatched and primitive billboards

219

hammered up along the western way, directing forty-
niners in need of rest and provisions to Lassen's land.
Harsh adventure had mutated Peter Lassen into a new
species unto himself, one with an entrepreneurial gland
instead of a brain.

Lassen's publicity campaign snookered two established and respected trail guides, J.J. Myers and Benoni
Hudspeth, who in the summer of 1849 led their reputa-
tions and immense company onto the Lassen Cutoff.
Like lemmings, vast numbers of forty-niners immediately followed their lead. The weather was inclement,
the way uncharted, and the Pit Indians, so named for
their habit of digging deep pits for game and enemies,
had grown hostile and plagued the caravans, stealing
goods and stripping wagons of their teams. The traveler
came across the carcasses of twelve hundred horses and
cattle strewn along the impasses of the Lassen Cutoff,
many of which had been slaughtered, as one owner put
it, "to avoid a visit from that lank, lean old monster,
Starvation." And many graves:

Sacred to the memory of
W. Brown
of the Rough and Ready Company
of Platte Co. Mo.
Died with skervy Sept. 19, 1849
Aged 35 years

When winter of that fabled year approached, and ten
thousand emigrants were still toiling in the wilderness,
the U.S. Army found it necessary to undertake a massive relief expedition, paid for by a $100,000 appropria-
tion from the federal government and private
contributions. (It is not recorded, incidentally, that Peter
Lassen was one of the contributors.) Four relief squad-
rons were dispatched, each of which quickly discovered
that the need and numbers of the lost greatly exceeded
their resources. Brevet Major D.H. Rucker, for example,
was besieged hourly with requests for food and forced to
dole out half-rations of bread and beef first to the sick,
then to the starving, then to families and usually not at
all to the single men who comprised the vast majority of

the gold rushers. By that time, the disgruntled wayfarers had taken to calling the Cutoff "Lassen's Horn Route," meaning that it was as much a shortcut as going around Cape Horn.

# 5 ❈ Haywire

"Stop it, Wolf." He is humming a little tune, a little tune that becomes littler in his tuneless mouth. "Stop that noise."

"Oh, was I doing it again?" He goes back to the business of grinning like an idiot and driving the car. We have not, of course, taken our left turn. We are back on I-70, at least until we run into the next 7-Eleven town. And another or the same little tune burbles to the surface of the bottomless well of Wolf's enthusiasm, toodles out of his nose, finds outlet from his mouth: "...the sun's so hot I froze to death, Suzannah don't you cry..."And without pause or bridge or change of melody—without interruption of any kind—he begins singing, "Oh my darling, oh my darling, oh my darling Clementine..." Wolf knows about ten songs; the problem is that he thinks they are all the same one.

I put the bell of the saxophone behind his head; I am going to let fly a tremendous diesel honk that will knock everything out from between his two ears. He pays no heed, his eyes riveted firmly to the inner landscape. I inhale deeply, place my mouth to the reed, and blow my heart out.

"blup-tweee?" says the saxophone. The reed is frozen stiff, and this plaint of an asthmatic mosquito is all it can come up with.

"You say something?" says Wolf, turning his head for the first time since the town of Vandalia and our last 7-Eleven.

I try to pull the saxophone out of my mouth—and my lips practically come with it. Christ! Never wrap your wet lips around anything eighty degrees colder than they are. "Mrmm!" I struggle to hold the saxophone absolutely still in the bumping car, keep it from tearing half my face away. "Mrmm!" I open wide alarmed eyes to Wolf.

"Hih, hih, hih, hih." Wolf's shoulders are hunching in slow serves-you-right laughter.

"Yerrr!" I sway and flop in the seat as the car weaves over the road in his laughter-loosened grip, until finally, bumpily, we stop.

Still giggling, Wolf reaches under the seat: in the Vandalia 7-Eleven we found food, drink, a boxed set of snow chains for our tires and a cryptic note in Eddie's infinitesimal hand concerning railroad tracks, the manifest destiny of man to westward tend and the joyful ease of floating oneself on the Great Salt Lake. Wolf reaches under the seat and comes out with a Lowenbrau. "Oh boy. I always wanted to do this to someone," he says, shaking the can of beer. "Always wanted to do this to *you*. Now, lean over, lean forward, that's right." He pulls the tab. Absolutely nothing happens. Wolf drops the can to the floor with a bonk.

"Frozen," he mutters. "I'll use spit." Closed-mouthed, saving saliva, he hums the Lowenbrau song; leave it to Wolf to mess up all the real tunes and save his perfect pitch for the commercial jingles. I am trying not to move my hands at all; the numbness has spread to my chin, and I can't keep my lips pressed together much longer or even tell how much skin's been ripped away. It's the ultimate test of my embouchure. Wolf spits copiously into a cupped hand, uses his other index finger as a Q-Tip, dipping and wiping the spit into my lip. It burns.

Suddenly the mouthpiece is sliding free, and I'm panting and glowering at the cursed instrument in my lap, feeling my mouth for blood and finding a little. "Well well well," says Wolf. "Man and saxophone."

Fire time. We have reached the point where we must go slowly because a rapid wind bores through our bones and blankets, and even so stop hourly to reheat, recharge and switch drivers. I don't know exactly how cold it is; the best that can be said is that when you spit it still hits the ground wet.

Now, in addition to our jeep-and-a-half and our thousand blankets, we are carrying twelve bricks. We line the fire pit with them, and when spit sizzles on contact, tong them out of the fire. The passenger gets four hot bricks for his feet and two for each hand; the driver gets the same but can only warm one foot and one hand at a time.

The fires themselves are a scientific matter now, thanks to the addition of lighter fluid and charcoal briquettes to our arsenal, and meals, the one thing we never expected to be easy, have become as easy as, well, Jiffy Pop, which product Wolf is currently shaking over the fire, maraca accompaniment for his salsa rap. "C'mon you little babies, c'mon now babies, snap crackle and pop for me." The Jiffy Pop goes shoosh ka-ka shoosh.

Our trail is marked with fire pits and the cans and wrappers of Wolf's favorite foods: Oreos, Green Giant Baby Peas, Rice Krispies, Kit Kat bars, Twinkies, alphabet soup, and best, Beef-aroni. It's a trail strewn thoughtfully, sparingly, just enough to get us from pit stop to pit stop. A trail that has taken us from unbearable to unbelievable cold, through Indiana and Illinois and Missouri and beyond argument. Eddie exists. Somewhere, Eddie does exist. "God o' Corn," says Wolf now. "Pop your babies." And the Jiffy Pop goes shoosh ka-ka shoosh, shoosh ka-ka shoosh.

Under our makeshift tube tent four king-sized blankets thick, strung up on a rope between stakes and sealed off at the ends with C-clamps that keep coming undone, I dream of a giant hand coming over and smothering me, but I don't mind because at least it's a warm hand, moist and hot and blanketing.

"Help me! I'm drowning! Help I'm drowning!"

The tent has collapsed again and Wolf churns under it, arms and knees stabbing out indistinguishably like six wildcats in a mailbag. I yank it all off him and he wakes up clawing blind. I give his face a slap and his eyes open; instantly, like a psychotic injected, his body goes slack. He peers at me blankly, erased, newborn.

I summarize the state of the world for him. "I'm Max, you're Wolf, the tent caved in, we are sleeping in Big Springs, Kansas, and you had a nightmare."

"Where . . . ?" he says weakly.

"Kansas, Wolf."

"Say it again."

"Kansas."

Wolf sits up dazed, looks around him, opening his eyes unnaturally wide as if to force consciousness straight through them into his brain. At these times he will often make announcements to the effect that BHT has been proven to cause cancer in laboratory animals or that the three angles in a triangle always add up to 180 degrees. Now, however, he simply makes sense. "Fire time," he says.

I assemble the ingredients as he sits and collects himself, arms around his knees, and I do not say another word until we are sitting in front of the flaming briquettes, hands extended toward warmth.

"Haywire," says Wolf suddenly. "That's what he used to call it when he went off his nut."

"Eddie?"

"Like when he was being held in county jail before the murder trial, and Dad and Mama made a pilgrimage to Florida, and Mama said, 'Honey, what happened now?'

"'I went haywire,' Eddie said. It was his word. And he could explain whatever he'd done, mug a friend, leave a wife, kill a man not just till it made sense but till it made such a strange kind of sense and so much of it you couldn't even think to argue with him. After Eddie was through with you, you'd swear you walked on your hands and ate with your feet. What I keep wondering is, has he gone haywire this time?"

I lean back on my elbows, sticking my feet near the fire. Got to be careful here: once I saw fat black droplets oozing from my boots; I thought they were blood, but it turned out that my Vibram soles were melting, dripping like candle wax. Gently I ask, "Second thoughts?"

"Yeah, and third thoughts too."

"Well, Wolf, if he's gone haywire I guess we're stuck with haywire. It's still getting colder. We can't last forever. The car won't hold together."

"No. And we don't have enough food to go anywhere but out on a straight line toward big brother Eddie." He presses his hands to his temples. "I feel like one of my rats being led into a trap. See food, eat food, wham!" He brings his hands together in front of his eyes. "Trapped."

# 6 ❋ Of the Old Dutchman and His Rascally Deceatfulness

Back at the ranch, naturally, Peter Lassen was doing a socko business. In Benton City, a tavern, grocery and general provision store, where flour, meat, wagons and livestock could be purchased by a captive audience at exalted prices, were flourishing. Not all were happy about it, but all paid. Chronicler and frontier artist J. Goldsborough Bruff reported that, just out of Benton City, four of Lassen's employees (whose names Bruff intimated he could readily supply), had accumulated a great deal of property by encouraging the emigrants to leave their stock and wagons and go ahead on foot because, according to them, the short piece of road that lay ahead was the worst "ever travelled by Christians." These unscrupulous fellows were "exceedingly prompt" in visiting arriving wagoneers and advising the owners "to abondon or leave them in their charge, &c." Oxen,

227

mules and horses were branded and "with some mysterious assistance, were transferred from one gorge to another, and finally *the indians stole them*."

The ground at Benton City was paved, according to overlander Simon Doyle, with "bones, rags, chips, sticks, skulls, hair, skin, entrails, blood," and cut-up beef parts hung from the trees. There, in the midst of the great waste that only great wealth can create, Major Rucker, head of the relief operation, was obliged to continue distributing food, because those who could not pay simply did not get. Doyle wrote an angry letter home:

> Some to pore forth Curses and
> abuse upon Lassin for his rascally
> deceatfulness in making the northern
> road in this all hands join and the
> Old Dutchman is in eminent danger of
> loosing his life and makes himself
> as humble as possible.

In addition to the profits reaped during the banner year of the gold rush, and on top of sums paid by the early settlers for parcels of Benton City, Lassen realized $30,000 for the sale of two-thirds of his holdings. Peter Lassen had parlayed his great mistake, getting lost in the mountains of Northern California, into a great success by getting others lost with him.

# 7 ❋ When Skidding

Up, up and up Mount Timpanogos we go, me driving a ribbon of white up into the night, the tire chains grinding the hard snow-covered surface, Wolf making his engineer's grumblings about the highway's "poor signing" and me rendering complaints of a more general nature, both of us wrapped head to foot in blankets, up and up and slowly up, in first gear all the way.

We reach the summit and poise exhilaratingly for a long moment, seem to be suspended there on the point where up meets down, on the point of decision, and then, in a moment that brings me back to the time I tried to stand up on a surfboard, start sliding, not rolling, sliding down the long straight steep incline, cut loose in the ocean of darkness, and I'm looking down from the curl of the wave at the surfboard stealthily, smoothly slipping out from beneath me and riding out toward the dry still haven of the beach. What happened next? I hit a rock, broke my arm in four places, spent weeks in traction watching *Days of Our Lives* on the snowy hospital TV.

"I don't like this," says Wolf, pitch rising. "Pump the brakes, don't hit them hard, just pump them."

So I pump them once, and the car jerks promptly left to ten o'clock and keeps slip-sledding down the road.

"Pump the brakes!" says Wolf.

I tromp on the pedal and the car heaves around to seven o'clock. We are being thrown down the icy mountain road, mainly ass-backwards and still gaining speed. I pump the brakes again and we are exactly ass-backwards, looking out over the jeep junk in the back seat to see where we are heading, then around the side of the car. We are spinning, four-wheel drive or not, extra weight or not, we are spinning, we are skidding.

Wolf speaks with the crisp well-informed desperation of a high school driving teacher. "When skidding," he pronounces, "turn in the direction of the skid."

"Right," I say, and do what any idiot would do, turn in the opposite direction.

Th-wow! We are whipping front by back at dizzying speed. The screams of girls on the Coney Island Cyclone. Two men in a centrifugal testing machine, their faces bulged and popping.

"Buckle up!" screams Wolf. And I'm digging through blankets as my side of the car slings itself five feet from cliffside—rocks and a long way down—burrowing through blankets until I have it! My right belt! Snick, and I'm snug in.

"You *idiot!*" screams Wolf as we head his-side-first toward an embankment. "That's *my*—"

We slam into the bank and my head jerks so hard it seems Wolf has flown right out of his seat.

He has. And is buried sideways in a snowdrift.

I jump from the car as Wolf levers himself free and sits on the snow, lit by one headlight, glaring at my approach, snow in his hair, snow in his shirt, a high pile of snow on one shoulder. "You know what I was thinking as we hit that skid?"

"What?" I say, trotting up.

He dusts off his shoulder imperiously, like a general adjusting an epaulet. "That it's a good thing nature's fixed it so I won't have to kill you."

My eyes are caught by a wide metal sign sticking straight up out of the snow not five feet from his head.

RESTRICTED AREA
Authorized Personnel Only

The rear end of the car rests in a break in the snowbank. There is a barbed-wire-topped Cyclone gate, and just inside it, a small concrete cubicle with a window: GUARD POST N.W. ALL VISITORS MUST SHOW SECURITY CLEARANCE.

Beyond the guard station is an utterly flat expanse of what looks like smoothly packed snow, a virginal plateau that stretches far into the distance and drops off with nothing below.

"C'mon," says Wolf. "Let's turn the jeep around and navigate this here Restricted Area."

The chains whip and churn as the jeep digs itself out of the snow. We skim across that wide lake, except that it is not a lake but some kind of minimalist military base, with KEEP CLEAR signs and guard stations and what look like dwarf traffic lights jutting up sparsely from the surface. We pass a sign that reads KEEP CLEAR 100 YARDS RADIUS AT ALL TIMES and I notice that the ground is broken, on closer look broken neatly in a wide circle ringed with four little traffic lights.

"Look at that," says Wolf, stopping the car. Off the edge of the plateau, maybe five miles distant, is a vast city. Down there, a flickering brightness, a live bonfire. "Salt Lake City." He puts a hand on my shoulder. "That's Eddie's city."

Has he turned on the ignition again? No. Then what is that vibration, yes, and that low rumble?

"Wolf? You hear that?"

"No, I—Christ!" All the traffic lights click audibly on, are bright blinking yellow.

"Wolf! Out! Now!"

The ground shakes; its icy sheath cracks, and Wolf and I jump from the jeep, and the ground shambles loosely under us as we skip and snag and skate across it and the roaring fills our heads. It feels like an earthquake, exactly like the earthquake that shook me out of bed in fifth grade, but it sounds like more.

We've almost reached the ring of traffic lights, and the roaring is so loud we can't hear them click to red, to blinking red, so loud we can't do anything but see, and as I yank Wolf along the ground breaks up into jagged slabs of thin concrete and the break is coming from the center of the circle, where the jeep! the jeep rears up like a horse, and before it can sink back to the ground a giant protrusion heaves up underneath it, hoisting it aloft. A thousand pounds of jeep junk rolls back out of the seat and Wolf and I are still skip-dancing backward, transfixed. Not an earthquake. A volcano?

A missile.

A missile the size of a ten-story building rising slowly from the ground. A blanket wafts slowly, gracefully, from the jeep at a height of maybe fifty feet, and finally the jeep itself is rudely upchucked, crashing soundlessly down the side of the missile.

U.S. ARMY is the last thing we see, then the painfully, piercingly bright tail of the missile as it shoots straight into the deserted sky. It's like looking directly into the sun, a giant sun that fills the field of vision: we see nothing but spots for the first mile or two of the missile's flight. We stand swaying, imbalanced, with our feet in a puddle of melted ice as our eyes readjust, and we watch and watch it, a bright arrow pointing at nothing.

Wolf finally takes his eyes off the missile. "Well," he says, alert as ever to the obvious. "There go our wheels."

On the broken concrete lies a smoking mound no more than two feet high: the jeep, the once-jeep, our one and only jeep, fused into a lump of metal-plastic-rubber-glass by the heat of the missile's exhaust. We are silent before it.

Was you ever bit by a dead bee? The missile has not yet reached its zenith, but we have found our nadir. Alone, foodless, blanketless, without compass and without ken; alone and stump-humble before the grimmest and grandest creation of our race; alone and shipwrecked by the accidental triggering of a robot circuit in an unpopulated military base, wholly ruined in the blink of an eye, the jerk of a knee; alone in the bitter cold quickly retaking the air from which it was chased, we are praying, we are crying, we are lost.

And now, suddenly, suddenly and loudly, somebody else, not me and not Wolf, a flesh-and-blood human being where none should be, bellows from behind us: "To the moooon, Alice!"

We turn our heads and there, there in a snowy ankle-length robe cut from a single piece of white fabric, there he is, Ezekiel Sheridan Dunster in the flesh, the quest's end, the doppelgänger, the legendary elder brother. No mistaking the Wolfish yellow-brown skin, the long jaw; but also no mistaking the unWolfish black eyes, eyes raised from the horizon at a degree that suggests divine inspiration, the eyes that possess at their center the lunatic gleam, the eyes that seem to behold and hold the moon at once: it is Eddie.

And Eddie speaks again in a soft voice. "To the moon."

# 8 ❋ The Honeymooners

Flanking Eddie are two men, one fat, wearing a dark uniform and a sort of police cap, the other tall, thin and befuddled, in a short-sleeved shirt, a squashed, low-crowned hat and an unbuttoned vest. At the men's elbows are women wearing fifties dresses and shortish hairdos cast-ironed into place with half a can of hair-spray. One has an apron. The women are shivering, and the thin man rubs his arms. I've seen them all before, in fact I know them well; but how, and when, I cannot say. It's as if I've heard a familiar tune but can't put a name to it.

Eddie opens his hands toward the men and women on either side of him, presenting them. It is a simple and somehow a religious gesture. "Meet the Honey-mooners."

And Ralph and Alice and Norton and Trixie step forward to link arms across one another's shoulders and bow.

Wolf looks up at the missile, opens his mouth, shuts

it, looks at the theatrical troupe, opens his mouth, shuts it, looks at me, mouth open. Wolf shuts his mouth.

Eddie lowers his gaze to his brother for the first time. "You're cold," he says, and turns, and the Honeymooners turn with him.

Wolf and I also try to turn, and collapse in a twisted heap: the ice around our feet, melted by the heat of the rocket, has refrozen and now holds our shoes fast. I'm able to lever my heavy boots free, but Wolf's low shoes sit there feetless in the cracked ice. He bends down to yank them loose, and we trot after Eddie and the Honeymooners. Back across the frozen lake they go, to the guard station near the entrance, through a tiny anteroom and into a closet barely large enough for our seven bodies. Two brushed-stainless doors meet and seal off; and we begin, almost without sensation, to move. Stanley Simone and His Silver Strings permeate the air with a version of "One O'Clock Jump" as we descend, green lights above the door tell us, to −2, −3, −4.

"You," says Eddie, turning to Wolf, "are Here." He pronounces the word with a kind of aspirate pride, as if it stands separate from everything around it, a word borne singly on its own solitary puff of air. Here is the name of this place.

The doors slide open onto a long beige corridor lined with multicolored plastic stacking chairs and olive green steel office doors, recent-institutional, lit and heated, overwhelmingly *indoors*. We stop before a coffee machine.

"Soup," says Eddie. Ralph Kramden and Ed Norton dig through the pockets of their capacious pants; Kramden comes out with a quarter. The machine drops a wax-coated cup onto a steel grate and Lipton Cup-a-Soup begins to trickle down.

"For you," says Eddie, handing the cup to Wolf. And we go on down the hall. It's an office building, a hospital, a community college. Eddie opens a door and through it, ladies first, go the Honeymooners. I can see only a sliver of the room: a run-down apartment with a dining table and plain hard chairs, a bare window; a familiar apartment, perhaps one lived in long ago by an aunt. The clapping of many hands comes back through that open door, thunderously instant like sign-prompted TV-studio applause. Ralph and Alice and Norton and Trixie have entered, as Ralph and Alice and Norton and Trixie are wont to do, onto the main set of *The Honeymooners*.

"Go ahead," says Eddie, waving us through.

We walk in, and a small auditorium opens up, a couple of hundred of curious faces all over us, sniffing us out close like dogs.

"EE!" roars the crowd. It is a short open-mouthed shout made in the back of the throat, deeper than speech, masculine despite the good number of women in the audience. Eddie has entered behind us. Wolf is by my side, leaning slightly, freeze-framed in the middle of a step forward or a jump back.

Eddie takes the stage, the Kramdens to his right, the Nortons to his left. There is no need for him to quell the noise; there is no noise. There is undivided attention, and when Eddie speaks it is into a void.

"Earlier this evening," he says, in a booming voice that bears no resemblance to Wolf's. "We sent a prayer to the sky in the form of a missile."

"EE!" roars the crowd, then falls instantly silent.

"That prayer was answered. A man saw and came Here. Ladies and gentlemen..." An emcee hand extends toward stage right, toward us. "Meet Charles Dewey. My brother!" The crowd begins to hubbub. Hundreds of eyes slither back to us, to Wolf.

"Omigod," Wolf murmurs under his breath, putting on a weak-growing-weaker smile. Eddie comes toward us, rounds the corner of the stage and descends a few steps to audience level. We follow him to front row center. Two people scatter for Wolf and me.

It's a whole, exact and unaltered episode: Norton sleepwalks, mooning for some long-lost love named Lulu, Luuuu-luuuu. Ralph finally discovers that Lulu was Norton's childhood dog. I squint and squint at the actors, but their makeup, their features are perfect. They are playing it as drama, and not once during the show is there laughter from any human in the audience. Who are these people? I want them to freeze in their seats so I can go picking over them, poking stomachs, palpating cheeks, slitting pockets and examining the evidence. But Eddie, "E," watches the show with his head as rigid as a dental patient's; Wolf takes his cue from him, and I from Wolf. While the real show is, must be, going on around and behind us.

When the show is over that cued applause comes on instantaneously. Eddie stands up, takes one step forward, turns and holds both hands high, the folds of his robe falling gracefully from his arms like the wings of some great white falcon.

"EE!" says the crowd. And slowly, meditatively, the small noises of his movements sounding clearly through the quieted theater, Eddie walks around to the side and climbs the steps, takes center stage, turns away from the audience momentarily, resting two fists on the table, turns back with open hands facing out and the same expression on his face as when he watched the sky, the missile and the moon in his upturned eyes.

"Today," says Eddie, his eyes swooping down to audience level. "We will talk about the Lost." A man sneaks on behind him with a carafe of water, pours a glass and stands ready to pour another. "In today's episode of *The Honeymooners* Edward Norton lost someone vital to him. You heard him—a man howling in pain, as Here, for months and months, you heard me. How many times did you hear me howling for my brother?" He pauses, continuing in a near-whisper. "How many times?"

"EE!" bellows the crowd.

"Well Jesus fucking Christ," Wolf says out of the side of his mouth.

"And how many times did I tell you he was alive? And how many times did I tell you that one day he would join us Here?"

"EE!" assents the crowd.

"Edward Norton was literally unconscious of his loss. When this show was aired, audiences laughed at him; in this harder world, no one would dare. We have lived Norton's sadness many times over. Lived and surmounted it. This is the key: a man who does not know what he has lost is himself lost."

"EE!"

"But a man," roars Eddie, riding the crest of the

noise, "a man who holds within him the knowledge of what he has lost is never lost." He holds up both arms. *"Is . . . never . . . lost!"*

"EE!"

Hands folded papally behind him, Eddie walks slowly around the table. "And that," he says quietly in the hush, "is the lesson of this episode, of this day, of this period in history.

"Know this now!" Eddie leans forward, hands spread wide on the table. "A man who stubbornly remembers, who refuses to forget, *who refuses to lose what he has lost* has lost nothing. Proof? That black man sitting in the front row." He takes a sip of water, and it is refilled in his hand. He holds up the water to Wolf. "That black man." He drinks deeply. "Know this now."

*"Know this now,"* says the crowd, giving each word exactly the same duration.

"Below us, in Salt Lake City," says E as the noise subsides around his voice, "a sizable group of the Lost squat upon precious land that is rightfully ours. We must not level the city merely to drive them from it. Nor, as the first skirmish showed, can we take the city with conventional arms under winter conditions. But the Lost have not our numbers, they have not our ability to draw from the lessons of history, they have not our destiny. All they possess is bare ignorant need." He has clenched his fists, and now curls them in to meet at his chest. "And when the thaw comes, nothing can, nothing will keep us from them."

"EE!" says the crowd. "EEEEEEEEE."

"The first commandment," E snaps out, continuing in a softer voice, "was 'Thou Shalt Not Kill.' It is a great teaching." He smiles slowly. "Provided we add to it three simple words: 'Unless Thou Needeth.' And in the great films of Stallone, of Norris, of Wayne and Peckinpah, thou needeth. In the world of which the great films were a part and reflection, thou needeth. On the brown Earth left behind by those who failed to learn its lessons, thou needeth. Know this now," says E, raising an eyebrow, nodding his head, speaking quietly. "Thou needeth."

"EEEEEE!" says the crowd, a sustained shout that

modulates into a cheer, into a solid, quieter murmur, and then into a lowing: "... eeeeeeeee ..."

Eddie's fists are still over his heart, and finally he extends them, opening his hands, very slowly outward. Everywhere around me rustling begins, but my eyes refuse to leave him.

"Amazing," says Wolf slowly. Though his voice is soft, it gives me a start; I'd forgotten that anyone but Eddie had a voice. "Perfectly fucking amazing. My brother the demagogue."

"Your brother," I correct, "the demigod."

Now that we can finally turn and watch the crowd, there is nothing to see except a few faces looking at Wolf; but when their eyes meet mine they jerk around, and their backs show nothing of them. Eddie watches until the last one leaves the room.

"Charles," says Eddie from the stage. "You have some people to meet."

"Fine, soon as I change. Hey, you got an extra one of those caftan things? I like the way it hangs on you."

"Always the frivolous one, Charles." Eddie smiles and hops lightly down, his robes billowing up roundly, then settling. He places a hand on Wolf's shoulder, distant-friendly, and suddenly, tightly embraces him. "It's good to see you. I don't know," he says simply, blinking wet eyes over Wolf's shoulder, "when I've been this glad. So." He pushes apart. "How was I?"

"You need to ask?" Wolf says drily.

Eddie laughs. "I don't need to ask. I need to ask *you*. Come. You must meet the Wise Men now." He leads us up the gradual stairs of the theater.

"The Wise Men?" says Wolf, tapping on Eddie from behind. "Who are they? Clue me in."

Eddie turns to smile. "But you already know them. You always have."

We walk through the corridor until we stand before a door with two signs, one engraved steel—WAR GAMES ROOM—the other hand-lettered, on cardboard: *Wise Men Only.*

Eddie holds the door for us, and there, around an oval conference table, six wildly different men stand at their swivel chairs, like a Board of Directors upon the entrance of the Chairman. Clockwise from lower left: a scowling young man, with bold dark eyes and bristlingly short black hair, in a white doctor's tunic, the top button rakishly undone; a patriarchal fellow in a dark jacket and narrow tie, hair comb-tracked straight back, who has about him a certain lesson-giving air and an infinite capacity for human foibles; a portly professional who wears a plain gray suit, with dark half-circles engraved concentrically beneath his eyes; a clean-cut, handsome blond in a pale greenish skintight knit shirt with a gold insignia on one breast; a rangy middle-aged man dressed country-style in a plaid shirt and overalls; and a rough-and-tumble bald guy with a prominent nose and a humorous gleam in his eye.

"Charles Dewey," says Eddie. "May I present Ben Casey, Ward Cleaver, Perry Mason, Captain James Kirk, Andy of Mayberry and Kojak." Eddie beams at them with a creator's pride. "I'll leave you now," he says after a moment. "With the Wise Men."

Wolf's brother is gone and the two of us stand stunned.

"Way-ell," says Andy of Mayberry, grinning, as always, baboonishly. "Why don't you folks grab a couple seats and just make yourselves right comfortable?" He brings two swivel chairs around the table to us. We sit down dazedly, and the six Wise Men take their seats. Each has a yellow legal pad and a pencil. Now, at close range, with the fluorescent light boring deep into their skin, I know what is wrong here, what was wrong with the Honeymooners, or rather what is too right about them all: the resemblances are far too close for makeup, coincidence, or a combination of the two. Cosmetic surgery, as the ads used to say, is the answer.

Now Perry Mason—not a man who looks like Perry Mason; not even the real Raymond Burr playing the fictitious Perry Mason, but Perry Mason in the flesh—stands up, hands in pants pockets, faced away. I could not be more agog if I were meeting Abraham Lincoln. "Mr. Dewey," says Mason, with an air of piercing insight. "Please tell us your mother's maiden name."

"Matthews and what the fuck *is* this?" says Wolf.

"I'll ask you to confine yourself to the subject matter

of this inquiry," says Mason, pivoting suavely to face us. "And the purpose of that inquiry is to determine if you're really Charles Edward Dewey."

"Charles *Eldridge* Dewey," says Wolf.

Mason smiles foxily. "Excellent," he pronounces. "No further questions at this time." He seats himself impressively.

"I'm glad you have no further questions at this time," says Wolf, getting to his feet and leaning low over the table. "Because you still haven't answered mine: just what in fuck *is* this?"

"A small community is similar to a starship. Consider." Captain Kirk speaks with the old gusty stop-and-go emphasis: "We are a relatively small number of men and women sealed off from a hostile environment. We place absolute trust in every crew member, and absolute trust can be established only"—his eyebrows peak—"by absolute security."

Ben Casey signifies disagreement by folding his burly black-haired forearms wooden-Indian stiffly across his chest. "Here is exactly like a hospital ward." An expert blinker, he blinks beligerently at Kirk.

"Naow gennelmen." Andy of Mayberry, ever the arbiter, holds up two large hands. "All this discussin is just fine and dandy, but seems to me we oughta be gettin round to askin Mr. Dewey our questions, stead of quibblin mongst ourselves."

The Wise Men grow serious, study their legal pads. Ward Cleaver entangles his fingers, leans forward genially onto the table. "Tell me something about, oh, your mom's intuition."

"A sham," Wolf says shortly.

"D'you happen to remember what kind of car your dad drove?" asks Cleaver.

"An Oldsmobile, as long as I can remember."

"E used to tote a piece," says Kojak. "Peashooter or bazooka?"

"Huh?" says Wolf, looking to Ward Cleaver for a translation. But Cleaver merely screws up his face and straightens his impeccably straight tie; the poor man is out of his depth, as if Eddie Haskell's given his Wally a slingshot.

Perry Mason, hip to such matters, explains: "Your brother allegedly carried a firearm. Lieutenant Kojak is seeking to establish the caliber."

"Ah," says Wolf. "A .22."

Cleaver lets out a sigh of relief, and affable informality washes over his features. "Your mom had a special nickname for you, didn't she?" The other Wise Men lean forward for the clincher.

Wolf shifts. "He told you *that*?" Under him, the swivel chair lets out a squeaky protest.

"*Mister* Dewey," Ben Casey growls impatiently, "just as a full medical history is essential for a correct diagnosis..."

After an uncomfortable pause, Perry Mason stalks to the center of the conference table, leans in on Wolf with both hands on the table and speaks sharply: "I must direct you to answer the question. *What did your mother call you?*"

Wolf's head retracts into his neck, which, in turn, becomes part of his torso. "Puppikins."

"Puppikins? *Puppikins?*" I dissolve into helpless, hiccuping laughter. And resolve into the realization, which comes in chunks, that no one else is laughing, no one even smiling, no one, in fact, doing anything but staring at me with dull I-don't-get-it eyes, as if I just bounded in through the wrong door from another discussion, another species, maybe even another medium, as if these men are the assembled Justices of the United States Supreme Court and I am Bugs Bunny. I am in a staring contest with six icons, and losing.

"So tell me, Dewey baby." Kojak cracks a craggy smile, jerks a thumb in my direction. "Who's the stiff?"

※

The vote of the Wise Men was unanimous: Wolf was indeed Wolf, that is, the brother of Eddie Dewey, E. Earnestly, fingers intertwined atop the conference table, Ward Cleaver told the story of how Eddie had rescued him from a house in Illinois where he was encamped before the fireplace, wrapped in defunct electric blankets and living off the warmth of the last Duraflame log; Ben Casey followed with a terse tribute to Eddie, who'd found him eating pickled things in a Kansas hospital. After the vote was in, the Wise Men addressed Wolf as Mister. They really are a kind of Board of Directors: Casey, a real doctor, is in charge of medical services; Cleaver heads the counseling unit, Perry Mason oversees the legal apparatus; Andy of Mayberry and Kojak command the overt and covert police, respectively; and Captain Kirk is the underboss for military planning. Eddie himself keeps a tight grip on the essentials: food and entertainment. The Wise Men accompanied Wolf and me to an open door, shook hands and departed.

The large square room had an overdressed hotel-chain consistency: everything—from the armchairs that faced in the same direction, to the night table to the lamp and Trimline phone on it, to the heavy drapes that could not possibly have covered anything but wall—was beige. There was a console TV of the kind of wood that looks like wood-grain Formica. There were two double beds. There was a sink and mirror. There was a writing desk. I had no doubt there would be a Gideon Bible in it.

Spider-Man, Dwight D. Eisenhower, Marilyn Monroe and Jesus Christ already crouched and grinned and come-hithered and blessed from our bedroom walls, new glossy posters straight out of the mailing tubes. Dirty Harry, however, was askew, and unable to stand a crooked picture, I went and fixed it. "Is he straight?"

"He's so straight," said Wolf, sitting down heavily on a bed. The spreads were plushy tan stuff, with raised gold fleurs-de-lis. There was a brand-new terry-cloth bathrobe, blue, on each pillow, and on top of each robe two envelopes.

Wolf held up the envelopes: MULTIVITAMINS and SO-MINEX. Somewhere upstairs a toilet flushed, and we stood listening. We lowered our eyes, dully, to each other. Finally, Wolf shrugged and tore open an envelope, and still watching, I got him a cup of water. Still watching me, he swallowed a sleeping pill and gave the cup back. We took off our clothes and got into bed.

A long time goes by without much sound. "Wolf," I say, my voice too loud and sudden in the Sominexed darkness. "I'm not too sure about your brother," I add very softly.

"Not *sure*?" Wolf bursts out. "Then let me set you straight. He's poison. He's a train that jumped the rails and shot straight into the ninth dimension." Pitch scaling with incredulity, he recites: "Spider-Man. Captain Kirk. Ike Eisenhower. 'Unless thou needeth.' Fooooooo," he exhales, and when he is about to talk, sighs again. "We are in deep shit."

Emboldened, I push it further. "I'm not entirely sure we should stay here."

"You're *what*?" he squeals, then gains control of his voice. "What else did you have in mind?"

"We could leave."

"We could, huh? On foot? I think Eddie'n you need to see the same lobotomist. Do you have any idea how fast we'd freeze?"

"Not necessarily. How far is Salt Lake City? Five miles? That's where the other group is, the one Eddie talked about. You know who they probably are?" No answer from Wolf. "Remember in Homestead, Sawyer or someone talked about an exploration group sent out by the government? We'd stand a chance."

"We would," says Wolf. "We'd stand a chance. One chance in seventeen quintillion. It's not the distance. You heard Eddie—he's already attacked those people down the hill once." His voice becomes see-Dick-run simple. "They have guns. They would use them to shoot us."

"Mmm." Got a point.

"Yeah, hmmm," Wolf snaps. "Scratch your head while you still got it. And if you can come up with one single reason why we should do the hara-kiri thang you tell it to me." His voice turns toward me. "I'm all ears."

"No." I shift position. My back hurts. My head hurts.

"No I'm wrong or no I'm right?"

"No you're right. I give up. Uncle."

Later on, haggard and irritable, I arise quietly and feel around for my shirt in the darkness. Perversely comforted by the filthy ragtag workshirt in the clean sheets, I fall asleep at once.

# 9 ❋ Showtime

Kojak comes a-calling. He raps once on the door, pushes in. It is morning. The night-table lamp is on. Wolf has slipped away, having murmured the word "Breakfast" into the backwaters of my unconsciousness, stimulating dreams of bagels and lox. I am the way I've slept, fully dressed down to my waist, fully undressed below it. Kojak does not seem to notice. Kojak has seen it all. He sits down on the corner of Wolf's bed, produces a red lollipop, goes to work on it.

"The Man wants to see you, baby."

"Me?" I stand up, rubbing my eyes with both hands like a child. "Eddie wants to see me?"

He thrusts out a stubby index finger. "You, baby."

"Well . . ." I pull on pants. "What about?"

Kojak regards his lollipop.

"Now?" I say.

Kojak sticks the lollipop back in his face. "Toot-sweet."

I'm done dressing, and Kojak holds the door for me.

There are two men with guns and holsters in the hallway. They step in toward me, latch onto my upper arms.

"What is this about?" I squeal, but Kojak's said his piece. Through a corridor, a left and right, up some concrete stairs.

"Aloha." E speaks from behind a half-acre of empty desk at the end of a long narrow room. He is dressed as he was, in flowing robes, except that the robes are black and a bit more flowing than yesterday's. "Aloha," he says, "means both hello and goodbye. Which will it be?"

"What do you mean?"

"Exile, baby," says Kojak, his short arms folded.

"Isn't that what you want?" asks E in a gentle tone. "Isn't that what you want anyway?"

"No, no. I'm comfortable here, I've got everything I need—"

E gives a nod, and the two armed men step crisply to my side.

"Go now," says E softly. "Go with the gentlemen."

I stand up. Kojak holds the door for me. "After you."

Everyone follows me out. Perry Mason, brisk of stride, with briefcase, joins us in the corridor. We are on −4, the same floor as the theater. We pass some multicolored chairs, a coffee machine. "Are we—" I sputter, turning around toward E. "Is this all going to be part of some . . . *show*?"

E. smiles. "The best kind of show. A show *trial*."

Kojak goes through the door first. There is mass applause. Next is Perry Mason, and the applause rises in volume. The stage is decked out in courtroom regalia: a huge judge's bench, a witness's booth and two long tables for opposing counsel, each with a goosenecked microphone. Only the jury box is missing. Curtains hang against the high wall behind the bench. Kojak stands inside, beckoning me with a finger and a smile. I enter the room and stand paralyzed as that instant-on, instant-off applause hits me like a gust of wind. My legs lose strength, go wobbly, go woozy. I take a deep breath and blunder toward one of the attorneys' tables.

The two guards step in and flank the doorway. One hollers, "All rise," and all do. The clapping reaches its crescendo and I don't need to turn around to know that

E has made his entrance. Nothing else happens until he has taken the judge's bench. And now all sit.

E looks down upon me. "Mr. Debrick," he says, his amplified voice reverberating through the room. "You are accused of third-degree treason. How do you plead?"

"Treason . . . ?" I repeat. I see Wolf in yesterday's front-row seat, mouth open, tongue pressed to the roof as if he has just murmured the same word.

"Have you heard the charge, Mr. Debrick?" E asks sharply. I nod. "How do you plead?"

This part I know. "Not guilty."

The crowd politely applauds; now they will see a show.

"You have the right to counsel of your own choosing," says E in a Miranda-rights drone. "Or if you wish, the Bench will appoint counsel. Finally, you have the option of representing yourself."

"Who can I choose from?"

"Anyone in the courtroom," says E.

Immediately, on media-reflex, I look to Perry Mason. He stares back hard at me from the other attorney's table. Della Street, as always, is by his side. She smiles demurely and turns up a placard that reads PROSECUTION. Just as well; this is not the Mason I know. Perry Mason for the Prosecution? I gaze out into the audience.

Wolf, fiery, locks eyes with me. "I choose," I say steadily into the microphone. "Charles Dewey." The crowd lets out a collective gasp.

"Very well," says E, reaching into a breast pocket and putting on a pair of half-framed glasses identical to Wolf's. "But I am obliged to inform you and your prospective counsel that under Section 39(e) of the Rules of Criminal Procedure, the attorney will share with his client whatever sentence is imposed. In the case of third-degree treason, of course, the sentence is exile."

"In that case . . ." I begin.

"Please speak into the microphone, Mr. Debrick," E booms. "There is a Jury of three hundred people trying to hear you."

*They* are my Jury? "In that case," I say, "I will represent myself."

"Now the trial will begin," announces E.

During steady prolonged applause, clapping that seems to result more from an ongoing state of general satisfaction than from any specific stimulus, three men with video cameras and tripods come onstage; one positions himself by my side, one by Perry Mason at the Prosecutor's table, and one below the bench, pointed up at E. A couple of men follow, scurrying low, disentangling wires, and then a natty fellow in a jacket, tie and fedora, who sits down at my table. A cameraman aims at him, and he begins speaking rapidly, urgently in a sharp-cheddar Walter Winchell voice. "We are here today at the jury trial of Max Debrick, Justice E presiding, where the alleged offense is third-degree treason and the atmosphere crackles with a grim, tense excitement." He pauses breathlessly, rattles a few sheets of paper and rushes on: "As you know, treason is a serious offense carrying appropriately severe penalties. In Section 111(b)(vi) of the Rules of Criminal Procedure (hereafter 'RCP'), treason in the first degree is defined as treasonous acts against the State, in the second degree as conspiracy to commit first-degree treason, and in the third degree as contemplation of second-degree treason. For purposes of determining the penalty to be imposed should a conviction be reached, treason in the third degree is considered the equivalent of second-degree treason, and treason in the second degree is treated the same as first-degree treason. Thus," he says, pausing dramatically, setting the script down, looking straight into the camera, "the case of Max Debrick comes full circle."

"Will the Prosecution have an opening statement?" says E.

Perry Mason looks up, hands folded atop the Prosecutor's table. "None, Your Honor."

"Does the Defense wish to make a statement?" asks E, his head bobbing fairly toward me.

"No, no statement."

"Does the Prosecution wish to call any witnesses to the stand?"

"Only one," says Perry Mason, rising to his feet. "If it please the Court," he begins, striding toward the bench, "we call Max Debrick."

Mill, mill, goes the audience, noise, noise. Rutabagarutabagarutabaga: the thing that actors say in crowd scenes. I get up slowly, a live defendant plucked from a jail cell and shoved onto a courthouse set, and make my way to the witness box. As I seat myself there is an audible mass inhalation, a leaning-forward of many torsos. Mason addresses me, faces them. "Mr. Debrick." He slowly turns. "Have you at any time since your arrival Here made any statements of any kind concerning our community or our leader? Specifically, have you made any adverse or critical statements of the aforementioned nature?"

Out in the audience, Wolf's head is shaking tick-tick No by millimeters. He will not say anything.

"I have made no such statements," I say boldly into the microphone. My amplified words come out a little too loud.

"Then will you kindly tell the Court your true sentiments toward this community?"

"I think you've done very well, all things considered," I begin slowly. "I believe you have created an amazingly comfortable world for yourselves. The search for lessons from the past has great validity." I'm warming to the subject. "Your focus on classic TV programs, and that's what they are, real classics, is fascina—"

"Wolf." I am interrupted by my own voice, but I am not speaking. "I'm not too sure about your brother."

"Do you recognize that voice, Mr. Debrick?" says Perry Mason, pacing in front of the booth.

Where is it coming from? Above and behind E, motorized curtains whir apart to reveal a video screen, and red-black forms move on a background of blackness. Infrared light, the bastards.

"Is that your voice, Mr. Debrick?" says Mason, stopping in front of me.

"Of course, but—"

"I'm not entirely sure we should stay here," says my voice. "We could leave." I am up in front of six hundred critical eyes, in the flesh, on live camera and on the screen, where I am dimly visible lying in bed, my knees up, quite naked, larger than life. Della Street hits a button in the table, and the words and image repeat: "We could leave. We could leave."

"Wait a minute!" I say finally. "You're using evidence that was . . ." What's the phrase?

"Objection sustained," says E immediately. Della hits a button, silencing "me." The big screen goes bright for a second, fades to a pinpoint. "The Jury," says E, "will disregard the evidence."

Perry Mason says after a pause, "You *could* certainly leave, Mr. Debrick, as you observed. Our door is always open, at least in the outgoing direction."

"I don't want to."

"Will you tell the Court why not?"

"I couldn't survive out there."

"That is not our primary concern," says Mason. "What will you add to what is already Here? Will you add your unquestioning faith in what we are doing?"

"Yes!" I bark. "Yes, I will."

"Do you think we are . . ." Mason touches his chin. ". . . warlike?"

"No, no, I wouldn't say that."

Mason smiles. "You wouldn't?" A few chuckles from the crowd. "Because we *are* warlike. It is necessary that we be warlike."

"Well, in a way, but I don't think—"

"Mr. Debrick," says Perry Mason. "Have you ever taken a polygraph test?" My heart sinks to the floor, bounces once, and lies there dead. "I mention this because," Mason continues, "such a test can be arranged without delay."

Three men dolly out into the middle of the stage a plush green reclining chair, another video camera and a cart with a large complicated device bristling with wires. The cameraman points straight down into the machine, and the screen lights up; he adjusts the lens and a huge VU meter comes into focus. Applause bursts forth.

"Cut the shit!" cries Wolf suddenly. Everyone in the room turns to him, uniformly startled. "You have me on the same videotape. Why aren't you asking *me* these questions?"

There is a pause. "Your Honor," says Mason politely, "I do not remember having called Mr. Dewey to testi—"

E silences him with a hand. "Charles has not been

called upon to answer because I have known Charles for
fifty years."

After a suitable pause, Perry Mason smiles, turns to
the crowd. "Your witness, 'counsel.'"

※

The vote was nearly unanimous: three hundred nineteen
to one. I would be allowed to sleep Here under guard for
a single night, and bright and early the next morning I
would be shown the door, wearing only the shirt, boots
and overalls I came with. I could carry my saxophone
and would in addition, as provided by the RCP, Section
115(e)(viii), be given one blanket and one book of strike-
anywhere matches. The gavel came down, the Walter
Winchell man wiped his forehead with a monogrammed
handkerchief and gave an eloquent summary with a lesson in it somewhere, and everybody went home satisfied.

"It's a wrap," someone said before they dragged me
off.

※

Up, up in the guard-station elevator we go, −4, −3, me
and Wolf and E and two guys with guns, toward the great
outdoors and its new improved version of winter, −2,
accompanied by the Muzak strains of "You Are the Sun-
shine of My Life." −1. After the skin-search Wolf exer-
cised visitation rights, so in addition to what I've been
allowed I have two cigarette lighters, two pairs of socks
and a half pint of peppermint schnapps.

"Don't wait around hoping for me to let you back in,"
says E as the elevator doors open.

Wolf steps forward, grabs my elbow. The thinness of
his face makes his eyes seem to stand in relief. Out of all
the possible nicknames, what will Wolf call me? Out of
all possible goodbyes, what will he say?

"I'm coming with you."

"No, Wolf. Two men, one blanket. We wouldn't make
it."

"*We* would make it," says Wolf, tightening his grip.
"*You* won't. You need me."

E recoils as if slapped in the face.

Wolf does not move his eyes from mine.

"Separate them!" cries E, too loudly, too sharply.

Wolf and I stand staring, and I pry his fingers from my arm. He latches onto my hand, clutches it, and his palm is wet, sweating.

The men stick their pistols in my back, push until I am outside the elevator.

"Max!" says Wolf as the steel doors close between us. "Don't die."

# 10 ⁂ A Park, a Map, a Peak

Peter Lassen, born in the old country in 1800, died fifty-nine years later, in the New World, at the hands of assailant or assailants unknown. Lassen was on a silver prospecting expedition in northwestern Nevada with Lemericus Wyatt and a man called Clapper, whose Christian name was known only to himself. An Indian approached the party and asked in mime for powder, caps and bullets. Over the strenuous protests of his two companions, Lassen sold the Indian everything he wanted. He patiently explained to Clapper and Wyatt that he was a personal friend of the great chief Winnemucca, and that he was so beloved of one of Winnemucca's tribes that its members called him "Uncle Pete." All Indians, Lassen assured Clapper and Wyatt, knew Uncle Pete and would never harm anyone fortunate enough to be associated with him.

One day, as they slept under a dawning sky, Wyatt heard the report of a rifle. Clapper, who was sleeping between him and Lassen, had already been shot through the temple. Lassen awoke as Wyatt ran off, exhorting

253

Lassen to do the same. But Uncle Pete did not run anywhere, not then, not ever again; he simply stood up where he was, shading his eyes against the sun and looking for the person who had dared to fire these shots in his direction. He might as well have had a target painted on his chest.

The widespread assumption, when Wyatt raced bareback to the nearest town and breathlessly related the bloody incident, was that Uncle Pete had been done in by one of his many "nephews." But Indians in those parts killed for property, and when investigators reached the Lassen camp three days later they found it undisturbed. Greatly expanding the list of suspects was the oft-circulated rumor that Lassen had carried a map showing the whereabouts of a vast silver mine.

It would not have been difficult, in any case, to find someone with a motive for killing Peter Lassen. No other man in California had earned as many enemies, with the possible exception of James Marshall, who had discovered gold at Sutter's Mill on January 24, 1848, and had since traveled widely over the state declaring that all gold found since then belonged to him.

Peter Lassen did have a mountain named after him, don't forget. Greater men can say less. Greater men have had to settle for statues. And which was the craggy peak so blessed? Saint Joseph's Mountain, now known as Lassen Peak, in the middle of the Lassen National Park, where lo these many years ago a lost Dane with guns at his back had walked the longest plank in history. It turned out, naturally, to be a volcano.

# 11 ❊ Winter Wonderland

I've given some thought to this moment. Watch me now in the guard station, preparing to pay a forced visit to nature in its glory, a smooth, oiled survival machine, doubling, tripling the blanket into a long strip, winding it once around my head, once around my face, once around my neck, and tying it off. I take off my boots, peel off a pair of socks, put my boots on, and wear the socks as mittens. It is 7:09 a.m.

The door is frozen shut. I kick it open. There is no wind. I can, I can make it to Salt Lake City, to whatever's left of the government expedition, to shelter and warmth. It can't be more than five miles. An hour and a half under normal conditions, two hours now. The thing is to keep moving. Survival machine.

I am past the entry gate, the desolate flats of Eddie's military base. Snow, not much, boot-high snow crunches as the fused lump of our jeep passes out of sight.

The road is snow over ice; I slip to my ass on the hill, and quickly slap the snow off before it has a chance to settle. The thing is to get moving, to keep moving. Snow,

255

snow and snow. How many different words did the Eskimos have for it?

It's no colder than it was when we came Here. I pick through the snow with a high plucky step, my breath heaving out large solid puffs of steam that hang in the still air like thought balloons. This artificial winter can't last forever. In another month, two or three, it's got to break. My chest and knees are the first to feel the chill. Another few minutes and they'll be numb. I'll need a fire, but what will I burn? It is colder. Luck of the draw: I've drawn a cold day.

The road turns, and a traffic sign comes into sight. The wooden signposts: there's my fuel! But not yet. My toes are cold; I wiggle them, keep wiggling them. Got to keep my feet warm. The sign says SALT LAKE CITY 14. Miles?

Miles?

Although I want to plump my dumb ass on the road and contemplate this new development, I go on. The cold dry air has reached the wetness in my nose; I try breathing through my mouth. No good, it wets the cloth over my face, and my lungs feel too much burning dry-ice air at once. Where was it written that the city was only five miles away? Five miles was one of those figures, I now remember with perverse satisfaction, that gets batted around until it is accepted as fact. Five miles? "I read it somewhere." The saxophone, wonderful conductor of heat and cold that it is, spreads an icy burning in my chest.

The road, in the way of mountain roads, winds and winds. Should I leave it and take the short way? No, too much snow, weird topography, no signposts to burn.

Less snow on the road. Strange how my lungs haven't warmed up again. Time to think serious thoughts about fire. At the next sign. My nose, if I touched it, might break off in my hand. A brittle beak, a brittle beak. You repeat yourself.

My toes no longer take literally the instruction to wiggle, and sort of undulate in a row. My hands, shoved up under my armpits, are warm. Thank God for small favors. Give me a sign.

I fall again and get up not at all easily, in sections.

New numb areas: the ass, the elbow: don't know the proverbial one from the other. Losing my coordination. Speech slurred if I spoke. The classic symptoms. Tough guy. Survival machine.

Toes report complete numbness. Keep moving. Need a sign. The wind kicks up, nothing fancy, just enough to drill through my legs, my stiff lock-kneed legs. Great. I fall down again. A little roll in the hay. Some snow gets through to my hands, melts, freezes. Does not bode well. Stop. Go. Keep moving. I need a. There is a sign. Blunder toward. Twelve, it says. Miles. Miles.

I side-kick the sign; as if in retribution it sends a vibration of pain, rattling pain, through my shin to my knee. The feet feel nothing. Kick again. Again. Tilting at windmills, losing my balance, falling down in the snow. The sign looms above, bent backward at an angle of mild surprise.

Kick, and kick again. Pain heats up my right leg. Heat is good; ergo pain must be good. Kick! Kick! The signpost craaacks, bows toward the snow. Victory is ours. Survival machine!

Fire time. I hold a cigarette lighter shiver-steady under a corner of the signpost. Silently, giving forth a single hair width of smoke, it burns. Got it going. Burns, and burns out.

I need kindling. Twigs? Too deep in the snowdrifts. My shirt? Insane. The lighter fluid. I lay the little plastic gem on the painted wood, smash it with my boot and watch the butane spurt off in all directions, into the snow.

One lighter left. A low blue flame spreads from it across the fluid-spattered patch of signpost. The paint cracks until it looks like alligator skin. Keep the flame on it, keep it on. The wood glows red, it glows! The fluid worked. There is a fire, I can even hear it in the windless air. Keep the damn flame on it, on it.

A real fire. I push my hands near, smell burning fiber. Too close. Feeling starts to come back into my fingers.

What to do with a fire? Take off my boots and warm my feet? Bad idea. The flame crawls up, slowly up toward SALT LAKE CITY 12. My face. The smoke makes me cough. I move around to the other side and see the black smoke licking the dry sky. Please somebody see it. Dot-dot-dot dash-dash-dash dot-dot-dot.

The fire burns for a good long while, and I lean parts of myself in toward the flame, warming leg, thigh, breast, tiny chicken parts of myself, while the rest, the great bodily mass, grows colder. I'll need a bigger fire, a much bigger fire, and then I'll need another. I get up from the wispy embers.

*Things I will need.* A winter coat. A car. A gas lantern. Down booties, blue, extra large. I've got maybe four more unwarmed miles in this body. Long underwear. Ski mask. Roasted chestnuts. Ninety-nine bottles of beer on the wall. Serve at room temperature. Serve in warm room.

On and on and on down and down and down I plod, an automatic marching machine, like those plastic toys you set on an incline and watch their legs shuffle forward by weight of gravity.

Exit 94 2 1/2 and two signposts. I'm a wild brute, kick down the sign in three savage blows. There, there in the jagged wood, I'll make my fire. I stamp on the metal face of the sign until I can roll it up with the posts and carry Exit 94 2 1/2 cradled in my arms. Interstate 15, a single signpost, is next, and I trudge on with my burden. Exit 94 1 1/4 falls prey to me too, the smart guy, the ultimate survivor. At Exit 94 I'll make my fire. And on I move, the cold spilling from the deep-frozen wood into my chest and arms, a wheezing, banging, clanging, asymmetrical bundle of wintertime fun, a very slow train coming.

My fingers begin jerking around under the strain, and my biceps pick up the idea, cramping, charley-horsing, hydraulic pumps with a bubble in their throats. I drop the bundle three times, once on my foot, certain there should be pain, but what I can feel of my body ends a little below my groin.

I unwind the blanket and make a sling to carry half the road signs in the state of Utah on my back. It's easy, until the cold wind, that airborne acupuncturist, begins to explore, to lay claim to and dig tiny point-bottomed flags into the pores in my cheeks and forehead. Exit 94, where are you? Give me a sign.

Careful: if I fall forward, I'm squashed: I keep my steps slow and small, because my legs have stopped obeying any but the simplest orders. A long straight-away, and at the end a sign? Must be, there's a great sweep of road to the side, but I can't read the sign because my eyes won't quite focus, are fixed only on things close to me like a stuck camera lens. Yes, that's what it says: Exit 94, with an arrow, and below that Salt Lake City 7.

I loosen the sling and drop the heavy load with a clatter. The legs attached to this torso will not kick down another sign. Why not throw my shoulder against the posts? Unh! Because it won't work. I pick up the bundle of signs and swing it like a great baseball bat. Again. Again. Again. Again. And the sign, the last sign, is down.

I bend the legs of the signs until the ends meet. Lighter fluid again? Not with my last lighter. The schnapps--alcohol! I overturn the bottle onto signposts, extend the lighter at arm's length, keep my face well out of range.

Nothing. The liquor must be too cold to ignite. And now I've lost my keg of brandy. Damn. God damn.

I place the lighter on a post, and rock my boot side to side across it until it cracks, just barely cracks. I hold the lighter over the jagged ends of the signposts and press the crack with my thumbs until the fluid drips out into the wood. And it just now occurs to me that those matches had better be dry.

They're not. Fiss. Fiss. I scrape one after another of the soggy things, wipe out half the black strip on the side of the matchbox. Images of the Little Match Girl occur to me; what a rotten ending I am concocting for the story, with the last poignant match a soggy dud. Three matches from the end I win the lottery, and the butane-soaked wood begins, gratifying, to burn.

Soon I have a fine fire, a big enough fire that I regain pain in my legs and nose and arms, and I sit down by it, know it's stupid but sit down by it, warming my face and hands and arms and torso at once. It's 10:10; three hours. Now I'll have the—oh. Have the schnapps. But I can: I taste the snow where it spilled: sweet and mint. I grab a handful of eighty-proof snow and suck it down, then another, quickly because the flame is melting itself down through the snow to the road's bare asphalt. The alcohol warms my insides, lightens my head, lowers my eyelids. This fire, no kidding, has stripped away the hard carapace of Nature to reveal a creation of Man, and I'm proud of it. A solemn column of smoke ascends from my fire, an I in the sky. Look at it, whipping, spreading, unfurling through the air: it's hair, hair underwater, hair on a pillow, hair in the wind. I don't even mind the weather right now; there are simply masses of white everywhere, if you choose to look at it that way. It's a winter wonderland, that's what it is, a wonderland. The last thing I remember before falling asleep was trying to sing "Ninety-nine Bottles of Beer on the Wall" and forgetting the tune.

I had one more lucid interval after that. I woke up with my face in the snow. The fire had gone out, but I didn't mind because the cold wasn't the problem. No, actually I was too hot and not only didn't need a fire but had to get out of all my clothes as well. I flung off my boots and pulled my overalls down from my ankles and tore the shirt off my chest, popping all the buttons. I didn't mind the saxophone.

"Goodbye!" I sang. I was dreadfully, fatally drunk. I was naked in the snow, as naked as an embryo in the womb. I was in the last stage of hypothermia. I was seven miles from Salt Lake City and not getting any closer. "Goodbye!" I sang. "Goodbye World!"

# 12 ❃ Phosphorescence

My arm swims in the darkness, glowing around the edges. I move my fingers in the black water and they too light up, five tentacles of some neon octopus.

Monica and I have escaped in the dead of a summer night from her family's beachfront house, having heard the wine-aided crescendos of laughter from both pairs of parents upstairs and known that we have hours before they will break up their party.

In the year since her family moved away Monica's changed, grown tall and stately, with enormous and enormously mischievous slightly slanted brown eyes and a closed-mouth smile that I can never figure out, mocking or inviting. At fourteen she looks twenty. At fourteen I look fourteen.

Nobody knows I love her, least of all Monica, who has been treated to my first fiction, to the effect that I've fallen for a girl at school. In letters I've concocted an elaborate fantasy life, movies and dances, Gail and me, me and Gail. Only the name and the facts have been changed.

Tonight I'm leaning against the four-by-four supports of the sun deck and gazing, ninth-grade romantically, at the moon. "Do you think I . . . ?"

"Think you what?" says Monica from the carpet, lying on her back with her legs up on the bed. Extended conversations, whether over the phone or in person, seem to bring out the contortionist in her.

"Do you think I love Gail?"

"Yeah, maybe." She tilts her head back, looks at me upside down. "Yeah."

And we've slipped out the back door and down the thousand wooden stairs to the beach for an illicit midnight swim. Our parents would kill us, which is the best part. We are running, we are wild, and tonight I will, I will tell her.

It's a cool black night, but the water's going to be warmer. We're sitting on the beach removing our shoes. And she's taking off her pants and I can't let myself look; I grip down into the damp sand, trying to get it under my fingernails and cause a little pain to blunt an incipient erection.

"Max."

"What?" I still can't look.

"Your hand."

Sparks in the sand; someone must have been here a few minutes before, tossed a cigarette. But the wide beach is utterly deserted, and the coarse sand heavy with moisture.

Monica scissors her legs across the surface, leaving a broad swath of sparks. It's in the sand, in the sand itself.

I really have to do something to conceal myself; I jump up and dash into the water. My arm swims in the darkness, edges glowing as if brightly lit from behind. Now Monica's in beside me, dog-paddling, her white bare arms and legs lit up.

"Monica, look!" I splash and the water is on fire. She's watching me tread water, watching my body, extremities glowing as they move, snuffed out invisible as they rest.

"Do you think it's bad for us?" she says softly, mesmerized. Her hair splays out on the pillow of the sea, slowly sinking in the warm water, lit by and lighting my fingers.

"Monica," I tell her, bobbing in the calm surf. "There's no such thing as Gail."

"What?"

"Gail is you, what I'd like to do with you."

Just then an invisible wave rose up out of nowhere and swallowed me, churning, gulping, milling, glowing, drowning, in it.

I awoke on my back in shallow water, and the first thing I saw was my own arm waving gently, borne floating, limp-limber in the foam like a bright sea plant.

✳

My arm swims in the dark, glowing.

"Are you alright? Are you awake?" she says, leaning over me, her features deep in darkness.

"Yeah." The ground is hard, not water, not sand, and quakes a little. "You're not Monica."

She shakes her head, and a halo of light surrounds her momentarily. She's a grown woman, but her eyes do look like Monica's. "No," she says, with Monica's smile. "Can you move your fingers?"

I open and shut my hands. They light up.

"Good," she says, and moves away. Splashes of light burst on the walls, snuff themselves out, where she is banging, not in panic, with her fists.

A man comes in, moving so quickly and giving off so much light I can make out not only his features but also the contours of the long narrow jolting room. He's wearing overalls. He gets down near me on all fours, and his head, a familiar mobile cannonball of a head, moves to speak. "How's my favorite buck?"

I'm mashing his fat cheeks with my hands, rubbing that bald head. "It's you. It really is."

Gary Tascheira smiles. "Of course."

"Garibaldi—" I say, my voice a startling shredded croak. He bends down close to me, and I whisper. "That woman—I love her."

"Of course," he says again. He feels my forehead, then his own. "Max, listen to me if you can. You are inside a broken-down Fruehauf truck being hauled by sixty-seven men and women. This light you see when people move is not an illusion. It's real. I found you naked in the snow outside Salt Lake City with the saxophone around your neck. You were nearly dead. I think you're delirious, so lie still and gain strength. Sleep if you want. We need you." He gets up and starts to leave.

I raise my head. "But who is *she*?"

"She'll tell you," says Gary Tascheira, exiting out a door in the side of the truck, ducking his fat head back in. "She'll tell you."

I am alone and unseeing with fever, God knows where, with this woman, God knows who, in a Fruehauf truck, God knows why. I am a sightless slab of meat and half a brain. "I love you," I murmur into a blind of hazy red capillaries. "I love you. Do you love me?"

"Not yet," says her voice, coming from very near me.

❊

In the lazy, murmurous, feverish aura, pieces of me, a left foot, an ear, some toes, seem to float down, to materialize within the wavering boundaries of my claim on life, pieces of me and pieces of information half-stated into the great glowing night, the phosphorescent night, for as I tell the woman somewhere between When and Where, phosphorescence is what you call it when the beach, the ocean and everything on or in them light up like this, pieces of information, for example that I am getting better and that her name is Catherine. She seems to pour her strength into me, Catherine, to lend me what is hers through the tingling agency of her hands. Hands that transmit, that exchange, and that grasp beyond their physical grasp and beyond the words which, with a strange lying tentativeness, we force into the air between us at irregular intervals, words which require engagement and interpretation and a whole host of mincing, pirouetting etiquettes foreign to hands.

I pass days or decades in this Hallmark-card delirium where all suns are huge and red, all moons are harvest moons, and all depth, all foreground and background is collapsed and telephotoed, where all sights—the slit of light in the truck's side that opens into a rectangle, fills with a human silhouette, becomes a slit and closes off into darkness again—and all sounds—the dry creak of the suspension, the kerosene heater going tk-tk-tk like an entropic metronome—are gauzy, pretty-pretty, all words are writ in script and *Everything Means So Much*®.

I'm forced to discount my perceptions: This week only, 50% off all items in our massive inventory. That's right, take what you see and subtract half. Limited time only. Everything must go. Numbers that represent nothing float obsessively by me in the darkness: if the Honeymooners = 22 and Wolf = 16, then Wolf + Honeymooners = 38, and 38-50% discount = 19. The price to you: 19. 19 dollars, 19 units, 19 ergs, 19 watts, 19 whats. Story problems. But what if Wolf = 2,009,009? Reality 50% off. This item as is. All items as is. Don't trust what you see. Floor models. Factory seconds. Demonstrators. Slightly used. This week only. Lost our lease. Everything must go.

My mind the liver, filtering out the irrelevant; the broom, sweeping the junk into a corner; the ragpicker, wading through the memory dump, selecting, discarding, selectively discarding; the divining rod: here is dirt, here is water. But what if the divining rod is bent? Here's what you want, it says; here is water. But you dig beneath the dirt and hit oil. Drink the water; don't drink the water. What to believe? Believe nothing. Believe everything. Apply 50% discount: believe half of everything. This week only.

And so it seems to me that I am in a spinning house in a tornado, with wizards and wicked witches and loved ones floating by. Where will you set down, house? Buena Park, 1957? Kansas, perchance? A missile base called Here? World's Fair, 1938? Hiroshima, mon amour? Now or Then? Harrisburg? Manhattan? Oh, where have you gone, Billy Bo, Billy Bo?

And so it seems to me that I am in a fish tank being pulled along a road. Sick fish, just lies there on the bottom of the tank. Is he dead yet?

And so it seems to me that two strange creatures, heads large and bodies small, hover over me in the darkness, fuzzy, glowing, their great eyes great with curiosity. Puppies-kittens-goslings-cubs. People, small size.

Hold on to that. Called...? Ah. Children. Children looking down on me. Could be. Could it be? 50% off.

And so it seems to me that I am on an abacus bridge. And on this bridge are rods, and beads, and other people; I have it all figured out. When one person slips, one bead slides over, knocks into other beads and other people on those beads also lose their footing. You don't even know all the people on your own rod until you lose your footing, until the person next to you loses his footing, and his neighbor, and his neighbor, until you are all falling through the bridge and finally see each other for the first time, while up above, on the surface of the abacus bridge, you hear dozens of people, dozens, hundreds, millions of beads slamming crazy, slamming haywire. The only thing like it, for quantity, for linkedness, for sheer slapstick, is a nuclear reaction.

And so it seems to me that I am being nursed by Monica: she loves me, loves me not; Monica, not-Monica, Monaica; girl, woman, girl; loves me, loves me not.

And so many things seem to me. Half of them seem; all of them half-seem. Half of one, six dozen of the other.

And one night—or day, the truck is dark as a cave, unless I move and by my movement light it up—I wake with an electric current buzzing solidly through me, through all connected all of me, my fever broken, alive, no doubt in the world, alive. The kerosene heater hisses calmly. The night, the truck, the great caravan of haulers and callers are still. So it is day; the truck moves only at night. Tk! goes the heater.

I sit up. And fall down dead. And wake up from my blackout and sit more slowly this time. The saxophone is somewhere to the left—I've seen it—and I, Max on percussion, go clumping, go tripping, go noising through the truck, the clanging, banging four-alarm truck in which everything seems to be made of metal. I have it, I have the magic flute. I sit and listen in the sudden quiet. No one, miraculously, comes. I blow silently, cautiously, loose-lipped soundlessly into the horn, I finger some scales, and I need no light, no help here. Tk! goes the heater, out of time. Tk! Tk!

And I wake as I've waked so often before, with Catherine's hand moving softly, water-softly, across my forehead. Long before I know what I'm doing I pull her hand down and kiss it. It's the first time I've done anything like that to her.

She sighs. Her face is large, with wide prominent American Indian cheekbones and a jaw line so strong and fiercely defined it is almost belligerent. A decisive face and one that, when lent to decision, will cling to it with the authority of passion. With her eyes closed she looks nothing like Monica, but all my need to see a resemblance to Monica has long since disappeared. "The patient is well."

"That's the idea, isn't it?"

"Yes," she says with an air of resignation. "That's the idea. It means I'll have no more excuse to come back here and take care of you."

"Oh. Well, I've been practicing. I could learn to be sick for a long long time."

She shakes her head, keeping her eyes on me. "Maybe would never be alive if we worked like that."

"Say that again." Makes no sense.

"Maybe would never—oh. Maybe is what we call ourselves." She smiles ruefully. "In honor of our chances for survival."

"Maybe, huh?" I smile. "E's group calls itself Here. Just Here. And they have a name for you too. They call you the Lost."

Murder comes into her eyes. "They'll kill us. Sooner or later, they will kill us. We've got to get as far away as we can." She scowls at me piercingly, even accusingly, her jutting jaw jutting.

"Don't look at *me*. I couldn't agree with you more."

"Then as soon as you are capable you must get up and help pull us along instead of being pulled. I am capable right now. Do you know what's in this truck?"

"No."

"Things that weigh. Hundreds of gallons of radiation-free water, six submachine guns, five thousand rounds of ammunition, lead-lined cases of seeds, bags of chemical fertilizer . . . The motor has a cracked block, so the only engine of this truck is us, harnessed up and hauling it. You get it? Hauling lead cases of seeds. Lead bullets. All that water. Cases of tools and medical supplies. A microfilm machine and library. And two bodies about to become one."

"Catherine . . ." I smile, holding my arms out to her.

She stands up. "Because I'm leaving. I'm going to help the rest of us drag your carcass."

"Please don't go yet." I'm desperate for her, and I make sure every bit of that desperation shows on my face. I wouldn't stand a chance if it were her need against mine; but it is only her duty that stands now against my need.

She looks at me, curious, and sits down, stiff and proper. "Survivor's syndrome," she says.

"No." I try to stop her with a palm. "Don't explain it."

"The tendency," she begins in a soft voice, "to fall in love with the person one perceives as having saved one's life." A soft voice that doesn't match the pedantry of the words.

"Put your hands on me again," I beg. "Please." She reaches out unwillingly, her hands hard tools plying my face. "Close your eyes now, Catherine. Close your eyes."

She does, and gradually her hands relax, mold themselves to me. I pull her down by those hands and kiss her very lightly on the lips. Her eyes are wide, startled, and her head rears weakly, unpersuasively away from mine; I bring a hand up over the nape of her neck, the base of her skull to her forehead, where I pull aside a few stray hairs pressed between our lips, and gently down, closing her eyes. Her fat lips, like her hands, soften and soften into mine.

"Tell me something," I finally say. She opens her eyes, and in them only a lazy pleasure remains, a pliable tiredness. "Are there any children here?"

"Three."

"So I did see them. And how many total?"

"Seventy-one."

"Did Gary tell me sixty-seven, or was that a dream?"

"That was ten days ago. We have four new people. They're in relatively good shape. They've been living in a Safeway, and they're going to lead us to it."

"How did they find you?"

"They saw the phosphorescence, I guess." A corner of her mouth turns up. "We advertise."

"What is it?"

She shrugs. "It doesn't produce any heat, and we're not giving off any radiation, so I can't explain it in any of the normal ways." She puts her head back down near mine. "I'll tell you about a dream I had."

I put my arms around her. I had imagined her, draped in her blankets, as a large woman. She's not. "A nightmare?" I ask.

"It was a dream about my mother," she says. "We were in the kitchen, and she was cutting vegetables for a stew. Suddenly she laid the knife aside and said, 'I'm tired.' She sat down at the dining table and took my hand. It all seemed very formal, almost rehearsed, one of those parental spiels. She told me something like There comes a time, Catherine, when everyone you love must leave you.

"'I know that, Mom,' I said. I was assuming that was it, a simple truism on life and death, but she started to explain the whole thing to me, how since her death she'd been doing what she could to help us. She and the others. How they were weak now, just about used up, and could only come to us when we were sleeping. It was easier, somehow, than to appear in the physical world. She told me, 'You're dreaming now, Catherine, as a matter of fact.' It made me jump, start to wake up. My mother put her hand on my arm like she could hold me down with her, and she said this was the last time I'd see her.

"She picked up the salt shaker and held it high, upside down. The grains of salt fell and caught fire for a second, like tiny shooting stars burned up and gone before they could hit the table.

"'That's just what we're going to do,' said my mother. 'That's just what we're going to do.'

"I woke up and knew she'd been right that I'd never see her again. I didn't understand anything else in the dream. I don't think I opened my eyes for a long time, just cried and cried, because the first thing I remember seeing was this aura, this Saint Elmo's fire around my body that grew more intense as I moved. And I looked down the rows of people and some of them were giving off this same weird light. Cheryl was sleeping next to me; when she woke up glowing she started to scream. She thought she was radioactive.

"Someone went into the truck and broke out the Geiger counters. We didn't register. Sleep was out of the question for the rest of the night, so we got up, made some food, that kind of thing, and when we moved we were so bright it hurt your eyes.

"It turned out we'd all had versions of the same dream. We couldn't figure out what the ghosts thought they were doing for us. The light didn't help us see much farther. It didn't keep us warm.

"Fifty-three of us had started out with the government exploration group. Sixteen had died; a group of five had refused to go any farther, just asked for their share of food and sat down in the road. Our big fancy truck full of the fruits and seeds of civilization broke down in the middle of nowhere. We couldn't move it, and we couldn't leave it. The cold was coming on; we told each other it was just an early winter, but we knew better. We were down to thirty-two people gathered around a house with wheels stranded somewhere on the Arizona freeway.

"The morning after the dream three stragglers came in, men thin as rails, with frostbitten feet. They said they saw our lights. They thought we were a city—that's how bright it was in the beginning. We found that with their help we could just barely budge the rig. It was very slow, but as long as we were moving we felt that we were getting somewhere. And every time we thought we had no chance, couldn't yank the weight another step, someone would see us, crawl out of a cave or a sewer and see us. We began to talk about 'making it,' and we didn't mean to the next meal. Somewhere along the way we started to view ourselves as the only thing between the human past and human extinction. Now we're twice as many. A rolling snowball. But from that night on the ghosts disappeared."

"Seventy-one," I repeat. She nods, and I hold her. Our bodies are hot together after all this time, pleasantly hot. "So seventy-one, counting you and me? Let sixty-nine pull the truck today, just today."

"I can't."

"This is the Little Wagon Train That Could. So you can." We kiss again, and kiss. We are hot together, restlessly, tossingly hot.

She smiles. "I can."

How can sex be so good sometimes between people who don't much like each other, or so bad between two people in love? Today it's the latter, to the extent it actually happens. We kiss, we roll around, and just when I begin to push up her sweater she says, "You're ready. C'mon."

"Yeah, but . . ."

"But what? No buts."

I'm poised above her, my hands spread beside her shoulders, my clothed penis pulsing obediently, patiently away. This is no position in which to collect one's thoughts. "Well," I say. "What about birth control?"

"Birth *control*?" she laughs. "The less the better." Deftly, firmly, she undoes my pants, yanks them to my knees, wets her fingers in her mouth, smears the head of my cock with saliva. "That's why I'm going to lie very still. It's supposed to be the best way for conception. Now c'mon."

She's dry, not ready. "Does it hurt?"

"Not much." She smiles.

Not *much*? What am I, a dime-operated horsie out front of a supermarket? Guess so; in an appallingly short time I'm a man-machine in heat.

"Go hard," she says, a simple order, not feigning anything, not even breathing fast. "Go deep."

And there I am above and inside the woman I love, shouting Move! move! and thinking that men are idiots and Portnoy could fuck a steak, and over and under and inside her now smiling, now laughing open red-mouthed refusals to move am coming, am squirting, am performing biologically, am making my deposit to the Sperm Bank of Greater Humanity, N.A., am sinking into torporous disappointment even as I do.

"That was nice," she says, too promptly.

"Nice?" I say. "It was fabulous, second only to peeing on the list of life's great pleasures."

"You don't have to get nasty," she says, shoving me unceremoniously to the side. I plop out more than half hard, and she pulls her knees tight up to her chest, puts a hand over her vagina, holding its lips tightly closed between her fingers.

"I wasn't aware that my sperm was that valuable."

"It is," she says. "More valuable than the water, the guns, the seeds, the fertilizer. More valuable than anything else we're carrying. Including the rest of *you*."

No insult intended? I look at her eyes, and they still hold the same sparkle of affection, but something new has entered, a patience, as if she is the teacher, I am the student, and she is waiting for me to catch on.

"I get it," I say slowly. "I get it, but I'm not sure I want it." I peel her sweater all the way up to her armpits. Her breasts are small but nicely round, with dark strong nipples, and it is strange that I am only now running the palm of my hand lightly over them. Her skin sparks at my touch.

She smiles. "What's this?"

"Foreplay," I narrate solemnly.

"You mean afterplay," she laughs.

"No, I mean foreplay. We've done our bit for Uncle Sam. Now it's our turn."

❋

In the truck, when I wake up, it is always night. And tonight or today I open my eyes, see Catherine sleeping next to me in a tight cold-weather ball, close my eyes, and let myself float as if on a still sea, lolling between the shores of dream and memory, letting the tide carry me wherever it will.

To a day almost twenty years ago, an early day or late night around five a.m., and since I'm up so late I've put on a jacket and am walking Frisky, the dog, the third sibling, through the empty streets of Buena Park.

Suddenly I am aware that we are under escort: Brenda the beautiful, the nymphet cat, has materialized some twenty human paces ahead of us, twenty noncommittal paces, as if, in the event anyone sees her, she can

say that she isn't with, can even, if chic or expedient,
disclaim all knowledge of these larger, clumsier creatures, these ludicrous galoots she may or may not happen to have seen before. But that is mere public
relations: Brenda believes she is our guardian angel.

When we slow, and Frisky sniffs a shrub or mildewed
newspaper, Brenda putters around in the yard two
houses ahead of us, until Frisky is done pissing or dis-
daining to piss, until Brenda can resume trotting ahead of
us, our advance guard, our Marines. One of her forepaws is orange, and sometimes it's the only part of her
that's visible, turning and churning in the darkness like a
leg-light worn by a bicyclist.

And when we reach the turnaround at the end of San
Paco Circle, Brenda materializes out of nowhere, twenty
paces ahead of us, suddenly and magically, in the home-
ward direction, her legs whipping effortlessly along the
sidewalk, pausing at our house and disappearing ahead
of us through the rubber pet door into the living room,
where we find her curled up in my father's armchair, as if
she's been waiting up for us all the time, reflecting on the
innocent foolishness of boy and dog.

I reach down into the reddish glow of the floor lamp
to stroke her side; no longer wild, no longer outdoors,
she begins to purr, and does not stop for some time.

※

I pull out Billy Bo's pocket watch; it reads 10:22, and
morning or night, it couldn't make sense. For the first
time I've let the watch run down without winding, and it
might have been weeks ago. I seem to remember Catherine getting up and bidding me a no-nonsense goodbye. It
is early evening, almost time for the caravan to begin its
nightly work.

Before very long Gary Tascheira pops in for what he
calls "Lesson Number One." This consists of the same
old puppy-dog prefatory We-who-are-about-to-make-
asses-of-ourselves-salute-you expression, an alto saxophone rendition of "All the Things You Are" that is, like
Tascheira himself, short and solid, and a blunt spoken
demand.

"Critique," says Gary Tascheira.

"Good," I say, smiling. It's the first time in memory that I don't feel like boiled toast. "It's nice to hear music. You're good."

His face goes sour. "For this I saved you? C'mon, Buckaroo, critique please."

"OK. You play with a fine lyrical feeling. Your technique is excellent, articulation crisp, especially up-tempo."

"What's up-tempo mean?"

"You're serious? You're *that* self-taught?"

"Like I said, this is Lesson Number One. A guy showed me the scales and where to put my fingers, and I picked up the rest from Hodges, Webster and Gonsalves. Ellington records, mainly Ellington. Old farts, like me. So what's up-tempo mean?"

"The fast stuff."

"Oh. Continue."

"Well, you tend to lose the chord changes once in a while. You could use dynamics more, but that's a matter of taste." He looks askance. "Dynamics: loud and soft."

"Ah. Anything else?"

"No. I'm honestly surprised that you never had a teacher. You're really quite good." He's crushed. "Really."

"Strictly living-room." He looks at the floor.

"Eat shit. I mean it, you're very—"

A sudden burst of noise, like many cars rapidly backfiring, cuts me off, and he's on his feet in a second, throwing crates aside, digging and coming out with a couple of submachine guns.

Guns? I sit up. He hands one to me. "Don't touch it until I say."

"Gary, what's going on?"

He throws open the side door and crouches to the side, silhouetted in the twilight, his gun up and pointed, G.I. Gary, ready or not. A voice comes faintly from outside: ". . . got one . . ."

"You idiot!" roars Tascheira. "You gave me a fucking heart attack!"

And the faint voice says "Sorry. . ."

"Yeah," says Tascheira, standing and closing the door and leaning his head against it, suddenly weary. "Sorry."

"World War Four?" I ask gently.

"No, just Fred," Tascheira says. "Fred," he adds with infinite contempt, "was shooting at rabbits. It's wabbit season."

"With a machine gun?"

"Yeah, well, it's all we have." He comes back to me, the gun dangling from his hand. "Fred *knows* he's not supposed to hunt this close to camp. By the way." He leans low, pointing out the features of the gun that lies inertly in my lap. "This knob is the safety. And this button switches it from automatic to semi."

"Uh-huh." I'm looking at him, not it.

Gary sits down heavily on a crate near me. "At least we'll have rabbit soup tonight." He puts his gun aside, pushes both hands up over his face and head. "There's a few things we want to know about those nuts in Salt Lake City."

"Yeah?"

"Like what in Sam Hill was that rocket?"

Mutely, I hold the gun up to him.

"Oh," he says. "Oh yeah." He puts the gun with his own.

"I think, Gary, I think it was a nuclear weapon."

Tascheira emits an old-fashioned low whistle. "Awful news," he says, and falls silent. After a while, he shakes his head, looking off. "They came at us in a truck. We saw it from a long way up the hill, got the machine guns out of cold storage. We didn't think we'd have to use them. Everybody who was unarmed hid. Then they all started piling out, fifty-one of em, waving guns, yelling like a bunch of movie marines.

"We had six grenades. When they started the blitzkrieg bit we threw all six. The grenades took down about half, most still trying to get out. More and more kept coming, too many to have fit in that truck. They tried to scatter. We had six submachine guns, well-spaced, well-hidden. If we didn't shoot every one of them they might have found our people hiding." His eyes plead with me. "It was a massacre."

"You had to do it."

His eyebrows go up. "You think so?"

"Yes."

"A usable truck shot to hell." Tascheira looks at the backs of his hands. "So what do they have, radar? Planes?"

"Maybe. Probably."

"Can they find us now?"

That hadn't occurred to me, and I don't want it to. "I would think so."

"Do you think they'll try?" He leans forward. "That's the thing: will they try?"

I avoid his eyes. "Christ, Gary, I was there for *two days*."

"Yeah, so will they try?" He's staring at me. "Even now that we've conceded them their turf?" He wants something from me, assurance of safety, permission to live, and I can't give it to him.

"Yes," I exhale. "They will try."

He sighs. "How many of them are there?"

That's easy. "Three hundred and twenty-three."

"Ah," says Gary Tascheira. He is quiet for a long time, fingering his jowls. "Three hundred."

"The first thing they'll do when everything thaws is occupy Salt Lake City."

"And then?"

"And then, if their leader whips them into enough of a froth, they might come out after you."

"Can he?" His eyes have a sharp light.

"Oh God." I make a peak of my hands and bow my head into them. "Yes," I say. "Yes."

"We don't stand a prayer," says Tascheira, putting his palms on his knees, pushing himself up onto his feet. "Not the whisper of a prayer of a snowball in Hell. All we can do is run as far as we can and dig our way into something hard to see from the air." He grins down. "And then enjoy life until it's over. Isn't that the way it always was?"

"Mmm," I say. "What do you mean 'run as far as we can'?"

He shakes his head slightly. "To that point where trucks don't roll anymore, they sink. To the West Coast. The Pacific."

"On foot? You're kidding."

"No," says Gary Tascheira, and the pause as my

smile fades is an awkward one. He stares steadily, daring challenge. It's the punk in him; I saw it in Homestead, saw enough not to press too hard on it. Then he breaks the spell, hunches his shoulders high. "So, uh, when you gonna play for us? I've got the whole wagon train hyped for the event."

"What." It is no question, just a small flat protest.

"I'm quite the junior concert promoter, you know. Quite the impresario."

"Soon," I yawn.

He smears a dismissive palm through the air. "Soon June Blue Moon. Be specific."

I stretch out, close my eyes, smile wanly. "Soon."

"I'm warning you: I'm authorized to torture you until you break. Every day until you play there'll be another lesson." Smiling down on me, with his bald head and his folded burly arms, Tascheira reminds me of Mr. Clean.

"I'm going to help pull the truck tommorrow."

He gets down on his haunches, gets stern. He rests an elbow on a knee, stabs an index finger out at me. "*That* you're definitely not ready to do."

"I think I can."

"Keep on thinking," says Gary Tascheira. "Someday you'll get good at it."

"Old line."

His brow wrinkles. "You've heard that before?"

"On TV."

He gets up, paces about two steps in either direction. "That's bad. I say it all the time." He opens the side door and stands in the night light. "I thought I invented it."

"Keep on thinking, Garibaldi," I shout after him. "Someday you'll get good at it."

# 13 ❋ Mormonee

William Lewis Manly was born on April 6, 1820, the eldest son of a miller, in St. Albans, Vermont, an afternoon's walk from the Canadian border. Manly's family moved to Ohio, then to Michigan and Missouri. In his seventy-fourth year he wrote a book about his accidental adventures in the barren California desert; in his twenty-ninth year he lived them. That year, add it up, was 1849.

Manly set out after gold with a Winnebago pony, a good rifle and a homemade buckskin outfit. He planned a rendezvous with a family friend, Asabel Bennett, and Bennett's wife Sarah and their three children, who had taken another route. In Iowa, Manly was hired by an affluent emigrant, Charles Dallas, to drive a team of oxen. At Independence Rock, near the Sweetwater River, Manly searched in vain among thousands of chiseled, scratched and painted signatures of travelers for the name of Asabel Bennett. At Deer Creek, Army officers told Dallas that he was setting out too late for California and would have to winter in Salt Lake City. Those of the teamsters who, like Manly, hailed from Missouri, did not relish the prospect of spending a season in the Mormons' isolated stronghold. Mormons had long memories of their persecutions in Illinois and Missouri, cursing residents of those states, according to one 1850 overlander, "even unto the fourth generation"; a few of the rougher Mormons on the western trail were fond of hinting darkly that some Missourians on the plains would not live out the year.

Manly and the other six teamsters parted amicably with Dallas at Pacific Springs, the first water that flowed into the Pacific Ocean, trusting themselves and their few possessions to a wobbly ferryboat. Manly was the only one who had any money, the proceeds of having sold his pony to Dallas; perhaps that was why the others chose him captain of the party. Manly's meeting with Bennett was, for all practical purposes, indefinitely postponed.

Soon they were on the Green River, borne forth on white water into a wild country that showed no trace of the white man except for one sign painted on a high rock: "*Ashley, 1824.*" The young teamsters, handy with horses but hopeless with a boat, had no idea where the river was so swiftly bearing them.

A band of Indians led by a chief who called himself Walker accosted Manly's party. Communicating in sign language, Chief Walker invited the white men into his tipi, where he displayed guns, knives and blankets, repeating several times the word "Mormonee." Deducing that the chief had received his goods in trade with the Mormons, Manly winked to his men, flung a hand to his own breast and solemnly intoned: "Mormonee." Chief Walker knelt to the soil, using stones and bits of bark to illustrate the location of the main emigrant route. Though two men refused, on general principle, to heed Indian advice, Manly took the rest along the way sketched by Chief Walker.

Near Salt Lake City Manly chanced upon his friend Bennett, who was headed for California, come Hell or high water. Manly bade his men farewell to join Bennett's party, a large group consisting of 107 wagons and about five hundred head of horses and cattle. They had drawn up a written charter, organized themselves into seven divisions, each with its assigned position in the march to the Pacific, and designated themselves the Sand Walking Company.

# 14 ❈ Hearts, Flowers, Amoebae and Violin

Maybe moves at night. Strapped into broad leather cross-your-heart harnesses and cocooned in rags and blankets, seventy-three men and women, seventy-three now, pulling thin metal cables strung through grommets at each hip and shoulder, all of it, truck, cables, legs, lit by phosphorescence: centipede, millipede, megapede, Maybe moves at night.

Old snow encrusts the road, and progress is gradual. Off to the side a much smaller group, including a man on crutches and another with a long white beard and a cane, struggles to match our pace. The air is hideously, all-invadingly cold, though I've been assured it gets better when you've been moving for a while. Front center, Gary tells Max, new arrival Max, "Don't be a hero. You're not ready yet." Two long-haired sixties kids, a girl around five and a younger boy, are skipping, footloose and burden-free, amidst my stiff-as-trees legs, mocking and celebrating the new arrival.

I blink, a hot blink of fever returning, say nothing.

"Shut up, Gary," says Catherine. "He knows his limits."

"He doesn't know his own name," says Tascheira. "Not since he met you."

"Do so," I grunt. "Hasbro Fensterwald, Sergeant First Class."

"Save your strength, Sergeant." Tascheira waves me aside. "For the USO show. Entertain the troops. More than anything else, we've got to keep our spirit."

"More than anything else," Catherine puts in harshly. "We've got to keep moving."

I say nothing. Red translucent spots are forming in my eyes, swimming dizzily, engaging in a lively game of tag like playful amoebae, swimming and swelling, reproducing by mitosis.

"We will keep moving, with or without him," says Gary.

"Nonsense," says Catherine.

"Horseshit," spits Tascheira.

"Tug-of-war," I comment. And faint. The ground slaps my chest, shocks me awake. I take a deep breath, scramble to my feet.

"Are you sure you're alright?" says Catherine.

"I'm sure he's not," says Gary, his hands burrowing under my blankets, searching to unhook me from the harness. "Listen to me," he says, his breath hot and urgent. "You go with the Sidesteppers." He jerks his head toward the little group of aged and infirm.

"I just slipped, damn it." I shrug him off, trot along the road. It is suddenly uphill. The truck has gained on me.

The amoebae divide and grow, become black, become opaque, divide and grow.

"Timmmm-ber!" shouts a child's voice.

I wake up in my old nest inside the truck. "Gary was right," says Catherine. She holds a canteen of water ready. "You did come back too soon. You're not walking with the Sidesteppers for another week, and you're not pulling the truck for at least two. We don't even want you playing your instrument."

I pull myself up by her arm into a sitting position and

suck down the water, let my body fall flat with a muffled bump. "Baby play my instrument," I murmur weakly.

"God what an idiot," she says. "Lie still and shut up. We're all very impressed by your grit and determination."

"Me too."

＊

At some point I am awakened when the back of the truck squeals and strains open like a rolltop desk, admitting three men and too much light. Soon I and the other contents of the truck are being tightly packed toward the front. Maybe is plundering a Safeway, and there is a debate over whether we should take tuna in oil or water (oil, decides Catherine; we need the calories) and another over whether or not we should take toilet paper (we do). And more and more, instant soup and instant chocolate, pasta and coffee and cookies and peas, until there is hardly enough space left in my bedroom to roll over.

＊

Some morning comes and Catherine returns, lies down next to me. A hand emerges from her sleep-roll, rests on my forehead. Warm relaxation pervades. She twitches, sticking a finger in my eye. I remove the offending hand and turn away.

The night arrives and with it early-bird Tascheira, first one up. He kneels by me until I wake under his gaze.

"Lesson Number Eight," he says quietly.

"She's sleeping," I say. My fever has subsided.

"Lesson Number Eight," he insists. "She has to get up anyway."

"Schmuck." I roll away.

"No? I told you before, Bucksters, it's put up or play up."

"The latter."

"Yeah? You're ready? You're sure you're ready?"

I forget myself and shout. "Shut up, Gary, goddamn it!"

There is a new voice, a new dim light of motion in the

darkness. "N'tonight," mutters Catherine, her jaw working, smacking gummily in her sleep. "N'tonight, Gary."

I whirl around, fix him in a stare. "'Not tonight, Gary'? What does that mean?"

He sits down on a crate. "The young lady," says Tascheira levelly, "is referring to the act of sexual joinder. Fucking, for the initiate."

"You asshole," I hiss.

"What are you two talking about?" says Catherine, propping herself up on an elbow. She opens one eye, looks at my knit-up red face and collapses. "Oh. I see."

"You assholes," I say, glaring at his impassive face, her impassive form. The two of them exchange weary, knowing glances.

"Yep," says Tascheira. "Time to tell our junior member about the facts of life."

"Max," Catherine sighs, sitting up. "I am of reproductive age."

I turn away from both of them. "So I'd gathered."

Tascheira prods my ass with his foot. "Then have you gathered that anything peculiar has happened in the last year or so? Like the human race has practically snuffed itself out?"

Cute. I reach back and whap his foot away from me.

"Max." It's Catherine's hand on my shoulder. "Maybe wants to survive. Not for a couple of months, for years, Max. Generations." She shoves me. "Turn around, goddamn it. I'm serious." I turn; her face is burning with pride, is burning with shut-up-until-I'm-finished, is burning. "We have twenty-six women old enough to bear children," she says, looking straight into my eyes. "Two of them are pregnant. We don't know how many of the rest are capable. Or how many of the men. So, Max." Her eyes rest hard on me. "To put it rudely, everybody sleeps with everybody."

My mouth, which was open, opens.

"Look at it this way," Tascheira says, clasping his fingers. "Most of us are probably sterile. We have to try as many combinations of improbabilities as we can."

Tascheira's powerful fat jaw is bursting with further argument, is aching to hold forth on the basic mammalian imperative to reproduce; Catherine's smooth high brow, the cheeks I know as soft, her wide-set dark eyes hold consolation but not apology.

I put a halt to all of it. "So this is life and love in Maybe? Every night you all tow the truck together, and every day you put on blindfolds and lie down with someone new to play Pin the Spermatozoa on the Ovum."

Catherine gets up with movements of brisk irritation and heads for the door. "That's a revolting way of putting it."

"Good!" I bark after her. "Then I am expressing my feelings clearly."

She slams the door with terrific force and the silence holds the sound. Tascheira watches me, sadly, for a long time. We both know what I am doing: I am exercising my inalienable right to be a martyr. "You," he finally says, like a doctor pronouncing a patient dead on arrival, "are an intractable relic."

Both my hands are on my forehead. "Beat it, Gary."

"Sure," he says, making no move to go. "But you think about this: what would you rather have, a chance for the human race to survive beyond the twentieth century—"

"Feh," I interrupt wearily.

"—or, for the sole and exclusive benefit of one Max Dimbulb Debris, no children, no future, but Love"—he lilts the word—"replete with hearts and flowers and a violin playing somewhere in the azure background?"

I have my watch out, am winding it, disguising disappointment as cantankerousness. "Leave. Go. Move. Shove off."

"Fine," he agrees. "When you give up."

"I give up."

"When you really give up. Let me say it like this: you can still have the woman you love, just not as often as you want and by no means exclusively. How dare you put yourself ahead of not only all the rest of us but your entire species as well?" He nudges me in the ass again with his foot. "So how do you dare, hmm? If it's expressive of your general maturity level I'll accept answers of one syllable."

"Moo."

"Well then, let me put it another way entirely: you

have nothing to worry about. Catherine and I don't love each other."

"Who could?"

"Under the circumstances? I'm not sure anyone. I'm also not sure it's relevant."

"It's always relevant."

"That depends on what you're comparing it to. If a man is crawling in the desert dying of thirst you don't trot up his longlost love and say, 'Do you recognize this voice? Because this is your life, Elmo Flemm.' The guy'll die."

"But it's not that late for us."

"No? Five thousand people, at most, remain in the entire country. Maybe one-tenth of them are women who could have kids, maybe one-tenth of those will. Maybe half the kids will be born with mangled genes. We're talking about twenty-five healthy children, Max. How many of those will be gunned down by nuts like Eddie or stumble into hot spots where the radiation is a hundred times normal, or just simply freeze their little peckers off so that *they* won't be able to reproduce? And the ones who do survive—what will they eat? Have you thought about what this winter is doing to edible plants and the animals that used to live off them? What will those twenty-five kids eat? Do you think *they* are going to chew their fingernails down on the great question of Love versus Reproduction?"

"Yes," I say, drawing on the power of simple contradiction. "Knowing human beings, yes."

He pats my thigh. "Max, you are indeed a rare bird."

"Thank you."

His eyebrows lift clean up into his scalp. "And do you have any idea how stupid birds are?"

The truck gives a jolt, wobbles, begins moving. Tascheira plants both hands on his knees and hoists his bulk to his feet. "Never mind. If there's one thing birds *can* do, it's sing." He grabs the saxophone, holds it out at arm's length to me. "Sing you must. When's the really big shew?"

I remain motionless. "Indefinitely postponed."

He shakes his head soberly, speaking on a long sigh. "You're not a particularly useful manual laborer, Max;

God knows you're no planner." He thrusts the sax into my face; his talking head floats, lit-up, disembodied, beyond it. "*This* is your implement of usefulness. *This* is your claim on life, Max. Take it. Hold on to it."

I do take my saxophone from him.

"Now," says Gary Tascheira. "Be a baby and pout for a few days, but practice on the saxophone. Don't speak to me, if it makes you feel any better; ignore Catherine if you want, but play the sax." Tascheira rises, opens the side door. "Good day." He stands framed in the doorway, in the dim glow of night. "We have work to do."

# 15 ✳ Captains of the West

A few days out of Salt Lake City, the Sand Walking Company was overtaken by a smaller wagon train whose captain possessed a map made by a local mountain man named Williams showing a cutoff that might make their trip much shorter than the established route the Sand Walkers proposed to take. For a day the Williams map was much exhibited, and speeches were heard in camp regarding the relative merits of the two routes.

The two wagon trains, incidentally, were encamped at Mountain Meadows, a site that achieved notoriety years later when high-ranking Mormons ordered the massacre of a hundred Missourians who had ridden through the Salt Lake suburbs breaking down fences and trampling Mormon fields, bellowing that all Mormon women were whores and whipping and swearing at oxen cleverly named after Brigham Young and the twelve Mormon Apostles. At this lucky spot, then, the two trains parted, a few choosing the original trail and the vast majority, including Asabel Bennett and with him young Manly, the Williams Cutoff.

Elsewhere at that moment, of course, thousands of emigrants were lost and hungry on the Lassen Cutoff. It was only three years after the famous Donner Party had taken yet another short-cut, this one known as the Hastings Cutoff. Cut off the Donner Party had been: cut off from known trails, from shelter and finally from food. Half the original ninety had survived by eating the corpses of those who did not. Cutoff was a word that should have had an asterisk (or the little cross used to mark footnotes and graves) attached to it by the time most of the Sand Walking Company decided in favor of the Williams Cutoff, but if it did, it was an asterisk pronounced, like the letter b in "dumb," silently.

Four days after the parting of the ways at Mountain Meadows, the wagon train paused for the reports of advance scouts. A good many wagons, impatient or wise, drove away to rejoin the Sand Walkers. Finally it was announced that the trail seemed clear for a crossing of the great West, and the owners of the twenty-seven remaining wagons hunkered down to choose their captain. Everyone was called "Captain" in those days; even Manly had availed himself of the title while on the Green River. The pioneers were forever holding elections, choosing captains, drawing up charters. Perhaps they were merely indulging an early and indiscriminate mania for democracy, or perhaps they were attempting to ward off, with tallies and protocol, the frighteningly uncivilized future that lay in front of them. When the results of the reconstituted and reduced wagon train's fiercely contested election were in, a fellow named Jim Martin had swept the honors.

Among the rejected nominees was Asabel Bennett. In a state of high dudgeon, Bennett announced that he would boycott the expedition. Only a few chose to stay behind with Bennett's family, including among others, J.B. Arcane and his family, elderly Captain Culverwell (this captain a real ex-sailor) and hardy John Rogers, the last remaining member of the original Green River gang. And, too, William Lewis Manly, for whom friendship was apparently stronger than blood or sense.

# 16 ✻ Seven Juries

So: the Fishlake National Forest, the red-clay mountains, the Utah cedars, broad and low, still and patient, sturdy and slow-changing, God's design for Better Men, and in a windless clearing rimmed with bonfires eighty-four phosphorescent nomads unhooked from their burden, eighty-four on a one-night holiday, a celebration of plenty and escape, bellies gorged on carved canned ham and fires on carved dead tree, eighty-four plus one, that one having been carried like some fragile sedan-chaired treasure to the spot where he now sits on three stacked truck tires, and the light of fire and eyes dances on the piece of brass tubing in his hands, eighty-five nomads not knowing what will come next.

"This is a Charlie Parker tune about forty years old," I begin, sounding too glib, the bandstand patterer. "The song was named for us—or almost. It's called 'Perhaps.' 'Perhaps' was written to the chord changes of a blues in C, which will make it easy for me to spin off into several other songs, which ones I'm not sure. If you feel like clapping, or dancing, or slam-dancing and hiccuping, or leaving, do it."

I close my eyes and feel the thousand ideas bursting for freedom, fighting for ascendancy, wait, the pressure building up until the only way to let out the steam in my head is to blow, and with eyes closed I take off into a swirling arpeggiated introduction, stop cold, take a breath and lay out straight the almost childishly simple tune of "Perhaps." I work it through a few choruses, knead it gently—time to stretch out comes later—bending and bending the last note until it's the first note of "All the Things You Are." Something they know or could know. I'm still flying straight, sketching the tune in black and white, adding a dash of color to one corner until that corner opens up into another song, "Begin the Beguine" here, a stutter-step tease of "Jeanine" there, using angular Benny Carter harmonies to jump sideways into "Perhaps" each time, first just the tunes, ma'am, only the dry tunes, then wetting them with a little spit-damp feeling until their real bumps and curves begin to show, until everyone is primed to move, then just the last note, once, twice, five times, tolling that note until it creates a tense surface of sound stretching from me to my listeners, connecting the player and the played-to in a solid sheet of expectation. And the song is the Sonny Rollins showstopper "Don't Stop the Carnival," a ragged happy calypso, and I'm on my feet for the first time since I tried to pull the truck, slamming my boots into the puff-dusty dirt.

They all perk up, up, you can see it, picking their heads up, raising their eyes, swinging their shoulders, slapping their hands against their legs. Cedar bark and cedar berries crunch under my feet. "Gary!" I yell breathlessly between choruses. "Catherine! Dance!"

And they do, bringing with them into the space between the seated and the standing kids, who jerk around in arrhythmic mimicry of grown-ups, and the three mothers, who group off with Gary and Catherine and me, for I am in the middle of all this hootenanny dust by now, dust kicked up and renewed by new entries into the dance, new feet so long danceless, the dust of joy, the Good Dust, the lusty dust, the swirling Fishlake dust.

"Yeah!" bellows Gary, as if cheering for a football team, when I angle the horn toward him. I move through the dancers, and where I go I egg them on, breathe a violent hurtling energy into the dance. The kids play a snake-charmer game with me: when I raise the horn high, they stretch up and wave their arms; the lower I bend, the lower they sink, bending dancers, belly dancers, baby dancers. And Catherine: it's Catherine I dance with, shaking her hair and strutting her stuff and jarring some bones loose, all angles, all ass and elbows. Until and until and until. Until Catherine's face leans in on mine with a worried expression, and now that you mention it I am about to plotz.

Softer and softer at the same tempo I play as Catherine leads me by shirttail to my seat, eighty-four sweaty faces assembled in front of me, seven juries of my peers, and I work into the oddest and only thing from TV in my repertoire, the theme from *Kung Fu*, a slow cry that sounds much better on *a cappella* saxophone than the original synthesizers, much better here amid the acrid smell of Utah Cedar smoke than on the small blue screen.

One more chorus of "Perhaps" and there's an ovation, a marching advancing standing ovation. Tascheira steps to my side.

"I want to propose," bays Gary Tascheira, holding up both hands like the new heavyweight champion of the world, "in honor of our resident artiste, that we change our name from 'Maybe'..."

"To 'Perhaps,'" say several faces quietly.

"To 'Perhaps'!" says Gary Tascheira. "Why not?"

And no one tells him why not.

I hold up the saxophone sideways in a kind of toast, the way Dexter Gordon used to. "To Perhaps."

※

With a great gnashing and neighing of metal, the wide back door rolls up to the ceiling. "Feel strong today?" says Gary Tascheira, stepping up into the truck. "Real strong?"

"Yeah, I think so. Yeah." In the week since my concert I've done nothing for anybody. I am afraid that my credibility in Maybe, in Perhaps now, is drying up.

"Good. Put your clothes on." He appraises me as I pull on my boots.

"We're not moving, are we?" It's no great deduction; beyond the back bumper one boy stands peering in at me, and two heads on either side of him are popping up and down, kids so small they have to jump to see in.

"That's what I've come to speak to you about. Ever driven a truck?"

"No. But the engine isn't working, is it? How hard can it be when you're going two miles an hour?"

Gary chuckles. "Oh, less hard than some things, harder than others. C'mon, up." He jumps nimbly off the back end.

"Gary, give me your hand. My foot's asleep."

He helps me off the truck and I follow him, hopping on one foot toward the front end. He opens the door and yanks me up, handing me half a pile of blankets. "Wrap up," he says. "No heat."

When we're ensconced in wool he comes over from the passenger seat, crams himself next to me. "As you can see," he tells me, "we're about to coast down a hill."

A mild little hill, in fact, steep but not too long; a ribbon of road perched, it's true, on a narrow straightaway with steep drops to either side, but a road with room for error, a four-lane undivided highway with our truck in the very middle of it. "Ah. Sounds easy."

He thumps my shoulder. "You just keep up that cheery attitude. Ignore the cliffs to the right and lover's leap to your left; follow the don't-look-down principle. Now then: you've heard of power steering and power brakes?"

"Sure."

"We don't have either one. Every drop of water in that engine is frozen solid, so we can't kick over the ignition and it wouldn't budge an inch even if we could. We have a block cracked in about seventeen different places, burst fuel lines, exploded everything."

I shrug. "You're the mechanic."

"And you're the hired help. Now what we're going to

do here is this: mash the clutch—that'll take the both of us—and put the truck into the lowest of its ten gears."

"OK. Ready."

"Sure you are. This is the clutch." He points the pedal out. "Both feet now."

It moves a little. He puts a fat boot on top of mine. "This may hurt. On three. One, two, three!"

He smashes my foot and we push and push. "Keep it up! I feel something," Tascheira grunts. A sweat breaks out along my legs. The pedal sinks slowly, fighting every millimeter, to the floor. "Hold it down!" gasps Tascheira. He grabs the gearshift, wrestles with it. "OK, leggo."

He slumps back against the seat, eyes closed, leg still extended to the clutch pedal, smiling, wrung out. "Piece of cake, huh?" He takes a long breath and straightens up. "You ain't seen nothin yet. How's the lad?"

"Remember I told you my left foot was asleep?"

"Yeah."

"Now it's in a coma."

"That's OK," he says. "We're done with your foot. Now it's time to work on the upper body. Get those pecs in shape, boy, those biceps and triceps, because..." Carny barker: "... Without the benefit of power steering or power brakes and without a safety net of any kind two gallant men are going to wrestle with thirty thousand pounds of pure inertia." He clambers over to the passenger side. "Ohhh-kayyy!" he shouts out the window.

"Yay!" say the kids, who begin trotting along outside on the left, the eight-year-old boy I saw before and a smaller girl and boy, shapeless jellyfish in their blankets. Cables pick up off the ground, pick up the slack, untangle, tighten like guitar strings as the eighty-nine bodies—eighty-nine now—strain forward. Tascheira scoots back over to me. "On, Donner!" he says.

"On, Blitzen!" says the girl immediately, as if answering a kindergarten quiz. We begin to creak, to move. The nimblest among the Sidesteppers hurry to the front bumper and unhook the cables, fast and furious.

"And now," says Tascheira, "Mack here is going to try to run off the road and dump us and everything we own into never-never land." He grins. "We've got to persuade him that's a bad idea." The cables are free, everyone is out of the way, and the truck blunders ominously forward.

"Great."

"Wait. It's less fun than it sounds." He crouches low by the steering wheel. "Turn right . . . now!"

We try to turn the wheel. Nothing doing.

"All your might!" grunts Tascheira, greasy beads of sweat on his brow. "Remember—no power-steering."

"You . . . are . . . kidding," I get out through clenched teeth.

"Brace your back against the seat. On three, give it everything you have."

"On four." Life is lived in four-four.

"On four," he agrees. "One, two, three, *otts!*" The wheel moves an inch. "Hold it there," he pants.

"What was that?"

"That noise? You've seen kung fu movies?"

"Yeah."

"Well whenever they kick or punch, they yell—it kind of summons up the whole effort. It's called a *kiai*. No, better." He rearranges his considerable mass, made more considerable by the mountain of blankets, until he is sitting atop and obscuring the steering wheel. "*This* oughta hold it." He grins. "I knew all along there was a reason I never joined Weight Watchers. Now the key is to keep Mack on an absolutely straight course, cause once he gets enough momentum in any given direction . . ." Gary's body turns clockwise a little.". . . it rapidly goes from bad to hopeless to worse. And then there's the whole problem of the brakes."

"Brakes?"

"Yeah," he says, turning a little clockwise. "The tenth gear is down real low, low enough to hold Mack to maybe ten miles an hour maximum."

"Sounds easy."

"Second time you've said that. The trouble is we can steer only if it stays under five. Now, the thing about the brakes—"

"Gary . . ."I say, a cautionary vibrato entering my voice as he turns a little clockwise atop the steering wheel.

"Let me finish. The thing about the brakes is that we

simply don't have them. Mack has two sets of brakes: the air brakes and the emergency. That's the only one left, after a fashion. What we're gonna have to—Yiii! Christ, get me outta here!"

His lower leg is pinned between the steering wheel and the driver's seat; the wheel is grinding him hard into the seat, and the truck is headed right, right, right off the road.

I try to yank the left side of the wheel down toward me. It doesn't move. "Harder!" says Tascheira. "Harder . . . !"

I strain until my tendons and forearms are hot, bursting, until my whole body is in a furious sweat:

"Owww!" he howls. And the truck lurches right, the wheel forcing him in on the seat, in on me. The compressed muscle and fat of his leg bulges out from the vinyl.

"I'm gonna do this." I curl up tight against the door, bringing my legs up and putting my feet on his thighs.

"Don't yak!" he yells. *"Do!"*

I push-kick his upper legs with all my might. His lower body jerks loose, goes spinning sideways in a flurry of blankets onto the floor, where he hits his head Clang! on something metal. And just lies there motionless.

With me in nominal command of the charging fifteen-ton truck. I hold the wheel; I'm barely strong enough to keep it from veering precipitously to the right, but not nearly strong enough to move it left. The front wheels are crossing the white line.

"Turn it left! Hey, you guys, left!" yap the chipmunk voices of the kids, who are still running beside us. I kick the Tascheira-body. No response.

I have little choice: I unlatch the door, push it open. "Someone!" I yell. "Help me in here!"

The eight-year-old boy and twenty-three elbows are in my lap; there's wool everywhere, and a face full of freckles and fear. "Are we gonna crash?"

"Oooh, *Jimmy!*" shrieks the little girl delightedly.

"Just grab the wheel and pull it left."

"OK," says the kid, looking off at the flapping door,

at the others like he wants to rejoin them. His blue eyes are wide; I can see the whites on all sides.

"Hard as you can!" I yell.

He starts to cry. "You're doing great! You're strong!" I say.

He is nothing of the sort; he's a child, twin puffs of fog spurting out his nose in a dragonlike mockery of fierceness, and we are still lunging for the great abyss. We are on the shoulder a foot or two from dirt.

"Where are we?" says Gary Tascheira, blinking slowly from the floorboard.

"About to die!" I shriek.

"That bad?" he says contemplatively, his hand touching a bloody gash on his scalp. The kid wails as we flatten a roadside reflector. Tascheira sits up, looks out the windshield. "Oh my," he says. "Kay team, turn left on three: one, two . . ."

"Ayyyyy," I yell, grasping the wheel.

"Whoa!" yells the kid.

"*Otts*!" yells Gary Tascheira.

The front end of the truck crosses left over the white line, crosses the lane until it is astride the double yellow.

Tascheira sits on the wheel, spreading his legs wide this time, well braced. He grins broadly, a trickle of blood running down across his forehead, the side of his nose, dripping off his chin. "The triumph of the *kiai*," he announces with deep satisfaction.

The truck reaches the end of the downhill stretch, begins to chug uphill and finally comes to rest.

"Imagine that," says Gary Tascheira. "We forgot all about the brake."

"Hey Gary," says the kid. "Are you gonna die?"

"Yeah," says Tascheira. "Someday."

# 17 ✳ Kill Me, Boys, for I Will Never Feel So Good Again

William Lewis Manly, easily the most experienced out-doorsman in the Bennett party, served as both hunter and scout. In the days ahead, Manly would see too little of the former duty—he did not discharge his gun in a month—and too much of the latter. Manly climbed hills, buttes, bluffs and mountains to look out over an increasingly desolate landscape, often reaching the summits after midnight, sleeping in the chilly heights and catching up to the party early in the mornings with his reports.

The country had become dry, had become desert, with vast parched lake beds. When the travelers finally found a small pool of rain water, one man threw himself onto his face and gulped down all he could, and then "told the boys to kill him for he would never feel so good again." It soon became apparent that white men had never traveled this way before. And it was not hard to see why: when Manly inadvertently frightened an Indian woman and child away from a small fire, he discovered that they had been cooking only cactus leaves. That night Manly climbed to the top of a butte, saw a desert that looked a hundred miles wide, and in it, no grass, no source of water.

Women cried when Manly brought this intelligence back to camp; Asabel Bennett, blaming the newsboy for the contents of the newspaper, told Manly to express his views less openly in the future. Their oxen getting shaky, the party discarded all that was not absolutely essential. Food and water were everything, and everything else nothing. These gold rushers had reached the point where, as Manly remarked, "a hoard of twenty dollar gold pieces could now stand before us the whole day long with no temptation to touch a single coin, for its very weight would drag us nearer death." Even stubborn Asabel Bennett, a carpenter who had brought with him a quantity of good tools from the east, was forced to shed his wares along the trail.

Nothing worked; oxen were starting to lie down in the dirt, were refusing to budge. The terrain grew uneven, slowing progress, and sharp stones cut the oxen's feet. The party slaughtered its first ox, a rite that would soon be repeated many times over, and used the hide to make moccasins for the other oxen. Manly, the designated hunter, had nothing to shoot at, and the reports from his nightly forays grew more and more discouraging. Now it appeared that they would be in the desert for a month or more; for the first time, Manly didn't think they could make it. Not a single bird flew in the sky.

On one of his explorations Manly was astonished to see a few figures gathered around a small campfire. He approached quietly and crouched in the darkness. It was the Reverend J. W. Brier, a remnant of an earlier party, calmly holding forth on the importance of education, with his young sons sitting in front of him, soaking up every word. And why not? There was certainly no water to soak up instead. The day was Christmas.

# 18 ❋ The Fire Men

"Drop-off?"

"Can't see yet."

Those are Watchers yelling to each other. The rest of us plod on blindly, our heads, along with everything else, wrapped in blankets. When I first heard the tantalizing syllables I tore off my headdress to see what they were looking at. It wasn't worth the cold.

"Time?"

"Yeah, is it time yet?"

Those are Watchers yelling to me. I'm one of the Lucky Six, as we call ourselves: those who are blessed and cursed with mechanical timepieces. The others had electronic watches, wiped out by the electromagnetic pulse, turned into mere bracelets, discarded on the road.

"No." It's not time yet; it never is, when they first ask. Three Watchers, left, center and right, expose their eyes on fifteen-minute shifts; the Lucky Six are on for two hours each.

The Watchers have developed a theory that our watches are sluggish because the lubricating grease has been partially frozen. The fact that all six time pieces are in agreement does not dissuade the Watchers, nor the fact that no one ever claimed before that watchers operated slower in winter than summer, nor yet the fact that there is no grease in a watch. Watches are lubricated by jewels, or not at all. The Lucky Six tend to look upon the theory with kindly indulgence.

"Time yet, Max?"

And so we march on. Everybody is learning forward at a slight angle, putting one foot in front of another, pitting body weight against that of the truck, the cables taut and keeping us from falling on our faces.

For the first three days, my hamstrings were vessels that carried liquid pain up to my buttocks, down to my heels. For the first three weeks I was a mess, a great twitching sleepless pulp always on the verge of major illness. I was told to expose my head as little as possible, but I couldn't help it. Try walking a straight line with your eyes closed: after only a few steps the compulsion to look becomes irresistible; potholes, people, road junk that wasn't there before fill your mind's eye, and before long, like Orpheus turning around to see if Eurydice was still there, you do, you must open your eyes. So I kept stripping off my headdress to see where I was going, to check my watch, to indulge the road-sign fetish I'd developed after my banishment from Eddie's city, and above all to see what the Watchers were yelling about. Mainly to keep their mouths moving, they might shout "Manderfield!" or "Paragonah!" or "Kanarraville!" and I would tear the blankets from my eyes to see what a place called Kanarraville could look like.

There was never anything to see; or, more accurately, what was there reminded me of our home movies, shot by my mother: we would sit in our darkened living room with individual bowls of buttered popcorn, having waited a long week after vacation for the film to come back, every shade pulled, every light in the house off. There would come on the screen a flickering snapshot of Mount Rushmore or Old Faithful or the Empire State Building, something just to fix the location, then a manic sequence of me digging elbows into a young, helpless, flush-faced Ellen, and her bursting into tears, and finally and predominantly endless footage shot from the passenger window: the front right edge of the blue Valiant, aerial quivering, a tongue of featureless pavement and a narrow strip of grass-bushes-trees moving interminably past amid telephone pole after telephone pole after telephone pole. One by one we'd turn around to stare accusingly at my mother, first me, then Ellen, then finally Dad.

"Scenery," my mother would say in a tiny, embarrassed voice.

That's what's outside our steamy opaque blankets now, our portable tents: "scenery," never worth watching, always worth missing. When it's this cold you learn to walk blind.

We rely on the Watchers: "Pothole, right," they'll say, or "Debris, stop the show." It took me some time to understand that they were not addressing me; the idea was to halt the caravan and clear the tire, bumper, tree or occasionally an entire stranded vehicle from the road. The Watchers do their job well, all in all, and they take it seriously. They talk mainly to each other; they imagine that they constitute a kind of elite corps among us, hardy, rugged, self-sacrificing. The few. The proud.

And once in a while the Watchers decide to perpetrate a hoax on the rest of us.

"Do you see *that*?" will come the word from the right wing.

"No," the middle, slow to pick up, will answer.

"*Oh my God*," says the left now. "Oh . . . my . . . God."

The rest of us tear our blankets off. Nothing is there, of course, nothing but "scenery." And the Watchers dissolve into helpless, staggering laughter. We, gullible group that we are, simple civilians, amuse them endlessly.

And so one night, when a Watcher says, "Hey! See that?" no one does anything but put one foot in front of another, one foot in front of another.

"Yeah . . ." says the other wing.

"It's a fire. I swear it's a fire," says the first.

"Miles off, though," says the middle. "Maybe fifteen, twenty."

Catherine's voice comes from next to me. "Max, you want to see something?"

"Really?" I bare my eyeballs.

There, in the far distance, is something to see: a matchhead on the horizon.

"What do you know?" says Gary Tascheira. "A fire. That's how I found you."

Night wore on, and the distant flame grew no closer. It was moving, being carried somehow along our Interstate 15. The next day the fire disappeared from view entirely, though an exclamation point of smoke ascended straight into the dusky sky. And at night, the smoke became invisible and the fire reappeared, miles farther than before. They had seen us too, and run. The next night the fire was closer; the next, farther again. When daylight came, and wind hit, the smoke of their passage blurred into a kind of skywritten question mark. Finally they made up their minds, and began to creep in our direction.

Three nights we crawled toward them, and three days they crawled toward us. When their smoke grew close we sent out a scouting party composed of Catherine, two other women, and me. The children were not allowed to come, though they kicked up a fuss. We carried samples of our goods in case it was necessary, as Gary explained, "to trade with them." It was thought that women would be less intimidating than men. I was along for the opposite reason. I was the enforcer. I carried a submachine gun beneath my blankets.

It was a lovely escape from the forced crawl of the human-towtruck business. Though we were laden with food and water and blankets, we had nothing quite so substantial as a fifteen-ton truck to worry about, and unharnessed, we were simply walking as human beings were intended to walk, stretching our legs, and as we did, something stretched out inside us, exulted. In a few hours we came onto a straightaway in the road; as we approached, two skinny, wild-eyed boys waited at the end of the stretch with a child's red wagon piled high to spilling with burning twigs, chips and logs.

One of the boys, with fuzzy, uneven hair, a kind of attempted crewcut, was well under five feet and appeared to be about twelve. Wearing only a T-shirt and an army officer's jacket ten years too big for him, its sleeves rolled up and most of the brass buttons still intact, he held in one hand a small hatchet with a cracked wooden shank, and in the other the handle of the red wagon, as if ready to turn and flee at any instant. The other, maybe fourteen and much taller, with long, greasy hair like everyone else I'd seen since Homestead, stood with his arms folded across his chest. He wore a filthy and incontinent down jacket, a striped red-and-white knit ski cap that said SNOWBIRD across the front, and the dissolute, drugged, heavy-metal-youth look, or maybe he was just hungry. With his twiggy kid's legs below the fluffy insubstantial profile of his torso he really did look like some odd lost bird who had gotten turned around and flown north for the winter, a scraggly flamingo, maybe, an incompetent stork. It was astonishing how few clothes they wore; but they brought a portable fire with them. Snowbird, who carried a bigger hatchet, was in charge.

Our three women stepped forward, and Catherine from among them.

"Hello," she said, holding both empty hands open toward them. "We come unarmed."

The teenagers said nothing, just stared wider. Their red wagon of fire was too small to have been what we had seen from so far away. They shivered, accustomed to more heat. They had evidently been dispatched from a caravan of children. I marveled that they could have survived.

"We have *things*," said Catherine.

"Uh-huh," said Snowbird, not breaking his stare.

"Water," said Catherine, producing a little clear plastic bottle of it.

"Huh," grunted the smaller kid, kicking at the snow that lay plentifully on the ground.

"Food," said Catherine. And the two women stepped up to flank her, showing Hershey's bars and peanuts.

The kids looked on hungrily, but made no move toward us.

"Blankets," said Catherine, fingering the ones that lay across her own shoulders.

The little one yawned. Snowbird folded his lanky arms.

"Cigarettes," said Catherine, an edge of desperation

in her voice. We had little left to impress them with. She put two cigarettes in her mouth and began feeling around in the nooks and crannies of her outfit for something. The kids' heads followed her movements with the quick alertness of cats watching a bird. Finally Catherine found a box of matches, and struck one to light both cigarettes. The kids were hooked. Emboldened, Catherine stepped forward to hand each kid a cigarette.

"Stay away," said Snowbird, raising his hatchet.

Catherine hopped back.

"Throw us the fire," said Snowbird. "The matches!"

"Oh..." Catherine's eyes met mine. *That* was why they kept their fire going; if it went out, they had no way to start another.

"Matches," repeated the small kid urgently, his eyes alight in reflected fire from the wagon. Snowbird's hand was still extended.

"Here." Catherine tossed the box of matches to the frozen ground in front of Snowbird. We had a million; they took up little space and weighed almost nothing. Rechargeable butane lighters started our daytime campfires.

Solemnly, as if to assure themselves that it wasn't a trick, Snowbird carefully removed one match and struck it. The two watched until it burned down to his fingers. Finally Snowbird asked, "What do you want?"

"For you to join us," said Catherine. "We're heading to the coast. We have a truck full of food and medical supplies. You'll be safe with us. Eighty-nine people. How many are you?"

"Wait here." The kids dragged their red wagon off a few feet and huddled, whispering like brothers planning a practical joke. Presently Snowbird turned around and came toward Catherine.

"OK, you go back to your people now," he said, and his voice cracked. "We'll go back to ours and show them your matches and tell them the other stuff. If they say OK..." He shrugged. "I guess we'll see you around."

The two waited there until we had reached the end of the straightaway, then turned their little red wagon of fire and went back the way they had come. That night their main flame moved closer, and the next day, in the middle of the day and the middle of sleep, it moved into our midst.

But not quite. The inert bodies of Perhaps awoke to the sound of a man's voice bellowing: "Where is your fire?"

"Nnna—go way..." someone a few carcasses down from me grumbled.

"Where is your fire?" bellowed the voice again. It was a deep voice, a voice with hair on it. "Where is your fire? We have seen it."

I opened my eyes. The owner of the voice stood, enormous, resolute, in a fiery bristling beard and a plaid woolen jacket, with a heavy cast-metal ax, at the head of a raggedy phalanx of scraggly creatures more like Snowbird than their leader. The men, like our men, had beards and long tangled hair, and there were two women. They were no caravan of children, as we had assumed; they had simply sent their only two, the weakest, most expendable members of their party, to meet us. None of them were wearing much clothing, by our standards. They didn't have to; they had dragged or pushed a railroad sidecar loaded high with logs, with fire. Gary Tascheira, our unofficial Greeter, hauled himself up out of bed with the air of one who had done this many times before, a giant baby swaddled in all his blankets.

"Our fire," Tascheira began phlegmily, and cleared his throat. "Our fire is inside us. It comes from the ghosts. We can't explain it because we don't understand it." He stepped forward. "We offer you equal shares in everything we have. We offer you peace, and a chance to survive."

"We survive," said the man roughly.

About half of Perhaps was sitting up now, whispering to one another and listening. We had previously reached general agreement that the fire people had lost half their minds and misplaced the rest.

"Yes," said Tascheira. "You do survive."

The leader of the fire people let out a little coarse damn-right grunt.

"But for how long?" asked Tascheira.

"We survive ... for now," said the leader.

"How about twenty years from now? Two hundred years?"

Snowbird spoke up. "He's talking trash."

"I am not talking trash, young man," said Gary Tascheira, approaching the group. "I am talking of genes, chromosomes, sperm, eggs, fetuses, babies, children, generations. I am talking about surviving."

"You can offer us hundreds of years?" said the leader, with a whistling incredulity in his voice.

"Perhaps," said Tascheira. "Just perhaps."

᠅

Now and for the past seven days the fire people go behind us, traveling at night when we do, hunting and eating their own rabbits, finding their own fuel, talking only to one another, and above all, keeping their fire, their own little piece of the apocalypse, lit. By turning over to them most of our matches, we seem to have insured, if not their undying support, at least their attendance.

These eleven speak English, use idioms, express themselves like modern Americans; but what they believe is that all good and all evil comes from fire, that, despite the matches we've given them, they must keep their fire continually burning, for without it they would die. They've allowed us to rig them to their sidecar with cables like our own, but not, emphatically not, to persuade them that their fire is unnecessary. Patient explanations about the impermanence of nuclear winter mean nothing to them; they know the cold will last forever. They even insist on sending around the small kid with his red wagon daily, like the Olympic torchbearer, to touch off all our little campfires. Anything else would be a waste of fire. Sometimes Snowbird comes along, sometimes not. Their leader's name is Bill, but it might as well be Thor. They are a people capable of both singing the complete lyric to the Mickey Mouse Club theme song and praying to a God of Fire.

And we, Perhaps and Attachment A, Perhaps and Appendix, Perhaps and Parentheses, Perhaps and the fire people, are now an even hundred.

# 19 ❋ In a Certain Sense

"In a certain sense we were lost," wrote William Lewis Manly in 1894, exercising the tact he had learned many years before at the hands of Asabel Bennett. Not merely lost, but almost out of food as well. The men reserved the remaining "civilized provisions" of rice and bread for the women and children, while they themselves would live on oxen alone; not ox meat but ox, eating even hide, intestines and blood. One day their luck ran high: they discovered a freshwater spring. The next morning it ran out: they marched up against a wide wall of rock, impassable by wagons. Bennett's party was not really camped there; they were surrounded, surrounded by a terrain that offered no hope of food or water, or even granted food and water, passage.

Now the men did what any red-blooded overlanders would have done; they held a meeting. William Manly and John Rogers were chosen to go on a rescue mission. An ox was slaughtered, and the women fashioned the hide into small knapsacks. The animal was so gaunt that its meat fit into the knapsacks with room left over for a kettle, two tin cups, two canteens and a half blanket.

In a few days Manly and Rogers came upon the body of Mr. Fish, an older man who had left the party some time before, refusing to discard the heavy bullwhip around his waist because, he had said, he might need it. Manly and Rogers ate stray blades of grass for moisture, chewed on flattened bullets, observed silence to avoid exposing their mouths. They couldn't wet the meat enough to swallow. "It seemed," Manly wrote, "as if we were going to die with plenty of food in our hand, because we could not eat it."

Soon they found several men who had split off earlier from the Bennett party. The men gave Manly and Rogers letters telling their families how and where they expected to die. It was now seven days since the two young men had left Bennett, Arcane and the others.

In another week they saw a few trees and a crow, a hawk and a California quail. Above them on a ridge, as their three-bird stew simmered in muddy water, wolves were tearing apart a large animal. Better game was nearby.

The two men finally crossed into a lush meadow where thousands of cattle grazed, sated and oblivious to the possibility of suffering. It was probably the second week of January 1850, although for the rest of his life Manly clung to the romantic belief that it had been the first day of the new year.

Ten days later, Manly and Rogers, returning with a mule and plenty of food, found the body of Captain Culverwell a few miles from the Bennett camp, perfectly preserved by the desert air, his face upturned and his arms outspread as if in plea. The Bennetts and the Arcanes, sick and emaciated but all of them alive, were the only survivors; the others, sure Manly and Rogers would not return, had fled into the desert. Captain Culverwell, unable to keep up, had died on the way back.

The young explorers piloted the families to safety, but before they did the entire party turned back for a last look at the thirsty land that had drunk the lives from thirteen of their number. Arrayed on the spine of a high ridge, they would have made an odd sight had anyone been there to see them: two men in their twenties who appeared twice that age, two older men leading oxen, two women walking alongside them and five squalling children packed tightly into canvas pouches on both sides of Asabel Bennett's ox. Mrs. Arcane, who had steadfastly refused to abandon her city finery, wore dozens of long multicolored ribbons that streamed out brightly behind her best hat, and tiny Charley Arcane was dressed in his Sunday suit.

"Goodbye," said someone in the party, and William Lewis Manly never recalled with certainty who had said it. "Goodbye, Death Valley!"

The Valley had been given a name.

# 20 ☀ Soon

If a tree falls in the forest, and nobody hears it, and nobody exists to ask the question, If a tree falls in the forest and nobody hears it, does it make a sound, does it—still, then—make a sound?

We are all out of trees. Live trees, dead trees that look like the veins in a leaf, radiation-deformed trees, petrified trees, frozen trees, fresh out of trees. We are in Death Valley. A town called Needles, my mother fainting dead away from the heat, a six-dollar air conditioner clipped onto the Valiant's passenger window spitting cubelets of ice. Death Valley, and it is getting warmer, so much warmer that in ten or twenty years ice might melt.

And we plod onward. Four ragged souls surprised us at the mouth of the desert, a man and three women. After the usual convalescent period, the women incorporated themselves into the reproductive scheme of Perhaps; the man was reluctant. Though I was none too glad to see them—three more women, three more days until I slept with Catherine—I was the one Tascheira assigned to give the man a talking-to. And we plod onward. Nothing new to report; the days are long, the nights are longer. The kids play war games, sniping at each other from amid the long legs of the adults as we haul the truck. The fire people are beside themselves; no wood. All except Snowbird, who seems to enjoy having the extra time on his hands. It is like a summer vacation, one he uses to investigate our camp, showing up in early evening to see us hook ourselves into harness, spying from behind the truck's wheels on a couple fucking, standing far off just to watch us eat our dinner. All his peregrinations are undertaken under a mantle of protective disinterest: if you try to talk to him he shuffles away; he was on other business all along. And we plod onward.

Today I am to bed down with Clare. Am to but do not; Catherine rushes up, whispers to Clare, Clare rises, scoots down the line. All very cloak-and-dagger.

"Kiss me, Max," says Catherine.

"Fine," I say stupidly. She holds my head, draws me down on top of her. Promptly, strictly according to protocol, I unbuckle my pants.

"Not yet," says Catherine. "I'm not ready."

"Not ready? Is this you? What's going on?"

"Max." Catherine pulls me to her with all her might, crushes the air out of me. "Max, I'm pregnant."

A thousand things occur to me to say; fortunately, I am without the wind to say them.

"I'm making you," she tells me, "the Honorary Father." It's a custom in Perhaps.

I pull up her sweater, rub her belly lightly. She's on her back, her eyes closed, smiling at the sun, wherever it is. I hook a hand around her soft side, pull myself close until my mouth is pressed against her ear. My tongue is broad, soft; I taste bitter wax. Baths and oral sex are things unknown in Perhaps.

I unsnap her pants, pry my hands in on her hips, move her pants down a little.

"Not yet!" Catherine says again.

"I'm *not* yet. I just want to take off all our clothes."

"Everything?" she says, eyes alight, with that peculiar closed-mouth smile of hers.

"Even your socks," I whisper. It's a dirty idea; no one in Perhaps removes more than what is necessary, usually just the woman's pants, and sometimes, if the man gets really carried away, his too. The idea of being naked is making us rub odd parts of ourselves against each other, my inner forearm against her thighs, her knee against my crotch, making us move in ways we never have together and making it damned difficult to complete the work of getting naked. It's a dirty idea, and because dirty, good.

It occurs to me that Perhaps is like Victorian England, where a well-turned ankle was enough to make grown men drool into their ascots. But nothing occurs to me for very long before being swallowed up in the sensation of skin on skin, of two chests and two pairs of legs rubbing sweat on sweat, two mouths pressed deep into each other, growing dry and finding new water, pressed deep until she shouts muffled into my mouth.

The night comes, warm and inevitable. By warm I do not mean I have a sudden urge to order iced drinks, but still by our Admiral Byrd standards it is warm, warm enough that sleeping under eight or nine blankets with no clothes on hasn't seemed to give us pneumonia. I am not tired, even after our frenzied celebrations. Catherine sleeps as if shot.

Midway through the night, when we're back in harness, it finally hits me. First my upper legs and buttocks lose their spirit, and then they gain a whole new spirit revolutionary in nature. They want to strike out against their oppressors, to sing the rebel song, to secede from the Union. My body is in civil war and my waist is the Mason-Dixon line.

"What's the matter, 'Dad'?" says Gary Tascheira. "All that siring take it outta you?"

"Go stick your face in a big bowl of soft shit," I tell him. I am operating on that level. It is the longest night of my life, a supernight, a thousand and one nights rolled into one.

Finally day dawns, freakishly warm. Mercifully, I've been exempted from procreational duty for the evening. I have about four hours before I have to go to sleep, and I am filled with false energy that will last for about thirty minutes.

It's the first day that feels warm enough to think about the saxophone. I retrieve it from the truck, remove the mouthpiece cover, test the reed cautiously with a wet finger. It doesn't stick. If I didn't know better, I'd swear the temperature was in the twenties, maybe even above freezing. Indian summer. Tan my hide.

I sit on the back bumper silently playing. The keys are warm because the saxophone was in the heated truck. I close my eyes, blow loose-lipped, fingering the notes to Rollins's "Alfie's Theme." My feet are swinging.

"You can't really play that thing."

I open my eyes. Snowbird is off to the side at his characteristic safe distance, speaking his few sullen words in his usual grudging way; uncharacteristically, he's staring right at me.

I avoid looking at him for fear of scaring him off. "Can too," I say childishly.

He moves a little closer, looking down. "I doubt it," he says.

I play five notes in the alto's screechy false register, the universal kids' jingle Nyaah-nyaah-nyaah-nyaah-nyaah.

"Don't you know any *real* songs?"

"One," I say. His body twitches slightly to attention. I play three horrendous measures of "Row, Row, Row Your Boat" liberally punctuated with fluffs and squeaks.

He turns around, begins walking slowly away; he, Snowbird, Mister Snowbird to you, has better things to do.

When he's a good twenty paces off, I tear into a Dolphyish "God Bless the Child," all blinding speed and arpeggio.

Snowbird freezes in his tracks as if my phaser were set on Stun. I ignore him, take it to the bridge.

He finally speaks when he's close enough to touch. "Well, that one you did before wasn't any good."

I raise my eyebrows at him, rip into the next chorus, quote "Pop Goes the Weasel," "Ring Around a Rosy," "My Country 'Tis of Thee," and "Beat It," coming back stop-on-a-dime to the sweet clean arpeggios of "God Bless the Child." At some point Gary Tascheira, drawn by the sound, shows up behind the kid, sees what's going on, salutes and silently slips away. Snowbird is transfixed; without pause I play him the unadorned theme of the song, draw it out again, musically explaining, into the arpeggios, take it further out, further out. His eyes are following. He sits down on the ground. I dare not break and lose him.

After a while Snowbird's red-wagon friend shows up, looks at me, puzzled, taps the older boy persistently on the shoulder, Snowbird absently swatting the hand away. Finally the child announces in the too-loud tones of the juvenile message-bearer: "Bill says you're supposed to come back."

"Shut up," says Snowbird.

The kid says, "You're in trouble *now*," and vanishes.

I finish off the song and set the saxophone aside, still avoiding eye contact. I pull Billy Bo's watch from my pocket.

"Can you show me how to play?" asks Snowbird.

"Maybe," I say. Reel him in slowly.

"Yeah, when?" he demands.

"Maybe soon," I say, winding the watch.

"OK," he says.

"You'd better go back now," I tell him.

"I don't hafta," he says, but gets up, pulls his knit cap low to his eyes, and begins to walk away. He turns around. "You said soon."

"I said maybe soon."

Snowbird walks away. I saw it in his eyes, saw him figure all the music out: *this* is what gives permission to do *this*, *that's* why he can play *that*. I can teach him.

Snowbird is a long way off now. He has made a resolutely unsentimental departure, steady as you go, pausing once to kick a rock, never turning back, never showing so much as an indecisive shoulder. Suddenly he wheels around and shouts: "You said *soon*!"

# 21 ❋ 9 Lives

We've reached the ocean, and we stand still, listening to it. There is nothing, never was anything that sounds like the ocean. There are louder noises in nature, but none so implacably regular: the tidal push and pull is a planetary heartbeat. Though the sea is the blood of the Earth, its sound is not essentially liquid, not from a distance; it is a dry rush, like a hard wind through pine trees. Closer, you begin to hear the splatter of water on water, of water on rock, of the last exhalation of the wave as it comes sheening onto sand. The sea is not frozen, probably never was. The cold cannot stand up to it. The cold will not return.

Hypnotized by the sound, I move out from the group to a bluff overlooking the beach.

Down there.

Phosphorescence?

No. A small fire glowing in the light beach fog, and a lone human being warming his or her hands against it.

"Hey!" I shout, to the person down there, to the people of Perhaps, to the Pacific Ocean. "Hey!" Snowbird hears me, breaks away from the others, and soon all of Perhaps clusters around me there on that ridge. It's late in our journey; the phosphorescence has died down to the point where you must look into the darkness and then look back at us to see it, has almost died out, and with it any good chance for anyone but Eddie to find us. And now, impossibly, we have found someone.

Quickly a contact party is dispatched, three women and submachine Max, four people trotting down the brittle, winter-broken wooden steps to that ocean, that fire, that human being.

A human being wrapped like a mummy from head to toe, rubbing her thighs and hands. Her; you can tell by her size, by the sloppy grace with which she moves, now delicately prodding the fire with a foot, now looking up at us, now settling to her haunches and rubbing the backs of her arms, that she is a woman. As we cross the beach, slowly, fighting dry sand, she makes no move toward us, no move of acknowledgment.

"Hang back, Max," whispers Catherine. "Her mind may be gone."

I wait there, my boots wrapped in cold sand, as the three women approach the stranger cautiously, circling slowly, one by one, around the fire. The stranger works a can of food open with a small metal tool. I hear their voices thinned by the noise and mist of the surf, but not the words.

What is it about this strip of sand that sets it apart from every Pacific beach I've ever seen? There are no birds, no seagulls, none. It's almost as if the entire landscape has been boiled sterile. Boiled or frozen: both extremes destroy. And there where the brown-green latticework of seaweed should be lacily dividing land from water, only the foamy edge of the sea is visible, slowly sinking into saturated sand. It's a different Earth, a new Earth, not even Earth but a planet newly formed on which life has yet to develop. A new planet, and we are the first or last human beings on it.

Now a single raggedy-ass seagull appears, waddling with a sailor's swagger right up to the women by the fire, emboldened by starvation. The squatting woman, perhaps in dim recognition of another lone survivor, throws the contents of the can into the sand, and the seagull goes to work, grabbing up the brown meaty stuff in its bill, raising its head to swallow. The woman waves Catherine and the others away from her, speaks; I cannot hear.

"Max!" shouts Catherine, beckoning me.

The woman turns her head to me as I get within speaking distance. I still cannot see her face, any part of her; she is as tightly wrapped as an Ace-bandaged ankle.

"Play me a song," says the figure in a voice that I know. But it is not a woman's voice: it is a man's.

And now, with one motion, the stranger strips his headgear off, revealing a long, long light-brown face, a tired smile. "Play me a song, saxophone man. Got one in mind."

I can say nothing. I lift the blanket to show him what bulges on my chest.

His eyes open wide, then crease as he points to me, finger moving with his body's silent laughter.

"So," he says. "Finally traded it in for something more sensible."

※

"How? How, Wolf?"

And Wolf eats. But eats is an understatement: sitting low, knees above chin, on a single truck tire before a bonfire on the bluff, Wolf falls to his food, pushing it into his face with both hands, slurping and snorting in a cacophony of comestibility. He tears at a five-pound ham balanced on his lap; he picks up a can of baked beans and drinks them like water. In a corner of the fire a large tin washtub rests on low stones, and in it a great mound of snow, Geiger-countered and declared fit for ration. Wolf pays no heed to the melting snow, to the one hundred and four faces that ring the flames, the children and the Lucky Six, the Watchers and the Fire Men, the Sidesteppers and the rank and file, watching him.

"How did you find us?" I ask again. "We could have taken any one of a thousand roads."

"Cat," he says simply, then goes back to his orgy of a meal. He sticks a hand out at ankle level. "'Bout so high. Got any more water?"

Somebody's arm thrusts a bottle forward. Wolf grabs it, sucks it down. "Little calico with one orange foot."

I sit on the ground opposite, watching him through breaches in the flames, waiting for an opening. Catherine is next to me, arms around her knees; Gary Tascheira sits cross-legged on the other side of the fire. No one else can say anything to him. They are, all one hundred and four, in awe: here, unlike everybody else who joined Perhaps, is a man who knew who and where we were, who followed and found us. Wolf wipes his mouth with his sleeve, burps copiously.

"I had a jeep from the beginning," says Wolf, out of breath from eating. "From Salt Lake." Eyebrows lower in incredulity all around the fire as Wolf drinks his beans; you can hear them glug down his throat.

"Alone?" says Catherine in a near whisper. "From Salt Lake City?"

"Yeah, that's where that little calico appeared in front of me, just walkin along like nobody's business. Didn't even seem to feel the cold. She'd sorta alternate between solid and gas; one second I'd see her, the next I could see through her, and then she'd disappear completely. She was a ghost cat. A she, I'm pretty sure."

"Yes, a she," I say.

Wolf nods. "Acted like a she. If I gave the jeep some juice, she'd run faster; if I gunned the motor as fast as I could, she'd turn around, hiss and disappear. She never let me catch up with her, not once." He squints at me as a wave breaks down below. "Wait. How do you know?"

Everyone turns to me. "She was my cat."

"It figures," says Wolf after a pause. "She was too contrary to belong to anybody else. Some more water? I, uh, like it cold, if you don't mind." He looks up and around. Snowbird seizes the moment to thrust his canteen quickly through the flames to the basin of snow-water. When it sinks to the bottom of the basin he retrieves it and rushes, arm dripping, to Wolf's side; now that he has earned his way up close he wedges himself into the half-space between Wolf and the man next to him, as if in the hope that whatever this stranger has will rub off on him. All around the fire bodies move a few inches to accommodate Snowbird's relocation.

Wolf nods his thanks, takes the water, gives a satiated gasp and continues. "Sometimes I turned off the road, looking for food or figuring this might as well be the way you'd taken as anything else. I'd be tooling along the road and see that damn cat, the headlights goin right through her, trotting down the pavement in the opposite direction. So I'd turn the car around and follow her, figured she knew more than I did, so why not? Every so often she'd put in an appearance in front of me just to let me know I was on the right track.

"Around Mesquite I was about to drop with hunger, and I just happened to look off to the side of the road. There was that calico pokin around an overturned truck. Goddamn truck was full of 9 Lives cat food."

"Wolf, how'd you open the cans?" I ask.

He smiles. "You know better'n that." He reaches into his pocket and flips something through the fire; it bounces off my chest before I have time to react. And my Swiss Army knife lies, red and silver, in the dusty tan soil at my feet.

Wolf squints up at the ring of faces surrounding him. "Tuna & Liver. Beef & Liver Platter. Liver Entrée in Creamed Gravy. And I never even liked liver for *humans*." He opens his face and a tongue comes lolling out. "Anybody want some cat food? I'm sick of it."

"Wolf," I say. "Tell me something. Where did you get the jeep?"

"Showroom in Salt Lake City. No fluid in it to freeze up, so it was in mint condition. I found a gas tank and some cans of antifreeze, just gassed that jeep up and drove it off the lot." Wolf grins. "Sign said EASY FINANCING. They'll never know how right they were."

"But first you had to make it down the hill from Here to the City. How?"

"How? Nothin to it. I went sledding."

"You what?"

"Went sledding, like kids do. You know, Flexible Flyer, Rosebud and all that."

"On what?"

"You know those road signs that say SALT LAKE CITY 7 MILES?"

I nod grimly, mouth tight. I'm not sure I want to hear this.

"Yeah, well, I took the screws outta the back of one of those signs, got on and sang 'Jingle Bells.' Took me right down to the bottom of the hill."

"Oh," I say icily. I look across at Tascheira's merry round face dancing above the flames. Before he can laugh I'm there with another question. "How did you get the jeep going?"

"Oh, in the cold?" says Wolf. He looks up. "You sure this isn't too boring?"

"Not to *us*," says Catherine.

"OK." He pops a whole canned apricot into his mouth. "Well, I warmed up water before I put it in the car. Had to have the motor running the whole trip, just to keep everything at room temperature, so when I slept I leaned a cinder block up on the gas pedal to set it idling." He yawns. "Could I see the knife?" says Wolf. "I consider it half mine, y'know."

I toss him the Swiss Army knife; he snatches it overhand and begins cleaning his nails with the small blade. "Seems like good food always makes a mess," says Wolf. "Doesn't it seem that way to you, Max?"

"Mm."

Tascheira speaks sharply. "What about *them*?"

"Who?" says Wolf, but everyone else knows who.

"The missile base above Salt Lake City," says Catherine. "Those people who call themselves Here."

"Yes," says Wolf. "You don't have to worry about them anymore." He finishes his left thumb, flicks the dirt off the knife and pockets it reflexively. "Nobody ever will, in fact," he adds very softly.

One hundred and four standing, sitting, kneeling, squatting bodies lean in toward Wolf. There are no longer any chinks of light between the forms around the fire. The ocean, between waves, slops around in the distance.

"I blew em up," says Wolf simply.

"You what," says Tascheira flatly, in a state of shock in which only his lips can move.

"Blew em up." He looks around at all of us. "I didn't *want* to. Had to. Just *had* to."

No one says a thing.

Wolf takes a deep breath, lets a name out on a long sigh. "Eddie . . . Well, Eddie's a nut. Guess that's obvious. He wasn't always. No," says Wolf, staring, melancholy. "Not always." He's looking off as though Eddie is there in the blackness out over the ocean, not someone named E but Eddie, who played with blocks and refused to eat okra.

After a while Wolf begins again. "Eddie trusted his brother. Trusted him entirely too much." He stares out. "He was already convinced that another man, an outsider, was the one who turned my head around." His eyes snap down. "That's you, Max. But I . . . well, I was born to be his right-hand man. It didn't take more than just a little time before he forgot all about everything cept the fact that I'm his brother. That . . . I *was* his brother.

"Excuse me," Wolf says abruptly in a ragged voice. "I gotta get up." Snowbird jumps out of his way, but Wolf doesn't just want to stand. He begins to walk very slowly, oblivious to the movement all around him as people clear a narrow path where, very slowly, pacing in the pauses, he circles the fire. "Eddie had himself fooled in half a million ways. And once a man makes up his mind to fool himself . . . Well. He had this plan to come after you and wipe you out, and not just you. Everyone who might be out there. In six weeks he showed me the whole defense system and how to operate it, in case anything happened to him.

"I set the missiles on a special course, time-delayed blastoff for two days, wrote Eddie a note how I was going down to the City to scout it out for us, see what resources were available, draw up a few plans. Then I slipped out in the middle of the night and belly-whomped down the hill."

Wolf's come to a halt where he started, across from me through the fire. "I got a hold of that jeep, drove off till Salt Lake City was a dot on the horizon." He starts pacing again. "Kept my eyes on the rearview mirror; there wasn't anything I could do about it, they were stuck. Couldn't look at food or anything else. Couldn't sleep. In two days . . ." Wolf stops himself. He is standing next to me. "What I saw was three nuclear missiles take off from Eddie's camp and..." He leaves off hoarsely. "And follow their flight plan."

The question is on everybody's lips; you can see them ask it but you can't hear a word.

"You ever see a boomerang?" says Wolf at last.

"You mean..." I murmur.

"Straight up," says Wolf, raising a thumb. "And straight down. Eddie never had a chance."

Wolf sinks very slowly, as if his knees are a hydraulic jack, until his heels meet his buttocks. He falls backward, sitting down with a jolt. "Shit," says Wolf, his knees tight up on his chest, his arms around them. "I didn't want to do it." He's rocking back and forth, and tears appear at the corners of his eyes. "Shit," he says again, burying his head.

I reach over to Wolf and put my arms around his compact form. For a long time, a long time that passes wordlessly but not quickly, until my knees are stiff, until the crowd breaks up, until Catherine bids me good night with a hand on my shoulder, until the fire is down to embers and Wolf and I are cold again, we are there together, rocking, rocking and rocking.

"So," says Wolf finally. He looks at me. We are alone on the bluff. A big wave crashes, thunders down below. "How bout some music?"

"Wolf, I'm never going to play you that damn song."

"Didn't think so." Wolf shakes his head, looking into or beyond the fire. "Didn't really think so."

# 22 ❀ Life

No one in Perhaps can sleep through all the unfamiliar night hours, through the bash and slash of the unfamiliar surf, through the existence of unfamiliar and unfamiliarly hospitable land all around us, through the unfamiliar circumstance of having to do nothing, to go nowhere in the immediate future, no one can and no one does. No one except Wolf.

There on the bluff from which I first sighted him, Wolf snores, lying face-up on a mattress of flattened cardboard boxes, a real pillow with a Winnie-the-Pooh pattern under his head, blatting and splatting through a deep long sleep. Catherine and I sit near him, sharing a crate, alternately gazing at Wolf and past him at the ocean. Snowbird is nearer, on the bare ground, eating Life cereal dry from the box. "He snores," announces Snowbird.

I nod, pressing a finger to my lips. Catherine and I get up and move the crate a little to the right, where we block the sun from Wolf's face. Out in the sea a long low form can be made out. "Catalina Island," I whisper to

Catherine. The sky is blue, entirely empty, and shadows are sharp.

Snowbird munches. "How come he's still asleep?"

"He's tired," I say.

"*I* was tired," says Snowbird, turning the box upside down into his hand. He fishes a paper packet from the last shreds of cereal and tears it open. "How come he's still sleeping? He's different. I think he's different."

I put a finger to my lips again.

"We won't wake him," says Catherine.

I watch Wolf's chest rise and fall. "Maybe not." He isn't even twitching.

"We're going to stay here until Cheryl has her baby," says Catherine.

"I didn't know she was that far along."

"Any minute now."

"Yeah," says Snowbird, peeling off a small Dodgers baseball-cap sticker from its glossy backing and carefully affixing it to his knit hat. "But she's not gonna let anybody watch, so it's gonna be boring."

"Is that so?" I ask him.

"Yeah." Snowbird gets up, bends each knee with a loud pop, and sits down again. He searches Wolf's form for new signs of life and looks out into the ocean. "Is it dangerous?"

"Sure," I tell him.

A jackhammer sounds in the distance. "New construction?" I ask.

"That's Gary." The left half of Catherine's mouth smiles. "Gary and Fred out hunting. Maybe they'll bag a lizard or two."

Snowbird is studying the side panel of the cereal box, is learning that Life contains L-Lysine Monohydrochloride (a protein fraction). "We gonna stay here?" he asks.

"Maybe." Catherine hunches her shoulders. "Perhaps."

"When you—" Snowbird cuts himself off when Wolf flops and grumbles and then, false alarm, resumes snoring. "When you gonna know?"

"We have to find fresh water first. We have to test the soil."

"Does it matter or anything if you like it?"

Catherine smiles. "Do you like it?"

"Yeah," says Snowbird.

"Good," says Catherine. "So do I."

Suddenly a tangle of fists and grunts and kicking knees and slashing elbows whips low along the ground. Seventeen Tasmanian devils! A horizontal tornado! Wolf is waking up.

Stark raving trapped-rat terror is in his eyes as he opens them wide too wide, all white and dilated pupil; they close themselves off little by little from the light of the sky; a weariness or sadness or relief enters those eyes, it is impossible to tell which; no, none of these things, no emotions, just a story, a long story writing itself across two brown human eyes: every blast and every woman and every model city those eyes have ever seen, every jeep they've ever seen every time they've ever seen it, every mother and brother those eyes have ever had, every turn in the road and every broiled bird and every bullet. It is like watching a child being born. Wolf shuts his eyes again, then opens them to slits.

"So," says Wolf. "What's new?"

## About the Author

MITCH BERMAN was raised in California and Oregon, graduated from the University of California at Berkley, and has a master's degree in writing from Columbia. One morning he was awakened in his Manhattan apartment by the door buzzer. "Hi," said the voice from the intercom. "We're in your neighborhood and we have a wonderful message for you about a future without crime, sickness or despair." Mitch Berman did not admit the visitors into his building but wants to thank them for giving him the beginning of a new novel.